CH

D0089011

DISCARD

SEP   2014
Westminster Public Library
3705 W. 112th Ave.
Westminster, CO 80031
www.westminsterlibrary.org

TO SAIL A DARKLING SEA

BAEN BOOKS by JOHN RINGO

BLACK TIDE RISING:

Under a Graveyard Sky • *To Sail a Darkling Sea* •
Islands of Rage and Hope (forthcoming)

TROY RISING:

Live Free or Die • *Citadel* • *The Hot Gate*

LEGACY OF THE ALDENATA:

A Hymn Before Battle • *Gust Front* • *When the Devil Dances* • *Hell's Faire* • *The Hero* (with Michael Z. Williamson) • *Cally's War* (with Julie Cochrane) • *Watch on the Rhine* (with Tom Kratman) • *Sister Time* (with Julie Cochrane) • *Yellow Eyes* (with Tom Kratman) • *Honor of the Clan* (with Julie Cochrane) • *Eye of the Storm*

COUNCIL WARS:

There Will Be Dragons • *Emerald Sea* •
Against the Tide • *East of the Sun, West of the Moon*

INTO THE LOOKING GLASS:

Into the Looking Glass • *Vorpal Blade* (with Travis S. Taylor) • *Manxome Foe* (with Travis S. Taylor) • *Claws that Catch* (with Travis S. Taylor)

EMPIRE OF MAN:

March to the Sea (with David Weber) • *March to the Stars* (with David Weber) • *March Upcountry* (with David Weber) • *We Few* (with David Weber) • *Empire of Man* (with David Weber, omnibus, forthcoming)

SPECIAL CIRCUMSTANCES:

Princess of Wands • *Queen of Wands*

PALADIN OF SHADOWS:

Ghost • *Kildar* • *Choosers of the Slain* • *Unto the Breach* •
A Deeper Blue • *Tiger by the Tail* (with Ryan Sear)

STANDALONE TITLES:

The Last Centurion

Citizens (ed. with Brian M. Thomsen)

To purchase these and all Baen Book titles in
e-book format, please go to www.baen.com.

TO SAIL A DARKLING SEA

JOHN RINGO

TO SAIL A DARKLING SEA

This is a work of fiction. All the characters and events portrayed in this book are fictional, and any resemblance to real people or incidents is purely coincidental.

Copyright ©2014 by John Ringo

All rights reserved, including the right to reproduce this book or portions thereof in any form.

A Baen Books Original

Baen Publishing Enterprises
P.O. Box 1403
Riverdale, NY 10471
www.baen.com

ISBN: 978-1-4767-3621-1

Cover art by Kurt Miller

First Baen printing, February 2014

Distributed by Simon & Schuster
1230 Avenue of the Americas
New York, NY 10020

10   9   8   7   6   5   4   3   2   1

Pages by Joy Freeman (www.pagesbyjoy.com)
Printed in the United States of America

As always

For Captain Tamara Long, USAF

Born: May 12, 1979

Died: March 23, 2003, Afghanistan

You fly with the angels now.

TO SAIL A DARKLING SEA

TO SARA,
DARLING

Once upon a night we'll wake to the carnival of life

The beauty of this ride ahead such an incredible high

It's hard to light a candle, easy to curse the dark instead

This moment the dawn of humanity

The last ride of the day

"Last Ride of the Day"
Nightwish
Imaginaerum

WELCOME TO
WOLF SQUADRON!

Wolf Squadron is an international volunteer search and rescue organization formed subsequent to most world governments falling in the face of the H7D3 "zombie" plague. Wolf Squadron is based around the megayacht Social Alpha, *formerly owned by the late internet billionaire Mike Mickerberg, founder of Spacebook, and includes as of this writing over twenty small craft as well as the oceanic supply ship* Grace Tan.

Wolf Squadron was founded by Steven John "Wolf" Smith, a naturalized American citizen, former Australian Army paratrooper and former high school history teacher. Mr. Smith and his family, Stacey "Momma Wolf," Sophia "Seawolf" and Faith "Shewolf" Smith began clearing boats and rescuing people just like yourself starting a mere two weeks after the cessation of broadcasts from the British Broadcasting System. As of the date of this pamphlet's production, four hundred and twenty-six persons have been rescued at sea including U.S. Army, Navy, Marine and Coast Guard personnel, with over one hundred and sixty coming from the cruise ship, Voyage Under Stars *alone. Most rescuees have agreed to join in on the effort and we hope you will too!*

Currently there are no land areas beyond desert and barren islands unoccupied by the infected. There are three known remaining governmental headquarters (USA: Strategic Armaments Command;

Russia: Strategic Rockets Command; China: 4th Strategic Military Command) as well as a small contingent of the CDC. If you are American, the National Constitutional Continuity Coordinator (see below: "What is the NCCC?") is Under Secretary Frank Galloway, who maintains a continuity of civilian control of the U.S. military. All of the headquarters personnel are uninfected and therefore must remain in their secure facilities due to the hazard of infected. Similarly, the submarines you may occasionally see or have seen surfaced are also uninfected and cannot open up until a source of vaccine can be obtained.

Here are a few frequently asked questions:

Q: *"Something" happened (rape, murder of noninfected human, incest, pedophilia, homosexual activity, "I'm pregnant by a guy I slept with after he killed my husband who had just turned into a zombie," etc.) when I was trapped in a compartment/on a lifeboat/life raft/small boat, etc.*

A. *"What happened in the compartment, stays in the compartment." If you feel you are in a state of threat from a person, relay this to your sponsor and you will be separated from that person. However, Wolf Squadron has no jurisdiction over actions taken prior to your contact with Wolf Squadron, and given the difficulties with prosecuting such issues, will only act to separate you from any perceived threat. If actions occurred in a compartment or lifeboat that fall under Uniform Code of Military Justice (including but not limited to sexual activity of a heterosexual or homosexual nature and/or sexual relations between junior and senior and/or disrespect for authority or any other violation of the UCMJ or standing orders) they are generally held under the same guidelines as agreed upon by the current NCCC and the current JCS. (Post-Fall DOD Regulation Nineteen.) Subsequent to rescue, military personnel are still under the UCMJ and there is a permanent "stop-loss" in place on all Military Occupational Specialties. As to issues that are not of a legal nature, what happened in the compartment, stays in the compartment....*

"Reloading!"

SSG Gregory "Janu" Januscheitis scrabbled for magazines in the red-lit compartment and realized he was down to only two loaded mags. And while his assault ruck had two books and a bunch of Copenhagen, it was also fresh out of ammo.

"I'm out!" Lance Corporal Derek D. Douglas shouted. "And I cannot get this *damned* hatch shut!" The tall and rugged corporal was pressing hard against the door but the infecteds had their arms through it and it wasn't going to dog.

Condition Zebra, which shut all the watertight doors of the *Iwo Jima,* had been set as soon as the H7D3 infection started to rampage through the ship. But then the "dual expressor" virus changed from a simple flu to a "neurological affector blood pathogen." And lockdown only worked as long as you weren't battling fucking zombies, which you had to when one second your Alpha Team sergeant is laying down fire and the next he's stripping off his clothes and howling.

Then the abandon ship call went out from the acting captain and the doors pretty much *all* got opened.

J's squad wasn't even close when the call went out. The boats were gone.

Running out of ammo and with no hope of getting topside they'd taken the next best route: head for the big food stores of the assault ship and try to hole up. If they could find them and if they could fight their way through the zombies.

"Leave it!" he called from the next hatch. "Hug left!"

Januscheitis was an airman, not an infantryman like Smitty, but multiple tours in the Sandbox when he'd been in support of "advanced air ops" had really ratcheted up the basic "every Marine a rifleman" thing.

"Aye, aye!" Douglas called. He let go of the hatch and slammed back against the bulkhead, shuffling down the corridor as fast as he could while keeping his back to the port bulkhead.

J and Lance Corporal David Toback began slow, aimed fire at the infecteds pouring through the hatch. The reason they were firing so carefully was that bouncers in the confined spaces of a ship were as much of a problem as infecteds. They'd lost two squad members when they were wounded by bouncers, then overrun by the fucking zombies.

"He's not going to make it," Toback said.

"Check fire," J shouted. "Dive, Derek, dive! Crawl!"

As soon as the corporal hit the deck, J switched to full auto, ripping out the remnants of his magazine. As the corporal slithered across the coaming, the staff sergeant tossed his last frag into the corridor and slammed the hatch shut. There was a dull thump and a pinging on the door followed by howling.

"Where the fuck are we?" Toback asked.

"Four tack 157 tack two tack lima," Januscheitis said. "The stores compartment with the water spigot is two compartments aft and one deck down." He pointed in the general direction. He had a bump for direction which had so far helped them survive. Helped.

"We got more this way," Douglas said from the far hatch.

"Frags?" Januscheitis said.

"One," Toback said, holding it up.

"Well, what are you waiting for?" Januscheitis said.

"Got nothing this way?" Derek said from the next corridor hatch. "Not close, anyway."

"If the frag didn't attract them, noth—" Januscheitis broke off as a compartment hatch undogged.

The Navy fireman at the hatch found himself the target of three M4s. He carefully raised his hands.

"Friend?" he said carefully.

"Talking, at least," Januscheitis said, lowering his M4. "You know a shortcut to five tack 159 tack two tack alpha?"

"No," the fireman said. "But we were headed to a dry stores compartment that's got a desal line."

"One deck down?" Smitty asked.

"Yeah."

"That would be five tack 159 tack two tack alpha," Januscheitis said drily. *Navy.* "Wait. We?"

With almost no ammo left, fighting their way through the zombies while escorting three Navy pogues was going to be a right bitch. And one of them was a split. Depending on how long they were trapped belowdecks... That could get to be even more of a bitch.

"Clear?" Toback said, listening at the hatch.

"It is or it isn't," J said, hefting his M4. He had six rounds left.

Then it was melee time. You could melee the zombies. Problem was, avoiding getting bit. The fireman, actually a helo handler, had duded up in bunker gear, which made sense. The split, a cook, and the other pogue, a storesman, were just in NavCams. "Time to find out."

It wasn't. But the fact that there was firing from somewhere on the far side had drawn the infecteds off.

There were about ten of the infecteds facing the attackers. But it sounded like the other guys were about as down on rounds as J's remaining team. As he listened, they went from three guns firing to two then one. On the other hand, they'd cut down on the zombies.

"Open fire," J said, firing carefully. The M4s were supposedly designed to wound. They were, in fact, just absolutely awesome at wounding infecteds. And the nudist bastards would eventually bleed out. Eventually. He'd gotten sick and tired of that fighting hajis who got hit and just kept coming. It was getting absolutely *infuriating* with the infecteds. They just, like, *shrugged* the damned rounds off unless you got a head shot. They weren't "undead," just infected, insane and naked. But the bitty little .223 round of the M4s just barely seemed to *faze* them.

Unless they had their back to you and you shot two of the last four in the head. The other two were engaged in melee with the group at the far hatch and he wasn't willing to try it.

A crowbar wielded by a sergeant did for the last two.

"Thank you, Staff Sergeant," the sergeant of the new team said. He had two Marines and another pogue.

"Semper Fi, Sergeant," J said. "Any rounds in your pack?"

"Air, Staff Sergeant. We are *clocked* out. Got cut off, trying to make the boats…"

"Same," J said. "Trying to find a storeroom."

"Ditto," the sergeant said. "Any clues where one is?"

"Down one more deck," the split said.

"And back a compartment from the ladder," J said, pointing to the hatch. "Bets on what's down there? Frags?"

"I've got one left," one of the new privates said, pulling off his pack.

"And they say never use frags on a ship," J said, holding out his hand. "Gimme."

☙ ⊖ ❧

"What's the status on the storage compartment?" J said, tossing his useless M4 on one of the infected bodies in the corridor. Useless both in that they had no remaining rounds and in that he'd bent it on an infected's head. On the other hand, he'd avoided getting bitten. As had become patently obvious, that didn't mean you wouldn't zombie. It just meant you weren't *guaranteed* to zombie. Anybody bitten went in about six hours.

There were infecteds at both ends of the corridor, closed away by the watertight hatches. So far, they couldn't seem to open them but he was going to tie the damned things down just in case. It looked as if they were going to be here for a long time. There had better be food stores and water.

"There's a fresh water line, Staff Sergent," Sergeant Christopher L. "Smitty" Smith said. "According to one of the pogues, we're below the level of the fresh water tanks, so it should gravity feed. And about a gazillion tons of stores. But no way to cook them."

"Cooking is so far down the list of problems we've got, it's not even in sight," Januscheitis said. "First things first while we've got light is a quick assembly...."

"Before we even get with getting a roster," Januscheitis said, "who's got para cord?" He pulled a coil of it out of his assault ruck.

"Here." "Here." "Here..."

Pretty much all the Marines had at least some of the strong, thin line.

"Right," Januscheitis said. "First we're all going to strip. And, yes, that includes you, Seaman...?"

"Gowen," the cook said. "Seaman Tonya Gowen, Staff Sergeant."

"We wash down," Januscheitis said. "We've all been exposed to not only the fucking flu but at this point the blood pathogen. Then do a bite check. Bites, cuts, abrasions, anything. I've got some betadine. Then back into light uniform. As soon as we're done, we're all going to secure ourselves."

"Secure?" one of the pogues said.

"Tied up," Januscheitis said. "At the ankles at the least. And we're *all* going to put in gags. And, no, I'm not being kinky. If we'd done this early on, half the *bites* we sustained, especially when sleeping, wouldn't have happened—"

"I sure as hell am not going to—" the petty officer started to say then growled and started tearing at his clothing.

Two of the Marines grabbed the PO by the arms and took him to the ground, face down, as he snarled and tried to bite.

"Oh, Jesus, Terry," Gowen said, turning away.

"Fuck!" Januscheitis said. He looked at the coil of para cord in his hands and sighed. "This isn't going to be pretty."

When Petty Officer Third Class Richard Samson's body had been placed in the corridor, Januscheitis began taking off his gear.

"I said strip, people...."

In two weeks they lost Toback, LCP Thomas Casad Mandell, one of Smitty's team and PO3 Patrick "Murf" Murphy, the storeman who had been with Gowen. For him the worst was putting down Deter. But you did what you had to do.

Murphy and Gowen had gotten pretty chummy in those two weeks. He'd stomped on that, hard. The subject of Gowen being the only split in the compartment had been raised nearly the first day. But he'd pointed out that zombie virus was a blood pathogen. Like, say, AIDS. Which had put the kibosh on fooling around. For a while. But you couldn't have five guys and one girl in a compartment for forever without something happening.

Which meant he had to have a "talk" with Gowen.

"According to our brief before things went to hell," Januscheitis started, "if you get the flu, you're asymptomatic for a week. Then you're sick with flu for a couple of days."

"I..." Gowen said. J had a long-duration watch with a glowing dial. It had never seemed bright until he was in a compartment in total darkness for two weeks. Now he could see her face panicking.

"What, Seaman?" Januscheitis said.

"I...got the flu, Staff Sergeant Januscheitis," the girl said. "But..."

"Not everyone who gets the flu turns," Januscheitis said, shrugging. "It's hit and miss. But the point is that while the neurological is building it can be a blood pathogen."

"Yes, Staff Sergeant," Gowen said, her face working. "And if...If Murf hadn't...It's not an issue, Staff Sergeant."

"Oh, it's a *huge* issue," Januscheitis said. The compartment was big. Big enough to have a fairly private conversation. "Once you're past that point, you're past it. Nobody, at this point, in this compartment, is going to infect through blood pathogen. Hell, we might even be immune to bites but I wouldn't bet on it. Thing is... Things can start to happen now."

"Oh," Gowen said. "Are you...hitting on me, Staff Sergeant?"

"No," Januscheitis said. "I'm getting to the point that this is going to be a huge issue unless it's addressed. There are five guys in this compartment. None of them seem to be homosexually oriented. And, in case you hadn't noticed, they've been expending H2O jacking off in the back of the compartment."

"I've...noticed, Staff Sergeant," Gowen said. "But..."

"And in case you hadn't been paying attention, things were going to hell in a handbasket back home before we hit the tipping point," Januscheitis continued, inexorably. "It has been two weeks and there's no sound of rescue, just howling zombies. Now, I think they'll die before we run out of food. Don't ask me about water. But we could be in here for days, weeks, months. Gowen, we could be in here for years."

"I— Yes?" Gowen said. "I don't know where you're..."

"Gowen, I've been holding the guys back by my rank and the fact of the blood pathogen," Januscheitis said. "Smitty and Derek both know the bit about it no longer being an issue. I think Patel probably does. Gowen, there is one female in a compartment with five males. The next part is the..." He stopped and grimaced.

"Staff," Gowen whispered. "If...If you really need to...?"

"I'm not the *only* one that will, does," Januscheitis pointed out. "If we knew when we were leaving...No problem. But this is like prison. Except with an unknown date of release. If it's not a death sentence..."

"So you want to *pass me around*?" Gowen said angrily.

"Keep your voice down," Januscheitis said.

"The hell with—"

"Listen, you little *idiot*," Januscheitis snapped, grabbing her arm. "I don't want to use you as MWR issue. I'm trying to make sure you get *some* control, okay? But that will only last so long if you keep playing cock-tease in a compartment where there are five testosterone-laden males who haven't had any in months and are thinking that you're pretty much *all* they'll have for the rest of their lives. So. There is no way in God's green earth that I can legally order you to put out. But if you don't agree to set up *some* sort of a schedule, if you think you're going to do the guy you *like* and not the rest and play petty games with your body in this hotbox, pretty soon you're not going to *have* a say. Hell, pretty soon *I* won't have a say anymore, and then we might as well all be zombies...."

CHAPTER 1

When bad men combine, the good must associate; else they will fall, one by one, an unpitied sacrifice in a contemptible struggle.

Sir Edmund Burke

Robert "Rusty" Fulmer Bennett III wasn't a guy to just sit around if he could help out. But he also wasn't, still, in the best of shape.

When he'd boarded the cruise ship *Voyage Under Stars* with his buddy, Ted, he'd weighed 337 pounds, nekkid. By the time the rescue teams from Wolf Squadron found him, Ted had long before zombied and Rusty weighed 117 pounds and *was* naked, covered in bed sores and mostly unconscious on his filth-covered bunk. Since he was still six foot seven and, honestly, big boned, 117 was pretty bad. The one nurse Wolf had found so far, no doctors, said it was a miracle he'd survived.

So he still wasn't in the best shape of his life when he sat down in the "Wolf Squadron Human Resources" office. In the four weeks since he'd been found he'd put on about twenty pounds but that wasn't much. And he could barely work out at all. He wasn't sure that he could hack it as a "clearance specialist" but he was all up for killing zombies.

He filled in his name on the clipboard and took a seat. Then he opened up a packet of sushi and started to munch.

"Still putting on weight, huh?" the guy next to him asked.

"I never thought I'd like sushi," Bennett said, offering some of the rolls. "Anything is, like, *the best food in the world*, now. Except hummus. If I never eat hummus again I'll be so glad."

"Gotta try fish eyeballs," the guy said, taking one and nodding. "Mmmm . . . tuna is sooo much better raw than dolphin. Brad Stevens."

"Rusty Bennett," Rusty said. "Actually, it's Robert Fulmer Bennett Third. But everybody calls me Rusty. Like, you ate a *dolphin*?"

"Not the Flipper, ark, ark, kind," Stevens said. "It's a kind of fish. But, hey, when that's what you've got." He shrugged. "I'd have eaten a, you know, dolphin, dolphin if I could have caught one. There were a couple of times I'd have eaten the *asshole* of a dolphin . . ."

"I'd have eaten the asshole of an asshole," Rusty said.

"You're like a string-bean pole," Stevens said. "How much did you lose?"

"Two hundred pounds," Rusty said. "I was kinda big when we got locked down."

"Oh," Stevens said, wincing. "In one of the cabins on the *Voyage*?"

"Yep," Rusty said. "One of the reasons I want to go do something is every time I walk in the damned cabin I'm afraid the door's going to close behind me and never open again."

"I thought I'd lost weight. I can't believe they cleared you for work."

"I just walked down here," Rusty said, shrugging. "The worst they can do is say no . . ."

"Stevens . . . ?"

"You're still in very poor shape, Mr. Bennett," the lady said. Like most he'd seen, she was pregnant.

"I really want to help out," Rusty said. "And I've got to get out of that fu— forking cabin, ma'am. I keep having nightmares that the door won't open."

"I took this job on the *Grace* because it's the biggest boat I could get on," the lady said, smiling. "Try having nightmares that you're back in a tropical storm in a life raft and you're suffering from morning sickness and starving."

"Yes, ma'am," Rusty said. "I'm good with my hands. But I'm not a mechanic or anything. I can shoot. I've been shooting my whole life. And I want to fight zombies, ma'am."

"You'd never make the medical requirements for clearance personnel," the lady said. "They carry tons of gear when they clear."

"I heard there's some thirteen-year-old girl that does it, ma'am," Rusty argued. "If she can—"

"Don't compare Shewolf to your normal thirteen-year-old girl," the woman said, laughing. "You haven't seen the video, have you?"

"No, ma'am," Rusty said. "I haven't gotten out, much."

"If you go up to the lounge, you can probably find somebody who can show it to you," the lady said. "Shewolf *led* the boarding of the *Voyage*. She wasn't supposed to, but it happened. The *Dallas* had used a machine gun to clear some of the zombies but while she was going up more showed up. She went over the side, anyway. There was a Marine in a little bit better shape than you, not much but a little, who was supposed to go right after her and got bogged down climbing. One of the reasons they want people in the best possible shape for clearance. At that point, most of the copies... You know that song, 'I get knocked down, but I get up again...?'"

"Sort of?" Rusty said. "Kinda before my time."

"Go watch the video," the lady said, looking at her screen. "Since you know she made it, it's a hoot. But... I mean you can go try to track down Nurse Schoenfeld and get her to clear you. But I'd suggest something lighter. At least for now. And I'd guess you don't like enclosed spaces..."

"I don't mind if I know I can open the door, ma'am," Rusty said.

"Being on a small boat is physically wearing," the lady said, "but they need people for light clearance. Clearing life rafts and small craft. Not many people want to do it because you get beat up on those little boats. But—"

"Ma'am," Rusty said. "Being out in the air on a small boat... That'd be like heaven, ma'am."

"How strong of a stomach do you have?" the lady asked.

"I... pretty strong?" Rusty said.

"You're on the assignment board," the lady said, making a definitive tap on her keyboard. "Since you don't have a defined skill that anyone is looking for right now, you've got a week to find something. After that, you get put on boat cleaning or you can go into the hold with the lame and lazy. People who don't want to help out."

"Cleaning?" Rusty said.

"Cleaning up a boat after zombies have trashed it."

∽ ⊖ ∾

"I don't want to have to clean out a new boat," Sophia said mulishly. "I've seen these boats. And I've cleaned them up. Rather get knocked around on a thirty-five."

Sophia "Seawolf" Smith was one of the founding members of the Wolf Squadron. As such, despite being fifteen, she was a shareholder and not a minor one, as well as being a member of the Captain's Board as skipper of the thirty-five-foot *Worthy Endeavor*. The boat had gotten beaten up by nearly six months at sea, not to mention the zombies that took it over, but it was still *her* boat.

"You won't," Fred said. "*You*, especially, won't."

Fred Burnell was the "Vessel Preparation and Assignments Officer" on the *Grace Tan*. The massive supply ship had an open center and rear deck. On it were, now, four "cabin cruiser" yachts on props in various stages of repair and refitting. Since all of them worked when they were brought alongside it was mostly a matter of cleaning them out.

"Things change," Burnell said. "We've got crews cleaning them up, now. But we're retiring the thirty-fives. They're just too small and don't have enough range."

"So, what am I looking at?" Sophia said.

"You don't remember me, do you?" Burnell said, smiling slightly.

"No," Sophia said, frowning. "Sorry. Should I?"

"No," Burnell said. "I guess if you've seen one castaway, you've seen 'em all. The *Endeavor* plucked me off a life raft. So let's just say I owe you one even if you don't know it. There's a very nice sixty-five-foot Hatteras Custom sitting out there. Not too beat up by zombies. The only ones on it were below, and we're changing out all the below materials. Good engines, low hours..."

"I appreciate it," Sophia said. "Sorry for snapping your head off."

"Not a problem," Burnell said. "Can't tell you how happy I was when you blew that foghorn. Oh, you'll need two light clearance personnel and deck hands. Bigger boat."

"I guess I need to go do some scrounging," Sophia said. "What happens in the meantime?"

"Support for the clearance of the *Iwo Jima*," Burnell said. "I think you know how that works?"

"Hopefully better than the *Voyage*," Sophia said.

"Okay, okay, *seriously*?" Faith "Shewolf" Smith said. The thirteen-year-old had gotten her height from her father and it had kicked in young. Nearly six feet, slender and with some of the look of a female body-builder, her fine blond hair was currently hanging limp and damp on her neck in the heat.

"You say that a lot," Sergeant Thomas Fontana replied.

The thirty-two-year-old black Special Forces sergeant had become fond of his... well he couldn't call her "protégé" since she'd taught *him* the ins and outs of close-quarters battle with infecteds. Partner was the right term but it was hard to apply to a thirteen-year-old girl, no matter how well she fought zombies.

"The middle of this ship is *missing*," Faith said, pointing pointedly. "There is a great big gaping hole in the *middle of this ship. Below* the waterline!"

The foursome were looking, in amazement in Faith's case, at the USS *Iwo Jima*, an Amphibious Assault Carrier the size of a WWII "Fleet" carrier. The combination aircraft carrier, troop ship and floating dock, while not as big as the *Voyage Under Stars,* was really, really big. Especially from the waterline looking into its cavernous well-deck.

"It's not missing," Fontana said. "It can't be missing if they never put anything there."

"That's the well-deck, Faith," her father said. Steven John Smith was six foot one, with sandy blond hair and a thin, wiry, frame. Although he was the putative commander of Wolf Squadron, so designated by the U.S. Navy no less, he did clearance as well. They still had only four hard clearance personnel and he was good at it. Besides it burnished the reputation and this "squadron" was all about force of personality. "Obviously, it's where they pull landing craft in and out."

"That doesn't make it not nuts," Faith said. "I know nuts when I see nuts. Letting water into a ship? That's nuts."

"The good news is the well-deck *is* open," Smith said. "You don't have to climb a boarding ladder up to the flight deck."

"They dropped the stern gate when we abandoned ship, sir," Lance Corporal Joshua "Hooch" Hocieniec said.

Hocieniec completed the foursome that had only recently finished clearing the cruise liner *Voyage Under Stars,* listed as the world's second largest "super cruise liner." Larger than any passenger liner in history, it was best described as a floating Disneyland and just about as damned large. While the *Iwo* was big, as large as a WWII aircraft carrier and with much the same look, it wasn't the *Voyage,* thank God. The only larger ships on the ocean than the *Voyage* were supertankers, which had relatively small areas for zombies to inhabit, and a supercarrier. God help them, the Hole was sort of hinting they'd like one of *those* cleared. Steve had flatly told them "Not until we've got *a lot* more Marines."

Hocieniec was the only survivor of the *Iwo* they'd picked up so far. There were sure to be more out there but all the life rafts from the amphibious assault ship found so far contained only the dead. And the few people picked up from the *Voyage* who might be potential reinforcements were still in too bad a condition to assist. With any luck there would be some Marines alive on the boat. They'd found that people were awfully inventive, given the slightest chance, at staying alive.

"And, look," Faith said, "a welcoming party."

Zombies, not so inventive. But very tenacious. It seemed like all zombies needed was fresh water. Which would seem in short supply at sea except their concept of "fresh" was about the same as a dog's. And if one died from the water quality, well, the survivors would just eat him or her.

Which was why there were at least thirty zombies waiting for them on the deck of a hovercraft inside the ship. Which was more or less exactly where they were going to have to go. Fortunately, the stern gate was down and conditions were calm. Very calm.

The *Iwo Jima* had been, deliberately, "parked" in the Horse Latitudes zone of the Sargasso Sea. The Sargasso—the only sea not bounded by land—was surrounded by, but not affected by, the various currents of the North Atlantic. The Horse Latitudes were, in turn, a zone where there was always little to no wind and only very rare storms. They were the bane of early explorers of the Atlantic for the constant calm. They were called "the Horse Latitudes" because those were the latitudes where you had to eat the horses.

The combination, along with the somewhat entrapping sargassum weed that gave the region its name, meant that the assault ship was going to *stay* there. Except for the minor waves transmitted from distant storms, the area was pretty much flat calm, a nice change from the storm they'd left behind in Bermuda.

Since they'd gotten in contact with the Hole in Omaha, center for the Strategic Armaments Control, Wolf Squadron had found out that *most* Navy surface ships as well as many major commercial vessels had been similarly "parked" for the duration. The opinion of the "powers that be" prior to the Fall was that that way they'd be more or less impossible, or at least difficult, to find and they wouldn't be blown away by hurricanes or other storms. The commercial ships had apparently gone into the normally untraveled zone to avoid the Plague and have a place where they could maintain minimal power. As far as anyone knew, none of them had been uninfected.

On the horizon there was a supertanker full of Liberian crude. The normally empty zone was, relatively, chock with *big* ships full of H7D3 infected.

"You know," Faith said, musingly, "if we get this running we're going to have to rename it the *Galactica*, right?"

"Ouch," Fontana said. "Geek points galore."

"What?" Hooch said.

"Wait," Faith said. "Does that make the infected . . . wait for it . . . *Zylons*?"

"Ow!" Fontana said, snorting.

"With due respect, Staff Sergeant . . ." Hocieniec said. "What the *hell* are you talking about?"

"Shall I shoot the Zylons with my Barbie gun?" Faith said, hefting a USCG M4.

Faith did not like the M4. Calling it a Barbie gun was an indictment not a compliment. She also didn't like Barbie dolls if for no other reason than her having a passing resemblance to the doll. Her main problem with the M4 came down to its round, the NATO 5.56mm.

It was hoary legend in the military that the 5.56 had been developed to wound the enemy so as to create a greater logistics burden on the enemy. The truth was that it was a light round with a high velocity, giving the M-16, the original of the M4, the ability to, ostensibly, fire accurately on fully automatic. The round also was light, permitting more of them to be carried by an infantry soldier as well as more moved logistically. And it, yes, did not "overkill" as had the previous .308 of the M14 much less the brute force .30-06 of World War II. It did *just enough* damage in the opinion of the technologist oriented defense department weanies and generals of the Vietnam era.

Faith's opinion could be summed up in one line, taken from a webcomic she'd enjoyed before the Plague: "There is no overkill. There is only 'Open fire' and 'Reloading.'" The first weapon she'd used for zombie clearance was a variant of the AK47 called a "Saiga" that fired 12-gauge shotgun shells. A zombie hit by a 12-gauge was not getting back up. When she ran out in a magazine and didn't have time to reload, she would switch to her H&K .45 USP. Zombies hit by .45 ACP also rarely stood back up. When they had run low on 12-gauge she had switched to her custom-built AK firing the original 7.62X39 round, again a decent zombie killer.

When, desperate and with one of the largest cruise liners in the world still to clear, they had started using M4s and 5.56mm salvaged from a Coast Guard cutter, her normally sunny disposition had taken a downward turn. She disliked that she had to shoot zombies four or five times to get them to lie down and be good.

"Or we could use a, you know, machine gun," Fontana said.

"Ah," Faith said. "There's only like thirty of them. Back the *Toy* up to this tub and let's just shoot them off one by one."

"I thought you liked machine guns?" Fontana said.

"The whole belt fed is so last week," Faith said. "I still think it's a design flaw that you have to let up on the trigger."

"We're working on some you don't," Steve said.

"How?" Fontana said. "I mean, the only way to do that is coolant and—"

"Coolant," Steve said, nodding. "I've got the shop over on the *Grace* working on a water-cooled Browning."

"Doing the sleeve is going to be a bitch, sir," Hocieniec pointed out. "And that whole pump thing is—"

"Tech has changed remarkably since World War One, Hooch," Steve said drily. "Think coiled copper tube and an electric pump. But that's for later. Shoot them off with aimed fire or break out the 240? As usual, I'm more worried about bouncers than anything. If we use the 240, even with these light rolls, we're going to have lots of bouncers."

"We could ask the *Dallas* to come up on it for us again," Faith said.

"That...is not a bad idea," Steve said. The subs' hulls were made of thick, high-tensile steel, which was largely invulnerable to small arms fire. "*Dallas*? You monitoring as usual?"

"*Wolf, Dallas.*"

"Got a zombie entry problem again," Steve said. "You up for some kinetic clearance?"

"*We're out of seven six two, Wolf. Stand by...*"

"Standing by," Steve said.

"They floated theirs off for us," Fontana said. "Remember?"

"If it was during clearing the *Voyage*, the answer is 'It's all a blur,'" Steve said.

"*Wolf, bringing up the* Boise. *Be about twenty. You might want to clear your boats.*"

"Roger," Steve said. "Squadron Ops, you monitoring?"

"*Roger, Commodore. We'll send out the word.*"

"Get them well back and to the side," Steve said. "Five miles by preference. Stacey!"

"Moving!" Stacey Smith called. She put the *Tina's Toy* under full power and pulled away from the assault ship.

"Okay," Fontana said. "The *Dallas* has been in contact all along. Then the *Charlotte* tows the Coast Guard cutter down. Now it turns out the *Boise*'s out there. How many fricking fast attacks are around us?"

"Your continued buildup of nuclear vessels in this region proves that you have access to vaccine!"

General Marshall Sergei Kazimov was the acting commander of Russian Strategic Forces or, as he frequently referred to it, Soviet Strategic Forces. He had bluntly stated that he was Chairman of the Soviet Union. Also that if the "renegade Anglo-Sphere forces" did not immediately "vaccinate all his crews" he would "turn all of America's cities to ash."

Every time he used the term "nuclear vessels," Frank Galloway, National Constitutional Continuity Coordinator, tried not to break into a hysterical giggle. The general had no capacity at all to pronounce the "v."

"Mr. Smith has stated, and our *very few* naval personnel who have gone through vaccination and quarantine have confirmed, that there are fewer than forty units of primer and booster in Smith's control," Galloway stated, again. It was always this way negotiating with the Russians. You just repeated the truth until they either gave in or the truth changed. "Our nuclear wes... vessels in the area are purely for what support they can provide to Wolf Squadron's clearance operations...."

"You lie!" Sergei shouted. "Wolf lies!"

"I wish he did," Galloway said, sighing. "I wish that he could immediately begin production of the vaccine. But until he has more clearance personnel and can clear a land base with the right facilities, that's impossible—"

"You will provide us with the vaccine or I will blow you to *hell*!"

"And we shall retaliate," Galloway said, trying not to sigh this time. "With what we have left. Which is, Sergei, far, *far* more than *you* have. You *will* be dead, I *might* be dead, there will be some radioactive wastelands that used to be infected-filled cities and what's the point? Oh, yes, there is the point that right now, Wolf is the only chance we have to get the world back in shape...!"

"Thanks, *Boise*," Steve commed.

"*You're welcome, Wolf Squadron*," the *Boise*'s commander replied. "*Please consider us for all your future kinetic clearance needs.*"

The team had rigged up while the *Boise* was potting zombies at long range with their MG240 and they now approached the wash deck of the assault carrier in a center-console inflatable.

Rigged up has a special meaning when zombie fighting. Troops in combat just thought they rigged up. Then there was "extreme hazard close-quarters biological clearance."

Each of the foursome was wearing multiple layers of clothes, including fire-fighting bunker gear, respirators, helmets and so many weapons and clearance tools it would have been ludicrous if they hadn't proven, at least once, that all of it was necessary. Not a single square inch of skin was uncovered or was in any way, shape or form "biteable." It was hot, it was heavy and it was cumbersome. It was especially hot in the Horse Latitudes, which were well inside the tropical zone.

It also meant that, as Faith and Hooch had proven, you could be absolutely dogpiled by zombies and still keep fighting. Faith, in particular, added a knife whenever she found a good one.

"Everyone remember where we parked," Faith said, stepping off the inflatable.

"Everyone remember to *drink*," Fontana said. "And how come you get to make the first landing, again?"

"I'm the cute one," Faith said. "You coming or not?"

"Faith, we've got to explain some language to you," Fontana said.

"Oops, live one," Faith said, as a zombie came loping down the catwalk above. She fired, missed and fired again. The second round hit but the zombie just stumbled then resumed running in their direction.

"Fucking *Barbie* gun...!"

CHAPTER 2

Amidst our arms as quiet you shall be,
As halcyons brooding on a winter's sea.

Dryden

"Paula and Patrick," Sophia said. "Paula's a mate. Patrick's the engineer."

"Sort of," Patrick said, shaking Rusty's hand.

"Where'd you find beanpole?" Paula said, shaking it in turn.

"Lounge on the *Alpha*," Sophia said. "He's sort of cleared for duty and he wants to do clearance."

"And I wanted to get out of the *Grace*," Rusty said. "I really don't like being in cabins."

"*Voyage* passenger?" Patrick said, wincing. "That explains the skinny."

"Yeah," Rusty said.

"We carried a lot of those over," Paula said sadly. "We lost a few, too. But, hey, you made it," she added, brightening up. "And I am nothing if not a good cook."

"She is," Patrick said, patting his stomach. "I was pretty thin when they found me, too. But I've been putting it on since."

"I read the whole thing about the rations schedule," Rusty said awkwardly. "I'm not sure . . . One of the reasons that I chose clearance, besides I like guns and I want to kill zombies, is the 'double ration' for clearance personnel. I was on a double ration when I could finally hold it down in medical, but..."

"Don't sweat it," Paula said, grinning. "We mostly do small boat clearance. When we find a boat, we pull off the good rations first. So we've always got plenty. I don't really get the rations thing, either. That's for the big boats."

"Positive to the big boats," Sophia said. "They're bigger and they're a lot more comfortable in any sort of weather. And we *do* get weather. Don't let this flat calm fool you. Downside, there's a lot more rules. Have to be. Most people who've survived are pretty sensible. You had to be to make it. Some real idiots made it, though. Usually being carried by sensible people. But they made it. People who fill up their plates with food then just sort of look at it. Food that people like us transferred from one boat to another in a storm after somebody had gone into the shit and killed zombies, so they could just *look* at it? Don't think so. So they've got the ration schedule. You get a big plate of food then just look at it, Rusty?"

"Ma'am, I get a plate of food, I chow it all down," Rusty said. "Now, I tend to take my time these days and savor every bite. But I don't let none go to waste if I've got the time to eat it all."

"Do we have orders?" Patrick asked.

"Once we get the bigger boat, we're supposed to move out of this area and start another search grid down in the area of the Canaries," Sophia said.

"The birds?" Rusty said. "Sorry, I..."

"Canary Islands," Sophia said, pointing to the islands on a map of the Atlantic on the wall. "We'll be working with the *Large* and we'll have to scrounge for fuel and supplies. PO Kuzma will be in charge of the overall operation. He's a nice guy and he's getting used to working with us civilians but he can be sort of a stickler for safety. Which I guess is cool. We'll be working in the Equatorial Current which means some tropicals, still. But just where they're working up to a real storm. We're not going to move into the rest of the tropical zone until we're past hurricane season. Until the...*No Tan Lines*..." Sophia hung her head knowing what was coming.

"*No Tan Lines*?" Paula said, snorting. "Seriously?"

"Seriously," Sophia said. "I'm going to talk to Burnell about painting a new name on it. But until we get it, we're to provide 'logistics support' to the recovery effort on the *Iwo*. Read, pick up any survivors and carry over ammo for my little sister to burn through...."

"*Finding the way back hoooome...!*" Faith sang, dropping a mag to the deck and reloading with practiced speed.

Faith had a perfect soprano voice which was barely audible over the continuous fire. Because half the time zombies appeared out of nowhere and hearing was the best protection, she couldn't listen to her iPod all the time. But in situations like this, when they'd opened up a hatch where they *knew* there were infecteds on the other side and had set up a kill zone, she'd hit her "blow them all to hell" playlist.

Currently it was Nightwish's "Last Ride of the Day" and she was screaming the words over the torrent of fire.

The hatch in question had been from the interior of the ship to the port catwalk of the well deck. The "big hole" in the back of the ship extended forward nearly to the forecastle and held a plethora of, unfortunately useless, hovercraft. Having cleared the well deck, they had to gain entry to the ship. So Hooch had popped the hatch he remembered as heading most quickly to the hangar deck, the next major area to clear, and had then more or less flipped off the catwalk to avoid the tidal wave of zombies. They had gone right past him since he was at this point hanging under the catwalk.

Steve had taken a position on one of the hovercraft in the well to take the zombies under fire as they passed. Unless, as some of them did, they jumped off the catwalk to come after him.

Fontana and Faith had taken the catwalk. And Faith was burning through magazines in two- and three-round bursts so fast it was like watching a human machine gun. The value of the 5.56 was finally coming into play. It might not kill very well but it went through body armor like nobody's business. And about half of the infected had managed to strip off their trousers before turning but hadn't managed the same with their body armor.

"*Wake up, Dead Boy, Enter adventure land,*" Faith caroled as Fontana tapped her shoulder. Despite the torrent of fire, the infecteds were closing. Kevlar was like that.

Faith stepped back, dropping another magazine, and continued singing without a pause.

"*IT'S HARD TO LIGHT A CANDLE, EASY TO CURSE THE DARK INSTEAD,*" she screamed the chorus, still in tune, reloading again. "*THIS MOMENT THE DAWN OF HUMANITY. THE LAST RIDE OF THE DAY!*"

The infected were getting close enough, about half the time she was double tapping one to the chest, one to the head. And she was getting at least eight out of ten head shots.

"She really gets into this," Fontana yelled.

Steve just stuck his thumb up, double tapping a zombie trying to climb up the side of the landing craft.

The infecteds on the catwalk were clear and Faith ducked behind Fontana to shoot the last few that were attempting to get to her father. She popped nine rounds in a rhythmic pattern, dropped her magazine and held the empty weapon over her head.

"Yes," she shouted. "Last one down *right* at the end of the song on the last ROUND, headshot through a *helmet*! That is AWESOME!"

"One just came out of the hatch," Fontana said, pointing.

"Oh..." she snarled, reloading. "Oh, that's just...upstager! Moment ruiner!"

"I got it," Fontana said, putting one in the chest and one in the head.

"Can somebody get me down?" Hooch asked.

"Okay, Hooch, how the *hell* did you *lose* this thing?" Faith asked, stepping over body after body. They were all well decomposed, most of them were infecteds, judging by the lack of clothing, and they were all shot to hell. "You guys put up one *hell* of a fight."

"We're Marines, Shewolf," Hocieniec said. "It's sort of what we do. But when half the guys in your squad turn on you...It's sort of hard to hold a position. *Any* position."

"And, Faith, note the *lack* of ricochet marks?" Fontana pointed out.

"Only Imperial Storm Troopers are this precise," Steve intoned.

"Tell that to Princess Leia!" Faith said. "Storm troopers can't hit the broad side of a *barn*!"

"You got any idea how hard it is to find your way around the Death Star!" Hocieniec said. "It's the size of a *moon*. I was on the Death Star for four years and I never *did* find the cantina on level Sixty-Nine! They were being *herded*!"

"Compartment," Fontana said. "I got it."

"I used to enjoy knocking," Faith said. She pulled out a billet of steel and banged on the walls. "Anybody home but the dead?"

"At least it isn't as complicated as the *Voyage*," Steve said, flashing a tac light at the ship schematics in damage control.

They'd *known* about the Damage Control Center in the *Voyage*. It was the obvious first place to go if you could get there. Modern damage control centers were mostly computer based and the Coast Guard had software that would allow downloading the schematics to even a smartphone. They also had detailed, hardbacked for carriage, maps that you could remove in case of loss of power or, oh, a zombie apocalypse.

The schematics for the *Voyage* had been *twenty-eight* six foot by six foot maps on a harder form of poster board. They'd taken one look and gone back to the brochures.

In this case, since they had Hooch to guide them at least this far, they'd decided to try to start with a plan.

"It's still pretty..." Hooch said, looking at the bare nine maps. "You're right, sir."

"Start looking for food storage lockers below the line of the main water tanks," Steve said, as Faith started pulling out the maps and arranging them around the room. She was having to step over bodies but that was so normal at this point it didn't even register. She propped one of the maps up on a lieutenant commander whose face had been eaten off.

"Let's get started," Steve said.

"You okay, Hooch?" Faith said.

They weren't finding many survivors. The few who had apparently been uninfected in the upper reaches of the ship were dead from starvation, dehydration or suicide in the face of either.

"I am five by five, Shewolf," Hooch said, closing the hatch of the compartment.

"I think I should do it," Faith said. "Trixie says you shouldn't look in any more compartments unless we hear survivors."

"Tell Trixie I'll be okay," Hooch said. "But thanks. Honestly, I didn't expect anything more on this level. And it looks like a lot of them saved the last round."

"So far I will admit to some disappointment," Steve said. "It looks as if this was the aviation officer's quarters."

"It was, sir," Hocieniec said.

"I was hoping to find at least one helo pilot," Steve said.

"Having a helo pilot would be cool," Faith said. "We could, like, drop in on these things instead of climbing. I don't like heights. Heights over water is better. Except for the whole we're wearing ten billion pounds of gear and there are always man-eating sharks. So, yeah, helo would be nice."

"Thank you, Faith," Steve said. "I had a broader reason but that's a good point."

"Just here to be helpful," Faith said, banging on the bulkhead. "Anybody hooome...?"

"*No Tan Lines*?" Steve said, trying not to snort.

"Oh, my God," Faith said gleefully. "That is so *you*, Soph!"

After the continuous nightmare of clearing the *Voyage*, Steve decided that there was only so much any one person could do. Not to mention he rarely got to see his kids who were still growing up. Okay, he probably saw *too* much of Faith. But the same could not be said of Sophia.

So while they were around he tried to have a family dinner, just the four of them, at least once a week. They were the only intact family in the squadron. They might as well make the most of it.

"All it takes to change it is some paint and a good hand," Stacey pointed out.

"You know, we talked about it and decided to keep the name," Sophia said, spooning up the ikan santen. Da's one real "perk" as the boss was that he had one of the better cooks they'd found. Sari was a real find. She'd had it as hard as anyone, harder than some, but she just sailed along. She didn't talk much about when the *Alpha* was in the hands of its "security contingent." The security, a group called Socorro Security run by a former SF major Fontana knew, and loathed, was one of the last, and worst, decisions Mike Mickerberg ever made. Dad had boiled it down to: If you have to use mercenaries, choose wisely. Socorro Security had not been a wise choice.

"That was somebody's pride and joy. It's a nice boat. Changing the name would be sort of dissing the dead. So we'll keep it."

"I'm sure you'll...overcome it?" her mom said.

"Actually, Mom," Sophia said. "Hate to tell you this but I don't *have* much in the way of tan lines."

"How's your new security guy?" Steve said, to fill in the gap in the conversation.

"I think he'll do," Sophia said, shrugging. "And if not, I'll find another. He's no Fontana. No real training. But he says he grew up with guns. Redneck, you know? I gave him a pistol and he knew which way the magazine went in. I had to explain that on my boat, you had better clear *every single time*. I'll make sure he stays safe. Best I can do for now."

"We haven't found any survivors, yet," Steve said. "But it's early days and the areas we're checking we weren't really expecting any."

"I hope they're in..." Stacey said then glanced at Faith.

"Better condition than the ones we found on the *Voyage*?" Faith said. "Me too. And when we don't get any response, I haven't been checking the compartments. Hooch has, which is sort of—"

"He's handling it," Steve said. "What do you think about the trip south, Soph?"

"Looking forward to it," Sophia said. "I want to get back to nautical, you know? Do some fishing, do some rescuing. Clear some boats."

"You're going to need a better, and bigger, base than the *Large* eventually," Steve said. "Keep an eye out for something. If it's too big for your group to clear, we'll send down a team. Hopefully, anyway. Assuming there's anything to find."

The problem with distress beacons was that they lasted a far shorter time than humans could. With a solar still, a fishing line or spear gun and some luck, people could survive a long time on rafts or lifeboats. One guy in the '80s had drifted across almost the entire Atlantic in a life raft. Some lifeboats had solar powered distress beacons. But their range was short. And boats' and ships' distress signals stopped when their batteries ran out. It was mostly a matter of "Mark One Eyeball" finding the boats these days.

"There'll be *stuff*," Sophia said. "There always is. I'm not sure about *survivors*. I'm sort of going to miss the tuna tower on the *Endeavor*. It was good for spotting stuff. The new one is lower even though it's a fishing boat, too."

"'Oh, I just get a pleasure yacht.'" Faith mimicked. "All *I* get is a ton of stuff and a Barbie gun!"

"Faith..."

So maybe a family dinner wasn't the best idea...

∽⊝⤳

Stacey Smith had decided there should be a law against using Volvo marine engines.

Stacey noticed, quickly, that as Wolf Squadron grew in size her role as the family's designated mechanic had faded. There were more and more pros who knew what they were doing. On the other hand, there were never enough even half-trained hands and she wasn't somebody to just sit around, so every day she'd wander over to the mechanic shop on the Grace and ask, "Anybody need a hand?"

Which kindness led to, for example, being upside down, squeezed into the narrow space between the port engine and bulkhead of the latest yacht brought in for "servicing," trying to get to the damned oil plug on this—did the designers even think about the fact the oil occasionally needed changing?—Volvo God Damned Marine Diesel. Because instead of putting the oil plug fore or aft on their engines, preferably with enough space for a person to get to the plug, they'd put it to one side. Easy enough to change on the starboard engine: Just reach under, put in a pan, and take off the plug. On the port engine, the only way to get to it was crawl over the engine, and remember to bring the pan, slither down the narrow gap between the engine and the bulkhead, kind of get on your back, more like your neck, then reaaach . . .

Bad enough that she was dealing with morning sickness. She had gotten over being seasick just in time for that little joy. Try being morning sick, upside down, on a rocking boat, trying to reach a God damned oil plug on a God Damned Volvo Marine Diesel!

"Mrs. Smith?"

"Yo," Stacey said.

Mrs. Sabrina Dunn wasn't sure where the voice was coming from. There didn't seem to be anyone in the compartment but there were some minor mechanical noises coming from somewhere under one of the engines.

She squatted down creakily, then got down on her stomach when it was clear she couldn't see under the engine that way. By peering under the engine she could just see one eye of, presumably, the commodore's wife. She appeared to be the source of the mechanical noises.

"Got you, you little bitch," the commodore's wife muttered. There were more mechanical noises.

This clearly wasn't the best time, but Mrs. Dunn was not about to be dissuaded from her self-appointed errand.

"Mrs. Smith, I request a moment of your time..."

The voice was polite but firm. All Stacey could see of the woman was some white hair and one eye.

"Gimme a sec," Stacey grunted as the nut surrendered to the ratchet. Whoever put it on the last time must have had forearms like a gorilla. The oil finally started pouring out of the overdue-for-maintenance engine and she began to contemplate how the hell to get out of her current position. "Whatcha got?"

"Pardon me?" the woman asked.

"I've got a minute here," Stacey said, then muttered: "Okay, how the hell are you supposed to get the oil out of the damned pan?" She hadn't gotten that far in her planning. The space between the engine and the bulkhead was too narrow to just pull the pan out even if she could. She'd have to tip it, and the oil, all over the deck. "Pump?"

"I... What?" the woman said.

"Never mind," Stacey said. "You had something you wanted to ask about?"

"Mrs. Smith, I understand that we are in rather difficult conditions..." the woman said.

Stacey snorted.

"You mean what with this being a zombie apocalypse and all?" Stacey said.

"Yes, that," the woman said, "as well as being still, essentially, stranded at sea. However, there are issues which I feel are not being properly addressed."

"Like making sure the fleet does not have Volvo marine diesels?" Stacey muttered. The good part about Volvos was they were reliable as hell. The bad part was, well... Might actually be a wash, come to think of it...

"I... what?" the woman said.

"What issues?" Stacey asked.

"The most notable is hair products," the woman said.

"Hair products?" Stacey said, trying not to snort. The woman was clearly as serious as a banker looking at a questionable investment.

"You have medium length hair, Mrs. Smith," the woman said.

"Do you wash it with the dishwashing soap currently being issued for showers?"

Stacey stopped and thought about that for a moment. She'd asked Sophia to scrounge some decent shampoo and conditioner for her on her trip south.

"No, actually," Stacey said. "You've got a point. But it's Isham's department, ma'am."

"I attempted to bring the issue to Mr. Isham's department and they frankly rebuffed me, Mrs. Smith," the woman said with not quite a sniff.

"Jack's a busy guy," Stacey said with, she knew, massive understatement. "So you want me to bring this up with Steve?" Like he needed that.

"If you would, Mrs. Smith," the woman said. "Both your husband, the commodore, and Mr. Isham have short hair. Most of the women in the squadron have medium length to long, and such hair does not respond well to Dawn dishwashing soap."

"Okay, point again," Stacey said. "I'll bring it up. What's your name, by the way?"

"Mrs. Sabrina Dunn," the woman said. "Widow of the late Mr. James Dunn of the Westland Dunns."

"Mrs. Sabrina Dunn, now that I've promised to do you a favor—just bring it up, not fix it for you, not sure if we can but I'll bring it up—can you do me one?"

"Which is?"

"Go find one of the regular mechanics. Ask them to come down here. Two reasons: One, I can't figure out how to get the oil out from under the engine; Two, I think I'm stuck."

"Hair products?" Steve said over dinner.

"She had a point," Stacey said. "Most of us are pregnant and feel like shit. You know how I get about how I look when I'm pregnant."

"Lovely in my opinion," Steve said, grinning.

"Letch," Stacey said, shaking her head. "We don't also need to have crappy hair. I guess the question is, how much do you want to improve female morale?"

"Point," Steve said. "Jack will just love to have this thrown at him. Anything else?"

"I'm getting a lot of this sort of stuff," Stacey said, shrugging. "That's just the only one I've brought up with you."

"Perils of being a commodore's wife," Steve said thoughtfully. "I hadn't thought about it before but . . . sorry."

"It's not my strong point, Steve," Stacey said unhappily. "People keep asking me to fix things. I mean, if it's an engine, I'll give it a shot. This kind of stuff . . . not my strong point."

"Unfortunately, it's important," Steve said. "This kind of back-channeling is the lube a society runs on."

"So now I'm the lube?" Stacey said with a snort. "Thanks."

"It's the reason that in the old adage about marriage in the military, 'Colonels must marry,'" Steve said. "There's more, necessary, information transfer in a society than just what occurs in meetings. It's arguably more important than changing the oil on an engine. It's changing the oil on the squadron."

"Great," Stacey said. "Again, not my strong point, Steve. I don't do tea and crumpets."

"Who brought the hair thing up with you?" Steve asked.

"'Mrs. Sabrina Dunn,'" Stacey intoned. "'Widow of the late . . . Somebody Dunn of the Westland Dunns.' I was clearly supposed to know who the Westland Dunns were."

"There's your answer," Steve said.

"What answer?" Stacey said.

"I couldn't run this lash-up without Isham," Steve said. "Appoint her your chief of staff. She clearly does know how to back-channel. It's been her whole life. Not necessarily her, you understand, but somebody like her. Just make clear that it can be taken too far. I don't need your chief of staff constantly bothering my chief of staff, saying 'I'd hate to have to bring this up with the commodore' or something. But get an assistant for this sort of stuff. Throw most of it on them. But still figure, especially as we get larger, you're going to be doing more changing the oil on the squadron than on boats. It really is important, honey."

"I get that," Stacey said, sighing. "Sort of. And you've got a point. I'll go look her up tomorrow."

"Now, about that special glow you get when you're pregnant . . ."

"Letch . . ."

"Oh, yes," Sophia said, pulling away from the cluster of craft around the *Iwo Jima*. They hadn't managed to sneak quite all of the *Endeavor*'s "special stocks" over to the new boat, but they'd gotten a lot of them. And she wasn't having to ferry stuff back and forth from the *Alpha* or *Grace* anymore. "The freedom of the open sea..."

"*Kuzma Flotilla, form line astern of Vessel One,*" Kuzma called. "*And when I say, 'form line,' I mean something resembling an actual line.*"

"You were saying?" Paula asked.

"Son of a *bitch*..."

"Son of a bitch," the sailor said, covering his eyes.

"I told you to cover your eyes and *not* open the hatch all the way up," Fontana said, tossing a chemlight into the compartment. "That will give your eyes some time to adjust. How many in your compartment?"

"Four," the petty officer said. "Left."

"Here's four pairs of sunglasses," Fontana said. "Put them on when we come back."

"You Coast Guard?"

"No. Nor Navy, Marines or Sea Scouts. Wolf Squadron. I'm Special Forces, she's some sort of psycho anime chick come to life..."

"Hey!"

"Long story..."

"I'm up for a threesome if anybody's interested...?"

When you were so bored and tired of being in a compartment with people you no longer could stand that you couldn't even get a *flicker* out of Mister Willy at a suggestion like that, you knew it was bad. And he was out of Copenhagen. Bad on toast.

Turned out that Gowen had never had group sex. Group sex hadn't been what Januscheitis had actually suggested but the idea got floated about two weeks after their little discussion. After the first time, she got really into it. By a couple of weeks after *that* it had been ongoing. There was flat *nothing* else to do in the compartment. He'd tried reading by the light of his watch and decided that was a bad idea. And he was out of Copenhagen. The senior NCO in the compartment had not been a happy camper for a few days when the Copenhagen ran out.

He'd maintained PT every day. Some of the guys thought that a go around with Gowen should count. They'd done PT, even Patel the swabbie. So had Gowen even after it was pretty clear she was preggers. How they were going to explain that, he wasn't sure.

They'd checked the corridors to see if the zombies had left. On one end the answer was they'd all died of dehydration. Which meant that the watertight doors on the other side were dogged. They'd checked that and run into more zombies. So their perimeter had expanded but that was about it. They'd knocked on a couple of bulkheads and found out there were other survivors in the area. But nobody they could link up with. The zombies held all the intermediate areas.

They'd used tap code to get a roster and passed their own on. They'd tried to use it to pass information and converse. That had worked for prisoners of war but there was no real point with this situation.

One of the compartments had run short of water after a short while. They'd tapped about ways to get some to them but they had nothing that could cut through the steel bulkheads. L-4-638 tapped that they drew lots and were going to "terminate" two to conserve water. It was three dudes and a split and the dudes had agreed that she wasn't in the lottery.

Semper Fi, dudes. Both of the Marines had "terminated."

Now 638 was just about down to the final male swabbie terminating. They were drinking piss mixed with water and everything that anyone could think of to hold out. L-4-642 had dudes slowly scratching through with a crowbar, trying to cut a hole to the compartment. Like their own, 642 had a tap and was below the main fresh water tanks. So far they'd had a steady stream and they were putting more into every ration can they emptied.

L-4-649 was low on food. But they figured they had about another two months on short rations, and 642 had reported that when they were through to 638 they'd try to find a way to 649. Eventually you could cut through steel with a crowbar. They weren't reporting their progress, though, which didn't bode well for either compartment.

"I wouldn't turn down a blowjob," PFC Rodas replied.

"Patel, you're up," Derek said.

"That is getting really old, jarhead," Seaman Patel snapped.

"Come here, honey," Derek said. "If none of these other gentlemen are up to the challenge of satisfying you—"

"Freeze," Smitty said.

"What?" Gowen said. "Why...?"

"Shut the fuck up," Januscheitis snapped. "Smitty?"

"Freeze," the sergeant replied. "Listen."

"Got noth—"

"I hear it," Gowen said. "Banging?"

"So somebody's banging on a compart—"

There was the clear echo of a burst of fire in the distance.

"Threesome hereby terminated," Januscheitis said, rolling to his feet. "Somebody survived with *rounds*! Git it on, Marines!"

"OORAH!"

"I think we got customers," Faith said, listening to the distant banging.

"Supply areas," Fontana said. "Makes sense."

"Hooch," Faith said, keying her radio. "We got more customers in Sector L."

"Good to hear," Hooch replied. "We've got some in M as well."

Rain had blown into some of the open outer hatches. That had, in turn, worked into pools in the upper area corridors, some of them all the way to the coamings. There were dead bodies and shit in most of the water but the zombies drank it anyway. It was amazing what the human body could withstand. Some anyway.

They'd been following a series of open hatches, finding live zombies all the way down. The surrounding compartments had all failed to respond to banging. Somebody else would have the fun of checking them later.

"This way," Fontana said, turning his head from side to side.

Faith banged on the hatch and was rewarded with the irregular banging, scratching and howling they'd come to associate with zombies.

"Right about now I'd like a grenade or something," she said, putting her hand on the hatch's locking mechanism.

"Never use a frag on a boat," Fontana said. "About the only thing I knew about clearing boats before this. Ready?"

"Hang on," Faith said, reaching for her iPod. "Or a chainsaw maybe..."

"Open the hatch," Januscheitis said.

"You su—?" Derek said then recalled he was a Marine again. "Aye, aye, Staff Sergeant."

They didn't have much in the way of melee weapons but if the rescuers needed help they were going to give it. Januscheitis figured that it must have been a group like themselves who had somehow held out long enough to access a magazine. And the rescue team's noise had drawn the infecteds away from hatch 943.

Derek popped the hatch and Januscheitis went through, crowbar up and at the ready.

What he had forgotten was that there was little or no way that any rescue group could clear without having lights. Derek popped the hatch at almost exactly the same time as the rescue group opened theirs. He wasn't even in direct line and the lights had him blinded. They must have been using about fifty tac lights or some sort of super-power spot.

Then he heard the singing. *Everybody* heard the singing.

"I'm one with the warrior inside," Faith caroled. *"My dominance can't be denied! Your entire world will turn into a battlefield tonight!"*

She was taking point, multitapping in time with the rhythm and dancing as she backed up from the oncoming infecteds. When she hit the end of the chorus she rolled to the left, popping out her magazine as Fontana took over. After a quick reload, she had taken the back position as Fontana continued to engage the infecteds. When he was out, she took over again. *"Come on bring it, you can't see it . . ."*

Januscheitis had taken cover behind the hatch at the fire from down corridor but while there were some bouncers from pass-throughs, the fire was remarkably accurate, given that the shooter seemed to be a split with an addiction to Disturbed. What was . . . disturbing was that the shots were in time to the music. There was a second shooter that took over with what was to his ears really solid timing. He'd tuned his ears to combat in plenty of actions and he caught the very quick reload, in time to the song again but fast. This was an experienced two-person team that had worked together *a lot.*

The firing finally settled down and Januscheitis stuck his head back out. The months had really wrecked his eyes but he could sort of pick up, from the singing and the way that the lights were flashing around, that the split had continued to dance after the firefight was over.

There were lights moving their way, though, and he slit his eyes against them, then covered them entirely.

"Sorry about her," a voice said. "Chemlight coming through.

Once she starts a song she's *impossible* until it's done. And that wasn't enough infecteds to run through 'Warrior.' Thank God it wasn't 'Citadel' or 'Winterborn.' We'd be here all day."

"No issues, dude," Januscheitis said. "Never been gladder to hear fire. Or meet new people. I guess you're not guys from the *Iwo*."

"One of us is," the dude said as the split continued to sing. And apparently dance. "Hooch is with the other team. But, no, Wolf Squadron. Volunteer group. Mostly civvies with some odds and sods of others. Staff Sergeant Thomas Fontana, Fifth Special Forces Group. And I was just a castaway myself."

"It's that fucked up?" Januscheitis said.

"It's that fucked up. Pretty much totally fucking gone. Chain of command is guys on a radio in the Hole in Omaha. And they're not moving."

"Jesus."

"*As I stand before you. With a warrior's heart now. I can feel the strength that will. Ensure my victory this tiiiiiiime...*"

"Okay," Fontana said. "I guess we can get going now..."

CHAPTER 3

You cannot exaggerate about the Marines. They are convinced to the point of arrogance, that they are the most ferocious fighters on earth—and the amusing thing about it is that they are.

Father Kevin Keaney
1st Marine Division Chaplain
Korean War

"Lieutenant, Lieutenant, Staff Sergeant, have a seat," said "Wolf," gesturing to the table.

Januscheitis sort of knew the Marine lieutenant. He'd been an XO in Charlie. The Navy lieutenant, equivalent of a Marine captain, he didn't know.

"Wolf" looked tired. He should, from the little Januscheitis had picked up. He wasn't sure how big the "*Voyage*" thing was but from what people had said it was the size of a supercarrier with about as many compartments. And now here the "commodore" was clearing the *Iwo* with one Marine, one SF Staff and a thirteen-year-old split. Who, admittedly, was pretty fucking badass.

"The pamphlet you were given only covers rough details," Smith said. "And it glosses over a lot of things. The Joint Chiefs is a group of colonels or equivalent and one general—"

"Excuse me, sir?" the Navy LT said.

"You heard me, Lieutenant," Smith said. "There are probably

more senior officers who've survived. Somewhere. But the current acting CNO, being someone who is actually in communication and in direct contact with the NCCC, is a *commander*. Given that our current count on Navy personnel who are not essentially trapped in subs is..." He consulted a list. "Seventeen, he's actually overranked. But we are, now, starting to have some semblance of an actual military force, U.S. military at that, and the question of who is legally permitted to give orders has come up. So, I had a talk with the chiefs and the NCCC and now *you* are going to have a chat with the chiefs, or at least the Navy commander in the Hole and a sub commander that slightly outranks him. Their decision...surprised me. And not in a good way. But they'll explain it to you."

He turned his laptop around and nodded as he got up.

"I apparently have to go find a uniform somewhere..."

"Lieutenant Joseph Pellerin?" the commander on the screen asked. It was split three ways. The person talking was in some sort of meeting room. One of the guys was a civilian, also in a meeting room; one was another commander with the background of a sub con.

"Yes, sir," Pellerin said cautiously.

"I'm Commander Louis Freeman. The gentleman in the suit is Under Secretary Frank Galloway, the National Constitutional Continuity Coordinator."

"I was formerly the Under Deputy Secretary of Defense for Nuclear Arms Proliferation Control," Galloway said. "I was number one hundred and twenty-six on the list of potential NCCCs or Acting Presidents."

"Hundred and twenty-*six*?" Januscheitis whispered.

"Also present is Commander Alan Huskey, skipper of the *Florida*," Commander Freeman said. "Although I am, technically, the head of the Navy by various regulations, Commander Huskey has me by date of rank as well as being a boomer commander. I have not yet had a command of any vessel as a commander. It's not a split in command in any way. But we thought he should be present."

"Yes, sir," Pellerin said, blinking.

"You're barely out of the ship, Lieutenant," Huskey said, his arms crossed. His uniform fit him loosely and he had the look of prolonged malnutrition. "Are you sure you and your people are up for a difficult conversation?"

"Possibly," Pellerin replied.

"That would be yes or no, Lieutenant," Huskey said. "Possibly is not the correct answer."

"Sir . . ." Pellerin said, with a touch of rancor. "It's not that I just got out of a compartment. Mine had plenty of food and water. I . . . maintained discipline . . ."

"I'll ignore the pauses," Galloway said, smiling thinly. "If you're wondering about the question of 'what happened in the compartment' . . ."

"I'm wondering about the whole thing, Mr. Under Secretary," Pellerin said. "From my perspective, I'm looking at some people in ill-fitting uniforms on a computer. You could all be sitting in the bowels of this ship for all I know. And, yes, I saw a sub on the surface and a couple of people in Coast Guard uniform. But . . ."

"You're suspicious," Huskey said. "Okay. You saw a sub. How many subs would it take to convince you that Mr. Galloway is, functionally, the Acting President and that I and Commander Freeman continue to control all military personnel who are in contact? Because, Lieutenant, that's the reality. As is the reality that we're still in a cleft stick. Which we need Wolf Squadron to pull us out of and thus we need Wolf."

Januscheitis tapped the Navy lieutenant on the shoulder and waved for some screen time.

"You have input, Staff Sergeant?" Pellerin said coldly.

"How many subs are there around here, sirs?" Januscheitis asked. "Can you say? With due respect?"

"Not many, frankly," Huskey replied. "Most of them are in position . . . elsewhere. Or deep. But are most of the attack boats in the Atlantic around Wolf Squadron? Yes. No reason for them not to be. There is not much else going on. The rest are generally maintaining security for our boomers—such as this one—and providing security to the extent they can for certain coastal installations. What is it going to take for you to recognize that you have a chain of command again, short as it is, Lieutenant?"

"Sir, I . . ." Pellerin said then paused as the compartment door opened.

"I was told I should be present for this, sir," the Marine gunny said. He was skinny as a rail and his eyes were glossy but his back was still ramrod straight. "Gunnery Sergeant Tommy J. Sands, sir, reporting for duty."

"Gunny Sands," Januscheitis said, breathing a sigh of relief. "Jesus."

"No, a Gunny," Sands said, walking over and shaking his hand. "But I can see where people get confused. Janu," he said, clapping him on the back. "Good to see you made it."

"Thank you, Gunnery Sergeant," Januscheitis said. He was clearly trying not to cry.

"Get your shit together, Marine," Sands said. "Sorry, sirs. Old home week."

"Not a problem, Gunny," Pellerin said. "We are discussing... We are discussing the CV of persons who are allegedly the remaining chain of command. I am not dismissing that, sirs, it's just..."

"I guess caution is in order," Galloway said drily. "Gunnery Sergeant, if you'd care to join us."

"Yes, sir?" Sands said. Januscheitis was already up and waved him to the seat. "And we're meeting with...?"

"The acting CNO," Huskey said. "Which is Commander Freeman on your screen, as well as the NCCC. Are you familiar with—"

"I'm familiar with the Succession act, sir," Sands said. "And the TS codicils, sir. Under Secretary... Galloway, is it? Sir?"

"Yes, Gunny," Galloway said, surprised.

"I heard since I got sprung that you was in the Hole, sir," Sands said. "May I ask if there's a Marine officer, sir?"

"Colonel Ellington," Galloway said.

"So that's where they stuffed that poor bastard," Sands said, shaking his head.

"Colonel Ellington is... present, Gunnery Sergeant," Galloway said, wincing.

"Sorry, sir," Sands said as Ellington came up on the screen. "I never got a chance to say it, personally, sir, but I was real sorry to hear about your wife. She was one in a million, sir. They broke the mold."

"Thanks, Tommy," Ellington said. "What with everything that's going on..." He shook his head. "And I'd agree about the breaking the mold if it weren't for the young lady doing clearance..."

"Shewolf, sir?" Sands said, grinning. "That girl *scares* me."

"You really have to see the video of her boarding the *Voyage*," Ellington said. "Especially one with her comment about a 'back-up plan.'"

"Bradburn from the *Dallas* literally fell out of his chair on that one," Commander Huskey said.

"You know each other," the NCCC said.

"The gunny was a security sergeant when I was a maintenance officer at Kings Bay, sir," Ellington said.

"And I was stuck in the Pentagon when you were working in prolif, Mr. Galloway," Sands said. "I recognize you. I was over in Colonel Grant's shop."

"Lieutenant Pellerin," Galloway said. "Does this satisfy your questions as to our validity?"

"Yes, sir," Pellerin said. "Again, sir, no disrespect..."

"Understood," Galloway said. "So, turning the matter over to Commander Freeman again. Commander?"

"Situation as it stands," Freeman said. "This was, apparently, the only headquarters uninfected by the Plague. There are no other U.S. command posts responding. POTUS was unable to access NEACAP due to possible compromise of the pilots, headed to Mount Weather in a heavy ground convoy and was never heard from again. Similar story on the VPOTUS although VPOTUS was headed for Raven Mountain and there was a definite report her ground convoy was compromised. Mount Weather, which held a good bit of the Congress and Cabinet, was responding for a period of time then reported they were compromised and stopped responding. Raven Mountain, President of the Senate, other half of the Cabinet, et cetera, simply went off the air. Boulder: compromised. Sunnyvale: compromised. I could go on but I won't. We appear to be it.

"There are a number of uninfected submarines, the exact number is still classified, at sea. They have limited stores. All of the subs are fishing for their supper."

"It's really amazing what you can do with active if you don't have to worry about being detected," Commander Huskey said.

"To free the submarine crews, as well as our own facility someday, hopefully, as well as, well, *save the world*, will require vaccine," Freeman continued. "There are two types of vaccine. One is made from vat-grown proteins. This is a very complicated process. The other requires certain materials and equipment that is unavailable at sea. At least, as far as we have been able to determine. Are you with me so far?"

"Yes, sir," Pellerin said.

"The second type mostly requires the spine of a zombie, if I remember right, sir," Sands said.

"What?" the, to this point silent, Marine lieutenant said.

"That is correct, Gunny," Freeman said. "Or any infected higher-order primate. The CDC and USAMRIID produced such vaccine from rhesus monkeys for their personnel as well as certain critical government officials. Unfortunately, there wasn't enough to get everybody that needed it. The way it is made is to separate the virus bodies from the spinal cord then irradiate them. The irradiation has to be extremely fine, more fine than can be done with a reactor. It takes either a radiation therapy machine or a certain type of dental X-ray machine. Also some specific lab equipment and materials. But with that and, yes, the spinal cord of an infected higher order primate, you have vaccine. And a bunch of other 'stuff.'"

"Wolf had access to that type of vaccine prior to leaving the States," Galloway said. "And someone close to him, we believe his wife, assisted in its production."

"Oh," Januscheitis muttered. "That had to be cold."

"At this point, I'm not going to pass moral or legal judgment," Galloway said then shrugged. "Given the . . . the way that the infected were 'cared' for was horrific. And it's been shown that the virus does permanent damage. There is no 'cure' as such. CDC has confirmed that in animal testing. Using them as a source of vaccine would have been, in retrospect, a much better choice. But that is twenty-twenty hindsight and no one was even willing to openly broach the idea prior to the Fall. The point is that not only does Wolf have the knowledge to produce the vaccine, he has a plan which may provide the equipment and materials. He also . . . has been and continues to be the main driving force of this rescue operation, which is the only such rescue operation ongoing in the world. At least of its size."

"This is it, sir?" Lieutenant Pellerin said. "Some small craft and a couple of ships?"

"That's it, Lieutenant," Huskey said. "Smith had the combination of being vaccinated and having a boat that was sufficiently stored, armed and safe to hold out until the Plague had run its course. There are one or two other small groups in other oceans but they are even smaller than what you've seen."

"We just finished a long conversation with the admittedly

fatigued commodore," Galloway said. "Our conclusion was to give the commodore a U.S. Navy Captaincy."

"Sorry, sir," Gunny Sands said. "A *Captaincy*, sir?"

"Yes, Gunnery Sergeant," Galloway said. "That would, we are aware, put him in command of not only yourselves but all of the Navy commanders at sea. Mr. Smith, pardon, *Captain* Smith, is fully aware that this is an ambiguous situation. The explanation for this decision is long. Would you like it?"

"I'm sorry, sir," Pellerin said. "I would, sir."

"Are you familiar with Wendell Fertig, Lieutenant?" Galloway asked.

"Oh," Gunny Sands said, nodding. "That makes sense, now, sir."

"No, sir," Pellerin said, frowning. "Was he a Marine?"

"Fertig was, prior to World War Two, a civilian civil engineer in the Philippines," Galloway said. "He was direct commissioned an Army captain shortly before the war broke out. He was rapidly promoted to major, definitely, and according to some reports to lieutenant colonel although the Army never confirmed that.

"After the fall of the Philippines to the Japanese, he began organizing guerillas. Recognizing that they would never follow a major or possibly lieutenant colonel, he styled himself a brigadier general. And it worked. By the time MacArthur landed, there were thirty thousand Filipinos under arms and MacArthur was greeted by a marching band.

"It was a matter of social values systems as well as competence. Various persons in history have styled themselves Generalissimo something or another. Fertig was, in fact, competent to organize and develop a guerilla movement. But he also needed the cachet of being a *general*, not a major. The entire thing was, as 'Wolf Squadron' is, a cult of personality. A barbarian band more than a military force. It is about getting lots of people to do stuff, quoting Wolf, 'for no other reason than that I ask.'

"You are currently the senior Navy officer who is not essentially trapped. But no one knows who 'Lieutenant Pellerin' is. Everyone knows of Commodore Wolf. He did not style himself that way, by the way; the moniker was given to him by his captains. Which is sort of the point. With an actual captaincy, he has both his cult of personality *and* controlling legal authority. And he is the man with the plan who, thus far, has been succeeding. Thus the 'competence' part. I will not say that there are not questions and a degree of angst. Captain Smith, himself, expressed some negativity about the captaincy. Among other things, he expressed that he intends to continue to consider himself essentially acting in independent command. His exact words were 'Okay, but don't joggle my elbow.'"

"This is an old fashioned approach," Huskey said. "Lieutenant, we are brought up in a professional environment of low-key officership. It's about standing out just enough. Stand out too much, make too many waves, and you're never going to make captain much less admiral. Just do your job professionally and stand out that way. But... Things change. There's been this thing called the Plague that has wiped out most of humanity. People need someone who *does* stand out. Someone to follow. A legend, if you will. Smith has created that."

"Half militia, half regular forces," Sands said. "Mixing that will be...difficult, sir."

"Regular officers will retain much of the actual control," Galloway said. "We're not going to give him the keys to a boomer and he sure as heck cannot order a nuclear strike. Be that as it may, the decision has been made. Steven John Smith is now a captain in the United States Navy and outranks everyone else he may run across for the time being. You are, Lieutenant, Gunnery Sergeant, shortly to be under his command. There remains only one small detail to complete."

"Which is, sir?" Pellerin asked.

"It is required by law that a commissioned officer swear in a commissioned officer," Huskey said drily. "And since none of *us* can so much as shake his hand..."

General Orders, Wolf Squadron...
Steven John Smith directly commissioned Ensign, USN.
Steven John Smith promoted Captain, USNR.
Captain Steven John Smith, USNR, appointed Commander, Atlantic Fleet.

CHAPTER 4

When the Himalayan peasant meets the he-bear in his pride,
He shouts to scare the monster, who will often turn aside.
But the she-bear thus accosted rends the peasant tooth and nail.
For the female of the species is more deadly than the male.

"The Female of the Species"
Rudyard Kipling

"Oooo," Sophia said, setting down the mike on the flying bridge. "Da's going to have the big head."

They were floating under a moonlit tropical sky. It was nearly impossible to spot vessels at night so they went to low power to conserve energy rather than continuing their search grid and just kept an eye on the radar. With the lights of the boat turned down, there was so little light pollution in the middle of the Atlantic you could see every satellite hurtling by. Sophia wondered how long they'd stay up. The GPS satellites were particularly important.

"You really think so?" Paula said.

"Actually, no," Sophia said. "But I'll have to twit him about it."

"*No Tan Lines, Alexandria, over.*"

"Who?" Paula said.

"Dunno," Sophia said. "*Alexandria, Lines, over.*"

"*Switch to channel twenty-two for retrans, over.*"

"Sub," Sophia said. "Roger. Up on twenty-two."

"Sophia, Da, over."

"Da," Sophia said, grinning. "Got the big head have we? Commander Atlantic Fleet?"

"Maybe once I find a uniform that fits. Not a personal call."

"Roger, Captain," Sophia said.

"I just got off the horn with Kuzma. He's going to be a Navy lieutenant as soon as we get an officer there to swear him in. I shot for Lieutenant JG for you but was overruled. They're willing to go Acting Ensign Third Class but not Ensign or JG at the moment."

"Wait, you want me to join the Navy?" Sophia said.

"You're already in the Navy in case you hadn't noticed," Steve replied. *"I want you to be an* officer *in the Navy."*

"Does that mean we have to join the Navy?" Paula asked.

"What about my crew?" Sophia asked.

"Crews, except for certain positions, can be civilian. Basic structure of the Wolf Squadron remains the same. Certain officers, both skippers and administrative, have been asked to become Naval personnel. It's a bit of a mish-mash for right now. But certain equipment has to be under control of Naval personnel, including Marines. Basically, you can only legally use big guns from Navy or Coast Guard ships if you're under Federal controlling legal authority. It's a technicality of a regulation they're not willing to overlook and I understand why and agree. Goes back to the Treaty of Westphalia. That's not the only reason I'd like you to be an officer, but it's one of them. Other than that, there's no real difference. You don't have to respond now. Contact Kuzma one way or the other. Any major questions?"

"Not right now," Sophia said. "I can think on it?"

"You can think on it," Steve said.

"Okay, I'll think on it," Sophia said. "No worries, Da. And take care of yourself."

"You too. Wolf, out."

"Alexandria, I think we're done," Sophia said.

"Roger, No Tan Lines. Be advised . . . You have a cabin cruiser sixteen miles south of your position. Don't know if you want to check it out."

"Roger, *Alexandria,"* Sophia said, starting up the engine. "We'll go check it. Did you visual?"

"Roger. No infecteds on deck. We have several other sierras in the area we're tracking including some lifeboats and life rafts."

"And they tell us *now*?" Paula said.

"Might have just got on station," Sophia said. "Might have been a change with Da getting promoted. *Alexandria*, got coordinates on that boat?"

"I wonder if this means... No, they *wouldn't*..."

"Gunny," Steve said, waving to a chair. "How you doing?"

"Ready to rock and roll, sir," Sands said, sitting down carefully.

"Bullshit," Steve said. "I won't tell you you can't work for a few days, but you're not going to be running around the bowels of the *Iwo* for now. Not until you're fit. There's too damned much gear to carry. We made that mistake with Hooch and he was in *better* shape than you are. You need to put on some pounds, first."

"And you, sir?" the gunny asked, looking over at Fontana, who was looking... closed.

"Alas, I think my days of clearing ships are done," Steve said, waving at his desk. "I'm conning a desk for a while. Isham has agreed to take a lieutenancy, temporary like mine, so he can tell Navy people where to get off. He's a bit of an asshole, but he's a competent one. I'll keep him as my Chief of Staff for now. But, no, I'm not going to be clearing ships. Some of the Marines we found are fairly hale and they can continue the clearance ops. But that gets to the point of this meeting..." Steve leaned back in his chair and thought for a moment.

"I understand you've met my daughter, Faith, Gunny?"

"Oh," Sands said, his face cracking into a slight smile. "That's the agenda, sir? Yes, sir, I have. She and Staff Sergeant Fontana cracked my compartment, sir. And, yes, sir, I think she'd make a fine Marine, sir. Even a fine Marine officer, sir. In about five years, sir."

"Then there's an issue," Steve said. "Because tomorrow, Faith will be the team leader for the first group of Marines to reboard the *Iwo*. We're going to be using it mostly as a training exercise. She will also be overseeing their kitting up. Because she knows very little, at all, except the best ways to clear zombies."

"Pardon, sir," Sands said. "Not Staff Sergeant Fontana?"

"*Lieutenant* Fontana will be managing the preparations for the assault, Gunny," Steve said. "And along with Lieutenant Volpe he will be managing the clearance operation as a forward officer. Miss Smith along with Lance Corporal Hocieniec will be training the Marines on the Wolf Way of clearance. It's like the Marine way but...different.

"This is a Marine thing. A temporary, out-of-the-blue, Navy captain is not going to tell a Marine gunny who should and should not be a Marine. What the captain is going to do is allow the gunny a week to think about his response."

"I understand your position, Captain," Sands said. "But, with respect, I'm not sure that I agree. Among other things... Pretty much everyone has heard about Miss Smith and we all think she's pretty damned great, sir. But...I'm not sure, sir, with respect, that they're going to listen and pay attention to a thirteen-year-old girl, no matter how badass she may be. 'Cause she's a thirteen-year-old girl, sir. I will, with your permission, sit in on the training, sir, to ensure that they understand that..."

"Gunny," Steve said, raising his hand. "Permit me to give you some semblance of peace in this matter. I appreciate you sitting in on the training. What I had not mentioned was that *before* the training session, there will be a brief familiarization class given by the lance corporal. I would recommend that you sit in on that as well."

"Yes, sir?" Sands said, frowning.

"When we, Faith actually, hard-boarded the *Voyage*, the *Dallas* was standing off," Fontana said. "And they recorded the boarding on their onboard video system. Then, apparently, someone made a video mash of it, including some of the discussion of whether she should begin boarding without nearby reinforcements..."

"By the time we got there it was all done," Steve said, smiling thinly. "And Faith was like 'No worries, Da! Bit of a scrum—'"

"Scrum?" Sands said. "Definition, sir?"

"Ever played rugby, Gunny?" Fontana said. "It's that bit where the two sides fight over the ball."

"Faith always enjoyed playing Aussie Rules when we were Down Under," Steve said, sighing. "Except Rule One. I don't expect the video to change your mind. Give it a week. She will, however, be acting as a civilian technical expert in infected clearance during that week. By the end of the week, we should be done with clearing the *Iwo* and begin salvage work. We'll discuss it again at that time. If you're set that she is not, currently, Marine material... then I will leave that on you and, no, no hard feelings. There are any number of other areas I can use her expertise."

"As I said, sir," Sands said. "I'd just like her to get some more maturity."

"I think you're thinking *age*, Gunny," Steve said. "Maturity is something slightly different."

The gunnery sergeant didn't crack a smile at the radio intercept of Faith's concept of a back-up plan, an intercept that had caused Commander Bradburn, skipper of the *Dallas,* to literally fall out of his command chair laughing. Sands managed to watch the video stone-faced as she boarded the *Voyage* and began her "fifteen minutes of mayhem," set in the video to the tune of Chumbawamba's "Tubthumping." He managed to keep a straight face the third time she popped back up like a jack-in-the-box after being dogpiled by zombies. He held it in during her overheard running commentary as the rest of the Marines, even the NCOs, started rolling on the deck.

It was when she got the Halligan tool stuck in a zombie's head and overbalanced that he snorted. When she unstuck her bent machete and it caught a male zombie in the groin he started laughing out loud. When the, admittedly not petite, girl stuck a boot knife in a zombie's eye then threw him over the side, tears started running down his face and he completely lost his composure as a senior NCO of the United States Marine Corps.

"Sometimes you get dogpiled," Faith said, latching the bunker gear on the Marine sergeant. "MOPP's not designed to prevent penetration. This is. And you can just get washed down in it no worries. And you *are* going to need a wash-down after we're done..."

"Seriously, a K-bar? You think one dinky little knife is enough in a scrum...?"

"Christ," Faith said, taking the Halligan tool away from the lance corporal. "*Here's* how you use a Halligan tool. *Ram* the son-of-a-bitch. Put some *welly* in it, Marine—!"

"Zombies don't like impolite people," Faith said, stepping over a fresh kill. "In general, you should knock first. The real point is that they seem to hibernate for periods of time. If you go *sneakin' around*, Sergeant-I'm-a-*recon*-scout, as you just discovered, you get *surrounded* by zombies who *used* to be sleeping and are now preparing to *eat you* ..."

"PFC, I swear to *God* if these zombies *did* go for brains they would *totally ignore you!*"

"So, this is five five six that *works*?" Faith said, looking at the round. Unlike the other rounds they'd been using that had green tips, this one looked like solid copper.

"It's superior," Januscheitis said. He was trying not to sound nervous. Faith had been running them around their own ship for six hours like privates on Paris Island and what was worse, she kept being *right*. "I don't think there's anybody who really loves five five six."

"Nope," Faith said, putting five rounds of 5.56mm into an oncoming zombie. "Unless you get a perfect shot, it's still sucks." She fired one round into its head and it dropped. "I don't suppose there's a few thousand rounds of twelve-gauge anywhere on this tub?"

"We don't use a lot of twelve-gauge so ... Not that I'm aware."

"Seven six two by thirty-nine?"

"Haji round. No."

"Forty-five?"

"Forty-five we've got," Januscheitis said. "Somewhere. Ordnance was not my billet."

"Find me 'somewhere,' Staff Sergeant."

"Found it!"

"Ooo, ooo," Faith said, stroking the box of ammo. "Come to momma." She bent over and hugged the pallet of .45ACP. "Mmmm ... There is beauty left in this fallen world ..."

"Oh, wait," she said, straightening up. "This is full metal jacket, isn't it?"

"Yes," Januscheitis said. "Hollow point is outlawed by the Geneva Convention."

"Damn," Faith said, then went back to stroking the boxes. "Oh, well, FMJ forty-five is better than twenty-two magnum. Sooooft ..."

she stroked the box a moment longer, then reached over her back and pulled out her Halligan. "What are you waiting for?"

"See?" Faith said, as the zombie dropped. "*One* round. Forty-five 'cause they don't make a forty-six. You can keep your Barbie guns."

"No range, ma'am," Januscheitis said. "And you've only got seven rounds in a magazine."

"We're fighting at close quarters, Staff Sergeant Januscheitis," Faith said. "And will be for the foreseeable future. We don't *need* range. Well, unless we have to clear another *freaking* cruise liner and I'll leave that to you big, tough Marines. Those damned hot twenty-twos just over-penetrate then start *bouncing* around. *And* they don't kill zombies. As to how many rounds you've got in a mag..." she said, reloading, then dropping one-handed a zombie that had reared out of the darkness.

"How many rounds of five five six, on average, to stop a zombie... PFC Kirby?" she said, reloading her expended magazine from spare rounds in a pouch.

"About five, Miss Faith, ma'am," the private snapped, standing at attention.

"Staff Sergeant, divide thirty by five."

"Six," Januscheitis said, then frowned. "Damn."

"As to only having seven rounds," Faith said, holding up her pistol. "*You* only have seven rounds because *you* use the ancient and renowned, sort of like, say, the *Titanic*, Colt 1911 whereas *I* use the *modern* H&K USP with *twelve* rounds, which has been *proven* capable of killing a hammerhead shark in sixty feet of water. *That* works out to *sixty* rounds of five five six in relative killing power in an actual zombie fight. *With* lighter total weight in ammo, *not* having to reload *and* it doesn't just zip through and go *bouncin' arounnnd* like you've dropped a frag grenade. Old and busted. New hotness."

"Yes, Miss Faith."

"Oh come onnnn Jannnn, let *me* throw the grenade. If I can't throw it, let Trixie. *Trixie* wants to throw the grenade...!"

"There is, in fact, a primary storage of twelve-gauge on board, Staff Sergeant," Gunny Sands said, his voice muffled by the gas mask.

The gunny was notably unhappy not being able to accompany the clearance parties. It just wasn't right for a gunny to be lolling around in the rack when his Marines were fighting zombies. He'd made a foray a day and spent the rest of the time eating, conducting physical therapy and, far too often in his opinion, resting. But the fatigue would just hit him like a hammer whenever he exerted himself.

Today, however, he'd moved forward to the clearance command post set up in the CIC of the *Iwo*. The bodies had been cleared out but it was still MOPP conditions in the compartment.

"I was unaware of that, Gunnery Sergeant," Januscheitis said.

"Security and control teams use twelve-gauge," the gunny said, pointing to a schematic of the ship. "There should be twenty thousand rounds in Compartment six tack 190 tack one tack mike. It should be, if memory serves, port side, aft in the compartment. The rest of the compartment is mainly devoted to M829 DS for the M1s."

"Check that out on the next sweep forward," Fontana said. "Which will be *after* we clear the Central Four and Five levels..."

"You told me there wasn't any twelve-gauge, Jan," Faith said, pouting. "There'd better be twelve-gauge."

"So I'm not The Gunny," Januscheitis said, throwing his hands up in the air. "He's a gunny, okay? They, like, know *everything*!"

"Well, there'd just *better* be twelve-gauge..."

"Oh," Faith said, panting slightly. "Oh...Oh..."

"It's not much," Januscheitis said.

"Not much?" Faith said, grabbing one of the cases of 12-gauge double-ought. "Not *much*? It's...It's...I'll be in my bunk..."

Januscheitis just stood there with his mouth open as she left the compartment.

"Do you think she meant..." Derek said then paused. "I hope she didn't mean..."

The hatch undogged and Faith stuck her head in the compartment.

"Reloading my Saiga mags, you PERVERTS!"

CHAPTER 5

I could not tread these perilous paths in safety,
if I did not keep a saving sense of humor.

Admiral Horatio Nelson

"Soph, got something funky," Patrick said.

"I suppose I should get some clothes on," Sophia muttered. She was currently adding some reality to the boat's name up on the flying bridge. "In a bit..."

She could tell "funky" was not an emergency by Patrick's tone. Paula was "a good man in a storm." She just sailed on regardless of the conditions. Patrick had a bit of a tendency to panic. Which was not great in your engineer, but he was fine with the maintenance and stuff.

"Define 'funky,'" she said over the intercom, readjusting her sunglasses. She picked up a pair of binos to check out something on the horizon but it was just a bit of junk. Her ostensible reason for being on the flying bridge was "visual search for survivors." Which was pretty much a waste of time. Which was why she was actually catching a tan.

The Atlantic ocean was really, really, really big. And boats, even commercial freighters and such, were really, really, really small in comparison.

Depending on which authority you asked, the North Atlantic

Ocean, which they were currently searching for survivors, was about twenty million square miles in area. Their radar had a range of around fifty miles, if the target was radar reflective, while visually they could see between twenty and thirty miles. Realistically, it was possible that one boat might spot a lifeboat within ten miles. Essentially, it was like one microscopic germ trying to find another germ in the area of a standard American living room. That was clean and really germ free.

When they'd first started clearing boats off of Bermuda, there had still been some distress beacons working. Not many, but they were there. And there had been a lot of boats. The waters between the U.S. mainland and Bermuda were some of the most crowded in the world under normal circumstances. With anyone with an ocean-capable boat fleeing the Plague, and the east coast of the U.S. having a lot of such people, they were definitely crowded. There were days when they had twenty or more radar contacts or lifeboats and small boats in *sight*.

The Great Equatorial Current... Not so much. Oh, there were boats down here. And life rafts. And freighters. And, somewhere, God help them, based on some of the lifeboats they'd been finding, some cruise ships including at least one super-max. But they were scattered. They were lucky if they found two or three vessels in a day instead of thirty.

They were only there, really, to keep them out of the storm belt in the North Atlantic and tropical storms in the eastern zone, give them something to do and get some people rescued. Unfortunately, as usual, most of the boats they were finding were empty. Of live, sane, people, at least. Bodies they'd found aplenty. People... not so much. Not even live zombies. In the last two weeks the *No Tan Lines* had only found four survivors. But four was a number greater than zero.

The only reason they were finding most of the life rafts was that they had some modern additions. Back in the 1980s, the USCG pointed out that the material life rafts were made of, plastic, was fairly stealthy. You could pimp them up in any color you'd like, they didn't turn up on radar. So most modern life rafts and lifeboats included Mylar radar reflectors in their construction. And, fortunately, the *No Tan Lines* had radar. So Patrick was manning the radar and other gizmos while she scanned "visually." And caught up on her tan.

"Well, it's a distress beacon," Patrick said.

"I probably would have led with that," Sophia muttered.

"But it's well inside the range where we should have picked it up. It's only about twenty miles out."

"Azimuth?" Sophia said.

"No Tan Lines, Alexandria."

"Stand by, Patrick," she said, then switched frequencies and straightened up to start the main engines. *"No Tan Lines."*

"Holy, hell," Commander Robert "Thunderbear" Vancel, skipper of the USS *Alexandria* said. Vancel was on his first tour as a sub skipper when the worst disaster in human history hit. It had not been a pleasure cruise. He'd been a bit heavy before this cruise. Now, not so much. "COB: Down periscope. *Now!* And tell me that's not being broadcast all over the ship."

"Looks like she's just trying to live up to her boat's name, sir," the COB said.

"Fifteen, COB," the skipper snapped. *"Fifteen.* And, for God's sakes, an ensign? Remind me to talk to that young lady about the decorum expected of a Naval officer at the first opportunity after we meet."

"Duly noted, sir."

"Alex, No Tan Lines," Sophia repeated. Usually the Navy was right up on calling back but there had been a distinct pause.

"Lines, Alex. Be advised just picked up an intermittent distress beacon, your bearing, one one four, range: ten point three nautical miles. Be advised, beacon was not there four minutes ago. Signal is intermittent. Our evaluation, persons operating manual generator for intermittent signal. Probable survivors. Proceeding that location at this time."

"Roger, *Alex,* keep us advised."

She switched to intercom. "Going full," she said and put the hammer down. No real reason for it, the *Alex* was going to be there long before they were . . .

"Okay, up periscope," Commander Vancel said.

"Isn't that redundant, sir?" the COB asked.

"Again, COB, *fifteen!* And, sweet Lord Jesus I Can't Believe They Did This, LANTFLEET's *daughter!*"

"As well hanged for a sheep, sir . . ."

∽ ⊖ ∾

"Da, Da!" Julie yelled. "Look!"

Lincoln Lawton stepped out onto the aft deck of the forty-five-foot *Gentle Breezes* and shaded his eyes against the glare. He stopped and his jaw dropped at the sight of a periscope not five hundred meters off the boat.

Lawton, formerly the general manager for Information Technologies of Wilson Gribley, LLC, Liverpool, UK, had just left port for a month-long trip to the Mediterranean when the news of the Plague had been released. He had, briefly, contemplated putting back into port to return to work. He knew the term "workaholic" was often used to describe him and it seemed that if there was going to be a major influenza outbreak, the Firm, which was in the biomedical technologies field, would need his services.

Susan, his normally accepting and supportive wife, had put her foot down. First of all, it was the first long vacation that he had taken in nearly ten years. During which time his children had grown up with a father who was a virtual stranger. Second, given that the flu bug was described as being *particularly* nasty and wide-spread, it would be better to just cruise along for a bit without encountering it. Let it burn out and they'd put into port.

As it turned out, Susan was right. A point she tried not to rub in. They were not infected by the "zombie plague." On the other hand, food and fuel only last so long. They had stocked well but eventually the food ran out. And the fuel. Fortunately, there was an emergency solar still onboard that produced barely enough water for the lot of them. And he had stocked quite a few rods onboard. About the only time he spent with his family was angling on the boat in the Irish Sea.

It was a constant surprise to him that when you were hungry enough, *any* raw fish was a delicacy. His family had also come as something of a surprise. He wasn't sure exactly why he hadn't spent more time with them. Oh, being on a small boat occasionally drove everyone nuts. But he had some great children and, given that he'd had little to do with them, he also had come to have a new appreciation for his wife. An appreciation that, as the tan got darker and they both lost quite a bit of weight, had eventually overcome their desire to avoid certain difficulties.

Which was why Susan was, as far as they could tell, about two months pregnant.

"Help William with the signs if you would, there's a good lass,"

Lincoln said, waving at the periscope. It was clearly looking at them. He hoped the submarine would not surface, however. As far as they could tell, they were uninfected. Raw fish or no, they wished to stay that way.

William, his ten-year-old son, and Julie, fourteen, came up on deck quickly with the cobbled together signs. They had made them from bits of stitched together plastic and can boxes to keep from damaging their sheets.

They carefully held them up to prevent them tearing in the breeze.

"'Do Not Approach.'" Commander Vancel said. "'Not Infected.' They're in the same boat we are."

"With less in the way of stores and no power, sir," his XO pointed out.

"Seem to be making it," the CO replied, touching a control.

A light began to wink on the periscope.

"If I understood bloody Morse maybe I'd understand what you were saying," Lincoln said through gritted teeth. The signal was repetitive, though, two flashes then two flashes...

"I think they're just saying they understand," Susan said.

"I was thinking the same," Lincoln replied. He waved and nodded. "I wonder if they're infected? Or not."

"See if the *Lines* is monitoring," Commander Vancel said.

"No Tan Lines, Alexandria, *over*."

Sophia had been expecting the call and already had the mike in her hand.

"*Alex, Lines,* over."

"*Sierra is forty-five-foot Activa motor yacht. No power. Four survivors, probable family, uninfected. Boat has British registry. Over.*"

"Roger, *Alex.* Just over the horizon. Have them on radar. Will come up from their lee and attempt to communicate."

"*Roger. Standing by.*"

"*Alex*, could you retrans to flotilla, then possibly squadron ops?"

"*Roger, stand by... Ready on retrans to flotilla, over.*"

"*Livin' Large, Livin' Large, No Tan Lines,* over..."

"No Tan Lines, Livin' Large, *over.*"

"We have a contact this area. According to the *Alexandria*, they're uninfected. Last I heard, the squadron still had a few units of vaccine. I'd suggest that it would be advisable, given these people's circumstances, out of fuel and in the middle of nowhere, to use it on them. Over."

"Stand by, Lines..."

"Standing by," Sophia muttered. She could see the yacht on the horizon. The wind was from the southeast and she was coming in from the northwest. Which would put her downwind, or to the lee in nautical speak, from the yacht. Which was where she wanted to be.

It was, at this point, extremely unlikely that casual contact with the people on the yacht, or the sub crews, would give them H7D3. Flu eventually became noninfectious as a person's immune system overcame it. She probably could come from windward, fuel up the yacht, transfer supplies, carefully...

"Extremely unlikely" was not the same as "could not happen." And nobody wanted to infect people who had survived this long. Families like hers were not so much rare as nonexistent. Nobody found so far had so much as *one* family member survive. The closest was Chris Phillips, captain of the *David Cooper*, and his former fiancé. And both believing the other one dead, they had sought opportunities elsewhere in the interim. Even if a family was on a life raft or boat, like this one, drifting, only one survivor had generally been found.

Preserving this family was, in her opinion, critically important. They probably felt the same way.

The problem was... The ocean was really, really *big*. Finding them in the first place had been a matter of luck and that "intermittent distress signal." If they left the boat behind, they *might* be able to find them again. They knew the currents in the area and they knew where they were, now. But it was, again, only "likely." And if they were left to drift... They could drift until they were all old and grey and died on the boat if they ended up pushed into the Sargasso Sea. More likely, they'd eventually run aground and either get infected or eaten. Sum it up as "bad things."

Kuzma knew all this and he had *way* more experience than she did. Maybe he'd come up with a good answer.

"...that's my take on it, sir," Kuzma said. "If we leave them drifting, even for the time it would take to go up to Squadron and get the vaccine, we'll probably lose them. I'm sort of lost for an answer here, sir..."

"*Roger,* Large," the *Alex* replied. "*We've been kicking it around as well. The only solution we see, and we'd have to get permission from higher, is for one of our subs to take them under tow and bring them up to Squadron AO. We're going to discuss that with higher.*"

"Roger, *Alex,*" Kuzma said, his face working. "I'm going to leave this on you and the *Tan Lines* for now if that's all right."

"Under control, *Large.*"

"*Livin' Large,* out," Kuzma said. He shook his head and looked at the helmsman. "That's a zammie."

"Definite zammie, sir..."

"Boat, Da," William said, pointing to the northeast.

"I'm going to assume they're with the submarine," Lincoln said, looking at the approaching yacht through his binoculars. "I hope they stay downwind."

"Leeward, Da," Julie said didactically. Lincoln had one manual on seamanship and his oldest had studied it assiduously.

"I hope they stay to leeward, then," he said, trying not to smile.

"Good afternoon," Sophia said over the loudhailer. "We get that you're uninfected. Which an amazing number of people find tremendously exciting. You're the first complete boat of survivors we've found. Which is why you are about to have a zammie, which is an acronym for a 'zombie apocalypse moment.' The pre-Plague term is 'what the heck?'"

"Da," William said. He was always the one looking around. "*Another* submarine!"

Forward of the ship an American attack sub surfaced.

"*The USS* Annapolis *is going to fire you a line. They are uninfected so there's no chance of catching the flu. When you get it, hook it up to your forward cleat. We have a small stock of vaccine back at our squadron, which is operating about six hundred miles north of here. It's going to take a few days for you to get there but they'll tow you up. They will also pass you some water since your still won't work being towed. No food, sorry, they're short on rations as well. Anyway, a billion-dollar nuclear submarine is about to act as a tow truck for one forty-five-foot yacht full of vacationers. Welcome to a zombie apocalypse moment. We hope that you consider Wolf Squadron and the U.S. Navy in the future for all your towing needs...*"

"Hoooh," Sophia said, adjusting the focus on her binoculars. "Sweet."

She keyed the intercom, powered up and turned to starboard.

"Rig for fishing ops!" she boomed, then switched to the radio. "Flotilla, *Lines*, over."

"*Flotilla.*"

"Spotted surface activity, probable tuna, moving to target-of-opportunity fishing ops, over."

"*Stand by*, Lines."

"Like I'm going to let these out of my sight," Sophia muttered.

Tuna moved fast and often the only sign you got was a cluster of birds. When the tuna were done eating whatever was at the surface they'd dive and be gone. That could take hours or bare minutes. You either went for them or you lost them. And since this wasn't a big migration period in the area, fish had been scarce.

Since the only fresh food the entire squadron got was fish, and tuna was at the top of the menu, fishing ops was right up there with searching for survivors.

"What do we got?" Paula yelled from the transom deck.

"Probably tuna," Sophia yelled back. "Look big! Three polers."

"On it!"

"Lines, *Flotilla.*"

"*Lines*," Sophia answered, keeping an eye on the birds.

"*Roger fish-ops. We need a cut. Report to* Large *after taking on fish.*"

"Aye, aye," Sophia said. "*Lines*, out."

Then she keyed the intercom again.

"It's on like Donkey Kong!"

"What are we doing?" Rusty asked, holding onto a metal bar.

He wasn't a big fisherman but he sort of knew how you did it with deep-sea fishing. There was a chair and a big reel and you sort of cruised around until you got a bite.

You didn't go charging across the ocean at full speed with the boat rocking from side to side like it was going to sink.

And there was one big rod with a big reel. Not what Paula

and Patrick were rigging, which was three really long rods with lines at the end that all led to one big hook. The hook didn't even really have a lure on it. Just a big plastic bird-feather.

"What we're doing is rigging the poles," Paula said. "What you're doing is waiting till we're rigged, then I'll explain."

"Got it," Rusty said. He couldn't even figure out what knot she was tying. It was complicated was all he could get.

"Right," Paula said, standing up easily despite the bouncing of the boat. "First of all, glad you're here. You're about to get one hell of a workout. 'Cause here's how it works. We stand by the transom, that's the bulkhead at the back of the boat. Sophia will drive over near the fish. We then all three, together, flip the lure out over our heads and tap our poles on the water. Just follow along with us. When a fish hits the lure, you just hold on tight, lean back and pick it up out of the water and *throw* it backwards over our heads. We gotta do that together and pretty hard. Then we go back and do it again. We'll stop from time to time to cut the fish up and store them. We've got a big cooler for them. You got it?"

"Got it," Rusty said. "I think."

"You'll figure it out," Patrick said. "First time we tried it it was a disaster."

"It wasn't a disaster," Paula said.

"You weren't the one that got hit in the face," Patrick pointed out.

"You were only knocked out for a minute," Paula said. "Reminds me, we need to get the helmets and face shields."

"Or pulled overboard," Patrick pointed out.

"And the life vests..."

"Then there's the smell..."

"And the chum. Can't forget the chum..."

"You're supposed to use live fish for this," Paula said, standing back from where Rusty was tossing chunks of decaying fish over the side. "But we don't have any. Anything will do, really."

Rusty had gotten used to not wanting to throw up from the smell. But apparently they were low on respirators or he'd be using one. The "chum" was all the "stuff" they hadn't used from previous fish. It had been kept cool but it had still started to rot and smelled just awful.

"And we have customers," Patrick said, looking over the transom.

"Toss a bunch of that crap over the side," Paula said. "And grab your rod."

The rods were longer than the aft deck. The thick lines attached to the ends were barely half their length. Rusty still wasn't sure how this was going to work. But there were fish behind the boat, rolling to the surface feasting on the heads and entrails he'd tossed over the back. They were falling behind quick, though, 'cause the boat was moving so fast.

"You take the middle," Paula said.

"And watch yourself or you'll get hit in the face," Patrick added.

"Okay," Rusty said.

"Just follow our movements," Paula said.

She brought her rod down overhead until it was dangling with the lure just barely in the water.

"Now, tap, like this," she said, dropping her rod and tapping the water's surface.

As he brought his own rod down, he felt the line go taut and was nearly pulled over the side.

"Get your feet," Patrick said as the three lines jerked each of the poles. Suddenly it went slack.

"Damnit," Paula said, jigging the lure again. "Pop it! And keep your balance this time!"

The line got hit again but this time he was planted.

"One, two, three, pull!" Paula said quickly.

On the "pull," she and Patrick leaned back, pulling the rods back and yanking a fish out of the water. It headed right for Rusty who was in the center.

He dropped his rod and dodged to the side as the fish came flying past his head.

"Try to be some help here," Paula said. "Grab your damned pole at least!"

The fish had thrown the hook already and was lying on the transom deck flapping its tail. It was bigger than any fish Rusty had ever seen except on TV shows. If he'd picked it up it would have been nearly to his waist.

He tried to ignore it and grabbed his pole. They started to flick the lure back out but he wasn't ready and it got tangled. By the time they were untangled, the school of fish was out of range.

"Coming about," Sophia yelled.

"You getting this?" Paula asked sharply. "When we get on

the school, we all three, together, toss out the line. Then we all three, together, pop it. It's called jigging. When we get a hit, we all three together, pull. I won't go one-two-three this time. Just when it's on I'll go 'Pull' and we all pull. Got it?"

"Got it," Rusty said.

"Try not to go over the side, drop your pole or get hit in the face by one of the tuna," Paula said. "That's pretty much the safety briefing."

"Patrick," Sophia called. "Throw some chum!"

"Got it," Patrick said, leaning over and tossing some of the chum into the water.

"That's bringing 'em up," Paula said. "Pop it," she added, jigging the lure. The line went taut again and Paula looked at him.

"Ready, pull!" she snapped.

This time, Rusty just dodged to the side as the fish came flying out of the water.

"Ready, flick it back," Paula said. The fish had already fallen off the half-hook.

"Got it," Rusty said, this time getting the flick right.

The line had barely hit the water when it went taut again.

"PULL!

"And flick...

"And PULL...!"

"I think that's all we can handle for now," Sophia said from the bridge. "Certainly all Rusty can handle."

Rusty had slipped on one of the big fish covering the deck and was now sprawled out in the middle of fish goo and blood. When the fish were hooked it caused them to bleed. Between their thrashing and being thrown through the air, the transom deck as well as the bridge bulkhead were covered in spots of blood. So were all three of the fishermen. Even Sophia up in the flying bridge had some spots of blood on her.

"Might as well get to dicing," Paula said, giving Rusty a hand up. "Patrick, knives."

"Sorry about that," Rusty said. He was looking sort of gray.

"It does take it out of you," Paula said. "It's all in the back. The first time Patrick and I tried it alone we could only get about half the small ones. The rest were just too big. Having you as a third was a real help."

"I should have been more," Rusty said, shrugging. "Just ain't got my strength back."

"Some fresh sashimi will help with that," Paula said, grinning.

"What are these?" Rusty asked.

"Big eye tuna," Sophia said, pointing to the eyes. She'd left the helm and slid down the ladder to the transom deck. "They're generally a deep fish. They spend most of their time at more than twenty fathoms. But they come up to the surface to warm up and if there happens to be bait they'll get on it. Good size ones, too. This will feed the flotilla for a few days."

"What's next?" Rusty asked.

"We'll cut off the heads, gut them, then throw them in the cooler," Sophia said. "We'll keep the heads and guts for chum for the next time. Those go in the freezer."

"Freezer?" Rusty asked.

"You need to flash freeze fish to keep it tasting good and the right texture," Sophia said. "We don't have a flash freezer. The *Large* does, but most of this will be used up in a few days by us and the rest of the flotilla. Cooler's good enough."

"Knives," Patrick said, opening up a box filled with fillet knives and sharpeners.

"Now to the *really* bloody part," Sophia said, smiling. "And they talk about Faith getting covered in blood..."

"Respirators," Rusty said, holding up a box.

"Too bad they didn't use them," Paula said, taking the box and looking at the manufacturer. "Some European brand. I don't think they'll work on ours."

Which was a pity, since they'd about used up all their filters. Doing this job without respirators made it damned near not worth it. And this boat wasn't even particularly bad. There were only two people onboard. From the pictures they'd found, husband and trophy wife. The trophy wife had been on the back deck, nude. Probably zombied. The husband had been in secondary cabin, ditto. Guessing, the wife had gone first, the husband had locked himself in a cabin then turned.

It must have been early on in going to sea because by the time the team boarded, the wife was a clean-picked skeleton from seabirds and the husband was a mummy.

Despite not having useable respirators, the seventy-foot sailboat was, otherwise, chock full of goodies. How people loaded to flee a plague was, in many ways, idiosyncratic. They'd salvaged one boat that was full of books. And they'd loaded as many as they could, since books were the main source of entertainment these days. Books could be traded for other stuff.

There were a few consistencies, though. Boats with women onboard loaded lots of toilet paper. Sometimes much or all of it had been used up by the time the crew died but generally not. They also loaded lots of feminine hygiene products. This one had both. They'd found one boat that must have been owned by a restauranteur or a chef. It was positively packed with spices as well as various tasty goodies.

But there were several consistent salvage materials. Just about every boat had loads, boatloads, of alcohol, jewelry and, often, fine cigars. It was, like, the first thing most people packed. They'd grab their jewelry and booze and smokes if they had them. Then there was the fact that they tended to drink the cheap stuff first.

So when they boarded a boat, they almost always found some really nice jewelry and high-quality booze. The kind of people who could afford yachts tended to have both.

"Lots of halfsies," Paula said, looking over the bar in the saloon.

"Mix and match," Rusty said.

To conserve space, they tended to combine partially full bottles. They tried to make sure it was the same "type," bourbon with bourbon, scotch with scotch. But mistakes happened. Gin and vodka was okay. Rum and scotch not so much.

"There is a god somewhere that is angry because we're combining stuff like Cutty Sark with fifty-year-old Laphroaig," Paula said. "We are one day going to run afoul of him and he will raise a great storm to punish us."

"What is . . . Famous Grouse?" Rusty said.

"Scotch," Paula said, hefting a box of pasta onto the deck.

"Got a case of that," Rusty said. "Now if I could just find some shoes . . ."

They'd turned up a set of max sized galoshes on a boat but so far the security specialist didn't have any real shoes. Or pants that fit. His jeans fit around his narrowed waist but stopped mid-calf and were a bit tight in the crotch. Not that Paula minded the latter.

"We could strap a couple of inflatables to them," Paula said.

"Very funny . . ."

"And we're clear," Sophia said. "There's a ship to the southeast the *Last At Sea* spotted. Said there were some infecteds on deck so they banked off. We're to check it to see if it's worth sending a salvage and recovery crew."

"I'll get my gear ready," Rusty said. "I hope I don't have to do one of those boardings like Faith did."

"Eh, I'll just pot 'em off with what my sister would call a Barbie gun . . ."

"What is this thing, a ferry?" Paula asked, fingers in her ears.

The vessel named *Pit Stop* was a bit over a hundred feet long with a large bridge and presumably crew area forward and a low-set rear deck that could clearly be opened up at the back. The back deck had a vintage car, an inflatable and four pallets of stores piled on it. It *sort* of looked like a ferry. The difference was, it was also rather thin and lean looking. The design was actually vaguely similar to the cutter they'd cleared.

"No clue," Sophia said. "But if you'd give me a minute, this isn't as easy as it looks."

Sophia was laid out on the flying bridge with earmuffs on and an accurized M4 with a Leupold 9x scope propped up on a cushion. She'd wrapped the strap around her arm and was carefully preparing her shots.

Sophia was more than prepared to give her sister props for close-quarters zombie fighting. Faith was a brawler, always had been. When they went to tactical ranges, Faith regularly beat her scores.

When they went to *target* ranges, Faith went home pouting. Sophia had been planning on trying out for the Olympic shooting team when she got a little older.

Faith was a brawler. Sophia was a *sniper*.

The problem was catenary, the relative motion of two vessels bouncing up and down and side to side on the ocean. It meant your target was always moving all over the damned place. Which just meant that you waited for the right moment to take the shot. If you tried to follow the target, you ended up chasing it all over hell and gone. The U.S. Navy SEALs might have figured out a way to chase the target. Sophia had time. She waited.

There was a crack and Paula flinched as one of the infected dropped with an almost unnoticeable hole in his forehead and the back blown out of his head.

"Damn," the mate said.

"Come to Seawolf," Sophia whispered. "Be good little zombies. Yuck...they *do* eat brains..."

"That's why so many survived," Sophia said.

As a skipper, and an acting ensign, whatever that was, she really shouldn't be doing boardings. But when they'd left the main squadron, Rusty was the only volunteer for "hostile boarding specialist" that she could scrounge up. And clearing something this size was a two-person job. Paula and Patrick were trustworthy to hold the boat. Not so good at clearing zombies.

Fortunately, one of the ships they'd cleared had some double-ought and a couple of pump shotguns. So they both had adequate firearms. Rusty had some body armor borrowed from the Coast Guard. It wasn't really his size, as usual. And he still didn't have real shoes.

Needs must.

The reason for the surviving infected was a set of bags of rice on the pallets. The zombies had gnawed into the rice bags and had been feasting on the rice. And from the looks of things, the occasional bird that had tried the same.

There was also freshish rainwater pooled in the inflatable on deck.

"Water, food, zombies," Sophia said, pointing. "No fresh water, no zombies."

"I wouldn't drink that," Rusty said. The water was clearly foul. Then he thought about it. "Yeah, come to think of it, if I had that on the *Voyage* I'd have drunk it."

"Interesting fact," Sophia said, cautiously rounding one of the pallets. "With water like that, the trick is to use an enema."

"Seriously?" Rusty said, grimacing.

"Your rectum sucks up water from your poop," Sophia said. "It's why it comes out solid. The water gets drawn out by the rectum. And it also filters out the bad stuff, obviously. So if you've got really foul water and you really need it, you just give it to yourself as an enema."

"I wish I'd known that on the *Voyage*," Rusty said. "I was mixing water and urine."

"Which was why you survived," Sophia said. "Won't work with salt water, by the way. But you can even survive, for a while, on small quantities of salt water. The problem is, it's actually the salinity of the human body. So your body can't really absorb it well. But when you're really dehydrated, your salinity increases compared to salt water and you can survive. For a while. Then you go fricking nuts and die. Also the problem with urine. When you're recycling, you're still losing water and the salinity, not to mention urea, gets higher and higher and you die."

"I really don't want to be back in that situation again," Rusty said.

"And, hopefully, you won't," Sophia said, regarding the open hatch on the deck. "Any zombies in there?"

"Want me to yell?" Rusty asked.

"Nah," Sophia said. "I'm pretty sure any that are alive would have come for the feast..."

The only "survivor" hadn't. He'd hanged himself in the small cabin he was trapped in. But most of the belowdecks watertight doors were closed. The engine room was in good shape, as was the bridge. Pretty much the only areas messed up by the infecteds was a companionway. And the cabin with the suicide was a bit rank.

"Good find," Sophia said, examining the main engine controls. When she'd first seen an engine room like this, she'd thought she'd never understand one. Now, while she was no expert, she generally knew how to get the engine started on something this size. If there was any fuel and juice. She went through the procedure for engine main start—it was an air-powered starting system—and hit the button to start it cranking.

"Come on, baby," she muttered. She could tell the batteries were low, but the starter generator did turn over. Then the big diesels rumbled to life.

"Beauty, eh!" she shouted. They'd both donned earmuffs.

"Nice!" Rusty shouted, grinning.

She went up to the bridge to check the systems. There were read-outs in the engine room but she understood bridge systems better. Besides, it was easier to talk. Everything, so far, looked in the green.

"Rusty, go get some of daddy's little crawlies and drop them on the bodies on the deck and in the cabin. Then head back to the boat. We don't have a prize crew so I'm going to con this back to the *Large*. Just follow me."

"Yes, ma'am," Rusty said.

"Don't fall behind," she said.

"Okay, so I've got to slow down," she muttered. The *Pit Stop* was not, by any stretch of the imagination, a speed boat. But it was faster than the *No Tan Lines*. A lot faster.

"It's a crew supply vessel," Kuzma said.

"Details?" Sophia said, yawning. She'd had to keep awake nonstop heading back to the flotilla.

"Details, sir," Kuzma said, without rancor.

"Sorry, sir," Sophia said.

"No problem," Kuzma said. "The Coast Guard is sort of easy on the whole 'sir/ma'am' thing. But the Navy's not. And I'm trying, at fairly long range, to get you ready to assume the mantle of a Navy officer."

"Yes, sir," Sophia said. "Understood. But...what is a crew supply vessel? Bringing supplies for crews or supplying with crews?"

"Both, either, depends on the configuration and mission," Kuzma said. "Generally they're faster than other ships their size and they're used to do things like run crews out to oil rigs or supply ships like the *Alpha* at sea or at least in out-of-the-way coves. That was probably what this one was used for, based on the, you know, antique car on it. Which means there's another megayacht out there somewhere. Well, there are probably *lots* of megayachts out there somewhere. 'Somewhere' is the key."

"Yes, sir," Sophia said, yawning again. "Sorry, sir."

"Been there," Kuzma said. "However, there is one other area to cover. I understand that you did not have a prize crew available. However, for the future, while I can understand your doing boardings until we can get you another security officer, you should have put two of your crew aboard the *Pit Stop* to con it back or called for a prize crew. The *Lines* is *your* boat. *You're* the skipper. You don't leave your boat. Understood, Ensign?"

"Yes, sir," Sophia said.

"When you're a bit more clearheaded I'll go over some of the very bad things that have happened in history when skippers leave their boats at sea," Kuzma said. "Repeat after me. Do not leave the boat."

"Do not leave the boat," Sophia said. "Aye, aye, sir."

∽ ⊖ ∾

Rusty was trying to stay awake. He really was. It was just there was nothing to do on what the Navy called "midwatch." The boat had an autopilot that currently had it cruising at just about walking pace on a general "southwest" heading. He just had to sit at the helm, not touching anything, keep an eye out they weren't going to hit a drifting boat or freighter and try to stay awake.

They'd picked up about a dozen refugees in the past week, mostly from one big lifeboat. They were dossed down below. Everyone was dossed down below except one Rusty Fulmer Bennett III who had drawn midwatch.

He stood up, walked around the small bridge and sat back down. Which was about when he noticed a small red icon flashing on the control screens.

He looked at it, rubbed his eyes and frowned.

"'Main breaker overload fault'?" He said just about the time the icon got brighter and the console started going "Breeep! Breeep!" Then another icon popped up.

"'Engine room fire alarm'?" Rusty said. There was a moment of confusion before it kicked in. "ENGINE ROOM FIRE ALARM?"

"What the hell is that sound?" Harvey Tharpe said, rubbing his eyes as he opened the cabin door.

Being on this yacht was better than being on the lifeboat but not much. They were packed in like sardines. There was food but being woken up in the middle of the night by a blaring "Squeee! Squeee!" was not his idea of fun.

The former businessman had been "robust" before being cast adrift on a lifeboat in a zombie apocalypse. He still had his height and some solidity. So he was more than a bit surprised when the short, blond skipper of the boat, wearing not much more than a camisole and panties smashed him out of the way like an NFL linebacker on her way aft.

"MOVE PEOPLE!" the boat captain shouted, continuing to hammer her way through the crowd of refugees.

"Fuck a freaking duck," Sophia said, opening the door to the engine compartment. The smoke wasn't so bad she needed a respirator but it was bad. And they were dead in the water. All the power except the shrieking alarm was out.

She threw the main battery disconnect, then picked up one of the industrial fire extinguishers and played it over the exterior of the main breakers, which were the source of the fire.

"Skipper?" Paula said, picking another one up.

"We need to get it open before we use them all up," Sophia said, putting her hand on the extinguisher. "Get Rusty to get all the passengers up, out and on the sundeck."

She slid one hand into a rubber glove and popped open the main breaker panel. The whole thing was smoldering so she played the rest of the fire extinguisher over it until it was cold. A tick checker showed that the whole thing was electrically cold as well. Now if only the batteries hadn't discharged their whole load into the panel and killed themselves as well.

"What can I do, Skipper?" Patrick said groggily. The "engineer" was wearing not much more than the skipper.

"Get a hand-held," Sophia said. "See if there's a sub in range. Tell them we had a major electrical fire. Fire is under control. No power at this time. May be repairable but we may need assistance. Don't at this time but may. Got it? Do *not* call mayday or PON-PON. Do not."

"Got it, Skipper," Patrick said.

"And get these people the HELL OUT OF MY ENGINE COMPARTMENT!"

"Not to alarm you, Skipper . . ." Paula said as Sophia was jumping another wire.

The whole damned panel was screwed. She was having to rebuild it from scratch. On the other hand, every time they cleared a boat they grabbed anything resembling parts and often stripped out things like the breaker box. They had a lot of parts, breakers, wire and whatnot stashed in various nooks and crannies in the boat. However . . .

"How full are the bilges?" Sophia asked.

The *No Tan Lines*, while a great boat and definitely better than her previous one, had its issues. One of said issues being a small leak somewhere. They'd tried and tried to run it down but never could. It normally wasn't a problem. They bilge pumps handled it fine. Unless they were off-line for six hours while the boat's skipper, with some fumble-fingered help from the boat's "engineer," completely rebuilt the main breaker box which, not coincidentally, supplied power to said bilge pumps. Sophia had been noticing the way the boat was slowly getting more and more logy.

"Little water in the lower deck," Paula said carefully. The skipper clearly didn't need more stress. "Just a skim."

"I love pressure," Sophia said. "I eat it for breakfast. Patrick, under the bed in the number three sleeping compartment there's a bundle of green wire in a box. Somewhere in that box should be another Westinghouse twenty-five amp. Just bring the whole box."

"Aye, aye, Skipper," Patrick said, scurrying out of the compartment.

"It's a beautiful day in the neighborhood, a beautiful day for a neighbor..." Sophia sang, listening to the slap, slap, slap of the rising water below as she ripped out another burned wire and tossed it on the deck. "Won't you be mine, could you be mine...?"

"*Alexandria, No Tan Lines*, over," Sophia said, leaning into the blast from the air conditioning on the bridge. The engine compartment, besides stinking of ozone and burned rubber, had been hot as hell.

"Alexandria. *How's it going, over?*"

"Please relay to flotilla that we are back in business," Sophia said. "Although we're completely out of parts for a main breaker box. On the other hand, the one we've got is practically brand new, now."

"*Roger*, No Tan Lines. *Will relay. Glad to hear you're okay.* Alexandria *out.*"

"And with that, I'm going back to bed," Sophia said, hanging up the radio. "Somebody's got it," she added, waving a salute at Paula.

"I'll take care of it, Skipper," Paula said.

"Paula," Sophia said the next afternoon as they were cross-loading refugees to the *Livin' Large*.

"Yes, Skip?" Paula said.

"Refresh my memory," Sophia said. "Did we have a fire in the engine room or did I dream that?"

"We had a fire in the engine compartment, Skipper."

"Last night?" Sophia said.

"Yes," Paula said, frowning.

"Did it get handled?"

"You put it out and rebuilt the breaker box. You don't remember?"

"I think I must have done it in my sleep," Sophia said. "I thought I was just dreaming. I'm getting too old for this shit..."

CHAPTER 6

Алты́ного во́ра ве́шают, а полти́нного че́ствуют.
(The thief who takes three kopeks is hanged.
The thief who takes fifty kopeks is praised.)

Russian Proverb

"I guess coming down here wasn't a total bust," Sophia said, waving to the group on the aft deck of the Russian megayacht.

The ship was about as big as the *Social Alpha*. She wasn't sure what the actual name was, because the name was in Cyrillic letters. And it had a bunch of survivors. They were all skinny as rails but it was more survivors in one place than they'd ever found. There was a real preponderance of females. And, like the ghosts of the *Alpha*, they looked like they'd been chosen for their looks rather than their seamanship.

"I think some billionaire loaded up on supermodels," Paula said, waving as well. "At least they were good at dieting."

"Boat like that is nineteen or so crew and about as many guests," Sophia said. "I'm counting at least thirty people."

"Vaccinated?" Paula said.

"Bet so," Sophia said, smiling.

"...can tie up..." One of the men on the wash deck was pointing to the cleats for her to tie alongside.

"Tell Rusty to break out the dinghy," Sophia said.

"It's not rough," Paula said. "And we're going to have to cross-load them some supplies."

"No offense, Paula, but I'm the skipper," Sophia said, smiling again and waving. "Tell Rusty to break out the dinghy. Load up a bunch of water bottles. They've got solar stills going but I'd bet they'd like some water."

"Okay," Paula said dubiously.

"And no weapons," she added. "No infecteds, no reason."

"It's a little bumpy," Sophia said over the loudhailer. "Middle of the ocean and all. We're sending over a dinghy with some supplies! The guy's got a radio."

Turning out the dinghy was old hat at this point and Rusty, Paula and Pat made quick work of loading cases of bottled water. There was always bottled water on boats they cleared and they kept it for times like this. They mostly drank the water from the ROWPU system. It was the same stuff as "filtered" water.

Rusty putted the outboard over and tied off. Before he even started to unload, the same "pop hatch" as the *Alpha* had on the back opened up and men with guns, AKs, came out. One of them even had an RPG. Of course, if he fired it there, he'd kill most of the people.

"Rusty," Sophia called over the radio. "Don't resist. Just give the leader the radio."

"You were expecting this," Paula said angrily. "You sent Rusty over as bait!"

"I was expecting *something*," Sophia said as the hangers-on made themselves scarce. "You didn't get attenuated vaccine by being *nice*. And there were too many women, not enough men. Where were the men? Where was the billionaire? Get downstairs and get a video of this. I want to be able to identify who's there and who's not."

"*You will turn over your boat or we will kill your crewman.*" The man was heavyset and armed only with a pistol. He had a thick Slavic accent but the voice was...cultured. Something. He didn't really sound like a thug.

"Hello," Sophia replied. "Greetings from Wolf Squadron of the United States Navy. I'm Ensign Sophia Smith, skipper of the U.S. Navy Auxiliary Vessel *No Tan Lines*. To whom am I speaking?"

"*This does not matter. There is no United States so there is no United States Navy. You will turn over your boat. We will spare your lives. If you attempt to drive off, we shall open fire.*"

"That would be the worst possible mistake you could make, sir," Sophia said, calmly. "If you fire, you will destroy this boat; then we would both be adrift. Please, do not be . . . *nekulturny*. We have time. It is a nice day for conversation. You have been out of contact for some time. I would acquaint you with the current conditions. I will not, as you say, drive off."

"What are the current conditions?" the man said. Like with most castaways, she could hear the hunger for information in his voice.

"All land areas are under control of infected," Sophia said. "As are most ships and boats. However, Wolf Squadron *is* part of the United States Navy. I *am* a Naval officer and this is a *U.S. Navy* boat. A U.S. Navy boat or ship, of even the smallest such as mine, has not been captured since the Barbary Pirates days. I am not going to be the first.

"Now, your actions have been aggressive. But they are not, so far, past the point of real difficulty. Castaways react in various manners. You wish to be able to get to some point of relative safety. You wish to have supplies again, some sort of a life other than eeking out a miserable living on raw fish and what water you can distill with your solar stills. I can sympathize. Most of the squadron has been in your situation at one point or another. We are more than willing to share supplies. We can even get you a boat so that you and some of your companions can go on your merry way. With your weapons. You'll need them to clear boats of infected so you can salvage.

"However, we have only two real penalties at this point. We don't have much in the way of prisons or brigs so you get either the 'leave us and other uninfecteds alone and we'll leave you alone,' the offer I'm making to you now—or death. There, really, isn't much in the middle. So, you might want to consider that in light of your threat to destroy a U.S. Navy vessel. Because, then, well, 'leave you alone' isn't going to happen."

"You are one boat and you are under my guns. And I still don't believe you are Navy. Where is your uniform? Why would the Navy use yachts? Where are your supercarriers?"

"Full of infected," Sophia said. "Although we're clearing a baby carrier at the moment. And I am the only vessel in *view*. There are others. So, what do you say? I'll get you a boat, full of fuel, full of supplies, you can sail off with your . . . henchmen and we'll let bygones be bygones. I'll even throw in a case of scotch. You like scotch? Me not so much."

"*The boat I am going to take is here already,*" the man replied. "*And you will either surrender it or be destroyed. You have one minute to tie alongside. I have a rocket launcher, in case you don't know what that is.*"

"You have a rocket-propelled *grenade* launcher," Sophia said. "Slightly different beast. And if we're playing one-upmanship, *I* have a submarine. *Alex*, you monitoring?"

"*Roger, Seawolf,*" a powerful transmission came in. "*Surfacing at two-two-six, range one thousand yards.*"

Sophia didn't bother to look over her shoulder, she just watched their faces as the *Alexandria* came to the surface a kilometer out.

"So, yes, there *is* still a United States Navy and yes, I *am* a United States Naval officer and yes, you *are* in a heap of trouble. But we can work that out. So far it's no harm, no foul. So you can put down your poxie little crap AK knockoffs and your dinky little RPG or I can sink you. I'll even give you the choice of machine-gun fire, torpedo, Harpoon missile or Tomahawk. Your call, fucktard."

Rusty had collected the AKs, dumped the RPG into the drink, left the water and come back to the boat. In the meantime, the *Alex* had contacted flotilla. After that it was a matter of a nine-hour wait until Kuzma showed up in the *Large* along with the *Midlife Crisis,* which was captained by another CG petty officer; the *Pit Stop;* and a sailboat Sophia had never seen before called the *Knotty Problem.* Appropriate name. The *Large* had a machine-gun team on the "sundeck" forward. Sophia knew that while the two "security specialists" were both "into" guns—civilian shooters, that is—neither of them had ever handled a machine gun before the Plague. So she was really hoping it wouldn't come to that.

"*See why the skipper doesn't do away teams?*" Kuzma radioed when he was alongside.

"Yes, and in agreement, sir," Sophia said. "On the other hand, wasn't going to in this case. Knew there was something fishy. How are we going to handle this, sir?"

"*Do we have some clue who are goats and who are sheep?*" Kuzma asked.

"When the guns came out we took video," Sophia said. "There were seven who were armed. We don't know who they are, but we know what they look like."

"*Roger.*"

"*Russian vessel, this is Commander Vancel, skipper of the United States Navy Attack Submarine USS* Alexandria. *There were seven armed personnel who threatened to hijack a US Navy vessel onboard your ship. Those persons will stand on the wash deck of the vessel. The sailboat* Knotty Problem *will be brought alongside along with two dinghies. We will toss you lines. Tie it up. Our crew will offload, taking one of the dinghies. Those seven will enter the sailboat. Anyone who wants to accompany the seven may leave with them as long as it is clearly of their own free will. Any evidence of coercion will be dealt with by lethal force.*

"*The sailboat has been resupplied and refueled. The engines, peripherals and all sailing equipment are in good running order. There is one, repeat, one pistol onboard for self-defense or light clearance for the purposes of salvage. The seven individuals as well as any others who wish to accompany them will then sail away. As long as you are not further known to engage in hostilities, stay away from us, don't pirate vessels, and don't kill uninfected, we'll let bygones be bygones. Come to our attention in a negative way and you will be dealt with. As I believe Ensign Smith pointed out, we have 'go away' and 'death' as our only current penalties. This is the 'go away' option. You have fifteen minutes to prepare.*"

The heavyset man was on the back upper deck, by the entrance to the main saloon. He still had the hand-set Rusty had been carrying.

"*Do you know who I am? I am Nazar Lavrenty! This is my yacht. You speak of piracy but you are stealing my yacht.*"

"*I didn't know who you were until I contacted higher,*" Vancel replied. "*They, in turn, contacted the Russians they are in communication with. General Kazimov's response was ебать твою мать.*"

The man was waving his arms and shouting into the radio.

"*KAZIMOV! KAZIMOV? HE IS NOT THE RUSSIAN GOVERNMENT!*"

"Think that name touches a nerve?" Paula said, grinning.

"Sounds like it," Sophia said.

"*He is what is left,*" Vancel radioed. "*We might have tried to work with you and left you in some control of the vessel, which we need, had you not shown your inability to be trusted. This has been authorized by higher, and what remains of the Russian government. That is all there is to it. You have fifteen minutes or*

U.S. Marines will perform a hostile boarding. If you survive that you shall be given a very brief trial, shot, and dumped over the side. The clock starts now."

The sailboat was brought alongside. Some of the crew on the yacht caught the tossed lines and secured it while the Wolf crew unassed into a dinghy and headed back to the *Large.*

In a bit more than fifteen minutes, "Lavrenty" came out with his henchmen and the same number of women.

"Coincidence?" Paula said. "I don't think so."

"Lavrenty, leave the women on the yacht. Board the sailboat with your personnel. Put the women on the radio, one by one, on the upper aft deck away *from the sailboat with the radio. We have to have assurances they are not under duress. Do not attempt to exit the boat while we are getting those assurances. The machine-gun crew on the* Large *will take you under fire if you try to exit."*

"These are girlfriends. And they don't speak English."

"You'd be surprised how many translators survived," Vancel replied. *"Pick a language. It was not a request."*

The following conversation was in foreign languages. Most of them, after a few gabbled words, dropped the, fortunately robust, radio and darted back into the interior of the yacht. Only two went with Lavrenty in the end.

"They're going to be busy," Paula said drily. "Not that they weren't already."

Most of the women were visibly pregnant.

"What happens in the compartment..." Sophia said. "I sincerely doubt any of them were virgins before they got on that boat."

"Point."

There was a good bit of arm waving and angst onboard the *Knotty Problem.* Apparently, while it *was* supplied, the supply crew had not bothered to clean it up. Then there was the issue of the women. One of the "henchmen" slapped one of the women right in front of God and everybody, which earned him a burst of machine-gun fire from the *Large.* Finally, the aptly named sailboat started up its engines and putted away from the megayacht.

"If there are any qualified crewmen left onboard, could you pick up the radio, please..."

"Permission to come aboard?" Sophia said, tossing the line of the dinghy to a sailor on the wash deck of the megayacht.

"Come aboard, please." The woman waiting on the wash deck was gorgeous. Most notable were long, incredibly shapely legs. "I am Olga Zelenova, and you are...?"

"*No Tan Lines*," Sophia said, hopping onto the deck.

"Never leave the boat" referred to boardings of hostile or potentially hostile vessels. Not to boarding the new flagship of the flotilla.

"I...yes, I have no tan...What?" Olga said, confused.

"Sorry," Sophia said. "It's a Navy thing. I'm the skipper of the *No Tan Lines*. Acting Ensign Third Class Sophia Smith."

"Ah," Olga said, brightening up. "The boat which found us. Thank you. Yes, 'You may have a rocket launcher but I have a submarine.' Very funny. And, yes, Nazar was, as you say, a 'fucktard.'"

"You know where the meeting's at?" Sophia asked.

"This way," Olga said. "I am greeting the visitors."

"Nice," Sophia said as they entered the main saloon. "Much nicer than the *Alpha*. Of course, you never got overrun with infected."

The saloon had taken a beating in use, no question. But it was still reasonably clean and very very ornate. And huge. If anything it was bigger than the *Alpha*'s. Now that the ship was under power again, it was even pleasantly air conditioned.

"It is very nice," Olga said. "At first. When you are on here with no power or water and people you really did not like in the first place... It is less nice. I am pleased there is new ownership."

"Were you one of the ones Lavrenty tried to run off with?" Sophia asked.

"Yes," Olga said, frowning. "I do not want to go. But they still had guns, you know, pistols. And they are...brutal. Still, all has come out well."

"I don't know about well," Sophia said as they entered the massive dining room. "But better."

"Ensign," Kuzma said, waving to a chair.

"I'm not late, am I?" Sophia asked.

"No," Kuzma said. "And we're still waiting on Captain Sava. Miss Zelenova, if you could see where the captain's got to?"

"Sava?" Sophia asked when the girl had left the room.

"Skipper of this," Captain Lloyd A. Behm II said.

"Who is, probably, going to keep on being the skipper," Kuzma said. "With some security onboard, of course."

"I am sorry I am late." The skipper of the ship was a man of medium height with dark black hair and a heavily muscled body. "One of the water pumps is still not working. I was discussing it with the chief engineer."

"You're actually right on time," Kuzma said. "All right, everyone, Captain Vladan Sava, skipper of the...akuba...?"

"Perhaps '*Money for Nothing*'...?" Captain Sava said. "It is the rough translation."

"Skipper of the *Money for Nothing*," Kuzma said. "From left to right, Captain Behm of the *Sea Hooky*. Captain Poole of the *Noby Dick*."

"Yo," Gary Poole said, waving. The skipper of the awkwardly-named seventy-three-foot Arquela was tall, still quite emaciated, wearing a Hawaiian shirt and a broad-brimmed straw hat. "So wish tradition let me change the name..."

After Sophia had decided it would honor the owners to keep the name "*No Tan Lines*," the tradition had stuck fast. Captain Poole just happened to draw a very short straw.

"Captain Richard Estep of the *N2 Deep*. Captain Elias Rostad of the *One Toy Two Many*. And Captain Richard Purser of the *Finally Fishin'*."

"It is good to meet you all and I look forward to helping in this endeavor."

"Captain Sava," Kuzma continued, "who is an experienced master mariner, thank God, has agreed to assist the efforts of Wolf Squadron. The *Money* will begin to act, immediately, as the Flotilla One's flagship. However, all personnel onboard are currently suffering from malnutrition due to lack of stores. We have stores already delivered to the *Pit Stop* which will be transferred, however all excess stores should be moved to the *Money* beginning immediately after this meeting. Anybody going to say they don't have excess? And, yes, I know you've got your little stashes, I'm talking regular excess?"

"Plenty," Behm said. "We were getting ready to shift some of it to the *Pit Stop* anyway."

"We will also begin rotation of personnel to the *Money* for crew rest," Kuzma said. "I know you all could use some time in a bunk that's not rocking quite so much."

"All for that," Sophia said.

"With the exception of the *Lines*, which I'll get to," Kuzma said. "You're going to get screwed a bit; sorry, Ensign."

"No worries," Sophia said.

"The first boat to unload will be the *Lines*. Soph, what's your fuel status?"

"Not full," Sophia said. "Close. More than three-quarter's tank. We unrepped from a sailboat we found that still had onboard."

"That should be enough for this," Kuzma said. "*Lines* will then proceed to 30.532,–28.169 where we have report of a small tanker. I'll send a prize crew and another security officer with you to check it out. If it's diesel, we're golden. If not, you'll need to rendezvous with the *Pit Stop* at another freighter we found. That had plenty of diesel in its bunkers. This ship is going to need way more than the *Pit Stop* had to deliver."

"What about Squadron?" Behm asked.

"As in getting it from Squadron, or their situation?" Kuzma said. "They unrepped to the *Grace* and *Alpha* from the *Iwo* so they're in good shape. If necessary, we can run the *Pit Stop* up to the *Iwo* to unrep but we should be able to get it from the freighter. Best would be if the tanker has diesel. From the reports, it sounds like it's one of those small tankers that is used to resupply local ports. Sometimes it's gas, sometimes its diesel. You never know.

"Once we have this boat fully resupplied and refueled, the squadron will form a rough line perpendicular to the Equatorial Current. The *Large* will take and hold the center point with the *Money* and any other support type vessels we recover in trail. Small boats will spread out on either side, each with a packet to cover. The ones to the center will come in to the *Money* for off-load of recovered personnel and materials. If we can get a supply ship like the *Grace* at some point, they may be taken aboard for repair. Start ripping out any parts you find. We'll find a place in the support zone to hold and inventory them. Vessels will stay inboard for a few days after recovery doing local support. Including 'fishing ops.' Turns out the subs have been using their active to knock out schools of fish. They generally get more than they can use. Most of you have cold fish storage. We'll scoop up their excess. That is the general outline of the plan until we're recalled to Squadron. Ensign Smith, do you have any questions?"

"No, sir," Sophia said, trying not to sigh. She knew they were planning on rotating people to any big vessel they found, and she'd been looking forward to a few days off. But...

"Get with Gary on your security and prize crew," Kuzma said.

"They're already detailed off. If you don't have anything, we need to get cracking on finding some fuel."

"Will do, sir," Sophia said, standing up. "Have a nice chat."

"Okay," Sophia said. "Here's the thing with tankers. You really don't want to fire onboard."

The "augmentation" for Rusty was a former Army armor cav sergeant named Cody "Anarchy" Mcgarity. With his nickname "Anarchy" she wasn't thrilled to have him as a clearance specialist, but he seemed more on the ball than Rusty. It's possible that Rusty was just fine before his experiences onboard the *Voyage* but he was not the sharpest tool in the shed. Maybe it was drinking too much ammoniacal urine.

She'd already circled the vessel named the M/V *Eric Shivak* and she knew two things. One, it *was* diesel. Two, as usual, there was a leak somewhere. It wasn't just a tanker, though. There were two ship containers chained down on the deck.

"So... Melee?" Mcgarity asked. "Half-life Two fail: No crowbar."

"We've got about six," Rusty said.

"And some hammers," Sophia said. "And Halligan tools. This is more a Faith deal than mine, but you really want to avoid fire and sparks. However, there are no evident infecteds so you may get lucky."

"*Three KIA*," Anarchy radioed. "*All appear to be former infecteds. Crew boat is missing. Plenty of supplies left onboard. I think some of them turned and the rest abandoned ship. Ship's clear. Well, we didn't check the containers but they've got seals on them so they don't look like they've been opened.*"

"Roger," Sophia said. "Sending over the survey and prize crew."

"Mixed groceries, general stores, some parts including auto parts," Captain Hebert said. The "captain" had been a mate on a freighter that had abandoned ship when the crew started to turn. "And the main bunkers are full which is a relief. The spillage was minor. It's got more pure fuel than the *Grace*. Not as fancy but it's what we needed."

"Can we unrep from it?" Sophia asked.

"We can tank you up right now," Hebert said.

∽ ⊖ ∾

"You know," Paula said as the two boats got back underway to rendezvous with the flotilla, "we haven't known Hebert all that long. We didn't even leave Rusty and Anarchy aboard. What's to keep him from just taking off?"

"You think there's *not* going to be a fast attack following him around?" Sophia said.

"Oh, yeah, those."

"Flotilla Ops, *No Tan Lines*," Sophia radioed.

"*Lines, Ops, over.*"

"One tanker tack islands-support-boat full of goodness delivered," Sophia said. "Orders?"

"*Proceed to 23.274,–27.949. Rendezvous, USS* Santa Fe *for fishing ops.*"

"What?" Sophia shouted. They were *supposed* to be the next on schedule to spend a night aboard the luxury yacht. She thought about it for a moment then keyed the radio. "Roger, Ops. Proceeding..."

"You're in the Navy, now," Paula sang. "You're in the Navy now...How do *I* get out?"

"USS *Santa Fe*, USS *Santa Fe*, *No Tan Lines*, over," Sophia radioed. "Come on, be around here somewhere." There was no sign of the sub but that was sort of the point. "I know you know where *I* am."

"*No Tan Lines, come to heading one-six-niner, range fourteen thousand yards, over.*"

"Heading one-six-niner, fourteen klicks, aye," Sophia said. It was back the way they'd come. "I *know* you had me on sonar. You could have told me to wait up there..."

She could see the ECM mast about two klicks out.

"*No Tan Lines, hold your position. We will intercept and engage the fish, gather ours, submerge, then you get yours.*"

"That sounds vaguely wrong for some reason," Anarchy said. "They get theirs first. And how are they going to 'engage' the fish?"

"Not sure," Sophia said. "Usually when we run across a school we just, you know, fish for them..."

The Yankee search was so powerful, reverberations of it could be felt through the hull, and her depth finder went nuts. As they watched, a school of yellowfin floated to the surface.

"What the *hell* was *that*?" Paula said, flying up to the flying bridge. "My teeth are rattling."

"And so we have another zombie apocalypse moment," Sophia said, shaking her head.

"Well, that's something you don't see every day," Gunny Sands said.

The USS *Annapolis* was towing behind it a small yacht that would, possibly, have made a decent dinghy for the football-field-length submarine.

There was already a medical and resupply team standing by in moon suits to bring the family vaccine and supplies. The moon suits weren't to protect the greeting party but the family onboard the yacht. The MREs had even been decontaminated.

"Welcome to a zombie apocalypse moment, Gunnery Sergeant Sands," Faith said. "Defined as a 'What the fuck' moment that could only happen in a zombie apocalypse. We tend to call it a zam or a zammie."

They were standing on the lead edge of the flight deck of the *Iwo Jima* after completing morning PT. They could use most of the ship for PT, now, running up and down companionways, climbing stairs, running the flight deck, jumping coamings, and generally having a oorah Marines afloat day, because the ship was just about completely clear of infecteds. They still had some areas to check for survivors but that was getting to the point of no returns.

The *Iwo* might even run again, someday—the infected had done a lot of damage, but most of it was repairable—given parts and trained personnel. They had gotten personnel from the boat but it was a grab bag and, for fairly obvious reasons, tended towards store keepers and cooks. They were in the areas that had stores when the abandon ship call went down. They'd found damned few engineering personnel. Alive and uninfected, at least.

"I'll keep that in mind, young lady," the gunny said. Two weeks "limited activities" and food and he was starting to look like a gunnery sergeant again. He still didn't fill out his uniform but he was PTing. Not exactly running the young bucks into the ground but he was getting there. Faith had to admit that, no, she could *not* keep up with most of the Marines, especially since they PT'd in gear. So she and the gunny had been working out together.

Turned out the gunny was, unsurprisingly, an A-Number One coaming jumper, a skill she was still trying to master.

He was, also unsurprisingly, a master of Marine lore and trivia as well as an expert tactician and weapons expert. He'd started off sort of disgruntled at the suggestion that he PT with a guuurl but had taken the opportunity to increase her store of professional knowledge. And while in agreement on "The Wolf Squadron Way" of clearance, he had put his professional knowledge and acumen to the subject and suggested useful "tweaks" that had been tested, then implemented.

"Thank you for increasing my understanding of this brave new world in which we reside and fight, ma'am."

"That wasn't meant as a..." Faith said. She really liked and admired the gunny and didn't want to insult him.

"That was not intended ironically, Miss," Gunny Sands said. "As I have been teaching you a bit about the hallowed lore of the U-S-M-C, the information transfer has not been all one way. That is an example thereof. Just as you previously pointed out that zombies do not retreat and, therefore, small teams can expect at some point to come to melee distance or, as you put it 'get into the scrum.' Which has now become Post-Plague Marine slang on the same level of commonality as 'FUBAR' and 'BOHICA.' And that, therefore, it is useful to keep multiple knives on your person when clearing in case you're in a 'scrum' or even worse 'in the dunny.' Rather than it being purely an affectation."

"Understood, Gunnery Sergeant," Faith said.

"Miss Smith, your father, tentatively, brought up the subject of making you a Marine."

"I don't think I've got what it takes, Gunny," Faith said, shrugging. "I can't keep up with the guys now that they're getting back in shape. Heck, I can only climb a hawser once in gear. The guys go up them over and over again."

"You are female, Miss Smith," Sands said. "Men and women do not directly compete in the Olympics for a reason. I would never expect you to compete head to head in PT with the troops. The question is not can you compete as a male in PT or even certain types of combat. Although you are one of the few women I could honestly see being qualified in all respects for infantry combat. You make the grade at the point of low-level male infantryman, which is all that's required if you were to be a regular Marine rifleman.

"The questions are many others. Are you emotionally mature enough for the job? Are you physically fit enough as a *female*? Can you handle the physical and mental aspects of this type of combat? The only traditional ways of judging those thing is by putting you through some sort of introductory training and testing. Boot camp, for example. Are you, in fact, tough enough to be a Marine? Boot camp puts stresses on you that even this type of combat does not inflict. We stop clearance after a certain point each day. Can you continue for days with little rest or sleep?

"Then there are the technical legal aspects. You are performing, would be expected to continue to perform, front-line combat. You are, again obviously, thirteen. When he suggested it, I found it ludicrous on its face but I was...polite. I told him you'd probably make a great Marine in five years."

"Thank you, Gunnery Sergeant," Faith said. "I hope I can make the grade in five years."

"He suggested that I spend some time examining the new reality and table the discussion," Sands said. "I have since revisited the issue. With the approval of the L-T and Colonel Ellington, and if you agree, you are to be sworn in as a probationary third lieutenant, U-S-M-C at noon tomorrow."

"I'm not sure that's...wise, Gunny?" Faith said. "I mean, I know I'm sort of a mascot..."

"Oh, you are far more than a mascot, Miss Smith," the gunny said. "The reality is that we have exactly thirty Marines in current manning. We are so very few. They can all serve as clearance specialists but most are not, in fact, infantry. Aircraft crewmen, tankers, mechanics. Cooks. We also have five oceans and seven seas worth of ships to clear. There are cruise liners still at sea. Entire Carrier Strike Groups. We need every single person who can make the grade and, Miss Smith, thirteen, chick and all, you make the grade in a *leap*."

"Thank you, Gunny," Faith said, her chin working. "I'll try to...I'll try to be a good Marine."

"Marine Officer, note," the gunny said. "The one thing I'll ask you to do is tighten up, a bit, on the decorum. Only a bit, though, because there is, also, yes, the aspect of what you call 'a mascot.'"

"If that is..." Faith said carefully.

"If I may, miss," Sands said. "What you call 'a mascot' is more what should be termed 'an icon.' A subject not just of morale but of veneration or even worship. These men are United States Marines, yes, and they will continue to do their duty. But they are Marines who have lost everything. Family, friends, buddies, country. We are one and all lost and adrift on a darkling sea. You, Miss Smith, have become not their pin-up girl but their heart and soul. They would follow *me* into hell. Charge any shore, face any fire. I am their Gunny. That's what Marines do. If *you* hinted that Satan had a case of ammo you particularly liked, they would charge in *without* a bucket of water. As Staff Sergeant Januscheitis said when he, separately, brought the idea up: 'The only thing we've got left, Gunny, is Faith.'"

CHAPTER 7

I, [name], do solemnly swear (or affirm) that I will support and defend the Constitution of the United States against all enemies, foreign and domestic; that I will bear true faith and allegiance to the same; that I take this obligation freely, without any mental reservation or purpose of evasion; and that I will well and faithfully discharge the duties of the office on which I am about to enter. So help me God.

Oath of the officers of the
Uniformed Services of the United States

"So, Captain, what now?" Galloway asked. The NCCC had his fingers steepled and was, in Steve's opinion, looking just a bit too much like Doctor Evil.

The *Iwo Jima* was cleared. They'd found forty-three Naval personnel and sixteen Marines, with Gunny Sands and Lieutenant Volpe being the most senior. There were two navy full lieutenants, including Pellerin and "various other ranks." No chiefs. The senior were three PO1s. No pilots, some aviation crewmen, both Marine and Navy.

It was not a great number out of a complement of twelve hundred Navy and nearly two thousand Marines.

"There are several options, sir," Steve said. "Do you want me to lay out my arguments for and against or just cut right to my preferred plan?"

"The main question is the vaccine," Galloway said. "The subs are surviving...surprisingly well. But they cannot operate indefinitely."

"I have the submarine crews very firmly in the forefront of my mind, sir," Steve said. "There's a whole list of materials we need for producing vaccine. We've been over that, I understand. Gitmo is my preferred target for that. The base hospital, as of just prior to the fall and according to anecdotal data, should have the equipment and material. Hopefully with the gear at Gitmo we can make vaccine."

"So you're heading to Gitmo?" Commander Freeman said.

"I would prefer not to do so at this time, Commander," Steve said. "The main reason is the continuing vulnerability of my forces to storm. My boats are mostly small, and while their crews have a lot of experience at sea at this point, I really don't think they're up to sailing through a hurricane. We can try to dodge them at sea but..."

"I'm a Naval officer," Freeman said drily. "I'm aware of the power of the ocean, Captain, as well as the fickle nature of hurricanes. With due respect."

The relationship between the two was tricky. Freeman had yet to be appointed a captaincy but was in some ways, technically, the Chief of Naval Operations and Steve's boss.

"That is, in a nutshell, my argument against Road to Gitmo at this time, Mr. Under Secretary," Steve said. "Cognizant as I am that, pardon, now *my* submarine crews are slowly starving to death. On the other hand, they are also fishing quite successfully and have adequate vitamins to prevent nutrition deficiency for the time being. The main ones that I'm worried about are the ones that critical systems busted and are now ashore on desert islands. Especially those on ones who are also subject to tropical storms. I was planning on having a brainstorming session with the sub skippers and Commander Freeman on that subject at a later time. However, to the main point. I really would prefer not to subject the squadron to a hurricane. The season ends at the end of November. At that time we can easily move to Gitmo and begin clearance operations. That is less than two months. I'm going to take a survey of which boats are unlikely to be able to hang on that long and determine other options. My current plan is a redeployment for aggressive at-sea search, clearance and rescue operations in low-storm zones as well as testing littoral clearance methods after some redistribution of personnel..."

"Nice uniform, Sis," Sophia said.

Faith was wearing Marine Pattern Camouflage, colloquially called both MarPat and MarCam, and was carrying a cloth shopping bag.

The *No Tan Lines* had been "redeployed" back to the main squadron for "refit and resupply." They were actually okay on the supply part. If anything, they were going to be off-loading. The flotilla had been stockpiling "excess supplies" on the supply ships. Not that Sophia gave up her *good* stash.

"Thanks," Faith said, tossing Sophia the cloth shopping bag she was carrying. "There's yours."

"Mine?" Sophia said. The bag felt extremely full.

"We got an *official* suggestion from the CO of the *Alex* that we find you a uniform," Faith said. "I got tasked to find your size in the uniform store on the *Iwo*. There's tactical boots in it, too. Then I got an *unofficial* message that you might want to think about wearing *something* a little more often. Been doing what you can to raise the morale on the subs, Sis?"

"Oh," Sophia said, breathing through her nose. "Those glowing green *bastards*!"

"Never trust a submariner," Faith said, giggling.

"How've you been?" Sophia said, waving her into the boat.

"Good," Faith said. "Getting there, anyway. Kicking the ass of Marines is sort of fun."

"Kicking Marine ass?" Paula said. "Do tell."

"They're good, don't get me wrong," Faith said. "But they'd trained for fighting hajis in the Sandbox. Fighting zombies in a ship is different. And they're supposed to be trained for fighting shipboard but it's not really something they'd concentrated on."

"We found you a present as well," Sophia said. "Paula, where's that case of the good stuff?"

"Right under here," Paula said, opening up the compartment under the bar.

"You know I don't drink alcohol," Faith said. "Much."

"Tada!" Paula said, pulling out a case of razzleberry tea.

"Oh," Faith said, panting. "This is nearly as great as when we found a stash of twelve-gauge on the *Iwo*!"

"You're welcome," Paula said, then opened up the fridge and pulled out a cold one.

"Found a boat that somebody was apparently an equal fan," Sophia said, pouring herself a glass of brandy. "Cheers, Sis."

"Up your bottom!" Faith said, then took a sip. "Ah, nectar of the gods."

"You're really in the Marines?" Paula asked.

"I have been having an abbreviated class on military decorum," Faith said, making a face. "I was going to get pinned right away but they decided to hold off until you rejoined the squadron. Since you didn't have a uniform or 'accoutrements' as I've learned they are called, we'll both get pinned this afternoon. And that's when I'll get sworn in as a 'probationary third lieutenant.'"

"So you're a 'probationary' lieutenant and I'm an 'acting' ensign?" Sophia said, shaking her head. "Is there a difference?"

"Not that I can figure out," Faith said, shrugging. "I still don't get most of this military stuff."

"How was the *Iwo*?" Sophia asked.

"Compared to the *Voyage* it was a walk in the fucking park," Faith said, shrugging again. "We went straight for the food supply areas after the first day of upper deck clearance and found about half the survivors. Most of the Marines, Gunny Sands and a couple others being exceptions, were in good shape. The rest of it was mostly training Marines on the Wolf Way of clearance. And once we found a big, beautiful store of .45 and double-ought... Then it was just a matter of rolling hot. Not to mention frags make a dandy compartment clearing tool."

"Sounds like you had fun," Paula said.

"Buttloads," Faith said. "It wasn't the *Voyage*. There was just something different about it. There was way less finding people who'd just died for one thing. Or people who might as well be dead. It was pretty much long dead, zombies, and survivors in pretty good shape. And most of the long dead had either been chewed up pretty good or were, basically, mummies. And no kids and it wasn't a fucking play palace that had turned into a horror movie. So, yeah, mostly fun. Fucking *Voyage* still gives me nightmares. How was your float?"

"Found a family that was uninfected," Sophia said.

"The Lawtons," Faith said. "Need to bring up the dad in a bit."

"Why?" Paula said.

"Just will," Faith said. "He wants to see you. Has a present for you. All of you."

"That's sweet?" Sophia said, puzzled. "Any idea what? It's not like they had zip on that boat when we found them."

"Yeah," Faith said, grinning. "He gave me the same present. But it's a surprise. Anyway, adventures. Something about a Russian mobster?"

"Oh, that," Sophia said, grinning. "Not mobster, exactly. Except that anybody Russian with money was basically a mobster. No real big deal."

"Hey," Paula said. "It was pretty tense at the time."

"Sort of," Sophia said. "We found another mega. Smaller than the *Alpha* but not much. Bunch of survivors."

"The big one with the Russian writing," Faith said, gesturing with her chin.

"Long story, 'nother time," Sophia said. "Any clue what's next? We've been sort of out of the loop."

"Local area rescue and clearance is what I've got," Faith said. "Dad sort of hinted that he's going to stick us together but I'm supposed to 'manage' the operation as a good officer should. Have no clue *what* operations."

"Well, we could use another clearance guy, that's for sure," Sophia said. "I don't know how it fits in but we're supposed to go over to the *Grace* tomorrow for 'refit.' Not sure what we're being refitted with."

"*I'm* wondering where we're going to hide the stash," Paula said.

"Stash?" Faith said. "Oh, salvage."

"That," Paula said. "Yeah."

"So I just found out that as a Naval officer, I'm no longer on shares," Sophia said. "On the other hand, the *crew* is..."

"Pat and I opted to stay civilian," Paula said.

"...and we resupply first from 'salvaged stores.' So what if we keep the good stuff? Besides, I figure Da probably needs some stuff for entertaining."

"And boy do we have some stuff," Paula said. "Is Sari still cooking for him?"

"Yes," Faith said.

"She's so going to like what we're bringing in." She paused and grimaced. "Speaking of chefs, how's Chris? We were going to spot him some of it, too."

"I've only run into him a couple of times," Faith said, shrugging. "Lost his girl, found his girl, lost her again. Gwinn and Rob are married. Got hitched by Captain Geraldine in a really nice ceremony on the *Alpha*. Gwinn's doing admin on the *Alpha* right now. Rob's doing survey and salvage. They're good people. Chris just ended up as odd man out."

"I need to stop by and see him," Paula said. "He's got to be heartbroken. I think I was the only one on the boat he'd talked to about Gwinn."

"It's Chris," Faith said, shrugging again. "He just cooks his way out of his misery."

"He's been doing ferry work," Sophia said. "So he hasn't been doing salvage. Why don't you make up a little care package for him and take it over? Dinghy's worth. Say I'll be by when I can."

"Okay," Paula said. "That's a good way to get rid of some of the stash."

"Not the Grand Marnier," Sophia said. "Or, no more than a bottle. I was planning on making that a gift to Da."

"No Tan Lines, *Squadron Ops, over.*"

"Hang on," Sophia said. "Squadron Ops, *No Tan Lines*, over."

"You have *got* to change that name," Faith said.

"Think *ours* is bad," Sophia said.

"Lines *scheduled to come alongside the* Grace Tan *at fourteen-thirty for off-load and refit. Crew will be shuttled to the* Alpha *for pinning ceremony, Master, scheduled for sixteen-thirty. Master will, say again, will be in proper uniform. Reception to follow.*"

"Oooo..." Sophia said. "I need to get some stuff back to Da for the reception."

"You've got time to drop it by before you're scheduled to go to the *Grace*," Faith said, looking at her watch. "I'm sort of at loose ends. Drop me on the *Alpha* with it, I'll get it to Sari."

"Works," Sophia said, keying the radio. "*Lines* alongside *Grace* fourteen-thirty, aye. Pinning ceremony, sixteen-thirty, aye. Reception to follow, aye."

"*Squadron Ops, out.*"

"You know I'm really proud to do this," Steve said, pinning one side of Sophia's collar while Stacey pinned the other. The pins were gold circles rather than the single bar of an ensign.

"Still not sure why I said yes," Sophia said. "And while this is not in any way an official bitch, Kuzma has been running our ass ragged."

"I know," Steve said. "He wanted to see if he could get you to complain. Congratulations," he said, shaking her hand.

"I figured that much out," Sophia said. "I can hack it. But it's not fair on my crew."

"We'll talk," Steve said, stepping over to Faith.

"Faith, Marine uniforms are always supposed to be spotless and perfect," Steve said.

"Is there something wrong with my uniform?" Faith asked, panicking. She didn't like being in front of a crowd, anyway.

"No, but there is something 'wrong' with these," Steve said, showing her the pins. "These were recovered from the body of Midshipman Lin Wicklund, in the CIC of the USS *Iwo Jima*. Midshipman Wicklund, whose intent after the Naval Academy was to be a Marine officer, was found with a clocked-out forty-five by her body. Wicklund was, as far as we can determine, the last remaining officer fighting for control of the ship. The pips have a discoloration on them. Do not clean that discoloration off."

"Yes, sir," Faith said, her chin tightening. "Understood, sir."

"Sophia has already been officially sworn in," Steve said after putting on the pins. "She just didn't have the pins. You have not. Raise your right hand."

"I, state your name..."

"*I, Faith Marie Smith...*"

"Lieutenant Smith," her father said when the ceremony was complete. "There is not a bloody word in there that says 'I'm only an officer to kill zombies.' A Marine officer's oath is to faithfully discharge her duty to defend the Constitution of the United States. That's it. Period. Dot. There is also nothing in that oath that has a time limit. It is an oath for life. Clear, Lieutenant?"

"Clear, sir."

"You looked like you were going to pass out, ma'am," Januscheitis said.

"I thought I *was* going to pass out, Staff Sergeant," Faith replied.

The "reception to follow" was all ranks and had heavy hors d'oeuvres in lieu of dinner.

"I don't do attention well," Faith admitted.

"Seriously, ma'am?" Januscheitis said, grabbing a bar stool while it was unoccupied. "You certainly don't seem to mind attention from zombies. For you, LT."

Somehow, over the last few weeks, Isham had managed to repair most of the damage to the *Alpha*'s main saloon. While essentially nothing matched, it had been rearranged to give the impression of "multiple styles" rather than "salvaged bits of junk from a dozen different boats."

"Why thank you kind sir," Faith said. "I accept."

"What'll you have, Lieutenant?" the bartender said. He looked vaguely familiar but most of the people at the reception were people she knew or she had seen at least once. There were a few "new" faces, you could tell the freshies, boaties with deep tans, "ghosts" from compartments with no tan at all and all with a "hollowed out" look, but most were people she sort of knew.

"Water," Faith said. "Unless you've got some good juice."

"I cannot believe we've got an LT that only drinks juice and water," Derek said. "There should be a law."

"A Marine officer shall be prepared for duty at all times," Faith said. "Says so right in the instructions manual."

"I've got a really decent pomegranate," the bartender said.

"I'll drink anything that's wet," Faith said. "Except wine and beer. Or coffee. Or anything with carbonation."

"Seriously?" Derek said. "No alcohol, no coffee? What are you, ma'am, Mormon?"

"Just don't like the taste of wine or beer," Faith said, shrugging.

"And for you, gentlemen?"

"Beer?" Januscheitis asked.

"We've got a very nice pale ale on tap," the bartender said. "Something called Seven Acres. Pretty decent. Didn't turn."

"Works for me," Derek said. "Now, about the Mormon thing..."

"I don't drink, don't smoke, don't do drugs, don't like the taste or smell of coffee," Faith said. "I don't do carbonation. I don't even like black teas. I prefer green. I just don't like the taste. I like good fruit juice and certain kinds of bottled water. I'm really, really, incredibly picky when it comes to taste or texture. Problem, Corporal?"

"No, ma'am," Derek said. "Just sort of mind boggling. I'm having a hard time with... with Lieutenant Smith, zombie killer, and Lieutenant Smith..."

"'Don't drink, don't smoke, what do you do...?'" Januscheitis half sang. "Kill zombies."

"Got it in one," Faith said. "I don't do it for moral reasons; don't mind if other people drink, though they get kind of stupid, but I don't like the taste."

"Ever tried straight booze, ma'am?" Januscheitis asked.

"No," Faith said, shrugging. "Doubt it would change my interest."

"Try this and see how you like it," the bartender said, sliding the glass of chilled juice to her. "And your beer, gentlemen."

"That is pretty good," Faith said, taking a sip. "It sat in plastic too long, but it's not bad. Sophia, bless her black little heart, turned up a case of razzleberry tea. Now *that* is good."

"Oops," Januscheitis said, setting his beer down and coming to attention. "Commodore, inbound."

"Easy," Steve said, walking up behind Faith. "No rank in the mess or something like that."

"Yes, sir," Januscheitis said.

"Then is it, 'Good evening, sir' or 'Hey, Da'?" Faith asked, grinning. "I get confused."

"'Hey, Da' works," Steve said. "So this is your posse. I haven't had time to get introduced."

"Corporal Douglas," Faith said, "Staff Sergeant Januscheitis, Captain Smith AKA Commodore Wolf. Derek, Jan, my Da, Steve."

"Good evening, Captain," Januscheitis said.

"Good to see you again, Staff Sergeant," Steve said. "You're looking better. I'd like to thank you and your men for clearing the *Iwo*. That had to be double tough."

"From what I've gotten, not as hard as clearing the *Voyage*, sir," Januscheitis said. "Lieutenant Fontana has had a couple of choice words to say on the subject."

"The *Voyage* fucking *sucked*," Faith said taking a pull of her juice. "The *Voyage* is why I wish I *did* drink."

"Choice words like those, sir," Januscheitis said.

"Clearing your own ship with your own personnel had to have its own issues," Steve said.

"Are we going to get it back in operation, sir?" Derek asked.

"Not right now," Steve said. "I wanted to use the hovercraft for future ops but after due consideration, we don't even have enough technical people, at this time, to flood the wash deck. Or maintain the AACs. We will need it for future operations, when we can use it. But not right now. That brings up a point that I need some honest and open input on. Our usual technique with something like this is to spread dermestid carrion beetles to reduce the logistics effort of clearing the remains. I'm taking an informal poll of how negative the reaction to that would be in the case of the *Iwo*."

"Carrion beetles, sir?" Derek said.

"Da's little black helpers," Faith said. "Da, did you know one of your nicknames behind your back is Captain Carrion?"

"No, but I'm not surprised," Smith said. "They are fast reproducing beetles that only eat dead flesh. Depends on how many you start with but open all the watertight doors to areas that have human remains, dump some in, wait a couple of months and what you have is picked clean skeletons. Oh, and decks covered in beetles. Which can then be vacuumed up and in many cases reused."

"Ugh," Januscheitis said, twitching. "That's, um..."

"Simple, brutal and effective," Faith said. "Sort of like a Saiga. The Coasties didn't particularly like it when we did it to their cutter. But a team of ten only took a day to collect all the skeletons and we could give them a decent burial. Even if we didn't know which was which."

"The infected, in case you hadn't noticed, even tear off their dog tags," Steve said. "I'm going to let the surviving Marines and Navy personnel have some time to consider it. But...clearing the dead from the ship is going to be a major undertaking. And while the few people we have left are doing that, they can't be doing something more useful. Not to mention, it, well, sucks. Bodies are heavy. Skeletons...not so much. Like I said, give it a few days' thought, discuss it amongst yourselves."

"So, different subject, sir?" Faith said.

"Preferably," Steve said. "What's next, right?"

"I understand you intend to clear Gitmo, sir?" Derek said.

"Once the tropical season is past, yes," Steve said. "We're working on methods of doing so. Which is, in fact, next. Tomorrow we'll be testing out a new weaponry system for heavy littoral clearance. We needed enough rounds just to do the testing, which the *Iwo* fortunately has. If the test is successful, we'll then move on to actual clearance tests to see if it really works. *They* really work, since there are two different systems. If those systems work, we'll use them to clear some minor islands in the Eastern Atlantic, then in early December, move down to Gitmo."

"That sounds like a plan, sir," Januscheitis said.

"So what are these 'littoral clearance systems'?" Faith asked.

"Oh, I think you'll like them," Steve said.

CHAPTER 8

37. There is no "overkill." There is only "open fire" and "I need to reload."

70 Maxims of Maximally Effective Mercenaries

"Ooooo..." Faith said. "Big guns. Biiiig guns. Me like big guns."

The vessel was a fishing trawler that had suffered all the normal fates. It had been "refurbished," then the outriggers and some of the winches removed. The hard points for the outriggers now held two modified M2 "MaDeuce" Browning .50 caliber machine guns.

"Faith, decorum," Steve said, facepalming. "Among other things, phraseology."

"Water-cooled, sir?" Gunny Sands said, examining the copper pipe wrapping the barrels of the machine guns. A flexible plastic hose ran from the pipes to a strapped-down fifty-five-gallon blue barrel.

The group there to "evaluate and support" the test included most of the surviving Marines as well as some pre-Plague Navy personnel and some "post-Plague, hostilities only" survivors who had volunteered for Naval service as gunners.

"Got it in one, Gunny," Steve said. "Hopefully, with enough cooling, the weapon will be able to fire more or less continuously and thus tear up large numbers of zombies close to the waterline. The question is whether the design will hold up to continuous fire. Both in terms of barrel heat and vibration from the firing."

"Ooo, ooo!" Faith said, holding up her hand. "Me, me!"

"Don't think so, kiddo," Rob Cooper said. The former maintenance engineer of the *Voyage Under Stars* patted the barrel proprietarily. "My build. *I* get first crack."

"However," Steve said. "This is an endurance test. And while the butterfly trigger has also been modified to be locked down, *everyone* will take turns maintaining fire. Because I'm fully aware that at a certain level even the gunny is going 'Oooo, oooo, me, me.'"

"Bit, sir, bit," Gunny Sands said. "I'd rather be shooting up zombies with it. Is this going to be a Marine weapon, sir?"

"Not primarily designed as such, no," Steve said. "The crew will be Navy. Marines will be used for landing parties. But, if everyone would don hearing protection..."

"Now I know why the swabbies were unloading all that fifty!" Derek shouted as he hooked up another belt.

"I'm glad somebody thought of snow shovels!" PFC Kirby said, dumping another shovelful of spent brass and links over the side.

The test had started with a fifteen-second continuous fire. When there was no evidence of heating, it went to a one-minute, then a two-minute, then a ten-minute test. While there was no heating at ten minutes, it was apparent the system needed some lubrication. The M2 Browning machine gun was living up to its name, working like an actual machine. The system fired between 475 and 575 rounds per minute. In ten minutes, that was five thousand rounds. And the .50 caliber was an unquestioned man-killer. Although the current target was open ocean, .50 caliber was considered a "light-materials" gun, i.e., designed to destroy vehicles and even small tanks. Even without its "armor-piercing" rounds, it would penetrate a car block. When it hit humans they tended to explode and the round kept on going.

The entire group, even Gunny Sands, had at one point or another gotten to fire the weapon. The "support group," both Marines and some Navy personnel, had been busy keeping one of the weapons fed and the brass and links cleared.

"Feeding these beasts is going to take some muscle," Seaman Apprentice (Gunner) Bennett said. Rusty had volunteered to join the Navy when Anarchy was "cross-service transferred" to be one of the gunners. As a tanker Anarchy was intimately familiar with the MaDeuce. "Fortunately, I've been getting it back."

There were two fifties mounted on the back of the converted trawler and both of them were in continuous fire.

"Check fire," Steve shouted. "Break them down and check for wear..."

"With them not getting hot, the barrels are taking the rounds just fine, looks like," Gunny Sands said, examining the modified barrel with a penlight. "I'm not seeing any real wear at all."

"The breech looks good," Gunner's Mate Third Class Mcgarity said, checking the parts with a loupe. "We'll have to keep it lubed if we're firing over a minute or so, but with continuous lube, I don't know *how* long you could fire one of these."

"The question, sir," Gunny Sands said, "is do we have a target?"

"We do indeed," Steve said. "We do indeed, Gunny."

"Pretty," Sophia said as the division pulled into the harbor of Valle Gran Re in the Canary Islands.

The small town on the island of Gran Re was surrounded by dry, rocky mountains and virtually cut off from the rest of the not particularly large island. The harbor consisted of a large, modern, outer breakwater to protect it from the heavy deep Atlantic seas as well as a smaller, older one interior. Both could be driven on by vehicles, as evidenced by the abandoned cars and trucks. The inner harbor was still scattered with shallow-draft small-craft painted in a variety of bright pastels, along with a few large sailboats. Two motor yachts, one at least the size of the *Large*, were tied alongside. The buildings of the town were mostly stone block, whitewashed or also painted in a rainbow of pastels.

"Scenic," Faith said. "So's the greeting party."

And there were infecteds. They weren't concentrated, ignoring the boats as usual, but they could be seen foraging for food on the water's edge.

"With due respect, Ensign," Staff Sergeant Januscheitis said. "Might I call your attention to the shoals forward."

"Got it under control, Staff Sergeant," Sophia said mildly, turning to port. "I haven't spent a lot of time in harbors, but I have been around this block a time or two."

"*We'll set up for fire on the inner jetty*," Lieutenant Zachary "Zack" Chen radioed from the USNA *Wet Debt*, formerly the Fishing Vessel (F/V) *Wet Debt*, a sixty-foot oceanic shrimp trawler. Lieutenant Chen was the division commander for Littoral Clearance Division One. The recently rescued Navy lieutenant had previously been an ordnance officer on the Arleigh Burke-class destroyer USS *Truxtun*. The *Truxtun* was also known to be somewhere in the Sargasso Sea but with the exception of the lieutenant and another survivor from a life raft, so far nobody had seen hide nor hair of it. It wasn't at its last reported position; Sophia had broken away from the division on the way down to the Canary Islands to check. Chen had elected to command the division from the fishing trawler. The *No Tan Lines* carried the Marine Assault Team and would act as a ferry for any survivors from the town who wished to evacuate.

"*Stand by while we anchor and watch the shoals.*"

The *Wet Debt* dropped anchor off the jetty seaward towards the outer breakwater. It dropped anchor nearly at the breakwater, paid it out, then used the pivot point to arrange itself so it was at a forty-five degree angle to the inner jetty about a hundred meters out. There it dropped two more "stream" anchors at points of a triangle and last paid in on the main anchor so it was about a hundred and fifty meters from the jetty.

The second fishing trawler, the *Golden Guppy*, did much the same thing at the reverse angles, starting from landward. Then Sophia dropped anchor with the *No Tan Lines* well back, in line with the end of the jetty and in parallel.

"You know," Januscheitis said. "The sound of an anchor going down used to be one of those great moments. Port call. Exotic wom— Port calls..."

"Join the Marines, they said," Derek said. "Travel to foreign lands, they said..."

"Meet interesting zombies and kill them," Faith finished. "I say we just party till tomorrow."

"More or less the plan," Sophia said, shutting down the engine. She flipped on the stereo and set it to full blast, then plugged in her new iPod, Mr. Lawton's "gift."

There had been a stash of iPods on the *Alpha*. Apparently Mickerberg handed them out as party favors. Problem being, nobody had the "permissions" to load anything on them.

Lawton's company hadn't been involved in hacking but Lawton himself had attained his degree in computer engineering at the age of nineteen. He was a past master of all things hardware and software. For him, creating a bot to fix the permissions issue was child's play.

Thus what he had given to Sophia was not just a newer and better iPod but a six terabyte hard drive filled with about a gazillion songs. She was still ooing and awing over some of the stuff that was on the hard drive.

On the way down she'd set up a playlist. The fishing boats didn't have the same system but she could retrans it to their radios and they pumped it through their loudhailers.

The zombies had been ignoring the boats until the music started. At the first blast of reverb guitar their heads popped up and they started moving towards the end of the jetty.

"'Becoming the Bull,'" Faith said, nodding. "Nice choice. Appropriate."

"I thought so," Sophia said as the *Wet Debt* fired a burst at the group of zombies. "Hell with taking the bull by the horns. We're gonna *be* the bull."

"And now they have something to eat," Januscheitis said, nodding. Seagulls descended on the dead infecteds and that must have been a signal for other zombies. More appeared from the town, heading for the pile of new carrion.

"I *knew* I forgot something," Sophia said, snapping her fingers.

"What?" Faith asked.

"Flock of Seagulls."

"Oh, please, ma'am," Derek said. "*Anything* but that."

"Who?" Faith said.

"*Okay, now we wait,*" Chen radioed. "*Like, say, crab fishing. Let the bait do the work for you. Good choice by the way, Seawolf. Crank it up.*"

"Hope you like the rest of the playlist, sir," Sophia replied. "Okay, let's party."

"*By the way,*" Chen radioed. "*Do you have Flock of Seagulls?*"

"Oh, God," Derek said. "No, no, no..."

"Not on this playlist, sir," Sophia said. "I'll have to check my hard drive..."

"What's wrong with this song, Derek?" Faith asked, writhing to the music.

The sun had slowly set over the harbor and the boats had all their lights on full blaze along with the booming music. They'd even been firing off flares from time to time as the party got into full swing.

Lieutenant Chen was an Annapolis grad and raised in the tradition, going back to the first Secretary of the Navy, of ships being dry. He also was trained in the tradition of "never give a rule you know won't be obeyed." They'd compromised on "light drinking" for the "zombie bait party."

"You okay, Derek?" Faith asked.

There were plenty of military rules, as well, about having a party involving officers and enlisteds. Chen, again, was smart enough to know that in this mix, that was impossible to manage. There were no "wardrooms" or "officers' clubs." Just tiny boats with people packed cheek to jowl. So the party on the boats was decidedly mixed. And Faith had been enjoying a chance to metaphorically and literally let her hair down. Until Derek stopped dancing.

"I just remembered why I didn't like this song, ma'am," Derek said, looking off into the darkness. There was a light sea breeze, a tropical night in a picturesque harbor. A perfect evening. "My parents used to play it all the time whenever we'd go on a long drive and sing it together. It was one of their songs."

"Oh, Christ, Der," Faith said, stopping dancing. "You want me to get Sophia to..."

"No, ma'am," Derek said, starting to dance. "I just decided it's one of my favorites..."

"Okay, try *this*, ma'am," Januscheitis said, setting down a shot glass with a clear liquid in it.

"What is this?" Faith said. She sniffed it and her nose wrinkled. "Seriously? A Marine *has* to drink?"

"Not *has* to, ma'am," Januscheitis said. "Just interested. And it's chilled vodka. Try it."

Faith tossed back the drink as the assembled group watched with sneaky smiles.

"Okay, that's not bad," Faith said, shrugging.

"No reaction at all?" Paula said, looking shocked. "No coughing? No choking?"

"Was there supposed to be one?" Faith asked. She picked up the bottle, poured another shot and tossed it back. "There, happy?"

"Try this one..." Sophia said, carefully sliding across a shot of dark liquor.

"Ick," Faith said. "That's not so good. What was it?"

"Twenty-five-year-old Strathsclyde," Sophia said.

"Which is?" Faith asked.

"Scotch, ma'am," Januscheitis said. "Good scotch."

"Tastes like piss," Faith said. "Not that I've ever drunk piss. Okay, what else you got?"

Thirty minutes later there were a dozen bottles on the table and Faith had had at least one shot from each.

"Okay, rum's pretty good," she said, smacking her lips. "Not as good as razzleberry tea but not bad."

"She's not even *slightly* drunk?" Derek slurred. *He* was, for sure.

"Isn't it supposed to be doing *something* by now?" Faith asked, taking another shot of 151.

"I mean, I'd just finished *seventh grade*," Faith said. "I've been to, like, *two* school dances! I'm never going to get to go to *prom*..." She took another drink and frowned. "That *sucks*. That's one of the reasons I hate fucking zombies. I'm never going to get to go to prom."

"Marine corps ball, ma'am," Januscheitis said. He'd stopped drinking when the LT started to get shit-faced. Which had taken enough straight booze to drown a Force Recon platoon. "Way better than prom."

"Really?" Faith said.

"Really," Derek said. "Marine Corps Ball is like prom for Marines."

"Christ, it's coming up, isn't it?" Januscheitis said. "Time's sort of gotten to be one of those things you forget."

"We gonna have one?" Derek said.

"Bet you," Januscheitis said. "Gunny will insist. Probably use the *Alpha* or the *Money*."

"That'd be cool," Derek said, grinning. "Use the *Alpha*. Marine Corps Ball on a megayacht captured from zombies? I can dig that. Besides it's more trashed out. You know how ball gets..."

"Semper fucking Fi," Faith said. "I get to go to prom."

"We'll make sure of it, ma'am," Januscheitis said.

"Great!" Faith slurred. "So why do I gotta puke?"

"Oh, I'm glad I'm not on the gun boats," Faith said, holding her head. "This is the other reason I don't drink. Can we turn the music down, yet?"

"More water, ma'am," Januscheitis said, holding out the tube of her hydration unit.

Dawn was breaking and there was a huge concentration of zombies at the end of the jetty. The *Debt* had occasionally fired during the night to make sure they had food to keep them sticking around. Now in the early morning light, they could be seen as a mass of naked infecteds, alternately feeding and concentrating on the light and sound from the boats.

"And now the last song," Sophia said as the music temporarily stopped.

"*In the quiet misty morning . . .*" Faith sang. "Another good choice, Sis."

"*When the summer's past its gleaming, when the corn is past its prime . . .*" Derek sang in a not bad tenor.

"*Set me free to find my calling, and I'll return to you somehow . . .*" Januscheitis sang. He really didn't have the voice for the song but nobody minded.

"*In the quiet misty morning,*" Faith and Sophia sang in duet. "*When the moon has gone to bed, When the sparrows stop their singing, I'll be homeward bound again.*"

"*All gun boats, open fire,*" Lieutenant Chen ordered as the second of official nautical dawn was reached and the song ended.

Both boats opened fire, the massive .50 caliber rounds chewing up the crowd of what must have been nearly two hundred infecteds. It took less than a minute of concentrated fire for the crowd of zombies to be reduced to so much offal.

"*Landing team is a go,*" Chen radioed. "*Drop some of Captain Carrion's Little Helpers on that pile on your way by.*"

"Time to board the boats," Faith said, hefting her AK. "And keep an eye out for some ammo for this thing. I don't care if it's a haji gun. It works. Let's take that jetty, Marines."

CHAPTER 9

[F]ar from being the Great Satan, I would say that we are the Great Protector. We have sent men and women from the armed forces of the United States to other parts of the world throughout the past century to put down oppression. We defeated Fascism. We defeated Communism. We saved Europe in World War I and World War II. We were willing to do it, glad to do it. We went to Korea. We went to Vietnam. All in the interest of preserving the rights of people.

And when all those conflicts were over, what did we do? Did we stay and conquer? Did we say, "Okay, we defeated Germany. Now Germany belongs to us? We defeated Japan, so Japan belongs to us"? No. What did we do? We built them up. We gave them democratic systems which they have embraced totally to their soul. And did we ask for any land? No. The only land we ever asked for was enough land to bury our dead.

General Colin Powell

"Permission to look for some wheels, ma'am?" Staff Sergeant Januscheitis said.

"Oh, definitely," Faith said, trying to keep from swaying. "There's no clearing this place on foot."

The lieutenant was in charge of, more or less, a fire team of Marines. But that suited Faith just fine. And they weren't wearing "full fig" zombie-clearing kit, just basic combat gear with the addition of Tyvek suits, gas masks and hoods to reduce the chance of bites on exposed flesh. They had military headphones

107

and mics for radio communications and two of them carried Halligan tools and other entry systems.

All of them had a tendency to rock in place as the ground seemed to be moving. This was the first solid land any of them had stepped on in nearly six months.

"See if you can get something running that's got a moon roof," she added. "We can stick somebody out of the top with a loudhailer. If my head can handle it."

"Aye, aye, ma'am," Januscheitis said. "Two-man teams. One checking for keys and functioning vehicles. One on sentry."

There was a large parking lot on the jetty but it was mostly empty and none of the vehicles would crank. There were more cars at the square at the base of the jetty but those were, also, nonfunctional.

"The boats always have a spare battery," Faith said. "Staff Sergeant, send a team back to get a battery while the rest of us clear these buildings. I think it was my job to think of that."

"Aye, aye, ma'am," Januscheitis said. "Derek, Kirby, hump it."

"Aye, aye, Staff Sergeant," Derek said. "Let's go, Kirby."

"Clear this one first?" Faith said, pointing to a café. "I'm supposed to get input from my NCOs, Staff Sergeant."

"I would suggest backing up the jetty, ma'am," Januscheitis said, pointing to a building that was probably the harbor master's office. "That way we know our rear is clear."

"Make it so, Staff Sergeant," Faith said.

"Pagliaro, Bearson, crack me that building."

"Aye, aye, Staff Sergeant," Lance Corporal Pagliaro said, hefting his hammer. "Come on, Bear."

"Knock first," Faith said. "Zombies don't like impolite people."

"I don't got nothing," Pagliaro said. He'd hit the heavy door with his hammer several times. "No scratching or nothing."

"Open it," Faith said.

"Open it, aye, ma'am," Pagliaro said.

Pagliaro and Bearson made short work of cracking the front doors with the firemen entry tools. When they had the locks bashed, Bearson kicked the door in and they both backed off, hefting their M4s. Nothing came through the door.

"I don't think anyone's home," Faith said. "Check it, though."

"Pag, Bearson, clear the building," Januscheitis said.

"Clearance ops, aye, Staff Sergeant," Pagliaro said. "I'm point."

∽ ⊖ ⌒

"One dead infected," Pagliaro said as they exited the building. "Usual mess. Old. Most of it's dried up. Looks like harbor master's office. Some boat parts but they look like they're for those bitty boats in the harbor."

"*Staff Sergeant,*" Derek radioed. "*We've got the battery and some jumper cables. Mind if we try to crank one of these down here rather than hump it back up the jetty?*"

The smaller jetty was nearly two football fields long.

Januscheitis looked at the lieutenant and Faith nodded.

"Makes sense to me," she said.

"Shewolf says roger," Januscheitis replied. "Shall we continue clearance ops, ma'am?"

"Only if you feel like it," Faith said. "We can't open and clear every house in town. We need to sweep through the streets and see if we can find any survivors. I just wanted to see if the basic methods worked. From a supplies perspective, I'd say clear the tavern and see what's up there while we wait for Derek to find us a ride."

"Roger, ma'am," Januscheitis said. "Pag, Bear, go break into that bar."

"Oh, aye, aye, Staff Sergeant," Bearson said. "We are all *over* that!"

"Ola!" Pagliaro boomed through the loudhailer. "Anybody home? Hello? Anybody home?"

The unit had broken down into two three-man teams with Januscheitis taking charge of one and Faith, with Corporal Douglas, taking charge of the other. Douglas was driving while Pagliaro stuck his head out the moon roof to try to find survivors.

The streets of the town were deserted. So far they hadn't seen one single remaining infected and while there was some sign of them, the usual mix of decayed and gnawed bodies and fecal matter, even that was scattered. And there was, so far, *no* sign of survivors.

"Is it just me or is this creepy?" Faith asked.

"Little creepy, ma'am," Januscheitis said, taking a slow turn around an even smaller body in the street. "Christ, I hope that some of these towns have survivors."

"There are more towns up the road according to the map," Faith said. "I suppose we could try to penetrate into the interior."

"With due respect, ma'am," Januscheitis said. "I don't think that was part of the plan."

"Plans change, Staff Sergeant," Faith said. "But, yes, we'd have to get permission."

"Hey, I think we've got customers," Pagliaro said. "Half a block, roof of the building."

"Really?" Faith said, looking up through the cracked windshield. "Holy shit."

A group of people were waving from the roof of one of the buildings. They were just in the process of hanging a sheet from the edge of the roof to try to attract the attention of the Marines.

"Hello," Faith said, stepping out of the car. "Anyone speak English?"

She took off her gas mask. The smell wasn't really all that bad and they hadn't seen a single infected.

"*Si!*" one of the men yelled. "Hello! Thank you? Are all the *infectado* gone? Who are you?"

"Lieutenant Faith Smith, United States Marine Corps, at your service, sir," Faith yelled. "We haven't seen any. Come on down. Olly, olly oxenfree as we say..."

"The building was a general stores house, *si*?" the man said, taking a sip of bottled water. "Ah, that is good. Very good."

Valerio Villa had been one of five policemen for the District of San Sebastian de la Gomera. He had done what he could as the Plague took hold, then fallen back on the warehouse along with a small group of survivors from La Puntilla, the small town Faith's team had been clearing.

"We had much trouble with water," Conchita Casales said. "There is little rain."

The five survivors—two women, three men—had found seeds and created "soil" from their "waste," fecal and urine, and sand for mixing concrete. They had even taken tubs onto the roof and buried the bodies of the dead in them, then planted on those. There had been a store of bottled water in the warehouse but that had run out eventually. They'd collected rainwater. Generally, they'd just dug in and survived.

"Have you seen any evidence of other survivors?"

"There were some," Villa said, shrugging. "Across the town. We could see them. They did not have the stores we had, the seeds..." He shrugged again.

"I think we are all," Conchita said. She took his hand and shrugged as well, then patted her belly. "But there will be more, *si*?"

"What do we do now?" Villa asked. "Is the U.S.—? Are we to be...?"

"The United States has fought on every inhabited continent," Januscheitis said. "And the only land we've ever asked is enough to bury our dead. So, no, we're not 'taking' this land. It remains a property of Spain, I guess. More or less independent right now, since there isn't really a Spain. What you do is up to you. We can transport you back to the squadron or you can stay here. We've been asked to ask if we can put off some people here, if it comes up. We don't have any land bases. But we're pretty much adjusted to being totally at sea. And we're planning on taking some U.S. land bases in the near future."

"If there are *infectado* left... I cannot clear this whole town by myself," Villa said. "Among other things, I'm out of bullets."

"We have plenty of spare M4s and five five six," Faith said. "We should be able to get authorization to pass some of those to you. We also have been clearing ships at sea and have some fairly sizeable stores. Or we can pick you up and take you back to the squadron as the staff sergeant said."

"Can you help me ensure that some of the buildings are clear?" Villa said. "We have seen no sign that there are *infectado* surviving in them but... This is not the place to stay in long term."

"Ma'am?" Januscheitis said.

"I'll clear it with Division," Faith said. "But I don't see that being an issue."

"You know best," Januscheitis said. "But I'd suggest concentrating on a traditional building and something near the waterfront. We can't clear this whole island for you. We're not even vaguely up to speed. The USMC is pretty much twenty something guys and the skipper here and we don't have a bunch of people to come in and fix your town. So you'd better be prepared to survive on your own. Food, power, water and security."

"I think we can do that, yes," Conchita said. "I think we stay."

"We shall stay," Villa said, looking around the shattered town. "If we can borrow some guns."

"Not an issue," Faith said. "But... would you mind if some people took some shore leave?"

∽ ⊖ ᵔ

"I'd say this has been a successful mission," Lieutenant Chen said, taking a sip of wine. He was leaning back in a chair in front of the *Restaurante Rincon del Marinero,* which translated as "Corner Restaurant at the Marina." Which was a description as much as a name. There were a couple of apartments over the restaurant that the survivors had already occupied, and between a generator and finding some stored food, it was more or less back in operation. "Our next objective is Playa De Santiago, followed by San Sebastian de la Gomera. I think if we find any survivors in either town we should encourage them to fall back on La Puntilla rather than remain spread out."

The group would have seemed right at home in Israel. Although they were enjoying the late afternoon sun at a tavern by the marina, they all had their weapons ready to hand.

"San Sebastian is much the larger town," Villa pointed out. "It is possible we should move there rather than they here. La Playa has the airport and the boatyard."

He had an H&K G36 assault rifle leaning up against his chair, barrel down. There wasn't a round in the chamber but a recently refilled magazine was in the well.

"Where you gather up is up to you, Officer Villa," Chen said. "I strongly urge you, however, to concentrate in *one* area."

"Preferably a defensible one," Januscheitis said. "There are still infected in the surrounding towns."

"Playa has much in its valley," Villa said. "But there it is entirely surrounded by mountains. Here in La Puntilla we are in the Valle, *si*? There are towns all up the Valle. I could see the *infectado* slowly spreading this way. La Playa not so much."

"You wish to move to La Playa?" Conchita asked, bringing out a platter covered in slices of sautéed albacore and tomatoes.

"It is easier to hold," Villa said. "The harbor is not as good, but with the *infectado* gone, no more will wander in, *si*? I worry about the *infectado* coming down from La Calera."

"Then we'll move up and clear La Playa," Chen said. "Then move your people over."

"*Si*, that would be for the best I think, Lieutenant," Villa said. "Conchita?"

"Yes?" the woman said, coming out of the restaurant. "I have more food coming. Thank you for the fish. It has been so long since we had any. And all the food; it is so wonderful. Gracias."

"De nada," Chen said. "This is the good part of this job. And having spent months on a lifeboat with starvation rations, I'm glad to have it, too."

Villa and Conchita chatted in Spanish for a moment, then one of the other men interjected and it scaled up quickly to argument.

"There are guns and wine involved here," Chen said, raising his hands. "Can I get a general text of the argument?"

"Some don't want to go to La Playa," Villa said, shrugging. "Others don't want to stay here because of the *infectado*. Even tonight."

"We've got some room on the boats..." Chen said.

"Permission to speak, sir?" Sophia said.

"Go ahead, Ensign," Chen said, slightly amused at the formality.

"I checked out that yacht tied up to the jetty," she said. "It's in good shape. I mean, we need to see if it starts, but if it does, we can just load people on that and pull it into the harbor for the night."

"Point," Chen said, nodding. "I'm still getting my head around grabbing any boat or materials that happen to not be nailed down."

"Zombie apocalypse moment, sir," Faith said carefully. "For example, sitting in a really nice restaurant on a pretty little harbor with a bunch of guns sitting around just in case a zombie turns up. Also, salvage is pretty much all we do. Like, say, an assault carrier, sir."

"Point again," Chen said, chuckling.

"I'm actually thinking about asking if I can grab it, sir," Sophia said. "The *No Tan Lines* is sort of beat up at this point and we could use more room. Or one like it, maybe, depending on what we find at La Playa and Gomera."

"Officer Villa, this raises an interesting point," Chen said. "Legally, a boat that is tied up or anchored in a harbor and abandoned is not general salvage, but property of the local government or the harbor owner if fees have not been paid..."

"If you want boats, you can have boats," Villa said, waving his hand. "I think I am the only government official you have found, *si*? Have boats. Except, one, perhaps, we should keep for ourselves. A boat, if it works, has power and such on it and we can pull away from the dock if there are *infectado*. But if there are more, yes, you can have them. There are always many at San Sebastian de la Gomera. There may be some at La Playa, yes. It has a small harbor but it has the best shipyard on the island. A moment..."

He turned and talked to the group in Spanish. There was a good bit of arm waving and a bit of shouting but finally it wound down.

"They agree in general," Villa said. "We will accompany you to La Playa and San Sebastian de la Gomera and see what the conditions there are, as well. We may find others who are familiar with firearms. Diego, he has been born and raised here in Puntilla and has rarely even gone to San Sebastian de la Gomera. He does not really want to leave. But I say we see what the other towns are like, what other survivors there are of the *infectado*, then decide. I go with you and I am the only one familiar with guns, *si*? So they go with us then we decide."

"Works for me," Chen said. "Can any of you drive that thing? Assuming it works."

"That is why I need Diego," Villa said, smiling. "He is captain. So, we eat, yes?"

"Pretty little town," Sophia said as the guns ravaged the "*infectado.*" "But the harbor sucks. Why would anyone put a boatyard in a town like this?"

There were about twenty yachts and smaller boats up on blocks in the small boatyard. It was pushed so far up against a cliff the road past it went through a tunnel. The harbor was barely large enough for the three boats to spread out in their standard formation and they were firing across the jetty instead of down it since the tip jutted straight out to sea.

"You're asking me?" Faith asked. "Hell if I know. Ask Villa or something..."

"We got customers!" Pagliaro shouted.

"Survivors?" Faith asked then racked her weapon at the sight of three "*infectado*" coming down the road. "Time to stop, Staff Sergeant."

"Stopping, ma'am," Derek said. "But if I may, I think Pag's probably got this, LT."

"Permission to engage, Corporal?" Pagliaro said.

"Sure," Faith said, sighing. She'd had it explained to her by the gunny and Lieutenant Volpe that the job of an officer was to figure out what the unit was going to do *next*. Not kill zombies, *then*, unless there was a specific reason. That was what privates and lance corporals were for. She was starting to wonder if maybe she should have asked to be a private.

"Engage, PFC!"

"Engaging, aye."

"Barbie guns," Faith muttered, tapping her fingers on her crossed arms as Pag and Derek engaged another group of infected.

The small, picturesque, seaside town turned out to be so *complicated*; all the infected hadn't made it to the harbor by morning. The two teams were running into scattered groups of zombies between bouts of getting totally lost.

She glanced to the side and saw a zombie coming down the alleyway they'd stopped by. Pag and Derek were forward, taking out the group of infected while she, the proper officer, waited in the car for them to get done. She debated if it was her job to tell Pag he had a zombie coming up behind him or what. Finally, she just drew her H&K and fired it off-hand, hitting the zombie in the chest. The woman dropped like a stone. She was a blonde, which meant probably a tourist stuck here when the Plague shut down travel.

Faith decocked, holstered and checked the mirror to make sure there weren't any coming up behind. Then she checked her, admittedly light, make-up and touched up her lip gloss.

"You guys done?" she said, leaning out the window.

"Yes, ma'am," Derek said.

"How's your ammo count?" Faith asked.

"Fine for now, ma'am," Derek said, starting up the Fiat they were using. "We're having to use a lot of rounds as usual but it's not like we're in an assault or anything."

"Barbie guns," Faith sighed. "Onward, Derek," she said, pointing forward.

"Did you do something different with your hair, ma'am?"

"I'm going to declare La Playa as a yellow zone," Lieutenant Chen said as the sun descended on the cleared town. There had been ten survivors found. None of them were in great shape but they weren't death camp survivors, either. They'd been gathered on the "local" yacht, the *Estrella De Mar*. "We can immediately transit to Gomera and start the evening festivities, then clear that tomorrow. It's bigger and may take more than a day."

"I don't think I'll be joining the festivities this evening, sir," Faith said, yawning. "Although I've mostly been riding around in a taxi, it's been a long few days."

"Oh, Jesus Christ," Faith said. "Not another one."

There was a cruise ship tied up to the wharf at San Sebastian de la Gomera.

"That's not all that big, ma'am," Januscheitis said.

"It's not the size that matters," Faith said. "I've got a real case of PTSD about cruise ships. The *Iwo*...you guys had a fighting chance. You *could* fight. You *did* fight. You weren't locked in your fucking staterooms waiting for help that never came and slowly starving to death. And you were Marines. You sign up to go somewhere Uncle Sam needs people killed. You weren't on your honeymoon or a family vacation. It's opening up the compartments and finding the *kids* with arms like *toothpicks* that didn't even really *bloat* because there wasn't anything *to* bloat that bugs the hell out of me, okay, Staff Sergeant?"

"Yes, ma'am," Januscheitis said.

"All that being said, it's a fraction the size of the *Voyage*," Faith said. "No real problem. Just take lots of lights."

"*No Tan Lines, Division,*" Chen radioed. "*Need to talk to the ground clearance officer.*"

"It's for you, Sis," Sophia said, holding out the radio.

"Division, Shewolf," Faith said. "To answer your probable question, two to three days depending on infected level. Probably not a lot of survivors at this point. Over."

"*Roger, we will clear ground infecteds, then you can proceed to clearance ops on the vessel. After that, the town.*"

"Roger, Division," Faith said. "Glad we brought the heavy stuff."

"Shit," Chen said. "This is not the optimum outcome."

The chosen spot for engaging the infected with machine guns was what appeared on the charts to be an old jetty, possibly the original harbor or an old marina. There was a shoal that was clearly an old seabreak that came out from land and made a dogleg to the south. There was a small bit of it that still extended above the water at high tide and connected to the land.

Their usual antics had attracted a huge crowd of infected to the spit of land where they'd brutalized them come dawn. Unfortunately, the main jetty to seaward was close enough that more infected had gathered there. He had notionally planned on turning the division around and engaging them second. But when the usual seabirds descended on the carnage left by the MaDeuce, the group had started to mill around and break up. By the time they did the usual bit of picking up their anchors and spinning around to engage, the group would be so spread out it would take forever to hunt them all down with the .50s.

"Division, Shewolf, over."

Just what he needed. A thirteen-year-old with a question. She probably wanted tips on playing with dolls.

"Go, Ground Clearance Officer."

"Infected on south jetty breaking up. Request permission to put a couple down by rifle fire. The snacks should keep them around until you can adjust to engage with the Mas. Over."

Or, he *could* have the Marines shoot a couple...

"Confirm, Shewolf. Good call."

"Staff Sergeant Januscheitis's idea, over. Engaging. Shewolf out."

And she gave credit where credit was due. Chen shook his head and made a note in his personal log.

"There's a couple over to the left," he called over the loudhailer. "Don't stint the ammo..."

There was a crackle of rifle fire from the *No Tan Lines*. It was nice to have proactive and intelligent subordinates....

"What is it with everybody putting holes in the side of boats?" Faith asked.

The current offense to the lieutenant's sensibilities was the embarkation port on the port side of the cruise ship. The large port had a gangway that led from the wharf, now clear of infecteds, into the dark interior of the cruise ship.

"So...*Boadicea*?" PFC Kirby said. "Is that Spanish? Sounds like 'BOHICA' to me."

"Are you asking me, PFC?" Januscheitis said. "It at least makes entry easy, ma'am."

"And I suppose we should do so," Faith said, sighing. "Lights."

"Okay, this is not quite the carnival of carnage I'd expected, ma'am," Januscheitis said. Most of the watertight doors on the ship were closed, and while they were finding infected, most of them were long dead. Some of them were, yes, children. And there were some well-gnawed bodies of others. But even that was minimal. The ship looked as if it had been cleared before the Plague took hold.

"Feelin' the same way, Staff Sergeant," Faith said. She was even checking cabins. Most of them had either no human presence or dead infecteds. Some of the lower, interior, "cheap" cabins had infecteds tied to beds. Some of them had gotten loose and fed but most had clearly died there. There were some kids and that was always tough, but not many. It looked as if the cruise leaned more to adults. She could handle dead adults. And none of them had the death camp look of the dead passengers on the *Voyage*. Which just meant they'd died of dehydration instead of starvation. They were finding essentially zero "dead of dehydration or starvation" clothed bodies.

"And not complaining," she said.

"Okay," Faith said. "Again, creepy. Where'd the *people* go?"

The team was on its second day of laboriously clearing the ship. It wasn't huge but it *was* complicated. And every compartment had to be checked, cleared and marked. What they were not finding so far were either survivors or even many infected. And all the infected they were finding had been trapped in interior areas without food or water. That spelt death for infecteds just as much as humans.

"Up to eight hundred and eighty passengers according to the brochure we found, ma'am," PFC Kirby replied. "And three hundred thirty crew. I think we've counted, maybe, a hundred dead, ma'am? So, I dunno."

They'd broken up into two-man teams to spread the wealth. It had been a toss-up between Kirby and Rodas to accompany Faith. Staff Sergeant Januscheitis had suggested Corporal Douglas accompany the LT. Faith had pointed out that the *corporal* was one of their *leadership* personnel, as was *she*, so he should take one of the lance corporals or a PFC. Which on its face was pretty hard to argue. Especially when she added "That *is* how we're going to do it, Staff Sergeant."

Besides, it wasn't like she couldn't do this in her sleep. *Had* done it in her sleep.

"I think this thing is even useable," Faith said. The ship was in surprisingly good shape. The infecteds hadn't penetrated into any of the machinery spaces they'd found and except for some minor damage it all looked shipshape. The bridge was in good shape, that was for sure. It had been sealed but they'd found a key-card that would allow access. And there were no infected in it. "Which would be good, since we're running out of space on the big boats."

Kirby went to open a watertight door and Faith put her hand on his arm.

"PFC?" she said. "Zombies don't like...?"

"Impolite people, Skipper," Kirby said, banging on the hatch with the butt of his M4.

It was only the four *hundredth* time she'd had to tell him.

There was a distant clanging in response.

"I think we've got customers," Faith said. "Open away, PFC."

The next corridor would have been pretty darned gross if she hadn't seen it all before. It was, now, a good sign. Five gallon buckets once full of rations now full of shit and piss. Dead bodies lined up against the bulkhead. The sure sign of survivors. There were four bodies that were still wearing clothing. She knew what that meant. One of a million reasons she hoped she was never stuck in a compartment.

"I'm going to crack the hatch," she shouted through the watertight door. "I'll toss in a chem-light so you can adjust your eyes!"

CHAPTER 10

*If you weigh well the strength of the armies, and the causes of the
war, you will see that in this battle you must conquer or die. This is
a woman's resolve; as for men, they may live and be slaves*

Queen Boadicea of the Iceni
Tacitus

"Bloody hell, I've never in my life been this happy to see Yanks."

Second Officer, Staff, Becky Kyle was the senior survivor they'd
found. And they'd found a lot of survivors.

"Feel the love," Faith said. The survivors had been escorted
up to a café on the lounge deck. There were some windows with
external light but it was mid-line and thus not brightly lit. They
were all still suffering from photosensitivity. The café was getting
fairly crowded and even some children had survived, which was
a rarity. "But I'll take that for somebody who managed to keep
this many people alive. How did you, anyway?"

"When the plague was announced, the government put us in
quarantine," Third Officer Darren Arras said. "It was already on
the island but they locked us down, anyway. We . . . segregated
the infected. We tried to manage them but . . ."

"We ended up taking them into some of the empty economy
cabins," Kyle said, then shrugged. "There wasn't much we could . . ."
She frowned and shook her head.

"We found them," Faith said. "If it's any consolation, New York City had warehouses that looked like that."

"The quarantine wasn't so much lifted as things just started falling apart," Kyle continued. "Some of the passengers left the boat to find someplace on land. The ship's officers left with some friends on a yacht."

"Gotta love the loyalty," Januscheitis said.

"Normal," Faith said. "Same thing happened on the *Voyage*."

"*Voyage Under Stars*?" Arras said. "I'm glad I wasn't on *that* bloody floating abattoir."

"Abat..." Faith said. "Oh, slaughterhouse. Yeah. Pretty much covers it."

"The team only got about a hundred people off the *Voyage*," Januscheitis said, then gestured at Faith. "The lieutenant..."

"Not important," Faith said. "How did you manage to keep so many people alive?"

"First Officer Zastrow," Kyle said. "When it came apart, the first officer requested passengers and crew fall back on the stores compartments. We...secured ourselves. There were water spigots from the main water stores. As long as that held out..."

"We did the same thing on the *Iwo Jima*," Januscheitis said. "But there was no plan. Just chaos."

"I'd like to officially say as a representative of what is left of the United States Government that you and your crew did one *hell* of a job," Faith said. "Better than any group we've found so far. In one of those stores compartments, I regret to tell you, the infecteds gained control. But you kept a lot of people alive. More than anyone could think possible."

"We had to..." Kyle said, then looked away. "There were some people, passengers and crew, in our compartment..."

"That couldn't handle the strain," Januscheitis said. "And had to be dealt with."

"Which is one of the reasons we hold to 'what happened in the compartment, stays in the compartment,'" Faith said.

"One of our stewards kept trying to open the door," Arras said, wincing. "We couldn't keep him from trying. And we couldn't keep him tied up all the time. Finally, there was an...incident."

"What happens in the compartment, stays in the compartment," Januscheitis said. "We'll get some of the 'Welcome to Wolf Squadron' brochures printed up. Mostly it's about making sure that people don't think that what happened in the compartment is still okay after you get out. As soon as we've ensured the ship is free of infected, you can have the run of it."

"However," Faith said. "There is the issue of usage. And support. We're almost entirely marine-based at this point. We've only cleared a few of these small towns and they're only rough-cleared. We need people to help and we need this ship to tote those people. We're running out of room with the ships that we've got. Which is good, it means more survivors. But we still need this ship. It's in good shape compared to most we find and it's fully ocean-capable. So..."

"I can't exactly contact the owners for permission," Kyle said drily. "I'm not sure how the passengers will take it."

"I generally start with 'it's better than being eaten.'" Faith said.

"Is your lieutenant as young as she looks?" Kyle asked Januscheitis when they had a moment alone.

"Younger," Januscheitis said. "Thirteen."

"Bloody hell," Kyle said. "How does one become a Marine lieutenant at thirteen?"

"Well, it helps that her father is the senior officer that's not trapped somewhere and is acting Commander Atlantic Fleet," Januscheitis said. "But mostly it's a matter of being one of the four people who cleared the *Voyage* of infecteds. And from what they said, about half the passengers and crew survived. As infecteds. How'd you put it? 'Bloody abattoir.' They went through twenty thousand rounds of ammunition in three weeks."

"Oh," Kyle said, clearly envisioning what the blindsided battle must have been like in the cave-black caverns of the massive "super-max" cruise liner. "Hell. That had to be..."

"Clearing this was a walk in the park for her," Januscheitis said. "You can tell she's happy we found so many survivors and bored with the few dozen infected. There's a video of her boarding the *Voyage* that's both frightening and hilarious. She gets repeatedly dogpiled by infected and comes up over and over again, having killed them all. Which is why we call her Shewolf and us big, tough devil-dogs follow her around like, well, puppies."

"You *do* know who *Boadicea* was, right?" Kyle said.

"No," Januscheitis said. "We figured it was Spanish or something."

"Really?" Kyle said, obviously trying not to laugh. "Seriously...?"

∽ ⊖ ∾

"Okay, so, mission for today is..." Faith said, then paused, flicking off her safety. "Kirby, two steps left."

"Two steps left, aye," Kirby said, taking two steps to the left. Faith lifted her AK and fired twice.

"Clearing this town," she continued, flicking her safety back on as the two infected that had been loping down Paseo de Fred Olsen dropped. "Which obviously needs some additional clearance."

"Ma'am," Januscheitis said, raising his hand.

"Staff Sergeant?"

"Point of order. Found out what '*Boadicea*' means. Sorta funny story..."

"Command, Team Two."

"Command," Faith said. She could hear the crack of rounds over the radio call from Januscheitis' team.

"We've hit a big concentration of infected on... Calle Mahona or something. About fifty. Oh, and we're sort of lost..."

"Can you break contact?" Faith asked, waving for Derek to stop.

"Roger," Januscheitis said.

"Try to rendezvous at... Calle de la Era. It's back towards the port. There's a little square on the map. We'll meet you there."

"We'll try to find it," Januscheitis said.

"We'll set up a kill zone there," Faith said. "Try to lead them back."

"Don't think that's going to be a problem..."

"See if you can get this thing turned around, Derek."

"Aye, aye, ma'am."

"So why don't we use three oh eight as a rifle round?" Faith asked looking through binoculars at the oncoming infected tumbling before the MG240.

"It's heavy, ma'am?" Januscheitis said, taking a sip of water. It had taken the team some time to find their way around the twisty streets of the town and back to the square at the intersection of Calle de la Era and Calle del Guincho. "It overkills?" he added as one of the tracers passed through an infected and pinged into the distance.

"There is no such thing as 'overkill,' Staff Sergeant," Faith said.

"There is only 'Open fire' and 'Reloading,' yes, ma'am," Januscheitis said. "You can carry more five five six. And, yes, I am doing the math, ma'am. Given five rounds of five five six, it would be less weight to carry three oh eight. You can't fire it on full auto. But nobody who has any sense fires full auto anyway. I dunno, ma'am. One of those mysteries of the military, I guess."

"I suspect it's some deeply laid plot," Faith said. "There were Pentagon weenies involved."

"There usually are, ma'am," Januscheitis said. "I think they're all winnowed down."

"And I can see survivors waving from a rooftop," Faith said, lowering the binos. "Now if we can just figure out how to find them in this maze . . ."

"Hello!" Faith said through the bullhorn. "This rescue is courtesy of the American taxpayers and the United States Marine Corps . . ."

"Where the hell are these all coming from?" Derek asked, reloading.

"See all these little alleyways?" Faith said. She'd unassed from the little Toyota SUV they'd been using and was covering the rear.

"It was sort of rhetorical, ma'am," Corporal Douglas said.

"Who gave you permission to use a three letter word, Corporal?" Faith said, dropping three infecteds with three shots.

"Freaking *Barbie gun*!" Kirby shouted, as the infected continued to stumble forward despite putting what felt like half a mag into him. "*Die* already!"

"Oh, let me handle this," Faith said, turning around. She dropped the remaining five infected forward and dropped her still partial magazine for a reload. "I swear five five six is designed to just piss bad guys off."

"I'm starting to see what you mean, Skipper . . ."

"Any other issues?" Lieutenant Chen asked.

Most of the survivors of the *Boadicea* were pitching in with a will to help clear it. A survey and recovery team, including a master mariner and a qualified engineer, were on the way from the squadron. The division was to stay in place until they arrived.

There had been thirty-two survivors found in San Sebastian de la Gomera. Together with the survivors from La Puntilla and La Playa, that made forty-eight survivors from a total of about four thousand inhabitants. Which was bloody awful.

"Patrick tells me we've sustained what appears to be a deadline," Sophia said, raising her hand. "Oil pump for the tranny is out. He can probably jury-rig something, but there aren't any parts in any of the parts places here in Gomera for it. And it would be a jury-rig. I'd hate to have it crap out on us at sea. You know how rough it can get."

"I'm sure," Chen said drily. "I find this convenient, Ensign. Wouldn't have anything to do with a really sweet seventy-five, would it?"

The marina of San Sebastian de la Gomera was huge compared to La Puntilla or La Playa. And it still had quite a few boats in it. Most were sailboats, which the flotilla couldn't use, or small "fast" boats, outboards or inboard outboards. But a few large motor yachts had been left behind. And one of them, a seventy-five-foot Maiora, *Bella Señorita*, was just sweet as hell. Benefits included that it was in working order and hadn't been torn up by infecteds. Not to mention the marble counters and hot tub.

"Well, sir, that's a point I hadn't considered," Sophia said seriously. "We *could* use a bigger support boat for the division, sir."

"There is salvaging and grand theft, boat, Ensign," Chen said, shaking his head. "I think your father has been teaching you bad manners."

"Such as stealing a five-hundred-*million*-pound cruise liner, Lieutenant?" Staff Officer Kyle said.

"Point," Chen said. "Officer Villa, you're the only surviving government official we've found. Your call."

"It is a *very* nice boat..." Villa said musingly, rubbing his chin and letting the ensign sweat. "But the government of Spain willingly cedes this fine boat to the United States Navy in thanks for the clearance of its towns on the island of San Sebastian de la Gomera. And, besides, there are others..."

"Approved," Chen said. "Mission orders. Division One is to rendezvous with 'Mechanical Clearance Division One,' whatever that means, in Santa Cruz de Tenerife harbor in two days."

"You are going to try to clear *Tenerife*?" Kyle said. "Good luck. It's not a big city but it is a *city*, not a small town."

The island of Tenerife was clearly visible from Gomera; the massive Teide volcano, nearly as high as Mauna Loa, reared up above the snow line in the distance. Given the basically tropical nature of the islands, the snow-capped mountain was quite a sight.

"We're just providing support and possibly doing a landing, depending on conditions," Chen said. "At least, that's what I got. But we'll be pulling out tomorrow when the recovery teams are supposed to arrive. Is there anything that absolutely needs to be done between now and then?"

"There are more weapons and ammunition coming with the support ships?" Villa asked.

"There are," Chen said. "M4 rifles and an ammo supply. Do you have anyone who can use them?"

"There are two former soldiers among the survivors here," Villa said. "I know them. They are trustworthy. We can ensure the security of La Playa. I would prefer to be here but it is... large for such a small force. And there are some of the people from the cruise ship who wish to stay as well..."

"The... I don't know what you'd call it, sir, but we'd call it a 'strip mall' by the ferry dock would make a very solid defensible position," Januscheitis said. "The upper stories could easily be used as quarters. The downstairs has a bit of glass, but that's reinforcible easily. And as you ensure the clearance you could probably spread out. Just the little strip center by the Marina Society or whatever would be plenty of room for the time being. Or the ferry building. Again, good defensible position if you board up those ground floor windows."

"I'd arm up everybody," Faith said. "You'll need to think in terms of defense from the infecteds for a while. And it's hard to know when one will turn up. Just three people out of fifty is...I mean, give them some basic training then I'd arm up *everybody.*"

"There are problems," Villa said, shrugging. "I will keep your advice in mind."

"Where you set up and how you set up is up to you and your people," Chen said. "We can do one more sweep of Gomera before we leave. After that...up to you."

"How long will the support teams remain?" Villa asked.

"They're here primarily to get the *Boadicea* up and running again," Chen said. "They may be able to offer some additional support. But, frankly, you've got three towns full of supplies and materials to draw upon, as well as plenty of functioning boats to fall back on or just live aboard. I think you can make it."

᙮ ⊖ ᙯ

"Tell me we're not going to try to *clear* this bitch, ma'am," Januscheitis said as the *Bella Señorita* came around a cape with a big volcanic cone and into sight of the main city. It sprawled for miles along the shoreline and up the sides of the volcanic mountains.

"Oh, I dunno," Faith said. "It might be fun. If we could get some of those tanks off the *Iwo*..."

"Okay, this is a new one," Sophia said.

The supply ship was similar to the *Grace Tan* except for being smaller. The back was low, almost flush to the water, with a high forward bridge. There was a large crane on the back deck and two mostly standard cargo containers. The "mostly standard" was belied by a cluster of spikes on top and both ends. There appeared to be lights and some sort of motor, center on the top.

"We bringing zombie supplies?" Faith asked.

The ship had backed up to a pier and, keeping a fair distance, deployed the crane to pick up one of the containers. It lofted it over to the pier and set it down, then lifted and repositioned until one end was jutting slightly off the pier.

The crane detached and pulled back to the boat. A moment after that, both sets of doors on the container popped open. From the distance they could hear some sort of announcement as the lights on top started rotating. Between the announcements there was a loud "whoop" of a siren.

"That's gonna bring 'em but..." Faith said as a zombie came snuffling down the pier. It examined the container and circled around it before entering. A moment later, a shredded body came flying out the end over the harbor, still somewhat alive. Sharks and squawking seagulls quickly closed in.

"That's gotta smart," Faith said.

"Oh," Sophia said, shaking her head. "I see Da's bloody-mindedness at work."

"I was thinking maybe artillery or claymores," Januscheitis said. "That's..."

"Simple and effective," Sophia said as another zombie came squirting out. "By tomorrow this bit of the harbor will be chock full of dead zombie bodies."

"And sharks," Faith said. "Don't forget the sharks."

"Señorita, *LitClearDivOne, over.*"

"*Señorita*," Sophia replied.

"*Got a bit of an issue in the north harbor. Head on up here. We're discussing it with Squadron right now.*"

"Moving out," Sophia said.

"Oh, no," Faith said. "No, no, no, no..."

The Tenerife harbor was fairly large for such a small city. And the south harbor had had several large ships tied alongside. Those ships had blocked a full view of the north harbor. Which had a cruise ship terminal. And three cruise ships tied up alongside, one of them a "supermax" like the *Voyage Under Stars*. One of the others was about the size of the *Boadicea* and the other somewhere in between. They were all *big*.

"There's no way they'd expect us to clear all those," Januscheitis said.

"Bet you a dollar," Faith said, picking up the radio. "DivOne, Ground Clearance Officer."

"*Shewolf,*" Chen said cautiously. "*What do you think?*"

"First, we'll need to somehow block the pier," Faith said. "We're going to head into the harbor and examine that. Then we'll determine the... Break... Need a word. Not possibility. Think it's got a z in it."

"Feasibility?" Sophia said, rolling her eyes.

"Once we've looked at blocking the pier from access by the infected, we'll determine the feasibility of doing an entry and clearance. But this is an all-hands evolution. Over."

"*Roger. I'm on the horn with Squadron on that subject. They were aware of these ships and were discussing it. What about moving the mechanicals over? Over.*"

"Stand by," Faith said, thinking. "My first response to that is they'll draw too many infected. I think we might be able to do this sort of on the quiet. Maybe."

"I'd agree, ma'am," Januscheitis said.

"Negative on the mechanicals, Division. They'll tend to draw too many infected. Keep them in the south harbor is my recommendation. Possibly they'll act as a... distraction, keep some of the city infected off us. This is something that we really should bring Squadron or Marine Higher in on, but that's my recommendation. Over."

"*Roger, stand by... Switch to twenty-three at this time, over.*"

"Switching," Faith said.

"Faith, Da. How bad in your opinion?"

"We haven't gotten close enough to do any serious survey," Faith said.

"The Boise *says they don't see any survivors in the cabins."*

"No way they'd make it this long," Faith said. "If they took the way the *Boadicea* did it, there could be a fair number. But I'd bet on another *Voyage* situation. Hopefully, with fewer infected. They're running out of any source of hydration at this point. It won't be *as* bad, but it'll be bad. And we'll mostly be using Barbie ammo. We're really going to need the *Boadicea* for this one. Anchor it mid-harbor if we can, shuttle survivors over. And we'll need...stand by."

She pulled out a pocket calculator and started figuring numbers.

"Based on my estimate of what we used on the *Voyage* versus what we used on the *Boadicea*, we'll need at least a hundred thousand rounds of Barbie ammo or twenty thousand rounds of shotgun if we all had Saigas. We're also going to have to block the pier from infiltration by the infecteds. We're working on that at this end. But you might as well load up the *Tan* with ammo and bring it over. Oh, and we could use a few more Marines and some more Barbie barrels 'cause this is going to wear our guns out, some of those H&K Barbie guns, and well, *help*, over."

"Barbie ammo?" Captain Milo Wilkes said.

The Marine helo pilot, the only pilot they'd found so far, had been plucked from a lifeboat more or less stationary where it had been dropped in the Sargasso Sea. There had been several lifeboats found in the area by a passing boat and seven more Marines as well as twenty Navy survivors had been found.

"Anything five five six, sir," Gunny Sands whispered. "The lieutenant is no great fan of the M4 or five five six."

"I see," Wilkes said, nodding. He'd been shocked to find that a thirteen-year-old had been commissioned a Marine lieutenant and even more shocked that the gunny seemed to think it not just a good idea but a great one.

He'd seen the video. He understood she was badass for a thirteen-year-old girl. But there was more to being a Marine officer than being a badass. Admittedly, it was sort of the cornerstone but...

"And my Marines want to know where we're going to hold the

Marine Corps Ball, Da. I think these are going to be a little too messed up. I'm recommending the main saloon on the Alpha. Might be able to use the Boadicea. It's not too bad. Might be a bit smelly, still, but we're Marines. We can take it."

"I think that's a discussion for later, Lieutenant," Captain Smith said, grinning tightly.

"Better put it on the agenda, Squadron. I never got to go to prom. I'm not missing my first Marine Corps Ball. I'll hold it on this supermax if I have to. Invite a few infected, have a few laughs. Roger, we can block this pier with two or three containers. There's some sort of fenced area but no gate. Why have a fence with no gate? Oh, it's to keep people from falling in the water... There's limited infected presence on the pier at this time. We're just going to do a hard entry off the Señorita *and recon the embarkation ports."*

"Is that wise, Lieutenant?" Captain Smith said.

"When I said 'light' I meant no more than ten in view on a mile-long pier, Squadron. I've no interest in dropping in the dunny on this. We just need to see if the embarkation ports are open. Want Señorita *to keep the channel open?"*

"Roger," Steve said, shrugging.

"Sir..." Captain Wilkes said. "If I may recommend against this? I mean, is there any real need? Why not wait until..."

"Older and wiser heads arrive, Captain?" the commodore said. "Because our enemy in this, always, is time, Captain. Ask me for anything but time. And if Faith says she can recon the pier then she can recon the pier." He keyed the radio. "DivOne, Squadron."

"Squadron, DivOne."

"What is the infected level on the cruise terminal, over?"

"Light. Very light. Or I'd tell Shewolf no effing way. We also are standing by for fire support, over."

"Roger, DivOne. We'll monitor. Keep us apprised if there is anything we need to know. Be advised, we're picking up all our toys and heading your way at this time. We're going to leave the *Pit Stop* to load ammo and additional materials. The rest of us are already on the way."

"Roger, Squadron, good to hear. This is... How did you clear one of these with four people, Squadron?"

"One compartment at a time, Division, one compartment at a time. Squadron to monitor. Okay, Gunny, who plans the Marine Corps Ball?"

"Seriously, sir?" Captain Wilkes said. "Is that really important right now?"

"We are underway, Captain," Steve said mildly. "All critical decisions have been made. Gunnery Sergeant? Or should I refer it to the captain?"

"The plans were already in place, sir," Gunny Sands said. "I'd already scheduled the main saloon in the *Alpha* for the evening, sir. Dunnage, including dress uniform, of all surviving Marines is in storage. The only person who doesn't have appropriate uniform and accoutrements is Miss...Lieutenant Smith, and I was going to bring it up with her when I had a moment, sir. All under control, sir."

"We'll probably be clearing on the tenth," Captain Wilkes said. "I believe you said 'ask me for anything but time,' Captain."

"We also clear a maximum of twelve hours per day," Steve replied. "Because if you try to do more than that, over time you start making critical errors. Like blue-on-blue fire. So...we'll schedule it for off-time in clearance. And if my Marines can't clear with a hangover...they're not real Marines, Captain."

"Squadron, Ground Team One."

There was a sound of continuous fire over the circuit.

"Go, Ground Team," Steve said.

"Tell Gunny to break out all the double-ought. There be weevils in the bread!"

"How heavy is it, over?" Steve asked.

"Oh, fair dinkum an all. Piece of cake if it weren't for these bloody Barbie guns. Embarkation port of the supermax had some food stuffs spilled about. Got water, got food, got zombies. Bit of a lark. Going pistol, Janu. Okay, going next pistol, Janu...LitClear, could we get some fire on our flank, over? Told you you should get a real pistol...Yeah...Got that...Go ahead and reload, you two, got this...Thanks, LitClear, keep up the fire...Gunny, we're going to need frags for this one...And...why do we want two-handed swords? We can't swing them in the...Oh, really? Staff Sergeant requests something called claymores...And we're clear... Or we were...Squadron, we've got this, but it's going to take some time...break...Take some time...Embarkation port on the supermax is, repeat, is open. There's a fair number of...Stand by... Fair number of infecteds...stand by...Fair number of infecteds in the...Stand by...Oh, jeeze, you have got to be shitting me?

Fair number of infecteds in the embark... In the embarkation... Stand by... We're going to lay in the... LitClear can you get a gunboat over between *the two ships? That's a fair posse heading this way... Stand by... Oh, jeeze, I've got him... Bloody Barbie guns... Reload, Kirby... Kirby, you're just pulling on an empty trigger, reload... We're going to lay in blockades to prevent... stand by... prevent infiltration then start active clearance of the perimeter until you arrive. LitClear, that's as close as we'd like, thanks... closer really... Is that a roger? Shoot him in the* head, *PFC. I thought you were an expert rifleman... It goes like this... There, one in the chest, one in the head, they fall down go boom even with a Barbie bullet. And at this range if you can't do that you shouldn't have an expert... rifleman's... Oh, just* die *already... badge... Squadron, you there...? Squadron? Is this working? Hello? Any station this net...? Hello? Oops... Damn open c..."*

"Ground team, Squadron, status, over," Captain Smith said calmly a few moments later.

"Embarkation area is clear, Squadron. Going to reammo and continue to check the other two liners. Over."

"Were you in the dunny, over?"

"Negative, Squadron, never even broke out my kukri. Honest. Big thanks to the Golden Guppy, *though. Over."*

"Continue recon ops. Do not, repeat, do not allow infiltration behind you."

"Got that covered, Squadron. We've got boats standing by. We can always jump it."

"Clearance Ops will be by the discretion of the local commander. DivOne, understood?"

"Understood, Squadron. Not exactly chomping the bit to clear one of these again."

"Squadron, out. Lieutenant Isham, ensure that all the shotgun ammo we can find on the *Iwo* is on the *Pit Stop* as well as any shotguns we can scrounge. Faith seems to positively enjoy scrums, but I'd like to avoid them if we can."

"Yes, sir," Isham said, making a note.

"And ensure we have pistols for all clearance personnel as well as sufficient stocks of forty-five. This is going to be a bloody one."

CHAPTER 11

The Sons of Mary seldom bother,
for they have inherited that good part;

But the Sons of Martha favour their Mother
of the careful soul and the troubled heart.

And because she lost her temper once,
and because she was rude to the Lord her Guest,

Her Sons must wait upon Mary's Sons,
world without end, reprieve, or rest.

It is their care in all the ages
to take the buffet and cushion the shock.

It is their care that the gear engages;
it is their care that the switches lock.

It is their care that the wheels run truly;
it is their care to embark and entrain,

Tally, transport, and deliver duly
the Sons of Mary by land and main.

"The Sons of Martha"
Rudyard Kipling

"Bloody hell," Faith said. She had gone through a decon shower in full kit then a "real" shower and now was collapsed in the saloon of the *Señorita,* as were the rest of the clearance team. "I'd started to forget what a real fight was like."

Night was falling on the port of Santa Cruz de Tenerife and the last sunlight reflected a brilliant salmon off of snow-capped Teide mountain in the distance. Calling sea birds circled the boats moored in the main channel, squawking over bits of what had been human beings and were now shark-torn offal.

There had been infected around the cruise ships. All three. Lots of infected. Stores had been laid in at the embarkation ports and the infected had been feeding on those as well as each other. Water should have been problematic but zombies would drink anything and most of them even survived it. There were puddles of rainwater on the dock. No rational human being would drink from them but zombies weren't rational.

"You guys used up quite a bit of our fresh water," Sophia noted. "We're going to have to find a source of resupply."

"Get some from the tender," Faith said. "We're going to be taking lots of showers."

"It's going to need your support getting containers," Sophia said.

"And that's for tomorrow," Faith said. "We didn't have any real problem with infiltration from the main city, today, but we still need to get the pier blocked off. I'll get with the captain of the tender. We'll need to..." She stopped and held her head. "I know I was going somewhere with that."

"I've got food coming up," Paula said. "You probably just need blood sugar."

"As soon as I get food in my stomach, I'm going to collapse," Faith said. "I know I was going somewhere..."

"Get with the captain of the tender, ma'am," Januscheitis said.

"Oh," Faith said. "We'll need to try to get any containers that are well down on piers. These piers are so long there isn't much in the way of infected infiltration from the city. So..." She stopped again.

"There's a commercial port on the other side," Sophia said. "You should be able to get some from there."

"Right, saw that," Faith said. "The ship...we should look for embarkation ports on the outboard side. If we can get them open we can extract into the harbor rather than onto the pier. I'd like to just get the embarkation ports pierside up and closed. That will prevent the problem of infiltration...Am I making any sense?"

"Plenty, ma'am," Januscheitis said. "We'll take care of the equipment."

"Equipment," Faith said. "I knew I was forgetting something...."

"That's what NCO's are for, ma'am," Derek said.

"We'll need to get the *Boadicea* up here for survivors..." Faith said.

"And that's above your paygrade, ma'am," Januscheitis said.

"It is?" Faith said.

"That would be Lieutenant Chen's call or Squadron," Januscheitis said. "You don't have to worry about that level of support."

"Oh," Faith said.

"Think about how we're going to clear off infected so we can get some containers tomorrow, ma'am," Januscheitis said. "I'll make sure all the gear and men are ready to rock and roll. And, really, you don't have to worry about that until tomorrow because we haven't seen what we've got to do, yet. It may be dead simple, it may be nearly impossible. We'll get it done. But you don't have to really worry about it until tomorrow."

"Oh," Faith said. "Are you sure?"

"At this point, there would normally be an after action report to write," Januscheitis said. "I'll write up the draft and you can read it tomorrow morning and correct it as you see fit."

"No," Faith said. "I'll write it up tonight. You'll be handling the equipment. I'll get you to check it."

"I thought you were going to crash," Sophia said as Paula served dinner.

"Mission, men, me," Faith said, picking up her fork. "Get some food in me and I'll be good to go..."

"Passed out like a light," Januscheitis said quietly.

"I thought she was going to fall asleep in her plate," Derek said, just as quietly. "We going to try to haul her to her bunk?"

"No," Januscheitis said. "Just do everything real quiet."

"Ugh," Faith said, sitting up and wiping drool off her chin. "I hate it when I do that. How long was I out?"

"Not long," Januscheitis said. He had her AK stripped down and was carefully oiling it. Using weapons around salt water meant having to keep them oiled to a fare-thee-well. "About twenty minutes."

"Power nap," Faith said. "Okay, Paula, you can stop trying to do the dishes quietly."

"It's Patrick," Patrick called. "Sorry about that. Banged a pot."

"Okay, some razzleberry tea and I'll be a report writing machine," Faith said fuzzily, pushing herself to her feet. "Where's some razzleberry...?"

"Yeah, I'm gonna need to write this..." Januscheitis said, pulling Faith up from where she was passed out on the computer keyboard. "'...it was, like, *awesome*...' is not going to pass review."

"Wazzat?" Faith said.

"We're going to have to talk about report writing language, ma'am," Januscheitis said, getting the lieutenant to her feet. "Tomorrow. Off to racksies, Skipper..."

"Okay," Faith said, consulting her notepad. A ten hour "nap," breakfast, some apple juice and she was ready to rock and roll. "Day objectives: Clear zone around containers of infected so the supply ship can pick them up. Block the quay with containers. Begin clearance of the supermax liner. Find a dress for the Marine Corps B— Oh, wait, that's a personal objective..."

"Anybody got a plan?" Lieutenant Chen said. "'Cause I'm thinking this is a bust."

The commercial port of Santa Cruz de Tenerife had been a bustling center for the transshipment of cargo. The island had to import basically everything except food, and it imported a good bit of that. And the commercial port was set up to support it. It had a long breakwater that was also used as a "tie-up" for ships awaiting transshipment or were doing minor repairs, a fuel transfer point, one of two on the island, and a main cargo transfer point with two massive cargo handling cranes colloquially called "AT-ATs" for their resemblance to the Imperial "tanks" in the Star Wars movies. There were two freighters tied up alongside, half unloaded.

Alas, it also had the usual infected roaming around. Quite a few.

"I don't know exactly how this stuff works," Faith said. "But there's a cargo handling crane on that freighter. Can we use that?"

"If we can get it into operation," Captain Jesse Walker said, rubbing his bald head. The master mariner, formerly a freighter captain, was clearly unhappy with the mission. "Then there's all them zombies."

"They're in the cargo yard," Faith said. "We board the boat and clear. There's a personnel gangway but it's narrow. We hold that point while your crew offloads the cargo containers onto your ship. Then we pull back and board the *Señorita*. Your crew moves to the *Señorita* for boarding. You only come alongside when the cargo is ready to move. And if it gets too hot, we pull back, reboard the *Señorita* and come up with a better plan."

"That...might work," Lieutenant Chen said. "I'd like a back-up plan other than your usual, Lieutenant."

"Help if we had some claymores, Lieutenant," Januscheitis said, scratching his chin. "I'm not sure if it's a back-up plan, but we're going to want to carry one of the MGs. We'll set that up on the boarding gangway to increase our firepower. Between that, and the LT's Saiga and our Barbie guns we can hold any gangway."

"And on the retreat?" Chen asked. "I'm more worried about how you're going to break contact."

"Which is why I wished we had some claymores, Lieutenant," Januscheitis said.

"Oh, here's a better idea," Faith said. "Can you cut away a gangway? From the ship side?"

"Not easily without a crane," Walker said. "But you can do it."

"Without the gangway, they're not boarding," Faith said. "How do you do it?"

"It ain't complicated," Walker said. "But...it's complicated."

"Got anybody who'll board to take off the gangway in a fire-fight, sir?" Januscheitis asked.

"Hey, Greg!"

"This is just about a dumb fuck idea," Greg Dougherty said.

The tall, lanky seaman and maintenance engineer had the look of having once been heavier. He'd apparently found a blue coverall from slops, recovered salvage clothing that was washed and piled in sizes on the recovery ships, and it still didn't fit right. Not to mention it had some stains that weren't grease. He'd been "loaned" a 1911 by the Marines and told "don't draw it unless you absolutely have to." But he was there on the *Señorita*, ready to board with his toolbag.

"We'll come alongside," Sophia said. She had her H&K in a holster and her AK by the seat on the flying bridge. Just in case. "Let Paula and Patrick put up the grapnels. Then get your boarding ladder set, board, and we'll stand by in case you have to book it."

"I'll need a line to get this up," Dougherty said, hefting his toolbag. "And I can throw a grapnel pretty well."

"You go up with a safety line attached," Sophia said.

"If you go in the drink, they try to reel you in before the sharks get you," Januscheitis said drily.

"You'll be going up last. Just use that."

"This is gonna be so much fun," Dougherty said.

"Patrick, Paula, you set?" Sophia yelled.

"Arrr, we're all set to grapnel this prize, Cap'n!" Patrick said. They already had large "beach ball" or "balloon" fenders set over the side of the yacht to keep it from slamming into the side of the freighter.

"And we're coming alongside," Sophia said, lining up to the freighter and letting the wind take her in the last few feet.

Paula was forward with the grapnel and Patrick to the rear. They both made expert tosses to the bulwark railing of the freighter then pulled the yacht alongside with the help of the junior Marines.

"I don't see a welcoming party," Faith said. The flying bridge of the *Bella Señorita* was nearly at the level of the cargo deck of the small freighter. "Generally we have customers by this point."

Paula threw up the grapnel to set the boarding ladder, then Kirby and Pagliaro pulled in on the running end of the doubled line. The ladder reeled up the side of the ship, the rubber "feet" making hardly a clatter, until it connected to the lock-point at the top. A heave and the ladder was solidly in place.

Pagliaro clipped on his safety line and took point. He was wearing light combat gear, zombie apocalypse style, basic load-out for an assault with the addition of a gas mask and hood. This wasn't a mission where, hopefully, they were going to need "full load out" zombie fighting gear. He also had two boxes of MG240, 7.62x51 NATO ammo strapped to the back of his kit.

"Time to go," Faith said. "Hold the fort here, Sister dear."

"Will do," Sophia said. "Do not get in a scrum, Faith."

"No way in hell dressed like this," Faith said.

Faith and Januscheitis followed Kirby up, then took defensive positions while Derek and Bearson manhandled the MG240 over the side. They weren't sure they were going to need it, but if they did they were *really* going to need it.

The ship's deck was half filled with cargo containers with narrow passages alongside them.

"We'll hang here while you guys sweep," Januscheitis said. "Try to keep the noise down."

"Will do," Derek said. "Come on, Bear."

"Kirby, on me," Pagliaro said.

"I don't like this," Faith said, making a moue. "I should be clearing."

"We're here as a back-up and to manage, Lieutenant," Januscheitis said.

"I know my job, Staff Sergeant," Faith said. "Doesn't mean I *like* it."

There was a burst of 5.56 fire from forward.

"One clear," Derek radioed. *"Presence so far is limited."*

"Let's hope that doesn't bring them up the gangway," Januscheitis said.

The two plans they'd discussed had been "find the gangway, set up the defense point, then sweep" or "sweep, then find the gangway." Sweep then find the gangway gave them the option of retreating to the boat if there were too many infected aboard. If they penetrated across the boat, they risked getting cut off and surrounded. So they went with the, hopefully, sensible plan.

There were two shots from .45, aft and from what sounded like the far side of the boat.

"Clear up to the bridge," Pagliaro radioed. *"But that's got some of the infected over-side interested. I . . . Yeah, guy's heading up the gangway."*

"That cuts it," Faith said, picking up two boxes of ammo. "Hold the gangway," she radioed. "We're on our way. You gonna pick up the machine gun, Staff Sergeant, or just stand there?"

"Aye, aye, ma'am," Januscheitis said as there was another burst of fire from aft.

"Better hurry, they're starting the party."

Faith dropped a box of ammo and fired offhand into an infected that had reared up out of the shadows. The few infected who had found hidey-holes on the deck of the ship were moving to the continuous crackle of fire from aft.

"Leavin' that," Faith said, keeping her side arm in her hand.

"Concur," Januscheitis said. He had the MG on a sling over his shoulder and his 1911 in his hand. He wasn't going to try to use the MG in tight quarters surrounded by steel containers.

They followed a set of stairs aft then came in sight of the embattled team. Both men were leaning over the side of the ship, firing down.

"Hello, we're your friendly reinforcements," Januscheitis said, leaning over the side to check the conditions.

Infecteds from throughout the container yard were closing on the sound of the fire and the flock of birds that had descended on fresh carrion. Crows and ravens might be smart enough to bank away from a fire-fight but seagulls carried on regardless.

The infecteds, by sheer weight of numbers, were starting to push their way up the gangway.

"Oh, that's just not happening," Januscheitis said, unlimbering the MG and setting it on the bulwark. He fired a burst into the group of infected trying to force their way onto the gangway and tumbled a half a dozen to the ground.

Faith leaned out and looked both ways then frowned.

"Division, Division, Ground Team One, over."

"Division, over."

"Should have thought of this earlier. We've got infected coming from in the yard. We also have them coming from fore and aft the vessel. Could you lay in gunboats fore and aft to manage that, over?"

"Roger. Redeploying at this time."

"Break, break, forward team. Status?"

"Not finding many customers, over."

"Sweep back to the boarding point. Get the technical personnel. Bring them up here and pick up any ammo along the way, over."

"Sweep to boarding point, aye. Get technical personnel, aye. Move to gangway with technical personnel picking up ammo, aye."

"Command, out. Pag, ammo."

"Roger, ma'am," the lance corporal said, taking the box and pulling out the links to ammo up the MG.

"Kirby, head back to the boarding point," Faith said. "Pick up the ammo pile there. Keep alert, this thing might not be fully cleared."

"Aye, aye, Skipper," Kirby said then dashed off.

Faith walked aft then leaned over the side to engage the infected who were managing to get onto the gangway through the fire of the MG.

"Pag, while you're handling the ammo, keep an eye on our six," Faith yelled. "But don't shoot the tech."

"Can I shoot Derek, ma'am?" Pagliaro asked.

"No," Faith said.

"Check six, aye. Do not shoot friendlies, aye."

"We don't have time to drop anchor and get stable," Chen said over the intercom. "You'll have to fire on the fly."

"Not an issue, sir," Gunner's Mate Second Class Mcgarity said, pressing the butterfly of the modified BMG. The big rounds tumbled infecteds closing on the freighter to the ground. The platform was a lot more stable than a moving Abrams main battle tank, which was his normal platform of choice and tracking around as it drifted was no big deal. He fired a moment longer then reached on hand up to key the intercom. "Sir, could you pull this thing in closer? Like, real *close* to the pier?"

"You're getting them from here, Gunner's Mate."

"But if we get in close, I can engage the ones closing through the yard, sir. I'll have the angle. They might try to jump and swim aboard, but we've got rifles, sir, and there's sharks."

"Make sense," Chen said, putting the boat into reverse and backing towards the pier. "Try not to hit the cranes. One, we may need them someday. Two, while those rounds will go into a container, they will bounce off a crane."

"Roger, sir," Mcgarity said. "Or would that be an aye, aye, thing?"

"That would be an aye, aye, thing," Chen said.

"Aye, aye, sir."

"Oh, sweet," Pagliaro said as .50 caliber BMG rounds started tearing up the closing infected. When the massive "anti-material" rounds hit, most of the infected literally exploded from hydrostatic shock. The majority of the rounds then continued on to hit any infected on the far side.

"Except for the bouncers," Januscheitis said. A tracer round that had already passed through two infected hit the reinforced corner of a container, bounced off, hit the side of the ship, then caromed wildly into the distance. "But, yeah, direct fire MaDeuce support is always a welcome sight. Now if we just had some tanks. *Those* are sweet."

"Friendlies," Pag said as pretty much everyone else arrived at once.

"Oh, this is just *so* much more fun than I'd expected," Dougherty said.

"We ran into an infected on the way," Derek said, dropping two boxes of MG ammo to the deck.

"We've got this," Faith said. "Kirby, hump ammo from the boat. Derek, Bear, go make sure we're clear otherwise. Topside and close all hatches. We'll worry about belowdecks when we have to. Tech, can you get the gangway off?"

The crew gangway started with a solid platform that was inserted onto the deck of the ship through a latched back "door" in the bulwark. The platform extended outboard from the ship about four feet. A sloped ramp was attached to it that led to another, similar, platform that rested on the pier.

"Maybe," Dougherty said, hesitantly. "If I don't get shot doing it."

He tentatively stepped onto the extended platform and looked over the side. Then he bent over the rail and ralphed.

"Watch where you stick your head," Januscheitis snapped. The engineer had nearly stuck his head into his fire.

"Sorry," Dougherty said, wiping his mouth. "This really isn't my gig. Jesus."

"Can you get the gangway off?" Faith asked.

"I dunno," Dougherty said. "I was gonna pull the hinges on the ramp. That was gonna be tough enough but with the weight of the...bodies...Only idea I've got is a bad one."

"Which is?" Faith asked.

"Pull the dogs," he said, pointing.

The shipboard platform was solidly attached to the ship while the pier-side platform moved to allow for tidal changes and sway of the ship. The attachments were latches into the deck.

"The platform's balanced so there's usually not a lot of weight on them," Dougherty said. "Right now...Hell, if many more of 'em die on it, it might go on its own. It's only designed to hold the weight of twenty people at a time. And if we pull the dogs with this much weight on it, I'm not sure what it's gonna do. Might fall, might stay in place, might stay in place for a while then fall. I just dunno."

"Pull the dogs," Faith said. "If we have to, we'll lever it over the side with a Halligan."

"I'll need a hammer," Dougherty said.

"Kirby," Januscheitis radioed. "Get a hammer and a Halligan from the *Señorita*."

"*Errr . . . Should I bring this ammo first or drop it and get the Halligan, over?*"

"Where are you?" Januscheitis asked.

"Right around the corner, Staff Sergeant!" Kirby shouted.

"Bring the ammo," Januscheitis shouted.

"Sorry, Staff Sergeant . . ." Kirby said, running up to the firing position. He had boxes of ammo on straps all over his body.

"Just drop the ammo and go get a Halligan and hammer," Januscheitis said.

"*Señorita*, Ground Lead, over," Faith said, trying not to grin. Given that Kirby had been a Marine cook, he was taking to killing zombies pretty well. But he wasn't the sharpest tool in the shed.

"*Ground lead. We've got the Halligan and hammer standing by. I take it you mean a sledge, over?*"

"You want a sledge hammer?" Faith asked.

"Yes," Dougherty said. "Right."

"Roger sledge, over," Faith said.

"*Just waiting on you.*"

"Hoof it, Kirby!" Staff Sergeant Januscheitis said.

"Aye, aye, Staff Sergeant!"

"I think we could probably hold this position indefinitely," Faith said. "But we're burning up ammo."

"Only so much on the boat, ma'am," Januscheitis said. "And I'm about to have to change barrels. So I wouldn't say indefinitely."

"Heave!" Januscheitis said, pushing on the angled platform. The heavy wood construct finally slid over the side of the ship and fell into the water with a crash. Bodies of infecteds and the few who were hale fell into the shark-teeming water.

The clearance team ignored the screams.

"Thank you for your assistance, Mr. Dougherty," Faith said. "We need to get the rest of your team onboard, now, to see if we can get the crane working."

"Gonna suck if this was all for nothing," Kirby said.

"Did we ask your opinion, Marine?" Januscheitis said.

"No, Staff Sergeant," Kirby said. "No excuse, Staff Sergeant."
"Just go escort Mr. Dougherty..."

It had taken a trip belowdecks, which turned out to be another place infected had found to hole up, to get the crane into operation. But it was running.

"I'd thought we'd have to start the mains," Faith said as the first container went over the side. The supply ship had tied up to the bigger freighter for the evolution.

"You don't use mains for anything but propulsion power," Dougherty said. "Pretty much everything else runs on secondary systems. The good news was the primary gen and hydraulics weren't damaged. If they had been...I probably could have fixed 'em but it would have been a pain in the ass."

"How much of a pain in the ass is it going to be to get these onto the pier?" Januscheitis asked.

"One of 'em, not so much," Dougherty said. "The one that's going water side will be easy. But the one that's going interior? We're going to have to get right up to the dock. And I mean, in contact. We can only swing it out so far."

"So...We'll go aboard the supply ship to make sure you don't get boarded," Faith said. "And this time we'll bring company. Division, ground team leader, over..."

CHAPTER 12

Arrogance diminishes wisdom.

Arabian Proverb

"God I *love* this system!" Anarchy said. He was stroking the trigger of the Browning in bursts because there just weren't enough infected to engage full-bore. "The only thing that would make it better was if it was duals or quads!"

The two "gunships" had moved to the end of the pier, right by a bright red harbor tug, and were engaging infecteds "infiltrating" from the direction of the city. The sound of the guns didn't really carry all that far, but infected from all over were converging on the usual flocks of gulls.

"It's sweet," Rusty said. As one of the more senior people in the squadron who had transferred over to the Navy, he had been chosen as one of the primary gunners. More junior people were humping the ammo. Which worked for him. "What's a dual?"

"Uh, oh," Anarchy said. A huge group of infected had just come into view. Previously they'd been trickling in in small groups or singles. This was a couple of hundred and it looked like more behind them. "Rock concert time! Rusty, get the leakers!" Anarchy started engaging at long range. The BMG could kill out to nearly a mile. This was less than a thousand yards. But the single gun wasn't stopping the tidal wave.

"Division, you see this? Tell them to get a move on!"

∽ ⊖ ↝

"Roger, I see it," Lieutenant Chen said. He'd taken a position well outboard from where the containers were being put into place just so his boat would be the primary on engagement. "Boat Two, stop the leakers. Rusty, engage long. Repeat, engage long. *Garcia, Garcia*," he radioed. "What's the status on closure, over?"

"Oh, my," Faith said, looking through binoculars at the oncoming horde. The away team had landed on the pier as the better way to keep the infected from boarding the supply ship. The *Alan Garcia* was tied up, stern first, to the pier and was just maneuvering the first container into place. "That's a bunch, all right."

"And there's a problem," Januscheitis said.

"Which is?" Faith asked, looking over her shoulder. "Oh."

The crane on the *Alan Garcia* was designed for dropping cargo containers onto piers at small ports or onto lighters in small harbors where there weren't better systems. It was not designed to move them *far* from the ship. Just get them "on dock." It had had to be modified just to get them to drop "inline" with the ship for the "mechanical clearance" devices. Getting it to drop them further out was out of the question. It would need an entirely different crane.

And the outboard container didn't *quite* make it to the seawall. Thus there was going to be a gap. There was a pedestrian walkway with lights along it on the seawall side. They'd already checked and the container was going to crush the lights when it landed on them. But it didn't, in fact, make it. There was a solid four-foot gap. Two sailors were straining at lines to get it to swing out, but it just wasn't happening.

"Ground team, Division, you seeing what we're seeing?" Captain Walker radioed. *"And by that I mean the gap not the oncoming football hooligans."*

"We see it," Faith replied. "There's a gap. Drop it and put the next one in place. We'll figure out the gap later."

"Doors," Januscheitis said.

"Squirrel," Faith replied. "Why are we playing word association games?"

"We open the doors on the container and tie them back, ma'am," Januscheitis said. "The one that's on the south side will push into the wall so the more they push it the tighter it will get."

"That is a brilliant suggestion, Staff Sergeant," Faith said.

"Infected are holding from the fire. Let's make it so. We're going to need to smash away some of the lights."

"Kirby. Hammer!"

"Yes, Staff Sergeant," Kirby said.

"Wait..." Januscheitis said. "Squirrel, ma'am...?"

"What the hell is this?" Faith asked when they'd opened the container. The container was filled with pallets of wooden boxes that were narrow, wide and about man sized. A short man, anyway.

"Dunno, ma'am," Januscheitis said, firing twice. "But we're going to need to be on the *other* side of the door when those infected get here."

The fire from the combined gunboats was slowing the tide of infected but a few leakers were getting through. And eventually that would be a lot of leakers.

Faith pulled one of the shipping manifests off a pallet and looked at it, tipping her head.

"Yves Saint Laurent...Oh, my GOD! It's DRESSES! We can't use *this*! They're going to get RUINED!"

"Ma'am..." Januscheitis said.

"I just need to find a size eight!" Faith screamed, pulling out a knife. "Okay, ten...twelve is the highest I'll go..."

"Oh, jeeze," Januscheitis said. "Derek! Get the 240 and a bunch of ammo! Pag, Kirby...Find the LT a dress..."

"...Roger, Division, we're...uh...reconfiguring our plan, here. There's some high value material in this container so we're jamming the forward door to keep the infected out rather than tying back the rear..."

"No. God no, that color would look *horrible* on me..."

"Be about...Could be a while, Division..."

"Seriously? That would barely fit my sister..."

"...got the door jammed open, reinforcing it, still working the exercise, Division..."

"No, Lance Corporal, I am not going to wear that dress in public...I'm not sure I'd wear it in private..."

"...Pag, go see if you can get one of those cargo-handlers moving. We'll jam it up against the door...And pick up some more seven six two..."

"Oh, God. Oh, God, yes. YES! YES! *YES!*"

"Roger, Division, breaking contact now..."

"Now all I need to find is a container-load of shoes...."

"Good Lord," Paula said. "That's gorgeous."

The long-sought dress was basically red but the holographic silk changed it to a rippling cascade of different shades from pink to burgundy.

"Can you alter it for me?" Faith said. "I got it sort of large..."

"Easily," Paula said. "We'll need some time to do a fitting."

"Annnd we have *more*," Januscheitis said, patiently gesturing to PFC Kirby who was more or less invisible under a pile of fabric.

"I figured you were about Sophia's size," Faith said, pulling the dresses off the PFC. "There's a bunch..."

"Ahem. LT? Now that we've got *that* emergency fixed?"

"Oh, yeah, the liner," Faith said, grumpily. "Right, where's that techy? We need to see if we can get the port side embarkation ramp open and the starboard side closed..."

"Are you sure that door's going to hold?" Dougherty asked nervously, looking around the interior of the cruise liner. He'd puked, again, when he had to walk nearly knee deep in dead bodies just to get to the hatch controls.

"No," Januscheitis said, sighing. "But we've got it chocked, braced and a cargo handler jammed up against it. And the other door is open and tied back. If the first one fails, well, they ain't getting' past the second."

"If the infected get into that cargo container, every woman in the Fleet will tear you apart limb from limb, Staff Sergeant," Faith said. "You're not a woman. You don't understand."

"No, I don't, LT," Januscheitis said. "But we were fine giving you cover fire while you found a dress. And it's damned pretty, ma'am. It will look good on you."

"Thank you, Staff Sergeant," Faith said, giving his arm a punch. "Sorry I went a little nuts back there."

"No issues, ma'am," Januscheitis said. "It's sort of why we follow you around."

"So...what do you need to get this hatch open," Faith said, pointing at the offending hatch, "and that hatch closed?"

"Power," Dougherty said. "And some time and tools. And not having to worry about getting eaten by zombies would help."

"Get the pierside hatch closed and you're golden on that one," Faith said. "But it would be nice if we didn't have to fight our way out of the ship to get back to the boat so ... water side open first, maybe?"

"I'll go get some tools...."

"The pier side embarkation doors are closed all three liners," Lieutenant Chen said. "And water side are all open. Infected have been cleared from all embarkation areas and the pier has been somewhat secured against infiltration from the city."

The rest of the squadron had arrived just before dawn. Captain Smith had called for a "command and staff" meeting at 0800 hours to prepare for clearance of the vessels. Given that getting the embarkation areas of the liners was the most critical step, things seemed to be going well enough.

"Reconnaissance and clearance has been conducted on the supermax up to the level of deck five. Ground team commander?"

"It is believed that stores were being prepared for distribution either to passengers in cabins or to secure areas," Faith said, looking at the notes that Januscheitis had given her. She was really uncomfortable speaking in public and especially to the command and staff meeting. She'd never met half the people there, including the new senior Marine, she was bleary from sleep deprivation and she was terrified she'd look like an idiot. Which led her to read slowly and in a monotone.

"The stores were stockpiled in the embarkation area. Most of them were in nonmetallic containers so the infected were able to ... access them. This led to high levels of infected in the embarkation area. The watertight doors between the embarkation area and the atrium on deck five were all open. Continued infiltration of infected into the embarkation area led to a decision to commence clearance for the purposes of finding the entries and securing them.

"Infected subjects were found in all areas up to deck five. There were indications that there is a significant infected presence above and below deck five as well as on deck four, the embarkation level. Primary watertight doors leading to the embarkation area were closed and partially secured. The doors don't have manual dogs on them, it's some sort of electronic locking mechanism, so the best we could do was jam them shut.

"On the other two liners we started by finding and shutting

the doors, first, then entering with technical personnel to get the embarkation hatches switched around." She paused and her lips worked for a second. "By midnight, all embarkation areas were converted to water-side entry. Significant infected levels, in excess of the *Boadicea*, were found on all vessels. No evidence of survivors. However, penetration was limited to embarkation areas and immediate surroundings.

"I would like to commend Mr. Gregory Dougherty, engineering mate from the *Garcia*, on his ex...emplary actions in getting the doors switched around, often under conditions of some threat. That concludes my report."

She sat down quickly.

"I know that you have the word 'exemplary' in your vocabulary, Lieutenant," Steve said drily. "But that really didn't sound like your writing."

"Staff Sergeant Januscheitis has been training me on...military report writing, sir," Faith replied. "But in this case, yes, the staff sergeant pretty much wrote the report, sir. We got the doors *configured* by midnight. We were still picking out and clearing infected on the pier at one. There were a bunch of the little bastards. The staff sergeant and I worked on the report last night but I think I passed out around four. The staff sergeant shoved the report into my hands on the way to the meeting, sir. I really don't know what I'd do without the staff sergeant, sir."

"So you're working on, what, two hours sleep?" Steve said. "Remember the thing about no more than twelve hours' clearance a day, Lieutenant?"

"That would be on me, sir," Chen said. "We were trying to prepare for the arrival of the squadron. I wanted things to be in place so you could begin clearance ops without issue."

"And it just took longer than we'd thought, sir," Faith said, shrugging. "I didn't go into detail on getting the doors configured. We had to have a generator to run them. And every time we cranked the generator, we'd find we'd missed a damn hatch and, hello, here come a bunch of fricking zombies! Then Greg would dive for cover while we fought our way through the infected to the hatch we'd missed and get it closed. Or hatches in one case. So it just took a long time."

"You're off duty until tomorrow morning after this meeting," Steve said. "As are the rest of the members of your team. We have sufficient Marines for this clearance and I'm not going to have you or your team clearing in your condition."

"Yes, sir," Faith said. "I can still clear, sir. Meetings not so good but I can clear in my sleep. But for my team I thank you. They really busted their...butts yesterday. Sir."

"Before Lieutenant Smith leaves, any questions? Captain Wilkes."

"Any intel on the ships other than 'there's lots of infected,' Lieutenant?" Wilkes asked.

"We found a security point on the supermax, sir," Faith said, tapping the report. "There are the usual brochure maps and one detail map that covers the non-passenger areas, sir. We also recovered several key-cards, one of them a senior purser's. They give access to some areas. We found one door we couldn't open but...that's as far as we got, sir."

"Numbers?" Wilkes said. "Useful intelligence?"

"I'll cover that, Captain," Captain Smith said. "For your general information on clearance of a large ship, you can never determine numbers of survivors or infected until you open a *hatch*, Captain. Infected only need water. They'll eat each other if there's no other food source. If there are reserves of water, you can expect infected. So when you analyze the map, assume infected in any area with fresh water sources. Survivors are generally, not always, found in areas with food storage below the fresh-water tanks. Otherwise, your guess is as good as anyone's."

"Look out for the spa," Faith said muzzily. "There's a spa listed. Spas aren't good. You get in the scrum in spas."

"Translated as use a large force for spa clearance, which I and Lieutenant Fontana can cover," Steve said. "Lieutenant, you're dismissed until tomorrow morning. Have your team ready for clearance ops by 0800 hours tomorrow. Understood?"

"Aye, aye, sir," Faith said.

"Your gear should already have been moved over here. Ask Mrs. Bailey where it is."

"Yes, sir," Faith said.

"That means you can get up and leave, Faith," Steve said, shooing her. "Go."

"Roger," Faith said, standing up. "See you tomorrow."

"As to 'useful intelligence,' Captain," Steve said. "The fact that the lieutenant's team was able to get us full deck plans is a blessing.

We might be able to make a rational guess where survivors are located and we'll concentrate on that at first."

"I was not meaning to imply any lack of confidence in the lieutenant, sir," Wilkes said, tightly.

"Captain, your lack of confidence in my daughter is writ large," Steve said, chuckling. "You don't care for her being a Marine officer. I get that. For that matter, you don't like that I'm an instant Navy captain and your boss. Get that as well. When you've had some experience clearing a large vessel, you can, as the Gunnery Sergeant did, revisit your calculation. It is experiential. You may retain your opinion or modify it. I really don't care which as long as it doesn't interfere with the mission. Now, we're going to pull out those blueprints the lieutenant's team found and try to go at this with an actual plan for a change...."

"Captain, a moment of your time?" Lieutenant Chen said as the meeting broke up.

"Sure, Lieutenant," Steve said. "What's up."

"I...I do not have Captain Wilkes' issues with Lieutenant Smith," Chen said. "Either Smith. I've found them both to be extremely competent especially given their age. They're...I'm not blowing smoke, sir, when I say they're a real credit to you and your wife, sir."

"They're..." Steve said then shrugged. "It's both a very proud papa and a trying to be dispassionate observer who agrees. Their achievements speak for themselves. I take it, though, that there has been an issue?"

"There was, sir," Chen said, reluctantly. "Any good officer knows that there are things to overlook. For example, there are shall we say 'special stores' on the boats..."

"Given that there's no real pay to be seen on the horizon, I've ignored the fact that boats like Sophia's are turning into floating treasure galleons," Steve said. "And as for the booze...I was once told by an officer I admired that there's no point in giving an order you know won't be obeyed. But if you want me to discuss it with Sophia..."

"I'm going to do that, sir," Chen said. "But that's not the issue, sir. Sir, in the middle of the battle yesterday, Faith went dress shopping."

"Excuse me?" Steve said.

"One of the containers we used to block the quay turned out to contain some formal dresses, sir," Chen said. "Faith...protracted the engagement to sort through them looking for a dress for the Marine Corps Ball, sir."

"Seriously?" Steve said. "I mean . . . Seriously?"

"Yes, sir," Chen said. "I haven't formally investigated it, sir, but . . ."

"I hear what you're saying, Lieutenant," Steve said carefully. "And I understand your concern. It . . . it just doesn't sound like Faith. She's not normally a shopaholic."

"The Marines think it's funny, sir," Chen said seriously. "Just another example of, well, 'Miss Faith.' But it put them in a dangerous position while the lieutenant went, well, dress shopping, sir. I understand she is your daughter, sir, but . . ."

"That's . . . Yes," Steve said. "She is. However, I convinced the gunny she was worthy of a lieutenancy on the basis that she's not quite as immature as she acts. This is a counter example. Did she give any argument in favor? I mean, I cannot find an argument but . . ."

"I haven't brought it up with her, yet, sir," Chen said. "It's a touchy subject. The Marines think the world of her and they think it was hilarious. But it was not only putting her Marines in jeopardy to go dress shopping, it was using them for personal privilege, sir. On the other hand, she's a Marine, not Navy, and she's your daughter, sir. I'd considered bringing it up with Captain Wilkes but . . . You're my chain of command, sir. And she's your daughter."

"Well, I'm her chain of command as well," Steve said. "I'd like to bring her in to discuss it. See if she has any reasonable arguments. If not . . . letter of reprimand?"

"I . . . wouldn't go that far, sir," Chen said. "Possibly a written counseling statement."

"Very well," Steve said. "I've got a slot at fourteen-thirty. Bring her by."

Faith woke from a dream that all the women who'd been raped and murdered on the *Alpha* were trying to talk to her. She couldn't understand their words, though. Just that they were warning her of something.

She really didn't like being on the *Alpha*. She'd had to clear it with her Dad and Sergeant Fontana and it was one of the clearances that gave her nightmares. On the other hand, she had a cabin to herself and a private bathroom. She'd put up with the nightmares.

Someone had kindly laid out a pair of shorts and a Marines T-shirt on her bed before she got there. And all her stuff was not only in the room but unpacked and put in drawers. Her hard-found dress was in the closet and someone had even put it in a plastic bag.

She'd just dropped her uniform on the deck, pulled off her bra and crawled into the sheets, she was that tired. The brown T-shirt and panties were fresh. Good enough.

She got up and went into the bathroom and examined herself in the mirror.

"Okay, now I get what they mean by 'death warmed over.'" Her face was drained. She looked like a recent kill. Maybe that's what the women were trying to tell her. "*You look like shit, Faith.*"

She wasn't even sure what time it was. She could see it was twilight. Probably the sun was going down, not coming up. If it was coming up, she was already late for assembly.

There was a sign in the shower stall: "Please conserve water. Wet down. Turn off the water. Lather up. Rinse off."

She turned the shower on full and just hung her head under it. Screw water conservation. They could get some from the fresh water tanks on the freighter. The freighter *her* team had fucking cleared. And if they ran out? Well, they'd just clear another fucking freighter. Or get it from the liner. Liners always had big fucking fresh water tanks.

The shower helped. She did some push-ups and sit-ups and stretches and that helped more.

By the time she'd gotten done with that, her stomach was rumbling.

"Time to find food," she muttered.

She was off duty so she just wore the Marine T-shirt and shorts and some flip-flops. If anybody had a problem with that, they could bite her.

When she got to the main saloon, there was a buffet laid out and it was about full of people. What got her, initially, was that there were very few she'd recognized. While her team had been clearing the towns in the Canaries, the rest of the squadron had been doing recovery ops at sea and apparently they'd been pretty successful. She saw a few of the girls from the *Money* scattered around but they seemed to be "sponsors." Mostly it was one to a table. And you could tell a lot of the people were "freshies," fresh off the lifeboat or out of a compartment. The "boaties" all had super dark tans. The "ghosts," compartment people, were all wearing shades and were either ghost white or sunburned.

She grabbed a tray and started filling up a plate. She'd always worried about her weight but clearance ops were calorie intensive. You could eat about anything you wanted when you were spending all day climbing stairs carrying a hundred pounds of gear, ammo and weapons and fighting zombies. Another benefit of a zombie apocalypse.

"Hey, LT," a voice said.

She turned around and thought about it. The face was familiar...

"Sergeant Smith," Smith said. "I was in the compartment with Staff Sergeant Januscheitis, Lieutenant."

"Smitty," Faith said, nodding. "He talks about you a lot."

"Marines are over on the other side of the messdeck," Smitty said, gesturing with a thumb. "The staff sergeant's still down. But Derek and Pag are over there."

"I'll be right over," Faith said. "Just let me load up with some carbs."

"I can get that for you, ma'am," Smitty said.

"I think I can carry my own tray, Sergeant," Faith said. "But thanks."

She skipped the desserts, her tray was getting overloaded and she could always come back, and headed over to the table.

"Room for one more?" she asked.

"Right here, Skipper," Pagliaro said, pulling out a chair.

"Why thank you, kind sir," Faith said, sitting down. "And I know you work for a living."

"How'd the meeting go, ma'am?" Derek asked.

"I only sort of vaguely remember it," Faith said. "I get the feeling Captain Wilkes doesn't like me."

"He's trade school, ma'am," one of the Marines said. "Citadel, of all places. He's not really that up on ROTC officers. And he's a pilot. They're *all* 'I'm a pilot so I'm hot shit.'"

"He's doing okay at running the clearance," another said, shrugging. "For a guy who's not infantry."

"How's it going?" Faith asked. She was vaguely aware that it wasn't a good idea for an officer to get into running down a superior.

"Lots of zombies," one of the Marines said. "Lots of fucking zombies."

"Lieutenant Fontana said it's almost as bad as the *Voyage*," another said. "But the cabins weren't locked down."

"How come so many survived?" Pagliaro said. "I mean, water, hello!"

"Fountains," Sergeant Smith said. "The place has fucking fountains and pools everywhere. And they were all full. There's also pools on the upper deck that caught rainwater. And most of the doors were open so they could move around. Some of the compartments below the water tanks had valves leaking or partially opened. It's a fucking zombie fest."

"Which Captain Wilkes has been careful to avoid," one of the Marines said. "He hasn't gone past the embarkation area."

"And he had us lay out all the bodies and 'prepare them for proper burial,'" another said. "If he expects us to do that with the whole ship..."

"Then we'll do it with the whole ship," Sergeant Smith said.

"Da'll just have us scatter beetles," Faith said. "There's no way to clear two or three thousand bodies."

"What I don't get is how you and your dad cleared one of these by yourselves," a Marine said. "Jesus, ma'am. I mean... We've only got two decks clear."

"One compartment at a time," Faith said. "And it wasn't just Da and I. There was Sergeant... Lieutenant Fontana and Hooch. But, yeah, it was a bit of a wanker. Really rather change the subject. Okay, we're all Marines, right?"

"Yes, ma'am," Smitty said.

"Not everybody in the saloon?"

"No, ma'am," Smith said, frowning.

"How come half the people in this room are wearing Marine and Navy T-shirts?" Faith asked.

"Oh, that," Smitty said, chuckling. "There was a big stash of them on the *Iwo*. You know how finding clothes that fit is tough, ma'am. So they just are handing them out to whoever gets found."

"Ah," Faith said. "That makes sense. It sort of makes it hard separating the sheep from the goats, though."

"Well, I guess we could give them all dresses, ma'am," Derek said.

"Bite your tongue," Faith said. "Those are works of *art*!"

"We heard about your little combat shopping spree, ma'am," Sergeant Smith said over the chuckles.

"Okay, okay, so I went a little nuts," Faith said. "Sue me. You're guys. You don't get it."

"We figure we'd do the same thing if it was a container full of Guinness, ma'am," Derek said, grinning. "Don't sweat it. No worries."

"Is the door still holding?" Faith asked.

"Yes, ma'am," Smitty said. "We did some reinforcing on it. Well, covered some Navy guys who reinforced it."

"We need to get those out of the container and into safety," Faith said. "Seriously. Those are works of art. You don't just leave them to get rained on or overrun by infected." She looked at her empty plate and sighed. "I really shouldn't do dessert..."

"I'll get you something, ma'am," one of the Marines said. "What do you want?"

"I appreciate it, again," Faith said, standing up. "But, you guys have been clearing all day while I was napping. I should do my own fetching."

"So that's Shewolf?" one of the Marines said as she walked away. He added a whistle. "Damn that's some fine jailbait."

"Olsen, I will personally ram a fork down your throat," Pagliaro said.

"And the rest of us will hold you down," Smitty added. "Not to mention disrespect to a superior officer."

"I wasn't being..." Olsen said. "I guess I was but, just...wow! And I am being very respectful of the LT, Sergeant. Nothing but admiration. But is she really...I mean, she's big for a chick, especially a, you know, *thirteen*-year-old chick, but is she really as badass as everybody says?"

"Worse," Derek said. "Dead killer combat shooter, rifle or pistol. She's killed so many infected she just does it without thinking. Muscle fucking memory. Sees an infected, kills it. I've never seen her use her kukri but Lieutenant Fontana said she's pretty much the same at melee range. You've seen the video, right?"

"Yes, Corporal, I have," Olsen said. "Just having hard time connecting Miss Hotty with it."

"Then there's the drinking thing," Derek said, shaking his head.

"Drinking?" Olsen said. "Isn't she a little young?"

"Rather the not drinking, usually, thing," Derek said. "She only drinks, like, water and fruit juice. Doesn't like the taste of beer or wine."

"But she's okay with straight liquor," Pag said, chuckling.

"Straight?" Olsen said.

"Drinks it like water," Derek said. "Isn't really into it 'cause it barely gives her a buzz. Just takes a couple shots 'Is this supposed to be doing something?' I've seen her drink enough to put down a gunny and it not even faze her."

"Damn," Olsen said, laughing. "Okay, I guess she can be an officer."

"As if it's up to you to judge," Derek said.

"She does have a tendency to pass out at a certain point," Pagliaro said, snickering.

"Pass out?" Olsen said.

"First night we were clearing the *Boadicea* she practically face-planted in her plate at dinner," Pag said, laughing. "Like 'I've got reports to write...Snore...'"

"She's thirteen," Derek said. "She's still growing. I'm always surprised she hangs as long as she does. And, Pag, you were ten minutes behind her."

"I get that," one of the Marines said. "Clearing is fucking hell on your adrenal gland. I thought the Stan was bad."

"Fuck, I'm a God damned *airframe mechanic*," Olsen said. "This shit is for Oh-Three-Elevens."

"We're all infantry now," Derek said. "At least, that's the way Captain Carrion sees it. And he is another Smith I am not going to fuck with. Hooch says her dad is as badass as Faith. And that's pretty fucking badass for a Navy captain."

Faith trolled the dessert tray but she'd filled up on "regular" food and wasn't quite ready to pile on pure sugar. The chocolate tray was tempting. Apparently someone had found a stash of Godiva. She ate a couple at the buffet then headed back to the Marine table. She was still tired and dessert could wait.

Halfway across the room a hand grabbed her arm.

"Hey, Tootsie," the man said, holding out an empty high-ball glass. "Get me another Glenlivet."

Faith just stood there in shock for a moment. The dude, who looked to be in his early fifties, was clearly a "boat" freshy. He had one hell of a tan.

"Uh, sir..." The table "sponsor" looked like one of the *Money* girls and had a slight Slavic accent. "That's..."

"Let go of my arm," Faith said. "The last person who grabbed me, I *literally* cut their fucking hand off at the wrist."

"Do you know who I am?" the man snapped.

"Somebody who needs to learn some fucking manners," Faith said, grabbing his thumb and twisting it into a lock.

"Ow!" the man said. "Jesus, let go of me you crazy bitch!"

Faith's eyes blazed and she threw the man to the ground, putting his head in a lock with his arm twisted behind his back.

"I don't know who *you* are, but do you know who *I* am?" Faith snarled.

"Lieutenant!" a voice snapped from behind her. "Let go of Mr. Zumwald!"

She looked over her shoulder and it was, of course, Captain Wilkes. Great.

She released the man and rolled to her feet.

"Sorry, sir," Faith said. "But I don't like being grabbed and I especially didn't like being called a bitch, sir."

"Mr. Zumwald, I apologize for the lieutenant's overreaction."

"*Lieutenant?*" the man gargled. "She's *insane*! She needs to be locked up!"

"I will, I assure you, counsel the lieutenant on actions becoming of an officer in the United States military, sir," Wilkes said. "Lieutenant, a moment of your time?"

Wilkes led Faith out of the main saloon onto the foredeck and turned around, hands on his hips.

"Lieutenant, would you care to explain your actions in there? You don't put a major Hollywood executive in a headlock!"

"Sir..." Faith said. She tended to get at a loss for words when she was being scolded and she really didn't know what to say. "He *grabbed* me, sir!"

"So you put him in a chokehold?" Wilkes said. "There *are* situations that can be resolved without violence, Lieutenant. Has anyone ever explained to you the term 'conduct unbecoming of an officer'? It means you don't go brawling with *anyone*, especially major film executives, in public!"

"What was I supposed to do, sir?" Faith asked, angrily. "Bat my fucking eyes at him and go get him his fucking drink?"

"Lieutenant," Wilkes said coldly. "You are being officially counseled on what actions are becoming of an officer of the United

States Naval Service. In addition, since you don't know shit from shinola about being an officer, let me add that you don't get to use a disrespectful tone or disrespectful language to the officer that is counseling you. These are articles of the Uniform Code of Military Justice, Lieutenant. You can be charged with conduct unbecoming for your recent actions. You also can be charged with disrespect to a superior officer for that outburst. Do you understand that, Lieutenant?"

"Yes, sir," Faith said.

"Do you understand that an officer of the United States Naval service does not start a brawl because someone asked her to get them a drink?" Wilkes said.

"Yes, sir," Faith said.

"And that an officer of the United States Naval service does not put someone in a chokehold, *especially* a major Hollywood executive?"

"Yes, sir," Faith said.

"In addition, while you have had to, of necessity, spend a good bit of personal time with your Marines, when off-duty, when it is possible as is the case here on the *Alpha*, your place is with the officers, *not* the enlisted. There was an officer's table in the saloon. Spend your time there."

"Yes, sir."

"You've had a trying few weeks," Wilkes said. "You really shouldn't have been sent out on a functionally independent mission given your age and inexperience. I will try to keep this incident from being reflected on your FITREP. But you had better start learning conduct becoming an officer or I will not be able to avoid reflecting that. Understood?"

"Yes, sir," Faith said.

"I'll go smooth things over with Mr. Zumwald," Wilkes said. "You should probably go to your cabin and get some more sleep. Understood?"

"Yes, sir."

"Dismissed."

Faith went back to her cabin, avoiding the saloon, wrapped herself around Trixie and cried herself to sleep.

CHAPTER 13

Me that 'ave been what I've been—
Me that 'ave gone where I've gone—
Me that 'ave seen what I've seen—
'Ow can I ever take on
With awful old England again,
An' 'ouses both sides of the street,
And 'edges two sides of the lane,
And the parson an' gentry between,
An' touchin' my 'at when we meet—
Me that 'ave been what I've been?

"Chant Pagan"
Rudyard Kipling

"Get some sleep, LT?" Januscheitis said the next morning.

They were gearing up for clearance. It took some time.

"Some," Faith said tonelessly. "I really hate the *Alpha*. Clearing the *Alpha* gave me more nightmares than clearing the *Voyage*. And . . ." she shrugged.

"Ghosts?" Bearson said.

"There's no such thing as ghosts," Faith replied.

"I don't know, LT," Derek said. "Every ship that's lost people has ghosts. They call 'em 'phantom watch standers.' The *Cole* had ghosts. I've seen 'em on the *Iwo*, plenty of times."

"Quit trying to freak your LT out," Faith said. "It's not working."

"I'm not sure if I believe in 'em or not, LT," Januscheitis said. "But...pretty much everybody sort of knows about 'em. I don't think they're trying to freak you, LT. The ghosts on the *Cole* are just sort of there. Like they call 'em, watch standers. Almost comforting."

"The ones on the *Alpha* aren't comforting," Faith said tightly.

"How bad was the *Alpha*, ma'am?" Pagliaro said. "You can see it got banged up, but..."

"If you haven't heard about what happened on the *Alpha*, ask somebody else," Faith said. "I'm not going to talk about it. It was...bad. It wasn't the fucking zombies, it was the people that had it before the zombies and what they did. I don't like the *Alpha*. And if you're serious then, yes, ghosts. They fucking talk to me when I'm sleeping. The women, anyway. They cry. I can hardly sleep on this fucking boat. Okay? On the other hand, I've got my own stateroom and my own shower. That makes up for a lot."

"I heard you had a little incident last night, ma'am," Januscheitis said. "Probably not the best change of subject—"

"I was counseled by Captain Wilkes on conduct unbecoming an officer," Faith said. "I now understand that one does not overreact and get into a brawl in public. And since it's an officer thing, I'd like to drop that, too."

"I heard the dude grabbed you, ma'am," Kirby said.

"What part of drop it did you not get, PFC?" Januscheitis said.

"Sorry, Staff Sergeant," Kirby said.

"Hopefully, despite being an 'officer of the United States Naval service,' I'll be allowed to kill some zombies today," Faith said, racking her Saiga. "Because I seriously need to kill somebody. And that's all we need to talk about that."

"Lieutenant?" Gunny Sands said, sticking his head in the compartment. "Captain wants to have a word with you?"

"Captain Wilkes?" Faith said, wincing.

"Captain Smith," the gunny said.

"Oh, joy," Faith said. "I guess I'll need to derig..."

"Faith, there's a couple of things we need to talk about," Steve said, waving to a chair.

"Yes, sir," Faith said.

"The first bit is about what happened last night."

"Yes, sir," Faith said.

"I know you in mulish mode, daughter dear," Steve said drily. "When all you do is say 'yes, sir' it means you're not actually communicating. Nothing's coming out, so nothing's going in. I've spoken to several people about what happened last night. You should not have been grabbed. Not just as a lieutenant but as anyone. Mr. Zumwald was totally out of line in ordering you around, as was his language."

"Tell that to Captain Wilkes," Faith said, crossing her arms.

"Lieutenant," Steve said. "I am not speaking to you as my daughter, here, I'm speaking to you as a lieutenant in the United States Marine Corps, one of my junior officers. And I will not have you say anything disrespectful of your superiors. Understood?"

"Yes, sir," Faith said.

"Faith," Steve said. "Eye contact. What I tell Captain Wilkes, what I discuss with him about the incident, is none of your concern. Do you truly understand that?"

"Yes, sir," Faith said. "It's just..."

"There is no 'just,' Lieutenant," Steve said, calmly. "If, and I said *if*, Captain Wilkes *may* have done something wrong in handling the situation, that is between Captain Wilkes and myself. This is the tough part about being in the military. You do not show, by word, action or deed, disrespect to a superior. Ever. Even, or especially, when you think he's a cowardly fucktard that's got his head up some Hollywood executive's ass."

"Oh, you *have* met him," Faith said.

"Lieutenant, that is exactly what I was warning you about," Steve said. "You may think those things, true or not, but you do not *ever* express them. Ever. You need to seriously learn that, or we might as well drop this experiment and you can go do something other than being a Marine officer."

"I'll try," Faith said.

"Okay, first of all, that would be 'sir' and second, you cannot 'try' at something like this," Steve said. "This is one of the most important aspects of military discipline. Even if you think someone is an awful superior in the military, and Wilkes is not by any means as awful as you think, you simply do *not* express it. Not in any professional environment. You *can't* go questioning a superior's competence. Not to a subordinate, especially. Just as if you have, say, an NCO you think is not competent, you cannot express that to his or her subordinates. When the shit hits the fan, the men have to know that they can trust the orders they're getting. If you, who is looked upon as more competent than you actually are as an officer, express resentment or lack of trust in Captain Wilkes, even by *body language* at which you are a past mistress, that will spread. Then people will start to second-guess the captain. Which we absolutely cannot afford.

"Seriously, Faith, we're still in a cleft stick, here. If you cannot support Captain Wilkes, one of the two of you have to go. And he's the officer with the rank and the position. You're just a newbie officer who happens to be a wild-child at killing zombies. There is, in fact, more to being an officer than that. One of the things is discipline. Enough discipline to work with a superior, or a subordinate, you do not like and the feeling is mutual. To train the subordinate where possible, to learn the good things—and Wilkes has real positives—even from superiors you don't like. This is part of being a Marine. It really and truly is."

"Yes, sir," Faith said.

"Again with the robotic 'yes, sir,'" Steve said. "I need more."

"It's..." Faith said then waved her hands. "Da, can we just... talk?"

"Sure," Steve said, leaning. "I'm good with that."

"Actually it's more like 'Captain, can we just talk?'" Faith said. "I'm not the one talking Captain Wilkes down, sir. I mean, I didn't really stomp on it when people were ragging on him. Maybe I should have. But he's not real popular."

"Okay, couple of things," Steve said, leaning back. "First, troops grouse. They're used to grousing around you so they do it without thinking of you as an officer. Which has some good points and some bad points. It's good if they feel comfortable enough to discuss their issues with you. Bad if they just talk around you without thinking of you as an officer. Because, they can't obey your orders because they like you or they're humoring you. We'll get to the subject of your combat shopping spree in a minute—"

"Oh," Faith said. "Ouch."

"Yes, ouch," Steve said. "But we're talking about the situation with you and Captain Wilkes right now. First of all, if a troop comes to you and brings up something like his questions about the competence or courage of a superior, you can counsel them on it in private, listen to their concerns, but you *cannot* support their position. You can't say 'Yeah, he's a fucking coward' or 'He's a fucktard.' You're not a troop. You're their boss. You say 'I hear your concerns.' I have not stated that I agree with you, Lieutenant. I have said those things as examples. Be clear about that. I neither agree nor disagree. I hear your concerns regarding Captain Wilkes' approach to managing the boarding. However, I'm counseling you on *your* actions and reactions. You with me, Faith?"

"Yes, sir," Faith said. "Sort of. So...Is he a cowardly fucktard or not?"

"I just said that as his superior and yours I can neither agree nor disagree," Steve said. "And I'll repeat that language like that about a superior is a major offense of the Uniform Code of Military Justice. This is a counseling session so I can hear it or not. You don't use it outside of this compartment. Need to be really clear on that one. Are we?"

"Yes, sir," Faith said. "No calling superiors names?"

"People got hanged for it in the old days," Steve said. "You do not speak disrespectfully of a superior. Then there's 'the troops are ragging on him.' Yes, you stomp on that. Just as I'm stomping on it with you. If subordinates start to say something disrespectful of a superior, you point out that that's not acceptable. I won't make this official but...Was the staff sergeant present?"

"No," Faith said. "There was one NCO. But not Staff Sergeant Januscheitis."

"Did the NCO say anything about speaking ill of a superior?" Steve asked.

"It was just before the thing with the dude and the drink," Faith said. "So I'm trying to remember...They were bitching about having to clear the bodies out of the embarkation area. And Wilkes not leaving that area and whether they were going to have to clear the bodies from the whole ship..."

"The embarkation area was going to be used as an operations center," Steve said, frowning. "Clearing that made a certain amount of sense. Putting all the bodies in body bags instead of in the harbor...Eh, possible sense. But, no, we're not going to clear the bodies from the whole ship."

"Sergeant...The NCO present said something like, 'if we're told to clear the ship, we clear the ship.'"

"Okay," Steve said, leaning forward. "That, right there. Did you get it?"

"No," Faith said. "Sir."

"The NCO perhaps should have stomped on the questions of Captain Wilkes' lack of initiative in moving forward," Steve said. "Wasn't there, can't really comment. But he reaffirmed the point that if given an order, they obey it. Can you see that?"

"Sort of," Faith said.

"Then pay attention to it and look for it," Steve said. "And emulate it. Discipline is what makes a military an effective tool compared to a mob. And one of the things that enhances discipline is the actions and deportment of an officer. It can be carried too far. There are officers who think that actions and deportment are the only thing that's really necessary. At this point you're mentally inserting 'Captain Wilkes' into that sentence, correct?"

"Yes, sir," Faith said. "Was that disrespectful?"

"If one of your subordinates said it and you blurted 'You mean Wilkes' then it would be an issue," Steve said. "So don't. But appearances have a point. Officers have not just the right but the duty to tell their subordinates to do something insane and suicidal. Your troops would probably kill themselves to keep you alive. Or, say, to get you a dress..."

"We were never in any real danger, sir," Faith said. "Honest."

"But the point is that they have to think of you as an *officer*," Steve said. "Not their wild-child kid sister. Which in part is *acting* like an officer. Carrying yourself like one, requiring that you be saluted and called 'ma'am,' snapping orders in a firm voice. Because when it really drops in the shit, they have to know who is in charge. Even if it's Captain Wilkes. And part of that is, yes, not putting a guy in a chokehold because he called you a bitch."

"So am I the only one getting dressed down, sir?" Faith asked.

"Again, does not matter," Steve said. "How I handle the rest is up to me. That's on *my* plate, not yours. I'll give you this much. I'm not handling Zumwald. I told Isham if I saw the fucker I was going to toss him into the bay. I mean, seriously, toss him into the bay with the sharks. Was not joking."

"Thanks, Da," Faith said. "Sorry, thank you, Oh, Captain My Captain. That really pissed me off. I mean, not that it was... You know, 'Shewolf, Zombie Hunter' but that he felt like he could grab just any girl and... order her around. Da, this is the *Alpha*, okay?

You know what happened here. That was what went through my mind. Sort of. Mostly I was just pissed but—"

"I hadn't considered that," Steve said, nodding. "It's . . . If this was official and if there were charges, which there wouldn't be under most circumstances, it would certainly be a mitigating factor and it explains why . . . I wondered why even you, Faith, would have gone off so . . ."

"Yeah," Faith said. "I was just out of . . . Da . . . Captain, this boat gives me fucking nightmares, okay? I mean . . . I'm okay on the *Señorita* but this boat just flips me out. But this is where the team's based and, hell, I've got my own room and head."

"How are you with the *Boadicea*?" Steve asked.

"I'm great with the *Bo*," Faith said. "The *Bo* is the first bright spot in a long time."

"We're getting it cleared out and prepped," Steve said, making a note. "This isn't personal, it's professional. And, okay, personal. But I'll see about getting the Marines moved over to the *Boadicea*. It's not a good idea to mix them with the civilians. There have been other incidents. Okay . . . So . . . That is not permission for you to go off in public, understood?"

"Yes, sir," Faith said. "Sorry about . . . No excuse, sir."

"Mr. Zumwald will be counseled as well," Steve said. "At a certain point, possibly I'll have the two of you sit down and you can give him your story of clearing the *Alpha* and why, particularly on this boat, automatic male dominance for the purposes of personal service triggers rather unpleasant memories."

"Rather not explain that," Faith said. "I can't even talk about it with the Marines. And . . . If I can input on it, I'd just as well not have to deal with him again."

"There are not many of us," Steve said. "More, thank God, every day. But still so few. Absent throwing him off the island or, rather, *on* an island, you'll have to deal with him at some point. On the subject of Captain Wilkes or any other superior—"

"Do not undermine his authority," Faith said.

"Except in one limited circumstance," Steve said. "And even then, *especially* then, you have to be punctilious with your professional demeanor. So it is not, in fact, undermining his authority."

"Which is?" Faith asked. "Which is, sir?"

"When you're an instructor," Steve said. "The fact that Captain Wilkes has not seen a live zombie since he jumped ship, by orders, from the *Iwo* has been brought up through other channels. He really cannot make rational judgments as to what is and is not normal and proper without some experience of the operations. He needs experience and he needs an experienced teacher..."

"Oh, Da..." Faith pleaded. "Have Lieutenant Fontana or the gunny—"

"No," Steve said. "What the gunny and Lieutenant Fontana are going to do is give you a quick class in how to be a subordinate and an instructor. From what I've heard, you have it mostly down. The Marines certainly think that you'd have made a great tactical instructor. At least when it comes to zombie fighting. I'll have the gunny and Lieutenant Fontana, both of whom have experience with training more senior officers, explain to you the dos and don'ts. Then you will train Wilkes with your team back-stopping. And you will treat him with due respect. Is this understood, Lieutenant?"

"Yes, sir," Faith said.

"Now, as to the combat shopping. Dress shopping, Faith. Seriously?"

"They were *Paris originals*, Da!" Faith said.

"It was my mistake using your first name," Steve said. "In this case, again, Lieutenant, it would be 'Captain.' Lieutenant Chen feels that it was a serious error in judgment on your part and I cannot disagree. Not to mention the wall against infiltrating infected as we clear these ships is rather shaky. Two lapses in judgment."

"In that case, Captain, I will repeat myself," Faith said. "They were, and are, Paris originals. May I state my case?"

"Go ahead," Steve said, leaning back in his chair.

"I am not sure that the argument will work," Faith said. "But I'll stand by it. And I've had time to think about this one. First, I agree that I had a lapse in judgment as well as, um, not sure what the right term is. But I shouldn't have looked for a dress at that time and with my team helping me. That was sort of stupid. But I wasn't sure that we could hold the position. As it is, I would strongly argue that we need to...word, starts with a p, means important, sort of like property—"

"Prioritize?" Steve said.

"That one," Faith said. "I would recommend, Captain, that we prioritize getting them out of the compartment and to a safe place."

"They're dresses, Faith," Steve said. "I get that you wanted a dress..."

"Sir, again, they are not *just* dresses," Faith said, frowning. "I don't know how to explain it. Maybe... money terms? The dress that I grabbed, on the rack, in a store, would run thirty thousand dollars, sir."

"Ouch," Steve said.

"Now you're getting it, Da," Faith said with a grin. "We never could have afforded these for prom. That container contains several *million* dollars worth of clothing. And it's more than that, sir. I guess it's an MWR issue. But all the clothes we've got are either slops that were from infecteds or pulled off of salvage or uniforms. Pretty... matters to a woman. Just about *any* woman. The reason we propped the door the way we did was to keep the infected from screwing up, like, the last pretty thing in the world, sir. Those are the *last* Paris originals anyone will probably ever see. I...I don't know how to put it any better, sir. A woman would understand, sir. But everybody in my chain of command is a guy. No offense."

"Not quite," Steve said, thoughtfully. "Stand by."

He leaned up and toggled his computer to video then hit the link to the *Dallas*.

"*Dallas*, retrans to the Hole, personal for General Brice."

"*Roger, Squadron, stand by.*"

"Captain," Brice said, nodding. "How's the clearance going?"

"Nominal," Steve said. "It helps having Marines, that's for sure. Still not finding many survivors but there's always hope."

"Is it going to affect your primary mission?" Brice asked.

"We've got the time," Steve said. "It's clear these or continue clearance at sea until the tropicals pass. If we'd left for Gitmo instead of Tenerife when we left—"

"I've seen the satellite imagery," Brice said. "You'd be getting pounded."

"We'll leave this area late November for Gitmo, General," Steve said. "But that wasn't the reason for the call."

"And the reason for the call is?" General Brice asked.

"I have a potential discipline issue which overlaps with personal and I need both a more experienced professional's opinion and, sorry, a woman's," Steve said. "Fortunately..."

"I'm both," Brice said, chuckling. "Personal?"

"My daughter, Faith, took time out during a mission to secure a container that contained what she states is valuable material," Steve said. "She also put her Marines somewhat at risk both securing the materials and finding some for herself."

"That's . . . not good," Brice said, shaking her head. "You don't put your people at risk for personal gain."

"She agrees that her actions at the time were . . . poor judgment," Steve said. "But to prevent the materials from being damaged by the infected, she also elected to weaken the defenses. The container was being used to block the pier we're holding and she had the Marines brace the outer door to keep the infecteds out of the container. Bracing the inner door would have made it functionally impossible for them to get onto the wharf, but also would have allowed them access to the container."

"Tell her what it was," Faith hissed.

Steve waved for her to be silent.

"I've seen the satellite imagery," Brice said. "We were wondering why you'd done it that way. That had better be some pretty important material."

"Well, that's the question, General," Steve said. "It sort of hinges on that. It was dresses."

"Dresses?" Brice said, shaking her head. "I didn't think Faith was a shopaholic, Captain."

"Tell her what kind!" Faith hissed.

"Faith is present and insists that I point out that they were Paris originals," Steve said.

"WHAT?" Brice said, leaning forward in her chair and grabbing the monitor. "*What kind?*"

"Yves Saint Laurent!" Faith said, jumping up and leaning around to crane her head in front of the camera. "They're, like, *gorgeous!*"

"How many?" Brice asked.

"A whole container full!" Faith said.

"Is there a four?" Brice said. "Tell me there's a four!"

"There's like, every size!" Faith said. "Pick a color!"

"Okay, okay, okay," Brice said, leaning back and holding up her hands. "Professional. How endangered were your Marines, Lieutenant?"

"Ma'am, if at any point it got down to close quarters, I would have drawn back and let the infected have the container," Faith said. "Reluctantly."

"I bet reluctantly," Brice said. "You shouldn't have endangered your Marines getting your own dress. What's it like, by the way?"

"Oh, it's like this really hot red thing with holographic silk," Faith said. "It turns like every shade of red you can imagine..."

"Oh, God," Brice said. "It sounds gorgeous... Still, I can understand your desire to ensure the security of the materials but remember, mission, men, me, Lieutenant. Your mission was to secure the wharf, not go dress shopping."

"Yes, ma'am," Faith said. "No excuse, ma'am. Will not happen again. Even if I find a container of Prada."

"Okay, *maybe* if you find a container of Prada," Brice said, chuckling. "But even Prada is not worth losing Marines, Lieutenant. Understood?"

"Understood, ma'am. Won't happen again."

"Captain," Brice said, then paused. "I'm not sure you'll get this, but I'm ordering you to divert any available resources not focused on clearance to emptying out that container and putting the materials somewhere safe. While Lieutenant Smith's personal salvage spree was ill-considered, I frankly can understand it. I'd recommend a verbal counseling, this will do, that she had a lapse in judgment in securing her own needs at the expense of endangering her Marines but that her decision to ensure the security of the materials was well considered. I'm not sure that you or anyone else in her chain of command would understand that, but, well, absent being overruled by Mr. Galloway, I'm the boss."

"Yes, ma'am," Steve said. "And I get it intellectually but it is, I suspect, a gender thing. Which was why I brought you in on it."

"I'm glad you did," Brice said. "And, Faith?"

"Yes, ma'am?"

"Could you find me a four in blue?"

"Absolutely," Faith said. "I think you're about my sister Soph's size, General. We'll hold one back for you."

"I feel terrible..." Brice said. "No, never mind. Captain, you should distribute those to females who... Those would make very nice bonuses, Captain."

"I take it you only have uniforms in the Hole, ma'am?" Steve said.

"Yep," Brice said. "Maybe it's a gender thing, maybe it's cultural. But...I love my uniform and I'm proud of it. But there is, and don't tell anyone this, a 'woman' side to me that really, really is dying for a splash of color."

"Ma'am," Steve said. "Absent direct order to the contrary, I'll have Faith, after we secure the materials and when she has some downtime, get on the video conference, closed, and have her show you some of them so you can pick one out in your size."

"I'm not sure that would be an advised use of resources, Captain," Brice said.

"Two points in argument, ma'am," Steve said. "One, the situation that you are in is psychologically extremely stressful. As you noted, you are dying for a splash of color. You need something to take your mind off of, well, the zombie apocalypse, being trapped in the Hole and all it entails. Two, absent direct orders, if you think I'm not going to try to butter up the acting CJCS, you're out of your mind already."

"I'll take your first point and ignore the second, Captain," Brice said with a laugh. "But, seriously, it's an order. Get those secured. They're probably the last Paris fashions on earth. Don't distribute all of them. We're going to have museums again, someday, and one of them should be in it."

"Yes, ma'am," Steve said, making some notes. "I'll order that right away."

"Don't do it if you're going to lose people," Brice said. "Not that important."

"Again, not an issue, ma'am," Steve said.

"Anything else?" Brice asked.

"No, ma'am," Steve said. "Thank you for your time, ma'am."

"Looking forward to meeting you in person someday," Brice said. "Both of you. Especially if you're carrying a dress. Out here."

"Okay, Faith," Steve said. "You were right on securing the dresses."

"I was still wrong on grabbing them right then and there, Da," Faith said. "And...I'm sorry I lost my temper with that...the guy in the saloon. I'll work on the officer deportment."

"The truth is, Faith," Steve said, sighing. "It's not that dressing you down feels like pulling the wings off a fly. The truth is that if things weren't so absolutely fucked to hell, you'd be a shoe-in for the Medal of Honor. And that's not just being your dad saying that. You are an absolute asset. A living embodiment of the best in us."

"Now you're going all Da," Faith said.

"No," Steve said. "I'm trying to judge this fairly. If you were a twenty-one-year-old second lieutenant straight out of the Point or Annapolis or ROTC, you'd still be somebody that people would follow into battle. And the way that you fight is just so over the top that every real warrior on this ship wants to have your babies."

"I think it's supposed to be the other way around, Da," Faith said, laughing and looking awkward. She handled praise about as well as she handled being dressed down.

"You know what I mean," Steve said. "All that is true. The other truth is that you have a lot to learn about all the other stuff in being an officer. And, believe it or not, I think that Wilkes can teach you that. And maybe, just maybe, you can teach him what actual leadership means. Sometimes when you've got two problems they can cancel themselves out. I'm hoping that's what this experiment will achieve."

"I'll do my best, Da."

"That's my Shewolf."

CHAPTER 14

'Cause I'm a pilot
I only care about me
I don't give a fuck if I bring your bird back
Code 2 or code 3

'Cause I'm a pilot
And I never make mistakes
I'll take the credit if it ain't broken
I'll blame you if it breaks

"I'm a Pilot"
Dos Gringo

"Captain Wilkes," Steve said, looking around the embarkation area. "How's the clearance going?"

After clearing the immediate area and cleaning up, a team under Janu had fought their way to DCC and brought back not only all the hardcopy maps but laptops that, huzzah, contained all the same information. The TOC was set up with several plasma screens connected to those as well as other computers brought aboard. It looked almost professional.

As areas were cleared they were "greyed out" so they didn't repeat. With four people clearing, that had not been an issue. With thirty Marines working on the boats it had happened.

177

"Nominal, sir," Wilkes said. "Would you care to examine the map?"

"No," Steve said. "Other things to do. How far are you into the ship?"

"We've reached deck six and are proceeding upwards, sir," Wilkes said. "There is a significant infected level throughout the ship. At least, according to reports..."

"Have you..." Steve said, then stopped. "Can you turn this over to somebody, we need to have a chat."

"Yes, sir," Wilkes said. "Gunny, come get me if anything comes up."

"Yes, sir," Gunny Sands said.

Steve gestured aft and Wilkes paused.

"Sir, the infecteds have officially been cleared from these decks, however..."

"You've got an M4, right?" Steve said. "And I've got a pistol. That should be enough. As I said, we need to chat."

They walked back into the bowels of the ship and Steve opened up one of the hatches. The smell of rot was strong.

"Been back here?" Steve asked, stepping over a bloating body. "Keep the hatch open. Decay uses up oxygen."

"Yes, sir," Wilkes said.

"But I think this is far enough," Steve said. "I understand Faith had an incident last night?"

"I thought it might be about that, sir," Wilkes said. "I take it she complained to you?"

"No," Steve said. "Nor the gunny nor any of the Marines. They know, even if Faith doesn't, about not jumping the chain of command. On the other hand, we're a mix of civilian and military. And while the military personnel have, in general, not spoken to me of it, I've been getting an earful from the civilian side. I was even told there was some sort of message from this Zumwald character. And since I had a previously scheduled meeting with her, I counseled her on this indiscretion as well. Would you care to give me your version?"

"Lieutenant Smith was asked by Mr. Zumwald to get him a drink," Wilkes said. "She responded with physical violence. I counseled her on conduct unbecoming of an officer and, when she reacted with foul language, on disrespect to a superior officer, sir, and I'll stand by that position. Sir."

"I agree that her actions were unbecoming, Captain," Steve said mildly. "She really should have resolved it with less force. Which I told her as well as a strong lecture on respect to a superior officer. On the other hand, Captain, Mr. Zumwald physically accosted her, grabbing her arm and, when she protested, called her a bitch. Were you aware of that, Captain?"

"She did say something about it, sir," Wilkes said. "However..."

"I also understand that you spent some time with Mr. Zumwald afterwards," Steve said. "Rather late. Did you at any time express to Mr. Zumwald that accosting any woman, much less an officer of... what was it? 'The United States Naval services' was unacceptable behavior, Captain?"

"Sir," Wilkes said. "Mr. Zumwald is a major Hollywood executive—"

"Was," Steve said.

"Excuse me, sir?" Wilkes said.

"Was a major Hollywood executive," Steve said. "Right now, Ernest Zumwald, Captain, is a fucking refugee off a fucking lifeboat. Period fucking dot. He's given a few days grace, like most refugees, to get his headspace and timing back, then he can decide if he wants to help out or go in with the sick, lame and lazy. And in this case he's a fucking refugee who thinks it's acceptable to accost some unknown chick and tell her to get him a fucking drink. Grab her by the arm and, when she tells him to let go, become verbally abusive.

"What makes the situation worse, Captain, is that the person he accosted was not just any passing young hotty but a Marine *officer*. He did not know that at the time; the Marine officer was dressed much like other women in the compartment. However, he does not have the right to grab *any* woman in my care by the fucking arm and order them to get him a fucking *drink*, Captain! Then, to make matters *worse*, following the incident, Captain, *you* spent the entire fucking evening getting drunk with a fucktard who had physically and verbally assaulted *a female Marine officer*! You *dumbshit*."

"Sir, I..." Wilkes said, paling.

"And not just *any* Marine officer, oh, no," Steve said. "Forget that it was the daughter of the Acting LANTFLEET. Forget that it was the daughter of your fucking *rating* officer, you retard. I'm professional enough to overlook that. I really am. There's personal and professional, and I do actually know the line. Except that it was, *professionally*, a *disgraceful* action on your part, Captain. But not just any Marine officer, Captain. No, this was a Marine officer that, *unlike* you, is fucking *worshipped* by your Marines, Captain. This is a Marine officer that the acting commandant thinks only uses boats so her boots don't get wet walking from ship to ship. This is a Marine officer who is the only fucking light in the darkness to the entire squadron, you dumbfuck!

"I'd already gotten the scuttlebutt that you were a palace prince pogue who was a cowardly disgrace to the Marine uniform, Captain. I was willing to let that slide because *maybe* you could run the fucking clearance from the fucking door. But you just pissed off every fucking Marine we've *got*, you *idiot*. You incredible dumbfuck, moron!

"In case you hadn't noticed, you are getting cold-shouldered by everyone you work with for brown-nosing some fucking useless POS who used to 'be somebody.' 'Your' Marines are spitting on your shadow and that includes your fucking *Gunnery Sergeant*! Captain, am I getting *through* to you? Are you even vaguely recognizing how *badly* you fucked up? Professionally, politically, *personally*?"

"Sir . . . I stand by my statement that Lieutenant Smith's conduct was unbecoming and . . ."

"Already agreed, Captain," Steve said. "And if you can get your head out of your fourth point of contact, in general, I'd appreciate you taking her under your wing and giving her some actual guidance on how to act like a Marine officer. Assuming *you* know. Because this is *my* official verbal counseling statement, Captain.

"You failed to stand up for a fellow Marine. And a Marine *officer*! So you could shove your nose up the *ass* of some dork who used to make movies and listen to him ramble on about stars! Your failure to protect the reputation and person of a fellow Marine officer over a 'major Hollywood executive' has reduced what little trust your subordinates have in you and has raised questions as to your conduct and *honor* as a Marine officer. Not just in the mind of a jumped-up Naval captain. The incident, which I had investigated by *several* sources, was discussed with higher level command, and Colonel Ellington and General Brice are in agreement that it has raised questions as to your value as an asset in this operation. Furthermore, your failure to move forward to observe operations as well as your near inability to step into *this* compartment has raised and continues to raise questions as to your personal courage, which is an *absolute* requirement of a Marine officer."

"Sir, I formally protest any questions about my courage, sir!" Wilkes said hotly.

"Then take your fucking Barbie gun *forward*," Steve said. "And, Captain, that's not a request, that's a fucking *order*. The specific order is, you, Captain Wilkes, will spend the rest of the day under the direction, not command but direction, of *Lieutenant Smith*, who will instruct you in the methods and means of infected clearance. Because, Captain, she is *your* number one *expert* at heavy clearance."

"Sir..." Wilkes said.

"Again, not a request, Captain," Steve said. "She trained the fucking *Gunny* at how to do clearance, Captain. *You* can God damned well listen to her. You've been telling people they should move faster. Possibly that's the case. But you don't really *know* what's happening up front, do you? Because you've been staying as far away from zombies as you can *get*. Well, you're done staying away from zombies, Captain. Gunny Sands can manage the flow of material. Lieutenant Fontana will manage personnel distribution. *You* will go fight zombies. As of *now*. Is that understood?"

"Yes, sir," Wilkes said. "But, sir..."

"What is it about 'go fight zombies' you don't understand, Captain?" Steve said tiredly.

"Sir... I'm out of qualification on my M4, sir," Wilkes said reluctantly.

"Okay," Steve said, drawing a breath of foul air. "Captain, I am going to give you the benefit of the doubt. That is either the lamest excuse to avoid combat I've ever heard, or you're actually saying you haven't dotted an I and crossed a T in a *zombie apocalypse!*"

"Hey, Ernest," Isham said, waving at a chair. "Have a seat."

"Thanks," the former executive said. "So you're the number two guy? Where's this Smith character? I need to talk to him."

"Over on the Love Boat," Isham said. "Checking on the clearance operations. So, you getting your head back into shape?"

"Well, except for that incident last night," Zumwald said angrily. "According to Milo, that bitch was a Marine. He said he'd talked to her, but she needs to be charged with assault."

"And that's what we're here to talk about," Isham said. "According to more than one witness, you grabbed her arm and told her to get you a drink."

"That's no excuse for trying to choke me to death," Zumwald snapped.

"Shewolf wasn't trying to choke you to death," Isham said, chuckling and waving a hand. "If Shewolf wanted you dead, you'd be dead." He held up his hand to forestall a reply.

"You work with people," Isham said. "You know working the politics of Hollywood. Let me just give you a little brief, okay? Some information you need. Okay? About the politics of this little hellhole called Wolf Squadron."

"Okay," Zumwald said, crossing his arms. "But that bitch is fucking nuts."

"Yes," Isham said, nodding. "Yes, she is. She is totally fucking bonkers. So's her dad. You read that little pamphlet?"

"The one about 'Welcome to Wolf Squadron'?" Zumwald said. "Read it. It could use a rewrite."

"Maybe," Isham said. "But here's the thing. The chick you accosted last night? That was Lieutenant Faith *Smith*. AKA Shewolf. Boss's *daughter*."

"Oh, crap," Zumwald said, shaking his head. "I guess that throws getting her charged with assault out the window."

"Bit more than that," Isham said. "The reason you're talking to me instead of Steve is he was ready to throw you off the boat. Into the harbor I mean. The one with all the man-eating sharks. And here's the part you probably aren't going to get real easily. He'd have felt the same way if you grabbed any of the little bobsies running around the saloon."

"Okay, what?" Zumwald said. "His daughter... I can get that. I suppose I should apologize to him..."

"Might want to back off on that for a bit," Isham said. "Some more info. First, Faith's only thirteen..."

"I heard that but I didn't believe it," Zumwald said. "Seriously? How'd she get to be a Marine? Oh, her dad of course. Duh."

"Sort of," Isham said, pointing out the window. "You see that ship? What I call the Love Boat. There are thirty Marines, including your buddy Milo, clearing it right now. Slowly. Faith and her dad, one Marine and a Green Beret sergeant cleared one that was a touch larger. *Before* they found the rest of the Marines. *Then* they cleared the fucking *Iwo Jima*, which is the size of a World War Two carrier, to find some Marines to, you know, help.

"Faith's like a goddess to the Marines, and she's actually good at her job, especially given she'd just finished seventh grade. Which is an important job. She does really important shit.

"Right now, you're just getting your head together. Like the pamphlet says, maybe you decide to help out. We can use people who know how to get shit done. Not just as military. I only took the lieutenancy they offered 'cause I have to work with the Navy and Marines to get my job done and it helps. But there's lots of ways a guy with your background and work ethic and general get-it-done attitude could help. Problem being, even if you *wanted* to, right now the only reason the Marines haven't gotten together to kick the *crap* out of you is that they're too busy. When they get less busy or, for example, this evening when they break from killing zombies, I would *not* want to be in your shoes."

"So what is this?" Zumwald said. "A military dictatorship? Beatings for free?"

"Yeah," Isham said, looking at him as if he was nuts. "We're on *ships*. And they are all officially *U.S. Navy* vessels. Even most of the dinky little yachts. The commanders, including this one, are all Navy officers, even if the ink is still wet on the commissions. And even if they weren't, captains of vessels at sea have a lot of legal control in any circumstances. By the way, I talked Captain Miguel, boss of this boat, out of pressing charges against *you* for assault. Because you don't get how badly you fucked up. I get that. She's another Faith lover, but it's also you don't get to just grab any cookie and tell her you want another scotch. You *don't*. This isn't Hollywood, and, sorry, you're *not* some big time movie executive anymore. You're a fucking refugee in a squadron that spends half its time on the ragged edge. Still. You got no clue how tough it is to keep these vessels supplied."

"This is bullshit," Zumwald said, shaking his head.

"This is a *zombie fucking apocalypse*, Ernest," Isham said. "It's not a movie version, either. It's the real fucking deal. And right now, the choices are, you help to whatever extent you can and you get some perks. You don't and we stick you in a hold with a bunch of other losers and you get water and sushi or you can feel free to jump in the fucking harbor or catch a boat to land. Now, Faith and her crew sort of half-ass cleared a couple of towns in this area. You can ask the Canaries if they mind you jumping ship to one of those. No problem. I'll give you a pistol so you can go scavenge in the ruins."

"Very funny," Zumwald said.

"I'M NOT FUCKING JOKING, ZUMWALD!" Isham said, leaning forward and banging his desk. "Those are the *choices*. You got an alternate suggestion?"

Zumwald thought about it for a second.

"Hell, I can drive a boat," he said. "I've got my own yacht back in the L.A. marina. Gimme a boat."

"Which is what Smith did for me when we had our first little run-in," Isham said, nodding. "Then I hit the problem that he'd foreseen. Where you going to get fuel? Where you going to get groceries when they run out?"

"You guys have got 'em," Zumwald said.

"You going to whip out the Amex black?" Isham said. "Won't get you far. I said, it's a *bitch* to keep this squadron supplied. Okay, we've got a bunch of ships and boats to get stores from at this point. You think we're going to give you all the coordinates? *We* need those supplies. Are you going to climb the ladders, board the boats, some of them still with infected onboard, haul the stores off the boats? Ever tried to refuel at sea from a freighter? It is not easy, bub, trust me."

"Shit," Zumwald said, shaking his head.

"That fucker Smith left me to rot on a boat in the Bermuda harbor," Isham said. "And that was *after* he'd put a gun to my head. I learned my lesson pretty quick. I'd much rather sit in an office pushing paper than fish for my supper. Or haul stores or fight zombies for them. I leave that shit to crazy fuckers like, well, *Faith*. So now that we've got some background to the situation, I'll bottomline it for you 'cause I got other shit to do.

"No, Faith ain't gonna get charged with assault. I'm not even sure the incident occurred 'cause neither are you. You get three days off on the *Alpha* to get your head back together. Then you decide if you want to help out or go in a hold. Or, hell, I'll drop you off at a little town and you can fight zombies for supplies and fish for your supper. If you decide you want to help, God knows we need people who can organize and you should be able to do that. But if so, you're going to have to *climb down*. And you sure as shit had better figure out a way to apologize to

Lieutenant Smith or at some point you're going to end up shark bait. Because the Marines, with the exception of Captain Milo 'I'm scared of zombies' Wilkes, just absolutely hate your fucking *guts*. And the one group you do *not* want pissed off at you in this squadron is the fucking Marines. And of all the Marines, the one you seriously do not want to get on the bad side of is Faith Marie Smith. They call her *Shewolf* for a *reason....*"

"If you would knock on the hatch, please, sir," Faith said.

Wilkes was lost. He knew he was lost and he didn't like it. The bowels of the supermax liner were one corridor after another, all of them pitch black. And he didn't like being 'instructed' by a thirteen-year-old girl.

"Why?" Wilkes said. He'd open the hatch but the little bitch was holding the key.

"Because the objective, sir, is to determine if there are infected on the far side of the hatch, sir," Faith said. "That way they can be drawn into our kill zone rather than entering theirs. The objective is, as much as possible, to engage at range, rather than entering melee..."

"If they're on the other side we can just back off," Wilkes said.

"As I was saying, sir," Faith said, patiently. "Infected often rest. The rest is extremely deep, similar to hibernation. Banging on the hatch gets them up. You can detect them by sound at that point and prepare a plan based on the estimated number. So, sir, if you would be so kind as to bang on the hatch, sir."

Wilkes banged on the hatch with his fist.

"Satisfied, Lieutenant?"

"Sir..." Faith said. "No, sir. Several reasons. One, there are many hatches. At a certain point, you begin to damage your hand, sir. Two, as mentioned, infected tend to sleep. That would be unlikely to wake them, sir."

"Just open the hatch, Lieutenant," Wilkes said.

"Yes, sir," Faith said, swiping the card. "The hatch is green, sir. Feel free to proceed." She waved a hand into the darkness of a large baggage compartment.

"Enlisted should take point, Lieutenant," Wilkes said. "That is what they are for."

"I would normally agree, sir," Faith said. "But I was told that you, sir, are here to learn the basics of infected clearance, sir. Not managing or leading, sir. Doing, sir. This compartment needs to be cleared, sir. I will be your wingman, sir. After you, sir." She swiped it again because it had locked while they were talking.

Wilkes cracked the compartment and flashed his taclight around the large compartment. It was half filled with bags and pallets. Some of the pallets had been broken open.

"It looks clear," he said quietly.

"It has to be walked, sir," Faith said. "The point is to *ensure* it is clear, sir. So that later salvage parties, sir, do not encounter any unpleasant surprises, sir."

"So which way?" Wilkes asked quietly.

"Left, right, center, take your pick," Faith said. "On compartments like this, I tend to go right and hug the wall at first. That way, if anything springs up out of the darkness, my barrel is pointing in its general direction. Sir."

Wilkes went right. Despite what he had thought of as an overabundance of lights, there were far too many shadows for his liking. And there was no way to "hug the walls." There were bags and pallets up against the bulkheads. He stayed as far to the right as he could, went down the first bulkhead then turned up the next.

He was halfway down the bulkhead, tip-toeing past a pallet, when he stepped on something soft. And the zombie came up with a low groan that raised into a howl.

"Annnd now we're in the scrum," Faith said, as infected started popping up in every direction. Including the ones the captain had missed on his way by.

Wilkes let out a yell and fired multiple rounds into the infected with its teeth sunk into his boot.

"Not into the *deck*, you idiot!" Faith yelled, dropping two infected coming up behind them with her Saiga. "They go all *over* the place! With due respect! Sir."

"*LT?*" Januscheitis radioed. "*Need a hand?*"

"No worries," Faith yelled. "Got this..."

Infected poured over the bags and pallets. Wilkes got two, missing far more than he hit, the missed rounds ricocheting all over the compartment, then got dogpiled.

Faith cleared the infected heading for her, dropping to pistol when she was out of 12-gauge, then reloaded her Saiga and pistol while Wilkes writhed on the deck, covered in seven infected. When she'd put fresh mags in the pistols...she reloaded the mags from ammo in her assault ruck. The captain had words to say. They were sort of muffled.

Finally, when it was clear he wasn't extracting himself, she pulled her kukri and started chopping necks.

"The objective of banging on the door, sir," Faith said, pulling a zombie off the captain, "is to *wake* the infected who are sleeping so as to bring them into *your* kill zone, not go into *theirs*, sir. Zombies are found anywhere there is water. If you had listened to *that* part of the lecture and maintained *situational awareness*, sir, you would have noted that there is some sort of leak on the port bulkhead. There is a puddle of water over there. Water equals zombies, sir."

"Understood, Lieutenant," Wilkes said, getting to his feet. "Speaking of water: I guess I need to go decontaminate."

"Why, sir?" Faith asked, wiping down her blood-smeared kukri. "Your gear is not penetrated and there are more compartments to clear, sir."

"You're serious?" Wilkes said.

"Sir, I've been in five or six worse scrums in a *day*, sir," Faith said, sheathing the kukri without looking. "From which I generally self-extract because, as you noted sarcastically earlier, I am *covered* in fucking knives and guns, sir. So, yes, sir, with due respect I am serious, sir. There are more compartments to clear, sir. So are we going to continue with this mission or shall you go bunk off to get cleaned up, sir? Would sir care for a lollipop to go with sir's shower, sir?"

"So, is this normal?" Wilkes said.

The captain was trying to hold a door closed against what sounded, to him, like about two hundred howling infected. At least five had their arms through the hatch and were scrabbling at his left arm. He had the hatch braced with his foot and was pushing on it with all his might but he was slowly and inexorably being pushed back by the weight of zombies. There were shoulders. It was not looking good.

"Yes, sir, pretty much," Faith said. "Zombies are not people as we understand it. No sentience. They are just aggression, hunger and occasionally lust. Sort of Marines without stops, sir."

"Would the Lieutenant care to instruct the Captain on what the fuck you're supposed to do *now*? Quickly?"

"It is recommended in a situation like this that the lead request support from his team mates in temporarily reducing movement of the hatch, sir," Faith said. "Given that this is not a hatch with a coaming, but flush to the deck, that is simply managed, thusly..." She pulled out one of her boot knives and jammed it under the door, then kicked it into place. "Better, sir?"

"Yes," Wilkes said, leaning back. Between his boot and the knife, the hatch wasn't going anywhere. "So now what?"

"Is the Captain familiar with the operation of the M87 fragmentation grenade, sir?" Faith said, holding up one of the little bundles of fury.

"The Captain has not used an M87 fragmentation grenade since the Captain was in Marine Officer Basic Course, Lieutenant," Captain Wilkes said. "Where he threw one, once. And please tell me you're not serious."

"The operation of the M87 is so remarkably simple that even, say, a thirteen-year-old girl is capable of figuring it out, sir," Faith said, pressing the grenade into his somewhat flaccid hand. "I am sure a Marine pilot can do far better, sir. Place the thumb of your strong hand on the lever. You are right-handed, are you not, sir?"

"Yes," Wilkes said, weakly. "Seriously?"

"Hold the M87 hand grenade firmly with your strong hand," Faith said, keeping her hand wrapped around his. "Straighten the cotter pin, then pull, thusly. Remember that once the pin is pulled, Mr. Hand Grenade is no longer your friend, sir. Now, and this is the one slightly tricky part, sir. Reach o-o-over the estimated heads of the zombies and the flailing arms and toss the grenade *through* the narrow gap into the *other* compartment, sir. Very important that it lands in the *other* compartment, sir. Really, really important, sir."

"This is insane," Wilkes said, tossing the grenade. Into the other compartment.

"And duck and cover, sir," Faith said, pushing his helmet into the hatch and down. "Scrunch your neck down, sir."

"Doin' it," Wilkes said.

There was a somewhat muted bang from the next compartment and a lot of shrill screaming over the usual keening and howls.

"And sometimes it takes more than one," Faith said, pulling out another frag. "You know what they say about hand grenades, sir?"

"Close only counts with them and horseshoes?" Wilkes said.

"The M87, sir," Faith said, pulling the pin. "When 'fuck you' just isn't enough. And I really like saying 'fuck you.' Sir."

Wilkes was trying not to barf at the carnage in the compartment. Most of the infected were just wounded and they were screaming exactly like, well, people screamed when they were ripped half to death by grenades.

"What do you do about...about the wounded?"

"We don't have an infinite amount of .45, sir," Faith said. "And no idea how much we are going to use in the long term. And no great store of other pistol rounds. Barbie rounds go right through and go *bouncin' around*. So no dice there. Sometimes, if we've got the time, we cut their throats to put them out of their misery." She drew her kukri and offered it to him, hilt first. "It's not a requirement and it's not a test, sir. It's an offer. Just that. Otherwise we'll continue clearance ops, sir. It's messy as hell and generally we don't bother, sir. They'll bleed out in a while."

"We'll continue clearance ops, Lieutenant."

"Now, sir, in just a moment, the team's going to let go of the rope..."

This time the infected were on the other side of a hatch that opened away from the team. Which necessitated a different technique involving partially cracking the hatch, then letting the infecteds pull at it while holding it partially closed with a long rope held by most of the team. That way the point could back up and give some distance to engage. The general term was "zombie tug-of-war."

"This time we would appreciate it, sir, if you'd get most of the rounds into the targets," Faith said.

"Sorry about the compartment," Wilkes said. "I really haven't used an M4 in a while. Not my thing."

"I was fully aware of the infected in the compartment, sir," Faith said. "I also knew that I could handle it without either of us coming to serious harm, sir. But tell me in flight school there's not a point where the instructors let you screw up, sir?"

"You'd make a real prick of an IP, Lieutenant," Wilkes said, shaking his head. "And that was actually a compliment."

"You're the only pilot we've got left, sir," Faith said. "Da told me if I lost you, he'd have me cleaning compartments for a month, sir. And here I would prefer you succeed, sir. Now, sir, this is kinda important. Don't get focused on the infected as screaming zombies or even people. Just get, well, zen. You're just on a target range, shooting silhouettes. Shoot through the silhouettes. They don't fall down like the pop-ups, either, sir. You're going to have to hit each silhouette several times but don't worry about that, either. They do eventually become good zombies. We'll be firing as well. They are *not* going to reach this point. We are not going to get in the scrum again. Just, please, fire right down the corridor so the through-and-throughs pass through the hatch into the far compartment and engage all targets until they fall. All clear, sir?"

"Clear, Lieutenant," Wilkes said, taking an off-hand firing stance. "Ready when you are."

"Let the captain initiate," Faith said. "Let go, Staff Sergeant."

"Let the captain initiate, aye, ma'am," Januscheitis said, nodding to the team. He wasn't holding a rope. He was aiming his 'Barbie gun' as back-up. "Let go, aye, ma'am. *Pull!*"

Unfortunately, the first infected through the door was a female. And even for a zombie who'd been stuck in a ship for months, not a bad looking one. With all the light that was patently obvious. The Marine aviator froze.

"Oh, crap," Faith said, taking the shot and splattering the still somewhat breasty brunette all over the compartment. The splurt of saline from the chest explained the 'still breasty' given the rest of the emaciation. "Fire, sir!"

Wilkes finally fired, putting round after round into a zombie until it finally dropped. But there was another one behind that one...

"Jesus, they're not stopping," Wilkes panted. He suddenly realized he was out of rounds. How did that happen?

"You're pulling an empty trigger, sir," Faith said, calmly servicing targets. "Reload," she said, switching to pistol.

By the time Wilkes had reloaded, all the infected were down.

"Are you on safe, sir?" Faith asked when Wilkes had reloaded and chambered a round. "Safety is sort of important, sir."

"On safe," Wilkes said. "I apologize for not taking the shot. That put the team in jeopardy."

"I can't shoot the kids, sir," Faith said. "Fortunately or unfortunately it looks like they've all been eaten on this ship. Lots of them left on the *Voyage*, sir. Shall we continue?"

CHAPTER 15

O makin' mock o' uniforms that guard you while you sleep
Is cheaper than them uniforms, an' they're starvation cheap;
An' hustlin' drunken sodgers when they're goin' large a bit
Is five times better business than paradin' in full kit.

"Tommy"
Rudyard Kipling

"Captain?" Captain Wilkes said, sticking his head in the compartment. "I was told you wanted to see me immediately following clearance ops." The captain was out of zombie gear but still wearing the same uniform. Which was fairly grungy.

"Grab a seat, Milo," Steve said, waving. "You're not flying any time soon. Are you a drinker, Captain? And what? Bourbon, scotch..."

"Scotch, sir," Wilkes said, taking a seat.

"My daughter, Sophia, has cleared two hundred and eighty-six small craft, according to a report I just read..."

"Good God," Wilkes said, shaking his head. "Where do you *get* them, sir?"

"My wife actually popped them out, Captain," Steve said, smiling. He'd pulled a bottle out of the drawer and poured two glasses, then handed one to Wilkes. "And, yes, I consider them fine little sheilas. But the point to it is that people seem to always take booze with them when they evacuate. I was rather remiss in that area. Apparently, I was supposed to pack along two-hundred-year-old brandy instead of guns and ammo. Who knew? But the rich people with rich yachts that took to sea tended to stock rather fine booze. And from experience, your first day of clearing the fucking bowels of a supermax liner requires a little snort. Cheers."

"Semper Fi, sir," Wilkes said, taking a sip. "God, that is good."

"We've got a post clearance meeting in fifteen minutes," Steve said. "This is not any sort of official meeting. This is a debrief, only one you'll get. Time to clear your head with someone you can, actually, be frank with. The first comment would probably be along the lines of the 'Good God' you already used or possibly 'Holy Christ.'"

Wilkes leaned back and put his hand over his mouth, clearly thinking.

"How about 'Holy fucking shit on a cracker?' sir," he said after a moment. "When I looked at the objective my first thought was 'I'm expected to do this with thirty Marines?' My second thought was 'There is really no way anyone did this with four people. This is a battalion objective.' I mean, sir, with respect, I just sort of thought..."

"We'd made it up?" Steve said, snorting. "There are plenty of people who were around for it, Captain. I'm not offended, but "

"It's not the sort of thing you go up to random people and say 'They had to be lying,' sir," Wilkes said. "And that was before I actually went forward and saw what it's like, sir. When I actually did it...Jesus Christ Eating a Holy Wafer in Hell, sir."

"Are you still wondering...?" Steve asked. "I'm curious, not upset."

"No, *sir*," Wilkes said. "Sir, I saw the video, sure. But working with Shewolf is a different deal, sir. I'm a pilot, sir. We understand muscle memory and how much time it takes to develop. And your daughter, sir, fights zombies with muscle memory like nobody I've ever seen."

"She fights them in her sleep," Steve said.

"Which is the next point, sir," Wilkes said. "She needs a break, sir. That is an official statement as her commanding officer, sir. I'm pretty sure she really does fight them in her sleep. Every waking moment and every night is not good, sir. Her going off in the mess deck is now much more comprehensible, sir. Did that report cover how many hours of combat she's had since the Plague, sir?"

"Do we count New York where she was a positive zombie magnet?" Steve asked. "No, there's another team working on that one. Two hundred and fifty or so of 'hard clearance,' what you're doing, on the *Voyage* alone. Week of twelve-hours days on the *Iwo*…"

"Lieutenant Smith needs some downtime, sir," Wilkes said. "R and R. Swimming. A beach. Pina colad— Well, she's thirteen, so…"

"And really uninterested in drinking," Steve said. "When we finish this clearance we're headed across the Atlantic. Two weeks, minimum. I intend to sweep for any rescues on the way to Gitmo. That do?"

"Possibly, sir," Wilkes said. "But that's an official recommendation and not because she is, as an instructor, an absolute prick, sir. That's actually a compliment, sir. She is one hell of a prick instructor."

"So what do you think of the actual methods?" Steve said. "Official question."

"I think that they're… institutional memory, sir," Wilkes said. "Not really developed SOPs. And they need to be developed SOPs. Some of them are rough, catch-as-catch-can. I know you think I'm… well, a regular military asshat, sir…"

"I also am aware that there's a method to the madness, Captain," Steve said. "I did actually counsel Faith on that, if you're wondering about my counseling session with her. That there is a value to even such things as military deportment. When we head off on our cruise, there will, again, be time to work on developing these as actual SOPs. Thoughts?"

"We certainly don't have time right now, sir," Wilkes said. "I can see why the pace is as slow as it is. And why we're using so many damned batteries. I was going to bring up the subject of cutting down on the use of so many flashlights in clearance at this meeting, sir. That was until I did it. No way in hell. We don't have *enough* light."

"Lieutenant Isham brought it up already," Steve said chuckling. "I told him I'd be glad to take him clearing and he could see what it was like. But it's worthwhile for you to reiterate that. Especially given that you'd identified the same issue and now have a different take. Couple of things I'm going to be bringing up at the meeting that touch on your mission. We're moving the Marines to the *Boadicea*. And they're getting the good cabins."

"Sir?" Wilkes said.

"Marines are supposed to be all about Spartan," Steve said. "But as you pointed out, what they are doing is fucking godawful. The cleaning crews see your results but not how they happened. Maybe it's just that I used to be a para and I've done it. But I think they need...I hate to call it TLC but that's what it is. They're specialists and they're the only ones we've got. So they're going into the first-class cabins, no more than two to a cabin. The officers and senior NCOs into the better staterooms. They sure as hell don't need to be stuffed into interior rooms, six to a stateroom, after clearing in the fucking dark all day. There's a limit and I don't want to push it."

"I'm sure as hell not going to argue for shoving them into holds, sir," Wilkes said.

"The second thing follows the first," Steve said. "When they're done with clearance, they clean their weapons. Gear goes to a team to be cleaned. That will have to be checked, probably by the gunny, and I'm sure there will be some fuck-ups at first. We're not going to get rocket scientists, or Marines for that matter, cleaning it. But I know how fucked up gear gets doing this, and after making the mess, picking bits of flesh out of your gear is the last fucking thing you want to do at the end of a long day of getting pummeled by zombies."

"You sure about that one, sir?" Wilkes said. "I mean, the officers, I can see it. We've got at least two more meetings to go through this evening. The grunts are just...off, sir."

"How many times would you like to go into that shithole, Captain?" Steve said. "That's not a threat, but the fact that it sort of sounds like it should answer your question."

"I won't disagree, sir," Wilkes said. "But who's going to do it?"

"I have some people who are on my shit list," Steve said. "All they need is the proper encouragement."

"Mr. Zumwald," Steve said. "Walk with me."

"You're Captain Smith," Zumwald said. "You don't have much of an Aussie accent. Where we going?"

"For a little walk, followed by a boat ride, followed by a little walk," Steve said. "This way."

"Walk in concrete overshoes?" Zumwald asked.

"You have my personal and professional assurance that you will return, alive, from this little excursion," Steve said seriously. "You're not an idiot. The damage to my reputation if I really *did* dump you over the side would be extreme. Management is, to an extent, about trust. Nobody could trust me if I took such a high-handed approach. I'd lose my position, with justice, and my agenda would be disrupted or destroyed. You will return alive and unharmed. Physically. We'll see about otherwise."

"Well, I'd still like to apologize about what happened with your daughter, Captain," the former executive said. "I was sorta drunk and real glad to be off that little boat. It shouldn't have happened and certainly not to a real hero like your daughter."

"Were you aware that the *Social Alpha* was the megayacht of Mike Mickerberg?" Steve asked.

"Yeah," Zumwald said. "I was even on it one time before the Plague. I heard he got whacked. Which serves him right, the bastard. I lost my shirt in that IPO."

"Faith, then Sergeant Fontana and I cleared it," Steve said, gesturing to a dinghy. "After you."

"No, you should go first," Zumwald said.

"It's an odd thing in the Navy," Steve said. "The junior boards first. That way the senior gets off the boat first. You first.

"Did you hear about what happened before it went fully infected?" Steve asked as Zumwald got in the inflatable.

"No," Zumwald said. "Sort of. Mutiny or something like that?"

"Mr. Mickerberg, possibly panicking at the thought of an apocalypse, hired a cut-rate security firm that employed mostly West African mercenaries. Child soldier types."

"Sounds like Mickey," Zumwald said. "He was great for the whole social networking thing, never got his head in gear on anything else."

"The mercenaries took over, led by a slightly insane ex-Special Forces major," Steve said, gesturing for the crew to take off. "They injected Mr. Mickerberg with live agent to make sure he went zombie. Shot all the male passengers and dumped them to the sharks. Then proceeded to have their way, if you will, with the women he'd brought along."

"Jesus," Zumwald said, shaking his head. "I was going to say it's like the script to some low-budget post-apoc, but—"

"Indeed," Steve said. "But. Then there was the usual falling out you'd expect, as more and more became infected. Faith was part of the entry to the main suite, which we currently use for a command post. Nobody with sense would want to sleep there. The major had apparently locked himself in with, presumably, the fairer of the fair ladies. When the evil overlord was to be overrun, he lined them up, flex-cuffed them, and shot them all in the head, one by one. Then shot himself."

"Fuck," Zumwald said, shuddering. "And your daughter—"

"Saw it all," Steve said. "Was part of the analysis team if you will. So . . . Faith takes a dim view of any man who thinks he quote owns a woman. Or feels that his needs override some cookie who is just wandering around the saloon."

"Okay, now I really realize how bad I fucked up," Zumwald said. "And, again, I apologize." He'd been watching where they were going and now realized it was to the lit hole in the side of the supermax. "We're going to the liner? I thought you said I was coming back alive?"

"We will be going only into cleared areas," Steve said, pulling out a Tyvek suit and a gas mask. "You'll want these, however."

"Shit, you cannot be serious," Zumwald said. "If you're trying to test my courage, you win. I'm a coward."

"This is not a test of courage," Steve said. "It's not even a test. It is what is generally called a learning experience. I'm aware you're a coward. Not all bullies are, but you are. That's okay, I can use cowards too. Jack Isham's a physical coward and he makes a perfectly adequate chief of staff. I'm not asking you to kill infecteds. You're just going to be taking a short walk. And I strongly suggest the Tyvek suit. It has booties. You're going to mess up your Guccis if you don't use the suit."

"Is this just you and me?" Zumwald temporized. The stink from the boat was evident even on the water. It smelled like shit and iron and the worst rotting garbage in history. He already wanted to puke. "No way you're getting me in there."

"Oh, I brought people who can carry you, Mr. Zumwald," Steve said. "While we will be in areas that have been cleared, by a pro I might add, I am not an idiot. And I'm not rigged for heavy combat. So there will be security. And I really don't think you want the indignity of Lieutenant Fontana and Staff Sergeant Januscheitis dragging you through the bowels of the ship. Put on the suit, Mr. Zumwald. There are things you need to understand."

∽ ⊖ ⌣

"Holy fuck," Zumwald groaned.

"If you are going to puke in a mask, sir, this is the procedure," the black lieutenant said politely. "Take a deep breath as you realize you are going to puke. Lift the mask up to your forehead. Puke. You will automatically inhale. Try not to smell the surrounding air. The puke will probably cover it up. Redon the mask, clear it as we told you then take a deep breath. If you have to puke again, and you will, lather, rinse, repeat."

Zumwald wanted to pass out, not just puke. It was dark as fuck in the ship and he was lost. He had a flashlight, but there was no way he was finding his way back. Even if he hadn't had heavily armed Marines following him. So far they hadn't said a fucking word and that scared him worse than anything.

"This isn't actually the part I'm interested in," Smith said, examining the bodies. "All Barbie shots. Where's the other?"

"This way, sir," the big black lieutenant said.

About all that Zumwald knew about the military was that generals were the bosses. But the black guy was the same rank as that little bitch that got him into this. And Smith had said they'd been together clearing the yacht, which was before they'd found any of the rest of the Marines. So he and the chick were probably buddies. Hell, he was probably banging her. Blacks were like that.

The interior of the boat was like a fucking Tarantino movie but for real. He mentally made the note that even Tarantino didn't use enough blood. In some of the rooms it was drying and still an inch or more thick. Walking through it was like glue. Each footstep gave this puke-inducing "suck, suck, suck" sound. Sometimes he couldn't step around the bodies. One time when he balked, the two Marines just picked him up by the arms without a word and carried him over the pile of naked bodies.

He puked. Couple of times. The boat smelled worse than it looked. And none of these fuckers seemed to even notice. Like it was a walk in the fucking park.

Finally they came to the worst. He wasn't sure what the fuck had happened in the room but the zombies weren't just dead, they were *fucked up*. Huge fucking holes in their chests. He puked, again, when he realized he was looking at ribs and shit. For real.

"Jesus, Smith, enough, okay?" Zumwald said, bent over. He was just puking in his mask at this point. There wasn't anything to puke up. "Enough."

"I think you've noted the difference in the wounds?" Smith said. "Big fucking holes? That's my daughter's signature. Then there are these," he said, walking over to a pile and picked one of the dead zombies up by its hair. "This is where Captain Wilkes, who was in training, got piled by zombies. Please try to stop puking long enough to note the cuts to the back of the neck. Do you see them?"

"Yeah," Zumwald said, looking then looking away. "You can see the fucking spine."

"I was given to understand that one of the things that Faith told you when you grabbed her arm was 'The last guy who grabbed me, I cut off his hand.' It was a tense moment; I'm not sure you remember."

"I remember," Zumwald said.

"She was being quite literal, I hope you understand," Smith said. "She literally cuts off the hands of infected that grab her."

"You've made your point, okay? She's a fucking badass. I'll make the movie."

"I doubt it," Steve said. "The likelihood of there being any significant movie industry in the near future is unlikely. What there is is this. Blood and death and shit and crap and horror. We are living, Mr. Zumwald, a much worse reality than any movie you could possibly make. Even given a budget. Okay? Or, perhaps you should just get a camera. This is reality TV. On steroids. Every fucking day, Zumwald."

"And if there's a star, it's the lady that you manhandled," the black lieutenant said.

"And this is, yes, very much like *Survivor*. Some people do get thrown off the island, or the boats as it may be, Mr. Zumwald. And, no, I won't give you a boat. We need all the boats we can get working. And no, as noted, I will *not* throw you in the shark-infested harbor. I will put you down in the town of La Puntilla, which is a charming place from what I've heard and has plenty of resources for a resourceful person such as yourself. It will be a bit like *I Am Legend*. Just you, scavenging for survival in the zombie apocalypse. Does that sound appealing, Mr. Zumwald? I'll even give you a pistol. If I'm feeling sufficiently nice, I'll even give you bullets for it. And more than one."

"You're insane," Zumwald said. "That'd be murder."

"No, throwing you in the bay, with or without concrete overshoes, would be murder," Smith said. "Because the sharks around here have developed a real taste for manflesh. Putting you off in Puntilla would be, at best, abandonment.

"But I want you to really look around. When you make this much of a mess, it's a bitch to clean up. We are not going to even attempt to clean this boat. But those Marines fight in this crap, every damned day, looking for the few, rare, survivors such as yourself. They do it because they are told and because they are fucking Marines and every Marine sees himself as a hero. Then, Mr. Zumwald, after walking through hell, they go back to the boat and have to clean up all their *gear*. Bad enough that they have to do *this*, then they have to clean it up. And they do that. Perfectly. Every night. Then the next day they go out and like the Spartans of yore—again, I'm sure you're aware of the movie—they burnish their shields and go forth to do battle."

"What's your point?" Zumwald said.

"What the movie failed to mention was that the Spartans only put a last coat of polish on, so to speak," Steve said. "Each of them had body servants that did most of the work. So the Spartans could concentrate on what they did best: Killing. Now, body servants have, obviously, gone out of style. We *organize* and *manage* things now. You're all about the deal in Hollywood. So here's the deal. The deal of a lifetime. You are now in charge of cleaning all this crap off of the Marines' gear. Every night."

"Oh, fuck you!"

"Do you know what this is, sir?" one of the Marines said. He pushed up against the former executive from behind and held out what looked like a baseball for a second.

"Shit," Zumwald said, trying to back up. There was nowhere to go. It was a wall of Marine behind him. "That's a fucking grenade, you... You're all fucking *insane!*"

"It's what Miss Faith says when '*fuck you*' isn't enough, sir," the Marine said. "Would you care to try the next step up from 'fuck you,' sir?"

"Please, Staff Sergeant," Smith said. "Some couth. I did not say nor suggest that you, Mr. Zumwald, would be wielding a toothbrush..."

"And you'll need to use a toothbrush," the other Marine growled, "'cause *I'll* be checking it. And if it ain't good, *I* ain't as nice as the Captain, *Mister* Zumwald."

The fucker sounded *exactly* like R. Lee Ermy. Zumwald had had to deal with that fucker one time and he *hated* fucking R. Lee Ermy. The prick.

"I said 'in charge,' Mr. Zumwald," Smith said, then drew his pistol.

Ernest knew he was dead but the fucker just pulled out the other things with the bullets in them and held both up in his hands.

"So, recruit and manage people to clean gear, to the *Gunnery Sergeant's* specifications, or one pistol, twenty-one rounds and La Puntilla. Such a *deal* I'm offering you!"

"Dude, you missed your calling," Zumwald said. "You should have been in *my* business. Deal."

CHAPTER 16

Me that 'ave watched 'arf a world
'Eave up all shiny with dew,
Kopje on kop to the sun,
An' as soon as the mist let 'em through
Our 'elios winkin' like fun—
Three sides of a ninety-mile square,
Over valleys as big as a shire—
"Are ye there? Are ye there? Are ye there?"
An' then the blind drum of our fire . . .
An' I'm rollin' 'is lawns for the Squire,
Me!

"Chant Pagan"
Rudyard Kipling

Faith looked up from the computer at a knock on her door and thought about it. She had a shitload of homework and this damned report to finish.

"It's open," she said after a second.

The *Boadicea* didn't smell like decaying zombies anymore. It smelled like a hospital. There was a thick reek of disinfectant everywhere.

The cabin she was in had had a zombie in it. But she only knew that 'cause there wasn't any carpet. But there *were* thick rugs,

Persian or something she thought. She wasn't sure where they'd come from but they were nice. The rest of the cabin, except for some minor fittings, was pretty much what she thought a cabin in a cruise ship was supposed to look like. She'd never been on a cruise until the Plague and she wasn't planning on going on one even if somebody hit a button and made the world like it was. But it had a big bed, bigger than the one she'd had on the *Alpha*, and a really nice head. Big shower and a bath tub which she'd put to good use more than once. The head wasn't as "refined" as on the *Alpha* but all the fittings were original at least.

They'd been clearing for a week. Faith wasn't sure if it was deliberate on Captain Wilkes' part but she hadn't been near any of the cabin areas on the supermax. All she'd seen was the bowels of the ship. The usual compartments and zombie mess. Some people might have thought that was punishment. For Faith it was sort of relaxing. Once they got past a certain point, there weren't even many zombies and they had found some survivors.

She had been in on the "spa" clearance. Wilkes had paid attention on that one and they'd hit it with every Marine they had from several different entry points. There were quite a few surviving infected but it was over in ten minutes. Not a single scrum. Faith had been mildly disappointed. But it was the "professional" way to do it. And she was starting to appreciate "professional."

What she did *not* appreciate was the homework. Captain Wilkes had scrounged textbooks for her to study. Not just Marine manuals, either. Math, science, English. Chemistry. Yuck! With weekly tests. *And* he was making her do all her platoon reports, then "annotating" them. He had given her a dictionary and thesaurus, among other things, and after the first report after giving them to her told her she was "not allowed words of more than two syllables." It was worse than fucking school. "Recess" was killing zombies.

"Hey, how's the report going?" Wilkes said.

"Fine, sir," Faith said, standing to attention.

"As you were," Wilkes said, coming in and looking over her shoulder. "I would say that 'fine' would be mostly done, Lieutenant. Not stuck on the first sentence."

"I was reading Lieutenant Fontana's report, sir," Faith replied. "And trying to determine a better way to say what I was trying to say, sir. But . . . sir, what's an 'action plan'?"

"An action plan is any plan which involves action, Lieutenant,"

Wilkes said. "Direct conflict. When you told me to prepare to fire through the zombies, multiple times, and try to aim my shots so that TnTs would go through the hatch, that was an action plan."

"Battle field preparation plan, sir?" Faith asked.

"Knock on the door and make sure the zombies are awake," Wilkes said. "You're preparing the battlefield to optimize *your* strengths, kinetic projectile fire, over *their* strengths, direct contact engagement."

"So it's another way of saying 'get them into your killzone, don't go into theirs,' sir?"

"It's a more modern way of saying it," Wilkes said. "Your father's background is historical. Useful, don't get me wrong. But he tends to phrase things in a way that would be normal in a staff meeting for, say, Operation Overlord."

"That's . . . D-Day," Faith said. "Sixth of June, 1944."

"Fifth and sixth, yes," Wilkes said. "I'd expect that of your father's daughter."

"Horrible with dates, sir," Faith said. "But there's this band, Sabaton, that's got this really rocking song about it."

"Okay," Wilkes said, chuckling. "Why am I not surprised. Lieutenant, the report will keep. It's time for some professional education."

"Yes, sir," Faith said.

"Accompany me," Wilkes said, waving.

They went out of the cabin, down the corridor and around the corner to what Faith remembered as being one of the "big" cabins, the real luxury ones.

"Senior officer's country?" Faith asked.

"We don't have many of those, yet," Wilkes said, wielding the key. As he opened the door, Faith could hear people laughing. "So we appropriated it. Officially. I wrote a staff study. It was approved."

Fontana, Lieutenant Volpe, Janu and the gunny were all sitting around a table playing poker. There was a bar set up on one bulkhead and some snacks laid out.

"There really aren't enough of us for an O club," Wilkes said. "So this is the Staff NCOs and Officers' club."

"The dues are we gotta scrounge the stuff," Fontana said. "Seawolf owe you any favors?"

"Being my big sister and a pain in the ass count?" Faith asked.

"I found you some razzleberry tea, LT," Janu said, pulling some out of a cooler.

"Staff Sergeant," Faith said, taking the can and popping it. "You shouldn't have. No, wait, you should, you really, really should. Ah," she said, taking a sip. "Nectar. I shall see what my sister, terror of the seas, has in her stash. That she'll give up."

"In that case, I'm a rum drinker, ma'am," Janu said.

"No rank in the mess, by the way, Faith," Wilkes said. "Same to you, Jan."

"Yes, sir," Jan said. "That's going to be tough to manage, though, sir."

"The point to the mess is that in here, you can say to somebody that they're as full of shit as a Christmas turkey and get away with it," Wilkes said.

"I've heard that quote somewhere before, sir," Gunny Sands said. "Brotherhood of War?"

"Love that series," Fontana said.

"It's also true," Wilkes said, picking up the cards and shuffling them. "Reports and after action meetings are important. This is important, too. You can just talk and without it being official. Figure out the stuff you don't figure out in meetings. Tell somebody they're fucking up, even if they're a superior. Although, I'd appreciate nobody telling me I'm a 'cowardly fucktard.'"

"You were out of your depth, sir," Gunny Sands said. "You're a pilot, not an infantry captain. And this shit really does suck."

"Appreciate that, Tommy," Wilkes said, dealing. "Five card draw. No wilds. I really am out of my depth in clearance. I can't wait to get a stick back in my hand."

"TMI, sir," Lieutenant Volpe said. "TMI." He tossed a penny on the table.

"What are we betting for?" Faith asked, examining her cards. She'd played poker before but not a lot.

"We are not *betting*," Wilkes said. "That would be against military regulations. We are having a friendly game of cards that happens to involve some items of no particular value being on the table. Purely for the purposes of examination."

"Each cent is a dollar," Fontana said. "Against back pay."

"We get paid?" Faith said.

"Eventually, assuming that we ever have an economy again," Wilkes said. "We should get paid. Armies that don't get paid have a tendency to wither and die or revolt. We Marines won't revolt. I won't speak to wither and die."

"I think right now we're basically getting paid in booze, food and loot," Januscheitis said. "Which goes a long way to making for happy Marines."

"Then you trade the loot to the skanks on the *Money for Nothing* and you've got all the bases covered," Faith said.

"Olga is not a skank," Volpe said piously. "And our relationship is one of the mind."

"Now I know where you keep your brain, Mike," Wilkes said.

"I have an issue with basing our pay on looting, sir," Gunny Sands said. "It is corrosive to discipline."

"Totally agree," Fontana said. "And this is from an SF guy. We've had that problem historically. When people start paying more attention to what they can pick up in an area than their jobs...It can get bad."

"Especially when an officer goes dress shopping," Faith said. "That really was a bad call on my part."

"Not absolutely sure, Faith," Januscheitis said. "It's one of those legend things. It's what makes you, you, LT. We thought it was a hoot. And it wasn't like the infected ever got close."

"Still, looting is an issue," the gunny said. "In general."

"Also the only way we're getting any disposable income, Gunny," Januscheitis said. "I think we need to come up with some regs about it. It's not looting, anyway. It's salvage."

"Salvage only counts on the sea, St— Januscheitis," Gunny Sands said, gritting his teeth over the "no rank in the mess" thing.

"Gunny, with respect, everybody in those towns is dead, okay?" Januscheitis said. "If we pick up some stuff from the houses, they don't know, their relatives don't know because they're dead, too. And, no, I don't like being a damned scavenger, Gunny. But like Miss Faith said, it's all we've got as disposable income."

"I suppose we need to discuss with command some sort of scrip," Wilkes said. "There needs to be a better system than loot."

"What would people buy with it?" Volpe asked. "They're given food, clothing and shelter."

"Better food, better clothing, better shelter," Wilkes said. "We need to have an economy."

"Christ," the gunny growled. "Next thing you know there'll be bankers and loans and pawn stores."

"There already are pawn stores, Gunny," Januscheitis said.

"At least, places you can trade loot for other stuff. Better stores, better booze."

"Boats like my sister's," Faith said. "They get loaded down with booze. And stores. They offload a bunch of it but they always keep some choice stuff. Not necessarily the Navy boats," she said hastily. "But a bunch of the rescue boats are civilian. I'd guess from those. And that is salvage. And you could always trade it for dresses. Or, yeah, better clothes. Just 'cause a girl gets something from slops, doesn't mean she doesn't want something better. Okay, again, bad example."

"What are they doing with all those dresses, anyway?"

"They haven't made the announcement, but first pick goes to Marines for the Ball," Wilkes said. Then he blinked. "For their dates, I should mention. Any Marine showing up at the Ball in a dress will be thrown out."

"Well, *thanks*," Faith said. "I'm supposed to wear MarPat?"

"I mean, any *male* Marine," Wilkes said, then sighed. "I give up. You know what I mean. They'll be given a voucher for a dress that they can give to their date. One dress. Some of them are being held back but most of them will be available to choose."

"I can see the fights now," Januscheitis said.

"Speaking of which," Fontana said. "Miss Faith: Do you have a date to the Marine Corps Ball?"

Faith blushed and glanced at Januscheitis. He was studiously looking at his cards.

"On a matter of professional development," Wilkes said smoothly. "As an officer, Miss Faith, your date needs to be an officer or a civilian. Not an enlisted man of any branch. And not anyone in your chain of command."

"I'd love to be your date to the Marine Corps Ball, Lieutenant Fontana," Faith said. "Since Mike's dating that Russian sl— lady, Olga, it was you or my sister."

"Hey, Olga's a nice lady," Mike said.

"She is, Mike," Faith said. "I was just twitting you. And that way Tom gets to go. 'Cause, like, he's not a Marine."

"I am accustomed to being the odd man out," Fontana said. "Try being pretty much on your own in RC East. But I'm delighted you accepted the offer. I'd been sweating it."

"I'm sure," Faith said, batting her eyelashes. "And, no, you're not getting laid. I will have a knife."

"Do you ever go anywhere without one?" Volpe asked, grinning.

"Of course not," Faith said, flipping out her tactical. "Duh."

"Looks like a trip to the *Money* is in my future," Januscheitis said. "Based on the LT's reaction, I don't think I'll have a hard time getting a date."

"I can just see it now," Faith said. "Marines cruising the harbor, voucher in hand. 'Would you like a Paris original? There are tryouts...' What is it with guys?"

"There's a very long explanation," Fontana said. "And there's the short one. Which do you want?"

"You sound like Da," Faith said. "And I know the long one. Da put me through the lecture in various forms, getting a bit more specific each time, from about the time I was ten. The gene is selfish. Males are broadcast procreators, women are conservative. Males want to breed with as many women as possible, at least reasonably high quality ones in terms of breeding, since that's the best way to spread their genes. Women want the optimum single male. I can talk about it in more detail if you really want. With hand gestures and a diagram if somebody wants to find me a white board."

"I think we'll pass," Wilkes said. "Thank you, Faith."

"Seriously, ever seen zombies going at it?" Faith said. "I have. Not sure I'm up for that, thanks."

"Complete change of subject before we get even deeper in the dunny," Fontana said, "I think the spa op went well."

"Sure cleared it in record time," Faith said. "Not even one scrum. Sort of disappointing."

"I'm not so sure," Janu said. "Sorry, sir. The multipoint entry was... We nearly had some serious blue on blue. I think we could have done a single point entry and been okay. Pot's light."

"Kinda agree, kinda disagree, Jan," Fontana said. "I think it would have been a nightmare with hajis. But you Marines have gotten pretty good at on-point targeting. Even with a little range."

"Don't think so," Gunny Sands said. "God damn accuracy is going to shit with all this short range shit. We need some range time to dial those Marines in. Preferably a KD. Three."

"And there speaketh a Marine gunny," Fontana said, laughing. "One shot, one kill or it's a no-go."

"And the problem with that is?" Sands asked.

"Barbie guns," Faith said. "Unless you get a head shot, you're not going to knock down a zombie with a Barbie gun, Gunny, one shot, one kill, even in the heart. They just squirt more. Sometimes I gotta use two or three with my haji. And I don't know when we're going to be fighting at long range. Even when we were clearing the towns we were mostly fighting at under a hundred yards. Okay, so we're supposed to clear Gitmo. There might be some places where we are going to fire at over a hundred yards, there. I dunno. But we've got the MGs for that, right? Mostly we're going to be doing what we've been doing for a long time. I mean, what are we going to clear on the mainland, if we ever get there?"

"You think we'll clear on the mainland?" Wilkes asked. "That will be . . . I mean, we're going to get *swarmed.*"

"Da doesn't say what his plan is beyond Gitmo," Faith said. "But his goal is clearing the U.S. and getting clearance started on places like Europe and Asia. How he's going to do it, I dunno. And he won't say. Except that he knows there's not enough bullets in the *world* so it won't be bang-bang shoot a gazillion zombies. That's what he said when I asked him are we going to just shoot 'em up. 'Not enough bullets in the world. Cross that bridge when we come to it.'"

"Maybe the mechanicals?" Fontana said.

"I could see that for port cities," Wilkes said. "Anybody know how that's going?"

"According to Seawolf, you don't want to sail into the south harbor," Volpe said. "Three mechanicals and the sharks are rolling to the surface with full bellies and even the seagulls are just sitting on the bodies."

"That's gotta suck," Jan said.

"And they're fabbing more on the *Grace* right now," Volpe said. "You can see 'em working on them."

"About the clearance and accuracy issue?" Wilkes said.

"Whatever Da uses, there's going to be stuff to be cleared. Buildings. Skyscrapers . . ."

"I just sort of winced at clearing a skyscraper," Jan said. "Then I realized that one of these damned supermax is just one on its side."

"Which is why you *should* wince," Fontana said. "'Cause there's a lot more skyscrapers in the world than supermax cruise ships."

"Okay, now I'm getting a long-range picture," Wilkes said, shaking his head. "Jesus. Clearing New York."

"Fuck," Jan said, closing his eyes and bowing his head. "Fuck a freaking duck. We're gonna need *a lot* of Marines. These things are seriously a battalion objective. How many batts to clear New York?"

"Well, be that as it may, Miss Faith," the gunny said. "They had damned well be able to *shoot*. That's a damned requirement to be a Marine. You gotta be able put the bullets on target. Whatever kind of bullets you're using."

"Agreed, Gunny," Faith said. "But I'm just wondering if concentrating on five hundred and a thousand yards is a good idea. I mean . . . Sophia's a hell of a shot with a long rifle. Did you know that?"

"No," Wilkes said, leaning back.

"She took long distance competitions in her age group back home," Faith said. "But give her twenty zombies coming at her, she'll nail five. Maybe three. I'll nail fifteen. I took the tac competitions in my age group. Including, yeah, zombie tac comps. You know *I* own a Barbie gun? Well, my Da owned it but it was mine. Sweet trick-out with an Aimpoint and hundred round Beta C. Used to smoke zombie comps, which are all head shots at under fifty yards. On the other hand, those zombies moved slow and they weren't shoving into each other and moving their heads back and forth. And they'd fall down go boom with one shot. I've seen infected keep coming after you shot them in the *head* with a Barbie gun."

"Where is it?" Fontana asked.

"Back home in the safe," Faith said. "We loaded out what we needed, not what we had. Some fucker probably broke into it, too. People knew we were preppers. Point is . . . I can see where you're going, Gunny. You want Marines to be accurate. I want Marines to be able to put down zombies in compartments and corridors, fast and accurate."

"Unlike certain pilots," Lieutenant Volpe said, grinning.

"Okay, this time *I'm* going to make the point," Wilkes said, shaking his head and grinning. "Yeah, *pilot*, okay? Gimme a Seacobra and a 20 and I'll show you who's the boss, Mike."

"Aye, aye, Captain Pilot, sir," Volpe said, saluting.

"I wonder if that's the plan?" Fontana said.

"What?" Faith said.

"Okay, your 'Da' has hinted that he needed a pilot," Fontana said. "In fact, remember when we were clearing the *Iwo* and he was sort of pissed that there were no survivors in the pilot's quarters."

"Didn't need to be reminded of that, Tom," Wilkes said. "Those were my friends."

"Sorry, sir," Fontana said. "But he's been practically biting his nails for pilots. Helo pilots. So maybe...hover a helo then blow them away with 20 when they cluster?"

"Oh, please, God, yes," Wilkes said. "If there is a loving God, yes."

"Not enough 20 in a LHD," the gunny said. "Not even in a pre-po. Not for the whole mainland."

"Finding a pre-po would be sweet," Volpe said.

"Pre-po?" Faith said.

"Pre-positioned support ship," Fontana said. "Just a big roll-on roll-off freighter, sort of like a ferry, that's filled with all sorts of goodies."

"All the material support needed for a Marine Expeditionary Unit and thirty days of combat," Wilkes said.

"Sweet is right," Faith said. "Where do we get one of those?"

"Norfolk," Sands said. "There was one tied alongside and there was no plan to punch it. Or Blount Island where the MPF ships are unloaded and reloaded. The truth is, we got more ammo and supplies on the *Iwo* than we got Marines to use it."

"Which gets back to shoot training," Faith said. "So, sure, you train them on accuracy. But to be a boarding guy, you need people who can put lots of rounds on target fast and accurate. At mostly short ranges. That's different than 'did you hit the center of the black.'"

"There's more to it than that," Jan said. "We had some training in boarding and clearance. Fair amount. But we'd need more. A lot more. In gear so they get used to the weight."

"In weighted gear," Gunny Sands growled. "*Over* weighted gear. The more you sweat, the less you bleed."

"Gunny, we have so got to get you laid," Volpe said. He grinned, then winced and looked at Faith.

"Hey, don't look at *me*!" Faith said, holding up her hands. "Hello? Thirteen?"

"I think he didn't want you to be offended," Fontana said.

"Since I was a kid, I've been hanging out with guys," Faith said, shrugging. "Which was fine. We played ball. I'd threaten to kiss them and they'd run like mad. Then, all of a sudden, all they can talk about is p— girls. It was, like, what? When did *that* happen? So I'm used to it. No issues. If you say anything I don't like, I'll start talking about what happens when you forget to bring along pads. It's really godawful, you know...?"

"Okay, okay," Volpe said, holding up his hands. "We surrender."

"Glad we got that out of the way," the gunny said. "And for your information, Lieutenant, I'm married," he said, holding up his wedding ring. "And I don't fool around on deployment."

"Sorry, Gunny," Volpe said as everyone very carefully did not look around. All the dependents were back at Lejeune. Which was zombie city. "I forgot."

"No problem," Gunny Sands said. "Just looking forward to the float being done with. Wanna get home to my cold-beer."

CHAPTER 17

Come away, O human child!
To the waters and the wild
With a faery, hand in hand,
For the world's more full of weeping
than you can understand.

"The Stolen Child"
William Butler Yeats

"The Royal Netherlands Liner P/V *Saga of Amsterdam* is officially clear," Captain Wilkes said. "Two hundred and fifty-six survivors, mostly crew and, as usual, mostly associated with food services or housekeeping."

"Can we use them?" Steve asked, looking at Isham.

"Nine engineering or maintenance personnel," Isham said. "They're all onboard with working in those areas. Three passengers with significant boating or yachting experience who are in good enough mental condition to take a small boat. One is a master mariner. I've told her we're going to save her for something that needs her skill. The rest are the usual odds and sods. Some of them are still getting their heads together but I figure most of them will pitch in. Nine that are pretty much round the bend. That's starting to be a problem. We've got forty people in that sort of condition and there's not much we can do with them

213

except lock 'em in a cabin. Which freaks them the fuck out. The support people are mostly Indonesian. Some of them are already working in cleaning crews finishing up on the *Boadicea* and the couple of boats we've pulled in and hadn't cleaned up."

"We'll take the next one down the line," Steve said. "Did you intentionally finish clearing just in time for the birthday of the Marine Corps, Captain?"

"Let's say it put a little relish in the hotdog, sir," Wilkes said, grinning. "I told the guys I couldn't promise them a day off if they finished by the ninth but I could try to swing it."

"Do you want it off the day of or the day after?" Steve asked.

"Short day doing initial reconnaissance on the Tenth, sir," Wilkes said. "Stop operations at sixteen-thirty. Then the day after off."

"I can live with that," Steve said.

"We believe we can increase the pace on the next one, sir," Wilkes said. "If we can get some logistics support."

"Define," Steve said.

"Lieutenant?" Wilkes said, turning to Faith.

"The guys can carry their assault packs on clearance, sir," Faith said. "But they clock out on rounds, anyway. We're averaging about nine rounds per infected. We need to get that down, but that's where we're at. That means that the assault pack and basic load only allows sixty kills."

"I hadn't done that math," Steve said, nodding.

"Nine rounds is really phenomenal, sir," Wilkes pointed out. "The average in Iraq was six *thousand* rounds per stepped on kill."

"Six thousand?" Isham said. "You have got to be joking!"

"It was *sixty* thousand in the Korean War," Steve said. "Lots of use of machine guns. Different situation. So, only sixty infected per Marine per reasonable load. And the answer is?"

"We have spare magazines, sir," Faith said. "We pretty much brought every mag we could find on the *Iwo*. If we could get support in having spares loaded and moved forward, the Marines wouldn't have to go all the way back to the entry area then reload their mags. The trip sometimes takes ten minutes and reloads take up to thirty. That's nearly an hour all around. They're not bitching about that, they just sort of think that's what you do. We discussed this with the gunny and he thinks we're coddling them, but it would just make clearance more efficient."

"Loading and moving are two different things," Steve said. "I can see finding people to load... Jack?"

"That we can find people for," Isham said cautiously. "Carrying it through the ship? That's going to be tougher."

"My gunners would do it," Lieutenant Chen said. "My shooters are really chomping at the bit."

"I've got an alternate, there, I was going to bring up," Steve said. "We've got weapons. Put out the usual recruiting call. See how many people we can scrounge up. Put some sort of bennie on it. If we can do it, we'll do it. At the very least, we'll get the mags loaded which is a big part of the time. Okay, next point.

"Littoral Clearance Divisions one and two: Your boats, as you just noted, are being under utilized in this operation. We really don't need the gunboats to hold the pier since it's blocked and we're detached from it, anyway. So I'm going to send you out on light town clearance, again. But sans Marines. You'll have to decide if you want to send people ashore or not. Overall command will be Lieutenant Chen. Chen: One of your gunners is a former soldier, isn't he?"

"Gunner's Mate Mcgarity, sir," Chen said.

"Is he familiar with medium machine guns?" Steve asked. "I don't think that if you go ashore you should be under gunned."

"Landings are sort of a Marine thing, sir," Captain Wilkes said.

"The majority of landing parties, historically, were Navy, Captain," Steve said. "The Marine Corps did not really start to study large-scale over-beach landings until the 1930s. Most of the force that took Tripoli were Navy sailors. And if I've got a choice of Marines clearing small towns and sailors fighting through the bowels of a ship or vice versa, guess which way I'm going to decide?"

"Point, sir," Wilkes said. "No offense."

"I'd thought about it, Captain," Steve said, waving. "And Mcgarity, at least, is really a soldier."

"Tanker, sir," Lieutenant Chen pointed out. "But he trained on foot patrolling for a deployment to Afghanistan. And some of the other gunners are more than willing. They sort of enjoyed going ashore in La Puntilla and La Playa. Some stayed onboard, of course. Could I make joining the teams voluntary?"

"As long as it doesn't interfere with discipline," Steve said. "Just cruise down the coast and clear the towns as you come to them and they look good. I hope I don't have to warn you to watch the rocks and shoals. Bring spare prize crews with you who can pick up any useful looking boats. I want a lot of boats for the Atlantic crossing. The more boats we have, the more footprint we have for finding survivors at sea. Clear the towns if you think it's worthwhile."

"Yes, sir," Chen said.

"You're going to have to mostly resupply on your own," Steve said. "If you run low on ammo, we can run some down to you. But other than that, independent command. Run with it."

"Yes, sir," Chen said.

"Jack, we've got more gunboats in preparation, right?" Steve said.

"Two more are undergoing renovation right now," Isham said. "And we've got four yachts that are ready for sea. We're running low on people who know how to run them."

"Lieutenant Kuzma," Steve said. "Start a class on basic boat operation. No more than three days. If they can drive it without hitting the sides of the harbor, use the radio more or less and put out a fire, they're good."

"You're serious?" Kuzma said, wincing. "For an Atlantic crossing?"

"Oh, yeah," Steve said. "And the big class is on how to unrep at sea."

"Oh, God, sir," Chen said, covering his face with his hands.

"One boat can cover, at most, a ten-mile radius for search and rescue," Steve said seriously. "Counting the small yachts we have, what, fourteen?"

"Yeah," Isham said.

"That's, only a two-hundred-eighty-mile footprint," Steve said. "A hundred and forty boats gives us a twenty-eight-*hundred*-mile footprint."

"That is a point," Kuzma said. "And a lot more ships that have to be cleared."

"We'll take the already experienced people and put them in a follow-on squadron or squadrons," Steve said. "With Marine boarding parties and prize and salvage crews. See if we can find another boat like the *Pit Stop* to shuttle supplies forward to the main flotilla."

"You know the sort of people who will sign up for that are the sort of people we need for everything else, right?" Isham said, shaking his head. "We only have so many people."

"They have to have done a scut job, first," Steve said. "Cleaning up gear, cleaning compartments, what have you. But if they can read a map, use a radio and sort of not hit stuff, we need the boats."

"And . . ." Isham said. "Steve, look, I'm up to my eyeballs in work already. You want to bump up the number of small boats? I mean times ten? You got any clue how much logistics that is?"

"Yes," Steve said. "Need a hand?"

"Oh, hell, yeah!" Isham said. "You see my enormous staff, right?"

"First of all, if you've got numbers to crunch, toss it to the boats," Steve said. "By which I mean the subs. And speaking of looking for craft, that's a group that's going to start being more actively involved. At a certain level, if it's not in an AO we can effect, I'd rather just not know. But they'll sweep one wing of the movement. They've got sonar, radar and people who will actually maintain a watch. They can't interact but they can spot. One flotilla of fast response boats with them."

"Suggestion, sir," Chen said.

"Always," Steve said. "Please."

"Cigarette boats," Chen said. "Based around one of the megayachts. Something needs to be cleared, the teams head out on those."

"They use gas, right?" Isham said.

"Yes," Chen said.

"So now I gotta not only find gas, but have a way to carry it," Isham said. "Thanks, Zack."

"Glad to be a buddy, Jack," Chen said, grinning. "You can pump the diesel out of one of the tanks on the megas."

"They've got a spare gas tank, anyway," Wilkes said. "And an avgas tank. Speaking of which, you can spot stuff really well with a helo. Hinta, hinta, Captain."

"Qualified on a Lynx?" Steve asked.

"Does it have a Dash one, sir?" Wilkes said.

"Are your airframe mechanics qualified on getting it up and running?" Steve asked. "We got parts? Thing's been sitting as deck cargo in storms for six months, Captain."

"Point, sir," Wilkes said, shrugging.

"We'll put that on the to-do list on the crossing," Steve said. "At least get it surveyed. If it's working, do you think it would make an okay trainer?"

"Want to learn to fly a chopper, sir?" Wilkes said.

"We're going to need a buttload of chopper pilots at some point, Captain," Steve said. "And airframe mechanics and all the rest. After we clear Gitmo, you'll definitely be turning in the rifle to start working on that program. But that's for later. Lieutenant Chen's concept has merit. So, Chen, look for fast ocean-going boats with range as well. And, yes, some source of gasoline for them."

"Tools, parts, fittings..." Isham said. "Seriously, Captain, I'm going to need some help, here."

"I'll find you some," Steve said.

"I could really use..." He paused and frowned and looked at Faith for a second. "You know, Zumwald is an asshole and I know he's on your shit list. But he's really underutilized."

"I kind of like that he's in charge of cleaning our gear," Faith said. "Serves him right. Sir."

"Your point is worth considering," Steve said. "Okay, Marine Corps Ball, continue clearance on Sierra Two. USCG personnel to shift to classes on small boat operations for available personnel. LitClear to go, well, LitClear and collect said vessels. Work on an expansion plan for an unknown number of small boats. Chen, you've got about ten days, tops. All clearance to be complete by last week of November. We pull out November twentieth. All clear?"

"Got it, sir," Isham said. "And get me some more staff."

"I'll work on that," Steve said.

CHAPTER 18

Freedom is not free, but the U.S. Marine Corps will pay most of your share.

Ned Dolan

"I'm totally freaking out!" Faith said, adjusting her uniform as she approached the doors to the ballroom. She'd been informed as the "junior Marine" she had to give the toast and was, therefore, required to be in uniform. Her beautiful dress was relegated to the closet. Worse, all she had was MarCam.

"You'll be fine," Olga said.

"Easy for you to say!" Faith said. "You get to wear girl clothes!"

"Take a deep breath," Olga said, hand on the door. "Ready?"

"Ready," Faith said.

"Do you think you could increase your father's knowledge base, Lieutenant?" Steve said at breakfast the next morning.

"I'll try, Da," Faith said, holding her hand up to her face. She was wearing oversized glasses and make-up, which was unusual to say the least. And she didn't seem to want to move her hand away from the left side of her face.

"Is there a reason that the gunnery sergeant is sporting one hell of a shiner?" Steve asked.

"What happens at the Ball, stays at the Ball, Da," Faith said, chewing carefully....

CHAPTER 19

They got the Library of Alexandria. They're not getting mine.

Bumper sticker (with quote flanked
by silhouettes of pistol and rifle)

"Hey, Ernest," Steve said as Zumwald tentatively entered his office. "Grab a chair. I understand you're a scotch drinker?" He laid out two glasses and pulled out a bottle.

"So what's this? Last drink before you put me on a desert island?" Zumwald said, picking up the glass and sniffing it. "Strathclyde? Where'd you get Strathclyde?"

"My daughter Sophia clears a lot of ships," Steve said. "I mentioned that. There's always booze left. Zombies don't drink it. Cheers, mate," Steve said, taking a sip. "By the way, is it Ernest or do you prefer to be called something else? I doubt, sincerely, it's Ernie."

"Nobody's called me Ernie since I was in grade school," Zumwald said. "Ernest, usually."

"Cheers, Ernest," Steve said.

"Seriously, why are you being nice to me?" Zumwald asked. "What do you want?"

"It's like any abusive relationship," Steve said. "I smacked you around, at least emotionally, you did what I needed you to do, and you did it well according to the gunny. Now I'm being nice."

"As long as I keep doing what you need, right?" Zumwald

said, chuckling. "Seriously, you should have been in my industry. What, you need a movie done?"

"No," Steve said, then frowned. "And, yes. But there's a kid who used to do documentaries, small things, and he's working on that. This is history in the making. I'm not...I'm not a narcissist. But that's the reality. At least if we manage to keep the ball rolling. Which is why, yeah, I'll slap you around or feed you good scotch, whatever it takes, if I need something to keep that ball rolling."

"So what balls do you need rolled?" Zumwald asked.

"You got someone who can take over the whole gear thing?" Steve asked.

"I didn't get the pick of the litter," Zumwald said balefully. "But, yeah, I got somebody who can probably handle running it. Do I get a reprieve, finally?"

"I only ever saw that as both something I needed done and something that you'd do well but still hate," Steve said. "And as I said, you've managed it well. Even though, yeah, you got the bottom of the barrel to do it. This is different. We're going to be closing out the liner clearance in about a week. Then we'll do some reconfiguration. After that, we're going to cross the Atlantic. Isham's been looking at the logistics of that and it's going to be tough. And he's buried in the day-to-day and can't concentrate on planning it."

"So you want me to plan it?" Zumwald said. "What's in it for me?"

"You get to quit being a washing girl?" Steve said. "There's not a lot in the way of really good staff available but you get your pick of that. As for the rest, we'll figure something out. This is... what was that movie, Ben Stiller thing about some movie that was being made in the jungle..."

"*Tropic Thunder*?" Zumwald said, frowning. "What a crock."

"I'd wondered if you were the original for Les Grossman," Steve said, grinning.

"No, I wasn't," Zumwald said. "And Cruise can bite my ass."

"He's probably a zombie at this point," Steve said. "Still, the point remains. This is the deal zone. What do you want? And don't say, 'the world back the way it was.' Nobody can do that."

"What is there?" Zumwald said. "I mean, really? What I'd like is a steak."

"Don't we all," Steve said, grinning. "You'll get the top ration level. Lieutenant equivalency. Isham's still only a lieutenant and I can't really put you ahead of him. But it's the same stuff I eat. I'm thinking of sending one of the boats up to do a lobster run to Bermuda. But we'll at least have that once we reach the Caribbean. And the same on booze ration. Which means by the bottle, which I happen to know you've already been arranging. But you can just hit the Class Six for it. And the good stuff when available," he added, raising his still barely touched glass.

"Better accommodations?" Zumwald said. "I'm getting sick of my roommate. Fucker picks his nose. I can't believe I *have* a roommate. I didn't have a roommate in *college*."

"Deluxe cabin on the *Boadicea*," Steve said. "To yourself. Share a steward. Probably with Isham. I'll see if one of the ones that's still intact is available."

"Reluctantly," Zumwald said. "It's not exactly the Ritz."

"I just realized the other day that I'm running a commune," Steve said. "Which is odd since I loathe communism."

"What?" Zumwald said. "Sort of out of the blue, there."

"Not really," Steve said, musingly. "I'm sort of puzzled by it myself. But the overall drive is from everyone according to his ability, to everyone according to their needs. More like classic Soviet economy, though. For example, I'm offering you the equivalent of a better apartment and access to the good stores to run some stuff that I don't want to be bothered with. You get the similarity?"

"Yeah," Zumwald said. "And they made lousy films."

"Oh, they made lousy everything," Steve said, chuckling. "But the military has a lot of similarities. Another fact I realized the other night. In the military you get relatively little pay and some generalized living support, not much, for what is really seriously lousy work. You've seen the results. Then there's the guys running the ships, the cooks... It's really a communism but there's a reason that it works. And that this works, sort of. Where you from, Ernest? Where's home?"

"I've lived in L.A. most of my life," Zumwald said, staring at him like he was wondering if Smith had lost it. "But really the City's home."

"Where?" Steve asked. "The City is many cities in one."

"Brooklyn," Zumwald said.

"Family?" Steve asked.

"I got the word that's not something to talk about, mostly," Zumwald said. "Slew of greedy ex-wives. No kids. Got myself fixed after my first close call."

"You like New York?" Steve said. "It's pretty clear you're all about number one. But is it something you miss?"

"Yeah," Zumwald admitted after a few moments. "Yeah. I do. What's your point?"

"We saw the bridges fall," Steve said, looking out the window at the relatively pleasant harbor. If you ignored the fins. "We were in New York harbor, the Hudson, as a back-up plan for my brother. We went to the last concert in New York city, in Washington Square Park. They had the final blackout that night. The concert had generators for its lights. The infected closed in. We figured it was time to leave."

"I went to NYU," Zumwald said. "I spent a lot of time in Washington Square Park once upon a time. Hell, I was beat up in a peace protest in Washington Square Park."

"I wouldn't have pictured you as a peace activist," Steve said, grinning. "That's a little too altruistic."

"Ah, there was this chick," Zumwald said, shrugging. "Nearly ex number one. I got out after the beating and finished my film degree. Did a couple of, yeah, documentaries about the horrors of capitalism. Then I realized the money was in doing the background work and went to the dark side. Never looked back." He shrugged again. "What's your point?"

"Want to walk in Washington Square Park again?" Steve asked. "No Tyvek suit. No mask. No zombies. No guns?"

"Good luck," Zumwald said. "You're not going to do that with thirty marines and some chick thinks she's Arnie. '*Hasta la vista*, zombies.'"

"No, I'm not," Steve said, leaning forward. "It's going to take a huge force. It's going to take thousands and thousands of people sacrificing their time and effort and intelligence to push that ball. It's going to take hundreds, thousands, of troops. And for every combat troop it's going to take ten people supporting them. And that's going take really smart, skilled, organizers. It's going to take one hell of an organization.

"Once we get the subs opened up, there are going to be a slew of those guys. But they're all military. They're . . . narrow on certain processes and concepts. It's going to take a lot of people, Ernest, to clear New York to the point where kids can run free in Washington Square Park. The question is, Ernest, whether you want to be part of that? I mean, seriously, what do you really want? Who are you?"

"What I want, yeah, you can't give me," Ernest said. "I want my fucking corner office, my fucking PA, a thousand people running around like a kicked ant-hill if I'm having a bad day. And the parties, and my mansion and the women and, yeah, the coke. You can't give me all that back."

"I can get you the corner office and the PA," Steve said. "Eventually. Assuming I can get done what I've said I will get done. And so far, so good. We've got over two thousand people in six months when we started with four. We cleared a supermax in a week where it had taken three. We've got a shot at getting vaccine for the sub crews. I've got a concept to clear the mainland. It's going to take one hell of a lot more people than we're going to find in Gitmo or crossing the Atlantic, but it's a plan. And it's going to need managers. And, yeah, that plan includes clearing New York. And DC and all the big cities. Not because anybody can really live in them, but they're going to be in the way. All the logistics run through them. And they're emotional targets. Hell, I even plan to clear L.A. some day. You can at least go back to your mansion and get your stuff."

"So what's this plan?" Zumwald said, interested. "Because you're talking about the fucking United States. It takes four and a half hours to fly across in a 747. Bit less than four in a G. It's pretty fucking big."

"I don't talk about plans until I'm sure they're possible," Steve said. "But I'll give you one for New York. You saw the mechanical clearers, right?"

"This is Tenerife, buddy," Zumwald said, laughing. "You're going to need a shit-load of those to clear New York."

"Hell, by the time we get to New York, we're going to have to have *thousands*," Steve said. "And a factory, probably in the Miami commercial port, churning them out. Not to mention dozens of barge derricks to put them into place. Guess who I plan on putting in charge of the factory?"

"Not me I hope," Zumwald said. "Although Miami's not a bad place. How the hell you going to really clear it, though? The zombies are only going to walk so far to get to the traps."

"Like I said," Steve said. "I don't talk about the whole idea until I'm sure it's going to work. And, not you: Isham. He knows manufacturing. He had a manufacturing company. One of the reasons I recruited him in Bermuda. Because I knew what I wanted to do back *then*. But I can clear New York. Make it zombie free? No. But close enough. I can let you walk in Washington Square Park. I can give you back Brooklyn. But it will take *you* working for it, too."

"You'll do it anyway," Zumwald said, shrugging. "You said so."

"It'll be easier with people who know how to organize," Steve said, steepling his fingers. "You're a test. How do I motivate people to help me achieve these goals who used to have everything? And who had everything because they're good at organization. You're about as selfish a person as I'm going to find. Most really selfish people died from this Plague because humans can't survive without other humans to help them. If I can find your levers, then it's potentially possible to, yeah, clear New York and DC and the Hole and, hell, the West Coast. So, do you want to be the King of Flatbush?"

"Not Flatbush," Zumwald said, snorting. "Please. Riverside if anything."

"Okay, Riverside."

"You're just going to give me Riverside?" Zumwald said, snorting again. "Like you've got that power?"

"By then, yes," Steve said. "There will have to be a way to redistribute resources. All of it, no. Most of it, yes. Can I absolutely promise that? No. If I have the authority when that time comes, you get all the property in Riverside not held by survivors or people with provenance."

"Seriously?" Zumwald said.

"Seriously," Steve said. "I don't want to live there. And there aren't going to be many people surviving in those mansions. There may have to be some lag period to vestment. Some of the owners may have fled elsewhere and survived. But when the vestment period lapses, it's all yours."

"You're just going to give people land?" Zumwald said.

"*Somebody* is going to have to," Steve said. "When Ohio was originally settled, the plots that were granted were about ten square miles per homesteader. One of the reasons it was so easy to colonize, by the way, was that it was well maintained by Native American tribes who had been wiped out by, guess what, plague. There will be scavengers before we're done clearing Miami. Distributing salvage will be one of the tough parts of this job at that point. As will enforcing it."

"That's assuming you can clear it," Zumwald said. "And you're still a bit cadgy about that."

"Yes, I am," Steve said. "It's going to be a massive endeavor. And most areas the best that we'll be able to achieve is something like La Puntilla. There aren't many infected. You can move around if you're armed and know how to use a weapon."

"That makes the property a little less attractive," Zumwald said.

"Oh, *think*, Ernest," Steve snapped. "You're smart. Apply your brain. You want it cleared out? You hire a salvage company that has some specific rights. They have the guns. They clear it out for some of the salvage. It's not hard."

"And if they turn on me?" Zumwald said, sourly.

"That is actually what government is for, Ernest," Steve said, shaking his head. "Enforcement of contract law. That is, at base, pretty much its entire purpose. Everything else just gets ladled on by idiots."

"That's not communism," Zumwald said.

"I said I'm running a commune *now*," Steve said. "Free market will kick in pretty quick once we're not stuck on these boats. Hell, it already has. There's trading going on. People think it's black market. I think it's great. I just need to figure out, again, what is and is not workable. Not 'legal' or illegal. Just workable. So contracts can be enforced by the government and not black marketeers. I'm a free market guy. Just doesn't work when we're all still on the ragged edge. Then it's tyranny and, yeah, communism. Or something like it. We'll get to free market. But we're not going to see L.A., or New York, as you remember it, any time soon. Not in our lifetime. Not in our great-grandchildren's."

"Yeah," Zumwald said.

"So, returning to the original issue," Steve said. "I need someone to do the pre-planning for our next float. And future missions. If you take the job, you'll start working with Isham today. You'll need to get a basis for what's required. Then build a plans and ops team and figure out the float. For which you won't have much time."

"Great," Zumwald said, frowning.

"And the quarters and the rest," Steve said. "The main thing, though, is the power and the prestige. The multitudes bowing and scraping. And, eventually, Riverside."

"If you can swing it," Zumwald said.

"There will be politics involved," Steve said, shrugging. "You're generally good at that. If you have a reason to support my position, that's a benefit. And, as with Isham, if you *fuck* me you had better run far and fast."

"You really did miss your calling, Smith," Zumwald said, laughing.

"Oh, thank God," Sophia said as the *Señorita* cleared the harbor and hit the first rollers.

A slight squall had come through the night before and the water was a bit lively. But nothing that the *Señorita* couldn't handle and it seemed as eager to hit the waves as its captain. Not so much the crew.

"I think I've sort of lost my sea legs," Paula said. "I am mildly queasy."

"Not me," Sophia said. "I am sooo ready to go see some new harbors that *don't* stink of rotting bodies and rotting liners."

"Can I come up?" Olga asked.

The girl had been a late addition. Turned out she had significant civilian shooting experience.

"Sure," Sophia said. "As long as you promise not to hijack the boat."

"Very humorous," Olga said, sitting down on one of the benches of the flying bridge. "You forget, I was the bait, not the hook."

"You're forgiven," Sophia said. "And I was joking. I wouldn't have let you on my boat if I thought you were going to take it over."

"How the hell did you end up on the *Money*?" Paula said. "You said you were an American. Where did the Russian accent go?"

"I can get it back if you want," Olga said, with a Slavic accent. "But I grew up in Chicago. And I'm not Russian, I'm Ukrainian. Yes, there's a difference and yes, I care. I moved to the U.S. when I was six with my family. My father sort of had to leave. The FSB had recruited him and he told them to fuck off. They did not take it well."

"FSB?" Paula said.

"Russian spy agency," Sophia said. "Was he normally a spy?"

"Sort of," Olga said. "He was mostly a foreign military attaché prior to that. FSB wanted him to . . . do some things in the Middle East he did not agree with. It wasn't even spying. It was, basically, money laundering. When he said no, well, there were issues? It was not even legal as far as legal ever matters in Russia. He became a liability. I don't really remember it very well except a safe-house in Turkey. We were there for some time. Then we were in Chicago where I grew up."

"So how'd you end up with Mr. 'I have a Rocket Launcher'?" Sophia asked.

"I was on a modeling tour in Europe," Olga said, shrugging. "You know, it is hard to get a job as an international model these days if you are *not* Russian? So I told them I was Russian. I speak Russian. And read it. And French. And Spanish. German. Italian. Ukrainian obviously."

"Wow," Paula said. "I mean, why?"

"*I* wanted to be a spy," Olga said, shrugging. "I applied to the CIA. I was turned down. I did not meet the psychological profile. Oppositional Defiance Disorder. Basically, I have a hard time taking orders from idiots."

"Don't think of me as an idiot and I won't give you an idiotic order," Sophia said. "But if I give you one, you'd better do it. Because it's probably going to mean surviving or dying."

"You I don't mind," Olga said. "Or I wouldn't have joined your crew. Don't ask me about Nazar. So I was in Spain with the troupe. When the Plague hit, they shut down travel. And all my guns were in America. In a zombie apocalypse. I was quite upset."

"You should have seen Faith when they told her she had to be disarmed in New York," Sophia said. "Then they gave her a taser and that was a mistake. What kind of guns?"

"I like that your family prefers the AK series," Olga said. "I really do think it's superior to the M16 series in many ways. Much more reliable. They say it is less accurate but that is at longer ranges. The round is not designed for long range."

"I can hit at a thousand meters with my accurized AK," Sophia said. "It's a matter of knowing the ballistics. It's not real powerful at that range, but try doing the same thing with an M4. I'll wait."

"Oh, jeeze, you two," Paula said. "Get a room."

"So continue with how you got on the yacht," Sophia said. "We don't want our cook getting all woozy with gun geeking."

"We were called by the agency and asked if anyone wanted

to 'catch a ride' on a yacht," Olga said. "When they said who owned the boat...I nearly said no. We all knew Nazar. Or at least of him. Not a nice man, as you might have noticed. We knew what we were getting into. But then we were told he had vaccine..." She shrugged again.

"Accepting Nazar's offer was perhaps not the worst decision I have made in my life. I survived. Not how I would have preferred to survive, but I was vaccinated and I survived. But I did not even hint that I knew more about his men's weapons than they did. They were pigs. Tough guys. But none of them were military and none of them really knew what they were doing with them. When they brought out the RPG, I nearly peed myself. Irinei had no idea what he was doing with it. I don't think he even knew the safety was off."

"You know how to use an RPG?" Sophia said.

"My family liked the United States very much," Olga said sadly. "We all like guns and anything that goes boom. And in the U.S., you could find people who had licenses for *anything*. I've fired an RPG, yes."

"Well, if we find an RPG you can have it," Sophia said.

"Oh, *thank you*, Captain!" Olga said, clapping her hands girlishly.

"But we'll be keeping the rounds and the launcher *separate*," Sophia said.

"Oh, my, yes," Olga said. "And both will have to be in a well-sealed container. This salt air would cause corrosion quickly."

"I guess you miss your guns?" Paula said. "That's not a request for an inventory and loving description of each, by the way. Got that enough from Faith."

"I do," Olga said. "But I miss my books more."

"Books," Paula said. "Now you're talking my language."

"I have more books than shelves," Olga said. "And I had many shelves. I collect old manuscripts when I can afford them."

"If we do any land clearance, look in the libraries and big houses," Sophia said. "I bet around here you can probably pick up some great stuff."

"This is okay?" Olga said. "We can, salvage?"

"If there's time and if we clear the town," Sophia said. "Sure."

"Oh, thank you, Captain!" Olga said, kissing her on the cheek.

"Okay, now you *definitely* need to get a room."

CHAPTER 20

The vote, I thought, means nothing to women. We should be armed.

Edna O'Brien

"Okay," Sophia said. "Don't think we're clearing this one."

The town of El Chorillo was not at waterline. The *marina* was at the waterline. The *town* was on top of a two-hundred-foot bluff. Most of it. The rest was condominiums built into the bluff in racks up to the top of what was a small mountain. There was a large public park right at the waterline behind a massive rock breakwater.

"Señorita," Chen radioed. *"Drive into the marina and check it out. All I see is sailboats."*

"Roger," Sophia said, engaging the motor on slow. "Paula. Get up forward and check the water."

"Roger," Paula said.

"Check the water?" Olga said. She'd changed into a bathing suit. The girl was about covered in fine scars including one on her chest that didn't look like a surgery scar. More like a knife. Sophia had decided she wasn't going to ask.

"There was a sunken boat in the harbor at La Playa," Sophia said, entering the marina carefully. "Nobody noticed it until the last day and thank goodness nobody hit it. But we're getting extra careful. There's no real channel here. That shouldn't be an issue. Hopefully."

"All clear so far," Paula called.

From the entrance, Sophia could make the same determination. There were some offshore power boats, though. And the usual zombies. Most of them were in shadow, asleep. But she counted at least six in view. When you saw six, you knew there were more like two dozen. Most of the sailboat cabins were open. They'd pop up like fleas if she cranked the radio.

"No really ocean-capable yachts," she radioed. "I mean, thirty-fives, but that's it. There are some big Bayliner kind of boats. Is that what we're looking for, over?"

"*Do they look hell on wheels fast, over?*"

"Negative," Sophia said. "Thirty maybe thirty-five knots."

"*I'd say this is a bust.*"

"Roger," Sophia said, backing and filling in the turning basin. "Headed back out."

"*Division, Guppy.*"

"*Go, Gup.*"

"*We going to shoot 'em up, over?*"

"*Negative. We're under time to find boats and such. Only where there's a good salvage target.*"

"*Okay, but you see the survivors, over?*"

"Survivors?" Olga said, sitting up and shading her eyes.

"*Top of the cliff. Set of condos. Waving a sheet. Bunch of 'em. Over.*"

"Shit," Sophia said, looking up. "Son of a bitch."

The condo had ropes hanging from several of the balconies as well as growing plants. There was exterior piping that looked as if it was used for collecting rainwater. Several groups of people were trying to attract their attention. There were quite a few survivors. At least thirty.

"*Boise, you got your periscope up, over?*"

"*Roger, LitClearOne. We confirm multiple survivors.*"

"*Can you get up with Squadron and retrans the video? I'm pretty sure this is not a security team objective, over.*"

"*Stand by.*"

"We could do this," Olga said. "We can't just leave them!"

"Olga," Sophia said. "You can shoot. You had to qualify for the position. That's different from fighting as part of a fire team up to the condos then clearing those. Hang on. Division, going noise hot to demonstrate the issue to my new security people."

Sophia had been barely puttering along. The *Señorita*'s exhaust was below the waterline and she didn't make much noise. Now she turned on the stereo and cranked it.

As the piano opening of "Roland the Headless Thompson Gunner" boomed across the marina, zombies started pouring from everywhere. Sure enough, they'd been sleeping in the sailboats. Now they were howling. And their howling started to set off every zombie in the town. It was apparent that there were at least hundreds if not thousands.

"Oh," Olga said, looking around.

"His comrades fought beside him," Sophia sang as she puttered over to the public park. There was a line of buoys marking a "no crossing" zone and she puttered right up by it then dropped her anchor. "But of all the Thompson gunners, Roland was the best..."

"So the CIA decided, they wanted Roland dead..." Olga sang in harmony. She'd gone below and gotten her M4 while the boat was being repositioned. "Permission to do some target practice, Captain?" she sang in time to the song.

"Division, doing some catenary target practice," Sophia said.

"*Roger*, Señorita."

"*Jeepers*," the skipper of the *Boise* said. "COB, I'm defining this as a morale boost video. Retrans to the rest of the boats."

"On that, sir," the Chief of Boat said. "*Bella Señoritas* indeed. Damn those are some fine legs."

"You betcha."

"It is hard to hit them with a moving boat," Olga said. She was laid out in the prone position on the sundeck forward. "Or are they not noticing the five five six? There is not much rocking."

"Each," Sophia said. "Both. Takes a lot of practice." They'd both put on hearing protection.

One of the group of zombies lined up on the waterfront finally stumbled over and fell. When it did, the group fell on it, ripping at it with their teeth.

"Gross," Olga said, continuing to fire.

Seagulls clustered around, trying to find a way through the infected. Which drew more infected. Some of them waded out into the water. Then one went under and the water turned red. The others didn't seem to notice. They just stopped, waving their arms angrily, slapping the water and howling, when they were low-chest deep. Another went under. Then another.

"Swimming is contraindicated," Paula shouted. She'd put in earplugs.

"Are those two screwing?" Olga asked.

Sophia picked up a pair of binos and looked through them.

"Yup," she said, lowering the binos. "They do that when there are these feeding frenzies. They stay away from each other till there's a source of food like this. Then they swarm and tussle over it. Sometimes they start screwing in the middle of the tussle. You'll see a male run down a female, or sometimes a smaller male, and try to eat it and screw it at the same time. Although usually it's screw then eat."

"Gross," Olga said, taking another shot.

"Don't get Faith started on it," Sophia said. "A couple of times when she's been in scrums, the males realize she's female. There's no way to get through on her gear but she still doesn't like it."

"What do you do?" Olga asked. "I mean, if you're in a . . . what was the word?"

"Scrum," Sophia said. "Basically, if you're at the bottom of the dog pile. There's a reason that Faith carries a lot of knives. Apparently they get less romantic when you cut their parts off."

"Lots of knives," Olga said. "Got it."

"Yes, you did," Sophia said. "Oh, you meant the knives. But you hit that last one."

"I was aiming for the one next to him," Olga said. "This is hard."

"Señorita, *Division.*"

"Division, *Señorita,*" Sophia answered in a Spanish accent. "*Aqui,* over."

"*Bringing up the gunboats. Squadron is punching down a Marine team. We're to do the zombie boogie, primary clearance at dawn. Sending DivTwo down to the next cluster to check it out.*"

"Roger, Division."

"I wonder which Marines they're sending," Paula said.

"Three guesses," Sophia said. "And Hope and Charity were unavailable."

"Zombie boogie?" Olga asked.

"We crank the music all night," Sophia said. "Have a party. Lots of lights."

"Flares," Paula said. "Fireworks, if we've got 'em."

"Then in the morning, well, party's over, we politely ask any zombies who have turned up to lie down, be good zombies and enjoy their afterlife."

"Now is when I would like to be on the gunboats," Olga said as the boats began to jockey into position. "If I went over there and asked them nicely, do you think they would let me play with their *big* guns."

"I'm sure they'd let you play with anything you'd like," Sophia said. "You can probably stop by during the party."

"So you're talking about a real party," Olga said, looking over at her.

"Pretty much, yeah," Sophia said. "Booze, snacks, trying to carry on a conversation over the music cranked up to atomic level. There's usually not nudity or anything. And since we're as close as you get to the cops, you don't have to worry about them breaking it up. But I need to get the boat turned around, now that the gunboats are in position. Have to have the speakers facing the beach, you know?"

Olga watched as the crews got the .50s set up and loaded. Then they opened fire.

The big bullets smashed the crowd of infected into zombie goo in seconds. The seagulls were properly thankful.

So were the people up on the cliff. They were waving fit to die. Olga could see that some of them were crying. Then someone apparently found some spray-paint and started waving a badly painted American flag. The stars were black dots but it was the thought that counted.

Olga waved to the group, then realized she really should have put on some sunscreen.

"Division One. Captain's call, Señorita, *Nineteen hundred hours."*
"Paula, we'll need to lay out some of the special stores."
"On it, Captain."

"Why am I not surprised," Sophia said drily, as Faith stepped onto the wash deck.

"Shewolf...Arriving..." Olga intoned over the intercom.

"Oh, good God, Sis," Faith said, laughing. "You're really going over the top, huh?"

"It's a captain's call," Sophia said. "Should we be less than formal? I didn't have a bosun's whistle. I looked for a wave file on my computer, but the closest I could find was something from Star Trek. And it ain't, actually, a bosun's whistle. Now get out of the way, Lieutenant, my boss is coming alongside."

"LitDivOne, Arriving..."

"Hello Seaman Recruit Zelenova," Chen said, waving at the girl on the flying bridge. She had at least donned shorts and T-shirt for the "captain's call." "Is she shooting for..."

"Played Starcraft, have you, sir?" Sophia said, laughing. "Hey, Olga, give 'em the Valkyrie thing..."

"'Valkyrie...prepared,'" Olga intoned.

"Oh," Chen said, bending over as if punched. "That accent. That's not even Russian. It's German or Swedish or something."

"She used to do voice acting," Sophia said. "And turns out she's Ukrainian. Sort of. So, now that you're here, sir..."

"Let's get started," Chen said. "After you, Lieutenant."

"One of the reasons to have this here is that Ensign Smith has the big plasma," Chen said. The music was being pumped to the gunboats, which had been refitted with big speakers and was turned down on the Señorita so they could discuss the plan. "And we have actual intel this time."

He'd already connected a laptop to the port on the TV and now brought up a video file. It showed the complex from a high, sideways angle. He froze it as it showed a group on the roof, then zoomed in several times until their faces were clearly visible.

"Is this Predator, sir?" Sophia asked.

"Satellite," Chen answered, drily. "Turns out it's pretty detailed. But that's not all. This is a recent satellite pass. They're not moving them for stuff but they sweep constantly and they happened to be in the area. You've got no idea how big this video file is. Nearly a terabyte."

He zoomed out until the rooftop was barely visible, then pointed with his cursor and zoomed in again.

"There are rooftops, like this one, with plantings on them, here, here, here, here, here and here. Also in this small, unnamed town over to the side, here. There are two there and they have..." he said, zooming in. "Catwalks between their buildings. This one should be easy. We'll pull out the people with the security teams from DivTwo. The main town," he said, zooming back, "is another issue. The Avenue de Colon follows the waterline for about a kilometer then bends back up the hill and joins the Calle Juan Sebastian Alcano. Then about another kilometer to the first site. The entrances to the primary building seem to be on top. They are blocked to prevent entry of infected. There are three buildings that have survivors and they are all connected on top. There are two additional buildings nearby and, well, several in the interior. It is the determination of command that those cannot be cleared at this time absent this being an easier clearance than it looks. Lieutenant Smith . . . *She*wolf, any thoughts?"

"I saw the sub video when we got punched down here, sir," Faith said. "This is bigger but not a lot. All I've got is the obvious. Land, grab some wheels, roll hot to the door, extract the survivors and roll back, sir. The one thing I've got is . . . Okay, couple things. You know, sir, and I know that with these screwy, twisty roads . . . Infected aren't that smart, sir. Most of them are going to get trapped up on the cliffs trying to go straight for the lights. So we're not going to get most of them down on the beach, sir."

"Yes, I do realize that," Chen said. "It's one of the reasons that I contacted Squadron and asked for support."

"And as we move along and engage, it's going to attract more of them," Faith said, taking a deep breath in thought. "We're going to have to create fall-back points, move a team forward, have them attract them, bring them back to the defense points and engage. Then do it again. It's going to be slow, sir."

"If I may, sir," Sophia said.

"*Sea*wolf," Chen said.

"Go straight, Sis," Sophia said. She took the cursor and went straight from the beach to the first set of survivors.

"That's a two-hundred-foot cliff, Ensign," Chen pointed out.

"No, sir," Sophia said. "With respect. It's a hundred and fifty feet of *condo*, a *fifty*-foot cliff and more condo, sir. The gunboats with security teams cover infiltrators down Avenue de Colon. Marines clear *this* condo complex," she said, pointing to one at water level. "Then they send up an assault ladder from the roof, go up and clear *that* complex, if it has infected internal, then extract the survivors down. It probably has internal infected. Otherwise they wouldn't be getting around with ropes on the exterior balconies, sir. But going straight means your supply and extraction line has less sides to get hit by the infected. Sir."

"You just like that one 'cause you like to climb," Faith said. "That's your sort of thing."

"But does it make sense to you, Shewolf?" Chen asked.

"Unfortunately, yes, sir," Faith said with a sigh. "We'll probably need support getting them down the ladders, though. And it doesn't cover extracting the other refugees. But . . . gimme a moment, please."

She zoomed the image in and out, then hunted around on it.

"Okay," she said, finally. "This is still going to take at least all day. Maybe more. We go up the cliff. Ugh. Then we put in machine-gun points here, and here," she said, marking two points on one of the condos. "That will give us coverage down this road here. Then we cross, go up this condo, which doesn't have survivors but is the shortest distance, cut over to this one, which does have survivors, and extract them. Pretty much the same with this one to the left. Sir, we're going to need *all* your ground-capable security personnel to man these points and help extract survivors, sir. I'd recommend that the extraction in the second village be held until we complete this one, sir."

"I'd agree with that, sir," Lieutenant JG Elizabeth Paris said. The instant lieutenant had been the sole survivor of her family on a sailboat. She'd been into sailing and boating since childhood, knew small boats and the ocean and was still sane despite her experiences. Now she was in charge of three.

"Concur," Chen said. "I will manage the overall operation. Lieutenant Smith, Shewolf, will be in charge of the Marine force and primary clearance. Ensign Smith, Seawolf, will be in charge of the forward security teams and extraction. Lieutenant JG Paris will be in charge of over-the-water extraction and the local security teams for that. Hand-off will be at the water. Seawolf will cover Avenue de Colon. Callsigns will be Team Shewolf, Team Seawolf, Team Paris. All clear?"

"Clear, sir," Sophia said.

"Let's start figuring out the teams and detailing it out as well as we can," Chen said. "After all, we've only got all night . . ."

"Ahem," Olga said as the captains were preparing to depart. "Lieutenant Chen, sir?"

"Yes, Seaman Recruit Zelenova?" Chen said formally.

"Since there is nothing to do for a while, would it be okay if

I accompanied you to the *Wet Debt*? I was wondering if I could play with your big guns. The Marines only gave me *little* guns and I'm *longing* for some *big* guns."

"We usually fire in the morning... Seaman Recruit," Chen said, rolling his tongue around in his cheek. He knew he was being played but sometimes being played wasn't all that bad...

"Can't I just... *stroke* the trigger on your guns a *little*, sir?" Olga said coquettishly. "I *really* like to fire off big guns in the dark. Maybe with a little light..."

"Sir, if I might suggest you just give in on this one?" Sophia said. "She's really into big... She likes weapons, sir. And there's no real issue with firing off some of the BMGs at night. The zombies don't care. Sir."

"All aboard, Seaman Recruit."

"I just love being a recruit," Olga said, clapping her hands girlishly. "I *like* being trained. On the way over, perhaps you can teach me something about seamen, sir..."

"Ooooh," Olga said, stroking the breach of the Browning machine gun. Her eyes were closed and she was writhing in time to the stroking. "Ooooh, ooooh..."

"You wanna..." Mcgarity said, trying to keep some professional demeanor. "You wanna..." He finally just started laughing.

"I think I need some alone time..." Olga panted.

"*You* need some alone time?" Rusty said. "What about *us*?"

"I dunno, big boy," Olga said in a perfect Mae West voice. "Is that a roll of silver dollars in your pocket or are you just glad to meet me?"

"So..." Mcgarity said. "You wanna blow off a few rounds on the big gun?"

"I'm not sure I can get my mouth arou— Oh, you mean *fire* it?" she asked. "That would be *swell!*"

"Where'd you find her?" Skipper Poole of the *Noby Dick* asked.

"She was one of the chicks on the Russian yacht," Chen said, sipping a beer. They were up on the flying bridge of the fishing boat watching the team prepare to fire. Okay, watching *Olga* prepare to fire.

"She's a pistol..."

∽⊖∾

Anarchy went through the procedures for arming and firing an M2A1 BMG Mod1 while Rusty opened up the battle box and got it loaded. The battle box was a customized waterproof rounds case produced on the *Grace Tan* that held ten thousand rounds of linked ball. One of the reasons to use the fishing boats as gunboats, besides hard points, was that they could handle the weight of all the rounds.

When they'd all donned hearing protection and the gun was ready, Olga let loose a five-round burst at the dimly visible cluster of infected on the shore. Most of the rounds were high but she didn't seem to care.

"Oooh!" she said. She fired another, longer, burst. That one was on target. "Mmmm..." she moaned. She held down the trigger...

"Oh, God! Oh, God! Yes, yes, yes! God YES, YES, YES, OH GOD, OH GOD, OH GAAAAAA..."

She stopped firing when all the infected were clearly down.

"Oh," she moaned. "I need a cigarette."

"Seaman Recruit Zelenova?" Chen called from the bridge. "A moment of your time?"

When Olga got up there, Chen gestured with his chin for Poole to find business elsewhere and patted the vacated seat.

"Sit, Seaman Recruit," Chen said. "You said you liked to be trained. Time for some training."

"Of course, sir," Olga said throatily.

"That would be 'Aye, aye, sir,'" Chen said. "I enjoyed, as any heterosexual male would, your little display. But this is not play time. This is professional time. Can you distinguish the difference?"

"Yes, sir," Olga said. She'd dropped the accent.

"The display was more or less what I expected," Chen said. "Which I didn't mind. It was good for morale. All good. But tomorrow, you're going to be over there," he said, gesturing with his beer bottle to the shore. "With a bunch of other people. With guns. Surrounded by infected. Trying to do a very demanding and stressful job. People will be barking orders. Some of them conflicting. Things will go wrong. Problems will have to be solved on the fly. Even if things go wrong, people will have to stay focused. They cannot, absolute can *not*, be focused on Seaman Recruit Olga Zelenova and her shapely ass and legs. Which means that Seaman Recruit Olga Zelenova has to be a nonentity. Just someone to be given orders and obey them to the best of her ability without being Olga the Great and Sexual. The question, S.R. Zelenova, is can you do that? Because if you cannot, you need to be back on the boats, not on the land."

"I can dial it down, sir," Olga said. "I can even turn it off without . . . turning people off, sir. Yes, sir."

"Good," Chen said. "I hope you're right. Because Petty Officer Mcgarity will be your boss tomorrow. And I need him thinking about the mission, not how he can convince you to get in a little quickie in an unoccupied condo. 'Cause sure as God made little green apples, the shit will hit the fan right when he's thinking about it. And, Seaman Recruit, if you actually do bunk off for a little bunk time, or wall time or floor time, I will put both of you off these boats so fast it will make little blue Cherenkov radiation trails."

CHAPTER 21

The most consistently successful commanders, when faced by an enemy in a position that was strong naturally or materially, have hardly ever tackled it in a direct way. And when, under pressure of circumstances, they have risked a direct attack, the result has commonly been to blot their record with a failure.

Sir Basil H. Liddel-Hart

"Go, go, go," Sophia said, waving for the crew to get off the boat. She'd been the first one from the security team to set foot on the island.

Olga stepped off the dinghy and looked around. A couple of the security guys were looking a little pale, but she'd been on one of the forensic cleaning crews cleaning up infected-held boats and the *Boadicea*. She'd seen messes before.

And there was a mess. A few more infected had trickled into the park overnight giving the gunboat crews something to fire up in the morning. Not many, though. She'd gotten most of them earlier in the evening. The pile of bodies was covered in shrieking seagulls, making it hard to hear the ensign.

Uniform for the day was Navy "bluecam," body armor and helmets. They were wearing Marine body armor since the Navy version was just a flak jacket.

She peeled right, covering "her" sector, as the team assembled to follow the Marines.

"Steinholtz," Mcgarity said. "Keep an eye on your sector."

Seaman Recruit Matthew Steinholtz had been a Brinks armed security guard who won an all expense paid trip on a cruise liner. It was the worst cruise of his life. But he sort of knew how to use a gun and that was about as good as they were getting.

There were seven security specialists considered "functional" for this operation. Some needed to stay back on the gunboats to provide cover. Others really weren't "up" for a landing in an infected-held town.

And the ones they had weren't really trained in this.

"PO, you take point," Sophia said. "We're going to swing down to the vehicle opening. Just follow the Marines."

"Roger, ma'am," Mcgarity said. "Steinholtz, again, look *that* way," he said, pushing the SR's weapon to the south. "If I hear one of you lock and load without my or the ensign's specific orders, I will personally shoot you. We're more likely to get killed by ADs than zombies. Move out. Slowly."

The group began to shuffle down the beach, stepping around dead infected.

"Zombie," Olga said.

"Where?" Steinholtz said, spinning around.

"Steinholtz!" Mcgarity said, grabbing him by his harness and spinning him back around. "Keep *your* eye on *your* sector!"

The Marines had spotted the infected loping down Avenue de Colon. They turned as if they were one mind and each fired a burst. The zombie was hit by at least thirty Barbie gun rounds and dropped like a stone. Then they all swiveled back to covering their sectors. It was over in less than a second.

"For any of you who saw that, that is *not* how we do it," Mcgarity said. "Cover *your* sector. Lock and load if I tell you. Fire if I tell you. Do *not* load, do *not* fire if I don't tell you."

By the time they got to the vehicle entrance to the park, the Marines were already across the road and into the far building. The building had a metal gate with an electronic lock that the Marines had "bypassed" with a Halligan tool.

"Okay," Mcgarity said. "We plant ourselves here until we get called forward. Olga, there," he said, pointing to one of the parked cars. "Steinholtz, there," he said, indicating the opposite side. "Hadley, Larson, on Olga north. Yu, Hill, on Steinholtz, south."

"Can we lock and load now?" Steinholtz asked.

"No," Mcgarity said. "Because we're going into that building over there. And I'm not going to have one of you idiots AD in a stairwell and have it bounce around until it hits me in the ass."

"Infected, Petty Officer," Olga said.

"Your sector," Mcgarity said, putting a hand on Steinholtz's helmet to forestall him turning around. "You have to trust me and Olga to handle it. How far, Seaman Zelenova?"

"End of the road," Olga said. She still hadn't charged her weapon.

"These things are trickling in from that direction," Ensign Smith said. "Stand by. I've got this. Keep them on target. *Golden Guppy*, Seawolf, over."

There was a burst of fire from inside the building and everyone flinched.

"Your sector, Steinholtz. Larson, I see *you* trying to turn around, *too*. Keep an eye on *your* sectors..."

"Golden Guppy."

"Jerry's Kid loping down the road. See it?"

"Roger, Seawolf."

"Take him out for me, please."

There was another burst of fire from in the building, followed by more from the .50 offshore.

"Your sector, Steinholtz, Larson, Hill. Do not look at the fire..."

Olga fortunately did not have to turn around to see the effects. Then again, she'd seen them from behind one of the guns. The infected splashed when the massive machine-gun rounds hit her.

"Okay, okay, Mcgarity," Steinholtz said excitedly. "There's one this way, too..."

"Hill's sector," Mcgarity said. "Keep on your sector, Steinholtz..."

"Noby, Noby, Seawolf..." the ensign said as there was another burst of fire from in the building. "Can you engage that infected headed north on Colon?"

"Negative. Our security team's moving to the beach and they're too close for us to want to risk it, over."

"Anarchy, one, say again, one of our people can engage..."

"Hill, your sector," Mcgarity said. "Lock and load one thirty-round magazine."

"Okay, okay," Hill said, pulling back his charging handle.

"The correct response is 'lock and load one thirty-round magazine, aye,'" the ensign said. "And keep your freaking finger away from the trigger."

"Lock and load one thirty-round magazine, aye," Hill said. "I'm loaded, can I fire?"

"Jesus, it's getting close..." Steinholtz said.

"Watch *your* zone, Steinholtz," Mcgarity snapped. "Hill, take a good firing position. Calmly. You're on a range. You want it to get close. Trust me, I'll take it out if it gets too close..."

"I got another one," Olga said. She was just barely following the conversation. *She* was paying *close* attention to her sector.

"*Guppy*, you got the Jerry Kid...?"

"Take your weapon off of safe..."

There were several bursts of fire from inside the building and another infected exploded with .50 caliber fire...

"Aim for the chest...Deep breaths, just on a range..."

"*Division, Shewolf. At the top of the building...*"

"Fire single, aimed, rounds..."

"Oh, just let him shoot it!" Steinholtz yelled.

"Steinholtz," the ensign said. "One more word out of you and I will pull the trigger on this pistol. Do you understand me?"

"Yes, ma'am..."

"*...we're putting up the scaling ladder now...*"

"Engage..."

There was a crack of a round from behind her...

"*Division, we got a posse up here, you see this?*"

"I got it. I got...her..." Hill didn't sound so much elated as deflated.

"*Roger, Shewolf.*"

"*We don't have an angle. We can scrum...*"

"And I've got another," Olga said. "Where are they trickling in from?"

"*Can you get these without hitting us or the survivors, over?*"

"Division, we have this infected," the ensign radioed. "Releasing support to Team Shewolf...Olga, lock and load one thirty-round magazine."

"*Oh, and now they're trying to climb down the ladder. Don't engage those, Division. We don't want the ladder damaged...*"

"Lock and load, aye," Olga said, pulling back her charging handle.

"Prepare to engage infected with single, aimed, fire..."

"How come she just gets to shoot—"

"Steinholtz, *shut the fuck up...*"

"Prepared to engage, aye," Olga said.

"Engage."

It took five rounds to drop the infected. The man had soaked up four and she was pretty sure she missed with one.

"Place weapon on safe," the ensign said.

"Division, Shewolf. Way is clear to the survivor building. Starting entry for clearance at this time."

"Seawolf, Division, move your people forward to key locations to screen survivor movement, over."

"Mcgarity, you've got Steinholtz and Larson..."

"Oh, thank you sooo much, ma'am."

"Hold this position. The rest of you with the exception of Olga. Remove your magazines."

"Why?" Hill asked.

"Because the ensign told you to, fuckhead!" Mcgarity said. "Pull out your fucking mag. Now!"

"Okay, okay," Hill said, dropping his magazine out of the well.

"Pull back your charging handles and ensure your weapons are clear," Sophia said. "Not you, Olga."

"Yes, ma'am," Olga said as the others cleared their weapons.

"Now, put the mags back in and do *not* charge your weapons."

"There's one this way," Steinholtz said. "Can I shoot it now?"

"Now when I say 'lock and load' you say 'lock and load, aye,' *then* you lock and load. Got it. And only lock and load and *don't* put your finger on the trigger till I tell you..."

"Order of movement will be SR Zelenova, myself, Hill, Hadley and Yu."

"Who?" Hadley asked.

"Me, you dumbfuck," Leo Yu said.

"Now you can fire..."

"Yu, keep looking back in case we get infiltrated," the ensign continued. "Only SR Zelenova or I can lock and load or engage unless I tell you to engage. Understood?"

"Yes, ma'am," the group chorused.

"I got it! I got it!"

"Good for you. You've only got three thousand kills to go to equal a thirteen-year-old *girl*..."

"Mcgarity. You keep your eyes on the entrance. Do not let any of these idiots AD us or any of the refugees. Let's roll."

∽ ⊖ ᴄ∾

Crossing the street was one of the oddest things Olga had ever done. And she'd done a lot of odd things. But it was absolutely weird. It was just a street. An empty street in an increasingly empty town with the wind whistling through deserted condominiums that had once probably cost a billion dollars apiece.

She checked both ways, automatically, before stepping onto the pavement. Not for zombies, for cars. Because you didn't cross the street without checking for cars. The problem being, there were no cars. None running. They were lined up, parked, cold and dead. There were no tourists. There were no retirees. There were no children laughing and playing. Just a slightly cold wind and the occasional howl of a zombie in the distance. And muted bursts of fire from far, far up the cliff.

She entered the gated courtyard of the condos and paused, looking around.

"It's clear," Seawolf said. "Proceed."

The main door of the condo complex had apparently been open because it was mostly intact. And it was pretty dark in the foyer.

"Lights," Sophia said. "Turn on your taclights."

Inside the foyer there were the usual mailboxes. There was a large sideways V spraypainted on the mailboxes. The paint was fresh.

"See that?" Sophia said. "That's the sign that means 'this way to the exit.' If you're following somebody, you go in the opposite direction. If you're trying to run away from zombies, that is probably your best bet."

"Or you can follow the bodies," Olga said. There was one at the base of the stairs.

"Or you can follow the bodies," Sophia said with a sigh. "Especially if my sister is involved. Hill, Hadley, move that out of the way as we go by. Don't want the refugees tripping on it. Let's keep moving, Olga."

Olga carefully stepped over the body, sweeping up with her weapon to check the stairwell then continued upwards. The stairwell, fortunately, had windows in it. There was plenty of light. And while she'd never actually done anything like this or trained for it, she'd grown up with the War on Terror and had seen the pictures and videos of soldiers fighting in Iraq. She also was an avid gamer so when she came to the landing she turned around and carefully stepped up the stairs, backwards, keeping an eye up the stairs.

"Very nice technique, Olga," Sophia said. "But we've got ten more floors to go up and this has been cleared. My sister doesn't leave kills behind if she can possibly avoid it. Besides, if they come pounding down the stairs, we'll hear them in plenty of time. Just walk and keep your eyes and ears open."

When they came to the next floor, Sophia pointed to the fire door.

"Hadley, Hill, chock these doors shut."

The team was carrying chocks and hammers. A few swift blows and the door was stuck fast.

"Keep moving," Sophia said.

"Hey, Sis, where you at? We got customers. Lots of customers."

"Chocking the doors," Sophia said, keying the radio. "You know, like we planned?"

"Just hurry it up. These people are ready to leave. Division, Team Shewolf, over."

"Division, over."

"We've got some survivors with mobility issues. They even managed to keep some of their old folks alive. We're clearing out the corridors so we can move them through the building but we're going to need help getting them down. Over."

"Done, ma'am," Hill said.

"Then let's get moving," Sophia said, gesturing.

"Roger, we'll get some DivTwo people up there with folding stretchers. Recommend, if there is anyone who has the knowledge, belaying them down from the balconies rather than carrying them down the stairs, over."

"Division, Seawolf, over."

"Seawolf, Division, over."

"I can handle that exercise. I don't have the bodies for more than putting in some guides, though. I'll need to use the Marines for labor. I'll also need some rope and shackles. Over."

"Sounds like my kind of party," Olga said.

"Not now," Sophia replied.

"Division, Shewolf, over."

"Go."

"There are climbing ropes all over up here. One of the survivors was apparently a professional climber who lived here. That's how they survived. They've even been scavenging empty apartments. So we've got the ropes. Over."

"Can that guy get them down, over?"

"He says he can, but we sort of need real stretchers. Over."

"They're on the way up, Shewolf."

"Roger. Just waiting on Seawolf, then. Out here."

"Seawolf, status, over?"

"Chocking the doors shut, over," Sophia replied.

"Leave a team to do that and move to link up with Shewolf's team."

"Roger, Division. Hill, Hadley, keep at it. Olga, hold up. Division, Seawolf."

"Go Seawolf."

"Be advised, I do not have enough people for two-man teams at each primary point. And I'm pretty sure the refugees are going to be freaked coming down this stairwell. I'm going to leave singletons at primary points and try to figure something out for the stairwell. We'll either have to have a security person walking groups down or . . . something. Left some details out of the plan on this, over."

"Roger. I'll see if I can scrounge up some more people. In the meantime, hurry up and link up with the Marines, over."

"Will do, Seawolf out. Yu, you okay with going down to the foyer on your own?"

"Yes, ma'am," Leo said.

"When the refugees come down, guide them out to the street team. Stand by. Anarchy, Seawolf, over."

"Go, Seawolf."

"Can you move your teams across the street and still maintain coverage? Yu is going to come down to the foyer. He'll handle the hand-off there. I do not want less than two there on the street. That's a primary threat point, over."

"Roger, we can handle that, Seawolf."

"Seawolf, Division."

"Division, Seawolf."

"Div Two will move two-man team and leader to ocean side of the street. You keep your people on the land side. Hand-off Div One to Div Two will be at the street instead of waterline. Over."

"Roger, Division. Anarchy, did you copy that last, over?"

"Roger, handoff at street, aye."

They'd finally reached the roof. The Marines were still up on the cliff at the second set of condos. There was a group of refugees up there as well, eyeing the boarding ladder askance.

"Faith, Soph."

"I see you finally decided to join the party."

"Yeah, yeah. I'm going to put myself at the bottom of the ladder. Olga's going to have the doorway. As soon as Hadley and Hill get here, I'll have them escort groups down the stairwell. But you guys are going to have to talk them down and belay them from up there. I'm stretched as far as my people reach. Over."

"We've got more clearing to do, over."

"I repeat, I'm stretched as far as my people can reach. Do you want me to explain it in simple Marine terms?"

"We were listening in. We'll handle it from up here. Over."

"Thank you. Seawolf out. Okay, Olga, you're on the door."

"Yes, ma'am," Olga said.

"Hill!" Sophia shouted into the stairwell. "How far you got to go?"

"Four more floors!"

"That'll do," Sophia said. "When I send them over, get them organized in groups of not more than, say, seven. Then let Hill or Handley escort them down."

"Yes, ma'am," Olga said.

"Seawolf, Shewolf, over."

"Go, Shewolf."

"Change of plan. Get your 'I Heart To Climb' butt up here. The climber dude is getting ready to get the old folks down and nobody with my team knows how to really belay someone. Oh, and like, none of them speak English. Guess that high school Spanish is going to come in handy. Over."

"Stand by. Division, you okay with that? I can't run my people at all from up on the cliff. Over."

"Sounds like the only choice, over."

"Anarchy, Seawolf."

"Anarchy."

"You need to stay in place. But tell Yu if he gets any orders yelled down from Olga, it's the same as getting them from me. I'll tell Hill and Hadley the same when they get here. Break. Shewolf. I am not going to leave this position until my last two people get up here. Then I'll head up there. Seawolf out. Olga, you're going to have to manage Hill and Hadley. Issues?"

"Not from me," Olga said. "Will they take my orders?"

"They will when I get done with them," the ensign said as Hadley and Hill finally made it to the rooftop.

"Thank God," Hadley said. "That climb *sucked!*"

"And you're going to be doing it again and again and again,"

Sophia said. "Here's the skinny. I got to go up there," she said, point-ing to the top of the cliff. "When those people get to the bottom of the ladder, they'll come over here. Olga will get them assembled in groups. You will then escort the group down the stairwell and hand off to Yu. Then walk back up, and get another group. I'm not going to be here. Olga is now in charge of that part of the evolution..."

"Why her?" Hadley asked. "I mean, why do *we* have to walk up and down and she stays here."

"Because I said so," Sophia said. "And there's a reason and you can ask about it when we're done for the day. But for right now, you do it because I'm the God damned boss. Do you understand?"

"Yeah," Hadley said.

"The correct response, Seaman Recruit, is 'yes, ma'am,'" Sophia said tightly.

"Yes, ma'am," Hadley said.

"You follow Olga's orders like they're mine," Sophia said.

"You coming, Sis? Or should we order takeout?"

"Take a breather, then get ready to hump the stairs," Sophia said.

"I still don't see why we gotta hump the stairs," Hadley mut-tered. "What is this, the Pussy Mafia?"

"Tú hablas español?" Olga said.

"What?" Hadley replied.

"Do you speaka the Spanisha?" Olga said. "How are you going to deal with them? Most of them probably don't speak English."

"Oh," Hadley said. "You speak Spanish?"

"Yes," Olga said. "And so does the ensign."

"Why's she gotta go up there, anyway?" Hadley asked.

"None of the Marines know how to belay someone down," Olga said. "So she's going up there to manage that."

"She sure can climb," Hill said as Sophia went up the ladder like a spider despite the weight of her gear.

"Let's hope she knows what she's doing up top," Hadley said. "Or bet you one of them goes splat."

"Hey, Sis," Sophia said, rolling over the wall.

"Took you long enough," Faith said, shaking her head. "What now?"

The area the survivors were gathered in was a small garden behind the condo complex. There were a number of recent kills blown around by fifty-caliber rounds and there were holes through the concrete wall that prevented a fifty-foot fall. The boarding ladder was hooked to the top of the wall.

There was a coil of climbing rope, somewhat worse for wear, on the ground and some climbing gear including harnesses and a pair of heavy leather gloves.

"The dude up there said this would do," Faith said.

"It'll do," Sophia said. "I only really need two Marines. One to handle security, one to belay. The belay guy should be fairly big."

"Bearson," Faith said. "Belay. Derek, you stay on security."

"Aye, aye, ma'am," Corporal Douglas said.

"That all you need?" Faith asked.

"Yep," Sophia said.

"Okay, the rest of us are out of here," Faith said. "Let's go."

"Bearson?" Sophia said. "You're going to need to set down your weapon at least."

"Aye, aye, ma'am," the Marine said, unclipping his weapon and leaning it against the wall.

"Corporal," she said. "Get some blankets or something out of these ground-floor condos."

"Aye, aye, ma'am," the corporal said. He went to the closest condo and stepped into the darkened interior over the broken glass of the porch.

"Bearson, come here," she said, pulling out the climbing harness. It was currently sized for a much smaller person but it fit the Marine. She had to get down on her knees to put it on. "Don't get any funny ideas."

"No, ma'am," Bearson said.

"Excuse please..." one of the survivors said. "*Este* to the..." he was pointing at the wall.

"*Hablo español*," Sophia said. "*Momentito.*"

"Got some blankets, ma'am," the corporal said, walking back out with an armload of blankets.

"Stand by," she said, putting a figure eight on the harness. "Fold them and put them on the wall to the left of the ladder, just in contact. Bearson, sit down on your butt. That's where you're going to stay the rest of the time."

"Aye, aye, ma'am," Bearson said, sitting down. "This I can do."

"I need to talk to the refugees."

"Yes, ma'am."

"Hello," she said in Spanish, walking over to the group of refugees. "I am Ensign Sophia Smith of the United States Navy, Wolf Squadron. We are all glad that you survived, but until we get you to the boats, the problems aren't over. There are too many infected in this town for our small force to get you down to the boats by the roads. So you are going to have to go back the same way we got here. It is, however, quite safe. I am an experienced climber and all you have to do is climb a ladder. We will attach a safety rope to you so that even in the slight possibility that you slip, we will be able to keep you from falling. I assure you, again, it is quite safe. I need one volunteer, please..."

The man who had approached her raised his hand.

"I will go. I am tired of this place. Terribly tired."

"Please raise your arms," she said. She tied a bowline around his upper chest, tight. "If you slip, just fend off from the wall and keep your arms down. You can't really slip out of this. When you get to the bottom, call to the girl at the door down there. Tell her that she needs to move over to the ladder to help people untie themselves. Can you do that?"

"Yes," the man said. "I can even untie this knot myself."

"Don't do that till you're on the roof, okay?" Sophia said, smiling. "There, now, Corporal, help me get him over the wall and onto the ladder..."

"*Habla Ustéd español?*" the first refugee said.

"*Si,*" Olga said. "Hablo español. If you will wait here, we will gather a group and one of these men will escort you down."

"The woman at the top? She said that you, the woman, needs to go to the ladder and untie people who cannot do it themselves."

"Oh," Olga said, nodding. "Okay, guys, I'll assemble the groups at the ladder, you take them from there downstairs. You got it?"

"Jesus, why couldn't they get this all figured out the first time?" Hadley groused. "We're just gonna stay in place in teams. No, now we're going to be by ourselves. No, now we're going to be..."

"Because we haven't done it before," Olga snapped. "Just follow the damn orders, Hadley!"

"Screw you, Olga," Hadley said.

"I don't have time for this," Olga said. "Just get ready to take the people down."

∞ ⊖ ∾

Slowly, one by one, with much coaching, the refugees were put over the wall. Only one slipped off the ladder, an elderly man who lost his footing. But he was only ten feet or so from the bottom and Bearson belayed him down easily.

More turned up as the Marines continued their clearance of the local area. There were more bursts of fire, at one point a lot of fire, but nothing on the radio. So far, so good.

"Division, Team Shewolf, over."

"Shewolf, Division."

"All the target buildings are clear. No injuries to refugees or Marines. We are bringing the last group back to Seawolf hand-off at this time."

"Roger, Shewolf. Good job. Seawolf, how's it coming with the infirm? Haven't seen any of those over the side, over?"

"I still haven't seen the stretchers turn up, Division," Sophia replied.

"Let me check on the stretchers, over."

"Division, Seawolf. Thinking about it, unless they're in really bad health, I really think that the stretchers are a suboptimal choice. We just lower them on a rope. Unless they physically can't take it."

"Shewolf, Division. Are you back in contact with the climbing guy, yet, over?"

"Not yet, Division. Moving this last group of refugees."

"Contact him and check on what Seawolf is suggesting, over."

"Aye, aye, Division."

"Gotcha, ma'am," Derek said, balancing the woman as she reached the ground.

The elderly Spanish lady was bitching about something a mile a minute in Spanish. Derek's Spanish was limited to "Dos cervezas, por favor" and "¿Cuál es el costo de un rapidito?"

"Any idea what she's saying, ma'am?" he asked the ensign.

"Do you call this a rescue? Where are the helicopters? Who are you people? Are you really from the United States? I don't believe it. Where are your ships? Where have you been all this time?" the ensign translated. She said something in Spanish and the woman babbled back at her, just as angrily. There was some back and forth and the woman finally stopped, shaking her head. She patted the ensign on the arm then pulled Derek's face down and kissed him on the cheek.

"What was that for?" Derek asked.

"I told her she's looking at half the remaining United States Marine Corps," the ensign said. "Now carry her over to the ladder. We're going to have to belay her down there as well. Then probably through the building."

"Hola! Hola!" a voice said from above them.

Rapelling down the rope was a very tan and handsome man in his late twenties. He landed with a bounce and waved and bowed as if wearing a broad hat.

"Señor Javier Eduardo Estrada, at your service, *bella señorita!"*

It was only when he hit the ground that it was apparent he was shorter than the ensign.

"My *boat* is the *Bella Señorita,"* the ensign replied. *"I* am Ensign Sophia Smith of the United States Navy."

"Ensign Smith?" the man said, then pointed upwards. "Teniente Smith?"

"My sister," Sophia said.

"Ah, the resemblance is notable," Estrada said, then held out a hand at chest height. "Except for the height."

"You're one to talk," the ensign said, chuckling. "Maybe because it's not such a long way down for me to look, I'm the one that can handle them. Corporal. If you'd move Mrs. Alvarado over to the ladder, please? We get her all the way to the boats and I think we're done."

"Not before time, ma'am," Derek said. "Sun's going down."

"And the zombies like the dark, no?" Estrada said. "Perhaps it is best to hurry."

CHAPTER 22

They shall grow not old, as we that are left grow old:
Age shall not weary them, nor the years condemn.
At the going down of the sun and in the morning,
We will remember them.

"Ode of Remembrance"
Lawrence Binyon

"Please God, we don't have another evolution like that one," Corporal Douglas said. "I am fricking beat!"

The sun had set on the town of Las Corrillas, "the trickle," and all the survivors that were recoverable were tucked away in the large yacht that had brought down the Marines. Sophia had invited the Marines over to her boat to hang for a while before they moved out to the next town.

"I think in retrospect we should have just fought our way through town," Sophia said. "But that's both retrospect and I don't do that stuff."

"I'm not sure I agree, ma'am," Staff Sergeant Januscheitis said. "We hit some big concentrations up on the hill. And that was a hell of a lot of survivors. Getting them down in vehicles would have been as much of a pain in the ass. And walking them would have been out of the question."

"Yeah," Faith said, sipping a cup of tea. "Infected density was

257

higher than you realize, Sis. Most of them didn't make it down to your teams. They were trying to find a way down. Which meant they were in our way." She drained the tea and stood up. "Sis, thanks for hosting my guys and for the beer. But we need to get back to the boat. We're headed back to Santa whatever to go, ugh, clear more liners."

"Take care of yourself, Sis," Sophia said, giving her a hug. "And don't let that Spanish climber talk you out of your pants."

"He is *cute,* isn't he?" Faith said, grinning.

"Señorita, *Division.*"

"Division, *Señorita,*" Sophia said, picking up the radio.

"Need to get the Marines back over to their boat. We are pulling out in thirty."

"Roger, Division. The party was just breaking up. *Señorita,* out."

"So where you going next?" Faith asked, headed to the away boat.

"Las Galletas," Sophia said. "Know nothing about it except 'intel' suggests there are some useable boats. Nothing about survivors."

"You be careful," Faith said, giving her a hug again before getting on the boat. "Especially with all these mall ninjas."

"We'll get it done," Sophia said. "Da wants boats and survivors, we'll get him boats and survivors..."

"We're definitely not clearing this one. Definitely not."

They'd arrived at the town of Candelaria just before dawn. Which wasn't good. It meant they couldn't draw any of the infected into a kill zone. And there were going to be infected. The town was huge, at least as big as Las Corrillas. But there were some big yachts in the basin. The question was whether they could get them out. They'd been told to just anchor offshore and wait for dawn. It was dawn. And it was a damned pretty one. But it didn't mean the boats were any closer to being in their hands. And there were infected moving around.

"Señorita. *Take your away boat and go recon. See if we can cut these yachts out. I'm told recon indicates some good deep water inflatables as well. Check on them.*"

"Roger, Division," Sophia said, her face working. "One question, Division, define 'cut out,' over."

"Remind me to assign you some reading material, Señorita. See if we can go in and grab them without actually mixing it up, much, with infected, over."

"Oh, sure, that should be easy," Sophia said. "Olga, gear up. I want somebody besides me on this run."

"Aye, aye, Captain Crunch," Olga said, saluting. "Gearing up!"

There were the usual bunch of sailboats in the harbor. Probably more than normal. But there were also two big motor yachts. They were both rigged as sport fishers but one was at least a sixty-five-footer and the other was enormous, probably a ninety or better.

There were nine or ten big offshore inflatables. They were rigged for fishing as well. It was apparent that sport fishing was a big industry in the area. But they'd be really useful as general purpose "get-around" boats. Better than her dinghy, that was for sure.

Then there were the infected. There were a lot of them and they were active at the moment. But they were scattered. The way the marina was laid out, there were only so many that could, easily, make their way to the boats. One of the yachts was tied up alongside the seawall. The other was butt-in to one of the docks.

She looked up at the sound of an outboard puttering along and wasn't surprised it was Lieutenant Chen.

"I'm glad you're here, sir," Sophia said. She held up her digital camera. "I was taking pictures, but I didn't know if they were going to make sense."

"What do you think?" Chen asked.

"I think it's going to take careful coordination," Sophia said. "And one of the gunboats. Just in case it drops in the pot. And our best people. We come up to that one that's butt in. Throw a grapnel on the front rail. Send a team aboard. One of them cuts the ropes, I'd suggest a machete for that, while the other two cover. If the infected react, the gunboats engage outside the boat, port and starboard, and the security team engages inside. Once they've cut the ropes, pull it out. Then we find out if it's going to run."

"And the big one?" Chen asked.

"Pretty much the same thing, sir," Sophia said. "Possibly with both gunboats. One inside and one outside. The inflatables will be easy. I'd suggest that we take out the one that's sternfirst, first. That's closest to the main entrance and most likely to attract a bunch of infected. The other one, we can cover it pretty good. There's only one way for them to approach and we can chew them up with the fifties if they come that way."

"Sounds like a plan," Chen said. "Rusty and Anarchy, for sure. Who else?"

"Olga," Sophia said, thumbing at the girl. "With the machete."

"Oh, you're going to give me a machete!" Olga said, clapping her hands happily.

"Are the other gunners going to be disciplined enough with Anarchy gone, sir?" Sophia asked.

"I'll be watching them, Ensign," Chen said. "We'll use my boat to pull it out."

"Okay, the first problem," Anarchy said, looking up at the bulwarks of the yacht. "How the hell do we get aboard?"

The side of the yacht was well above the level of the inflatable. At least at the front.

"I'll creep back to the stern," Paula said quietly. As one of the people with the most experience driving small boats, she'd been elected to drive the inflatable. She really didn't like being this close to infected, but she knew she was the best choice.

The sun was well up and most of the infected had gone to ground. They mostly moved at night and around dawn and dusk. But it didn't mean they weren't there.

"Hey, boss," Rusty whispered.

"Yeah," Anarchy said.

"We get back there, I can boost you and Olga over," Rusty said. "Then you give me a hand up."

"Okay," Anarchy said. "Let's try to keep this quiet. If we don't fire at all, I'd be just as happy. I'd like these guys to keep sleeping. Okay, Paula, let's do it."

"You said *boost*," Mcgarity muttered as he was more or less hurled over the bulwark. Rusty was a big boy, Mcgarity not so much. And Rusty had gotten back pretty much all his strength, then some, handling the big fifties and their ammo.

The problem being, there was an infected sleeping in the shadow of the superstructure of the yacht. It woke up at the clatter of the arriving infantryman and scrabbled towards him on hands and knees, hissing.

It hit Mcgarity and tried to bite. The security specialist wasn't wearing full zombie fighting gear and it nearly managed to get his neck. He fended it off and got a hand on its throat just before it let out the standard zombie howl.

Mcgarity drew his side-arm and shoved it into the infected's stomach, pulling the trigger repeatedly and trying to angle up. Being in contact muffled the sound of the shots. Something must have given because the infected stopped struggling.

It was only when he pushed it off that he realized the infected was a teenage boy, shrunken and emaciated by privation and covered in scars including bite marks.

"Fuck," Mcgarity said, shaking his head. "Looks like fucking Gollum..."

He rolled over, then reloaded and holstered his 1911, looking around to see if the scuffle had attracted any attention. None immediately apparent.

"Gimme a hand getting this body in the harbor..."

Between the two of them and a rope, and Paula pushing on his ass and boots, they managed to get Rusty over the side.

"We gotta figure out a better way to do this," Anarchy said. "Olga, get the ropes."

"Okay," Olga said, drawing her machete.

An infected came down the wharf, on hands and knees, snuffling at the boards of one of the buildings.

"Target," Rusty said, raising his weapon.

"No," Anarchy said. "And inside voice. Just be quiet. Olga!" he hissed.

Olga lifted her head and looked at him. She was just about to chop one of the ropes.

He held his finger up to his lips, pointed at the infected, which was no more than thirty yards away, then motioned for her to cut with a knife.

There were six thick lines to cut. Anarchy watched her cutting through one then tapped Rusty and pointed to another.

Rusty pointed at his chest, puzzled, then made a cutting motion.

Anarchy nodded, furiously, and made another cutting motion and pointed at the line.

Rusty made the same cutting motion then held out his hands.

Mcgarity rolled his eyes and pulled out a tactical knife, handing it to him.

Rusty started cutting lines while Mcgarity watched the infected. It finally found what it was looking for and grabbed something. It was a rat. The infected didn't bother with cleaning. The squeaking rodent went down pretty much whole.

The building was some sort of convenience store. The doors were locked and there were bars on the windows. Even if there had been infected, or noninfected, in there, they were long dead. But the rats could get in and eat. Then the zombies ate the rats.

Zombies could probably survive a long time on rats. And there was going to be lots of food for rats.

Mcgarity suddenly realized that some of the assumptions people were making about zombies running out of food were optimistic. Maybe on ships. Land, not so much.

The infected continued sniffing, then looked around, searching for another source of food. It looked at the people on the boat and appeared puzzled for a moment. Then it scurried away around the corner.

"What the fuck?" Mcgarity whispered. He'd been fully prepared to start the party. But the zombie had just run off. They'd pile into a wall of bullets but this one had just run off. "Seriously, what the fuck?"

The last line was cut and he stepped, quietly, to the side and waved for the boat to pull the yacht out of its slot. They bumped a couple of times on the way into the basin but not bad. It was still seaworthy, anyway.

Once it was clear of the slot they tied it off to one of the pilings, away from any other boats, and the engineer from the *Wet Debt* boarded carrying a toolbag.

"Can you get it running?" Anarchy asked.

"How the hell should I know?" the mechanic said. "I don't even know if it has fuel."

"It has fuel," Olga said. She'd pulled the cap on the tanks and sniffed. Then she looked in. "It's mostly full."

"Which means it's probably got water in it," the mechanic said, handing her a bottle. "And it will have separated. Pour this in the tank. It might help. I'm going to be at this a while. After I get the door open," he added, pointing to the hatch.

"I've got a hammer," Rusty said.

"You've got a hammer but you don't got a knife?" Mcgarity snarled. "We need to talk about your priorities!"

"I've got a jimmie," the mechanic said. "If that don't work, then I maybe need a hammer. I'd rather be able to use the door, you know?"

The mechanic was able to get the door open without too much damage, then he waved at the interior.

"I don't do dark spaces that might have zombies in them."

"I'll check it," Anarchy said. "You two, don't fire unless a zombie swims aboard."

"Sharks," Olga said. "Don't think they'll make it."

"Then don't fire," Anarchy said.

He swept the interior of the boat but it was clean. Probably nobody had been aboard since the Plague.

"All clear," he said, stepping out of the saloon. "What's next?"

"Get me the batteries out of the boat and I'll see if it will crank," he said. "I'm still gonna need somebody to keep an eye out. Not going to have time to be looking around for zombies."

"Olga," Anarchy said. "Rusty, get back in the boat and hand me up the batteries."

"You got lights?" the mechanic said. "I got a headlamp but you're gonna need lights."

"I've got lights." Olga turned on her rail light and pulled out a headlamp. She also had a hand taclight.

The mechanic checked the oil, humming in apparent satisfaction, then disconnected the batteries from the engine.

"How's it going to run with no batteries?" Sophia asked.

"I'm going to install the ones I brought," the mechanic said. "These have been sitting for so long, not only are they D-E-D, dead, they're probably shot. I'll check 'em back on the Debt. The way things are going, we'd better find a container of batteries soon. So, you're the Ukrainian chick? Why no accent?"

"I was born in Ukraine," Olga said. "I grew up in Chicago."

"Enjoyed your little orgasm on the boat," the guy said, grinning. He was missing his middle front teeth.

"I tell you what," Olga said. "You concentrate on fixing the engine. I'll concentrate on not wondering if you're going zombie and I should shoot you."

"Okay," the guy said, holding up his hands. "Sorry."

"There is a time for fun and a time to concentrate," Olga said as Rusty came in hauling one of the big marine batteries. "Know the difference."

"Where do you want it?" Rusty said.

"I could make some suggestions," Olga said, leaving the compartment.

Cutting out the larger yacht was equally simple. The first time they had to fire was when they were securing the last of the offshore inflatables. The inflatable didn't have an outboard and the deck was teak. It really didn't look a bit like the others. But it did look fast.

They'd just boarded when an infected came stumbling up out of the previously unidentified cabin. It charged Mcgarity, screaming at the top of its lungs.

The former specialist reacted by grabbing it by the hair and tossing it over the side. Unfortunately, that sort of scream was zombie for "dinner time" and more heads started popping up all over.

"Let's get this cut out," Mcgarity said.

"I can just untie it," Olga said, running forward. There was only one line securing it.

Infected were trotting down the wharf and Mcgarity pointed right.

"Rusty, starboard," Anarchy said, keying his radio. "Division, fire support, over."

"Roger." Fifties started booming from the gunboat and the infected did their usual dance.

"Anarchy!" Paula yelled. "Little help?"

She'd tied the dinghy to the bigger inflatable, as they'd been doing, and when Olga got the lines free she'd started to pull out. Unfortunately, the infected had grabbed the tow line and was in the process of pulling himself aboard the dinghy.

Anarchy walked onto the transom deck of the inflatable and put three rounds into the infected, just as it got a hand onto the side of the dinghy. Just about that time the tension in the tow-line snapped. He lost his footing and went over the side into the water.

The weight of his gear sucked him down immediately and the sharks were already showing up for the shot infected.

"RUSTY, OLGA!" Paula screamed. "Anarchy's in the water!"

The water was crystal clear. Olga looked over the side and could see the former specialist struggling to get out of his gear.

But the sharks closed in. There was a gush of air and blood and the struggling stopped mercifully fast.

"What'da we do?" Rusty said, rubbing his rifle and pointing it then lowering it. It was clear the big guy had no clue what to do next.

"We go get a grapnel and try to get back as much as we can," Olga said. "Hopefully, we'll be allowed to give him a decent burial."

". . . Understood, Squadron. LitDiv, out."

Mcgarity's loss had been a huge morale blow to the division. That was bad enough. But in Chen's eyes, professionally, the worse blow was the loss of experience. Mcgarity was the only person he had who was school trained on the MaDeuce and had extensive experience with it. Not to mention the only one with combat experience prior to the Plague. Or, for that matter, more than Navy boot camp. He had one, count 'em, one Navy seaman who had been a seaman apprentice prior to the Plague and was now a PO3. Midshipmen and ensigns who had had "some prior civilian boating experience." The DivTwo commander was a semi-professional, female, yachtsman. And not much older than Sophia.

And now fucking Squadron wanted him to crew these new boats with the odds and sods they were carrying and "continue the mission"! "If any combat personnel become available, they will be moved to your location. Continue the mission."

"Sir," Seaman Recruit Erlfeldt said. "Seawolf just boarded. Requests a minute of your time."

"Send her in," Chen said. Just what he needed.

Sophia was carrying a bottle of booze. With a shot glass on top.

"Not what's needed at this time, Ensign," Chen said.

"Booze is officially forbidden on U.S. Navy vessels, sir," Sophia said, cracking the top and pouring a shot. "Except for two, count 'em, two shot bottles of medicinal bourbon per person aboard carried on all large vessels in the event of a significant trauma that requires broad tranquilization of the crews, sir." She held out the shot. "And this was Anarchy's favorite tipple."

Chen took the shot, toasted and downed it.

"Specialist Cody 'Anarchy' Mcgarity," Chen said. "May he rest in peace."

"Paula is taking the big yacht," Sophia said. "Patrick is going aboard the smaller one as engineer. There is a guy with boating experience in the prize crews. He'll take over as skipper. Ensign Bowman and I detailed off people to the boats and they're being shuttled around. That should take about another thirty minutes. Then, we need to leave, sir."

"Continue the mission," Chen said, handing the shot glass back.

"Yes, sir," Sophia said. "With due respect, recommend stopping offshore for burial at sea."

"Concur," Chen said. "Continue the mission."

CHAPTER 23

When a soldier looks up on the battlefield he will not see his first sergeant, sergeant major, company commander, battalion commander...he won't even see his platoon sergeant! He WILL see HIS sergeant...the squad leader, crew chief, team leader, tank commander...and this NCO will principally provide the leadership, advice, counsel, and firm and reassuring direction on that battlefield.

Gen. Paul F. Gorman (U.S. Army)

"Grab a seat, gentlemen," Steve said, tapping at his computer. "Be with you in just a second..."

He looked up after a moment and frowned.

"I used to get to kill zombies," Steve said. "These days I spend most of my time reading spreadsheets and reports. Which one is retired Chief Petty Officer Kent Schmidt?"

Both of the men with him were probably pushing sixty. They weren't alike, visually, but he had only been given the names.

"Here, sir," Schmidt said in a gravelly voice. He was silver-haired with dark brown eyes, nearly black, and a compact frame.

"And that would make you retired Sergeant Major Raymond Barney, her Majesty's Royal Army," Steve said, looking at the second man. He was had the look of being formerly heavyset with sagging jowels. He'd recently shaved his head but it was apparent he was mostly bald, anyway.

"Yes, sir," the sergeant major said.

"There are a million places I could use two former senior NCOs here in the main squadron," Steve said. "God knows we need the experience and stability. That being said, we have an... opportunity with our littoral clearance flotilla. It's already gotten a bit large for one Navy lieutenant to manage and they've just lost their only ground combat leader with any significant experience. U.S. Army tanker specialist. He was the best they had since the Marines are all busy clearing these liners. Sergeant Major, do you have any experience with the fifty-caliber BMG?"

"We used them on our Ferrets, sir," Barney replied. "Extensive."

"I've got experience with them as well, sir," Schmidt said. "And in a marine environment. Which I take it this is."

"Small boats," Steve said. "Yachts and fishing trawlers converted to gunboats..."

"Sounds like we're back to the War, sir," Barney said.

"My master's thesis was on the defense of Malta," Steve said. "I'm familiar with Her Majesty's Navy's ingenuity in the early part of the War, Sergeant Major. So, yes, very much so. The flotilla needs some experienced hands. If you turn it down, no foul. As I've said, I have plenty of places to put you. This is small boats out on the sharp end. Rocks and shoals and falling over the side in a shark-infested harbor in full kit. Which was how we lost Anarchy."

"I spent my whole career in Scouts, sir," Barney said. "Except for the boat part, it will be old home week, sir."

"I spent my entire career on carriers," Schmidt said. "But there ain't nothin' I don't know about the Navy, sir."

"Few more points I want you both to consider," Steve said, leaning back. "You're never going to get what you think of as 'discipline' out of these crews. You never do with small units that are frequently out of contact with higher. You didn't with motor gunboats in the War, you didn't with PT boats. They're small boat crews. That's what they're like. It's about motivating, not alienating. That doesn't mean they shouldn't follow orders if given orders. They've been doing that. But... it's not carrier ops and it's not Her Royal Majesty's Scouts. They're a bunch of mostly kids who signed up to go shoot zombies without so much as a day of basic training. And you're going to be the only professionals, except Lieutenant Chen, in the flotilla. That can be, assuredly will be, frustrating. That's the first point and it's an ongoing one.

"The second point is getting to the flotilla. It is continuing operations down the coast. It is, currently, two hundred miles away and getting farther away as we speak. Which means we're going to have to run you down there in an open inflatable fast-boat. It's not rough today, but it's going to beat the ever living shit out of you, anyway, gentlemen.

"Last. I'm not quite sure how this happened but about half of the sailors and commanders in the flotilla are women. Some of the boat commanders are civilian, some military. The gunboats are all commanded by Navy ensigns and midshipmen, two out of three are women. They're willing to take direction but unless you want me to make you officers, and I can in your case, Chief Schmidt, most of your bosses as well as coworkers are going to be women. And they are, even for women, a screwy bunch. You know what the compartments are like. And you're going to have to manage that, as well. I suspect it's especially bad with losing Cody. He was a great kid and everybody liked him.

"So, last chance..." Steve said, raising an eyebrow. "Yay or nay?"

"I'll need some bloody Dramamine for the ride, sir," Sergeant Major Barney said.

"Scopolamine patch," Steve said. "Takes about twenty minutes to kick in and it works better."

"You're still going to puke your guts up," Schmidt growled. "If the Limey's up for it, how can I say no?"

"By saying no," Steve said.

"I'm Irish, Chief Petty Officer," Barney said. "So that would be Mick, Yank."

"I'm in," Schmidt growled. "Reporting for duty, sir."

"Sergeant Major, we have no contact with the British Government," Steve said. "I therefore cannot reactivate your enlistment nor make you, as a British citizen, a sergeant major, or chief, in the U.S. forces. You are therefore a civilian given control over U.S. military personnel due to exigencies of service. There are precedents. I'll ensure that Lieutenant Chen knows to have you referred to by your former rank. The rank and file won't have a fucking clue about the difference."

"Understood, sir," the sergeant major said.

"Chief Petty Officer Schmidt," Steve said. "With the concurrence of the Acting CNO and the National Constitutional Continuity Coordinator, you are hereby reinducted into the United States Navy with no loss in rank for the duration of hostilities." Steve slid a piece of paper over. "Sign at the bottom."

"Married forty-three years, four months, nineteen days, sir," Chief Schmidt said, pulling out a pen. "Twenty-three of those were in the Navy. Dorene was a great Navy spouse but she never liked it. She said she'd strangle me if I ever joined the Navy again. I guess it's a good thing I had to do it to her when she turned, sir."

He signed on the line.

Puerto de Gulmar was just another damned town with another damned marina. With more damned boats and more damned zombies. And sharks.

"What are you doing?" Sophia asked, walking up on the flying bridge. The pop, pop, of an M4 discharging had made the answer obvious.

"Shooting sharks," Olga replied. She had her M4 pointed at the water. "You shoot one, the other ones close in for the kill. Then you've got a target rich environment. And they're not at the bottom of a fucking marina and out of range."

"Olga," Sophia said carefully. "Unload your weapon and hand me the magazine."

"They *ate* Cody!" Olga said angrily.

"I saw," Sophia said. "Helped pull him out. Remember?"

"You weren't there!" Olga said. "You didn't see him. He was *trying*! He nearly got his—"

"Seaman Recruit, put down the weapon," Sophia said. "Put it down. Now."

"Screw this," Olga said, throwing the M4 down. "Screw this. Screw this Navy shit—"

"Olga," Sophia said. "Sit."

"No," Olga said, crossing her arms.

"Sit," Sophia said. "Now. That was not a request."

Olga sat down with her arms folded. She looked like she was saving up spit.

Sophia picked up the M4 and unloaded it. She noticed that Olga had put it on safe before tossing it down, which showed she wasn't really round the bend.

"Olga . . ." Sophia said, then paused. "Okay, let's start with, 'this Navy shit.'"

"It's stupid," Olga said. "Aye, aye this and three bags full and port and starboard and sheets go on a *bed*!"

"That's not a big town," Sophia said. "And tomorrow, whoever we get to climb aboard a dinghy is going to go in and pull out survivors. And you are going. You're going not because you want to. But because I'm going to order you to. And if you don't, Olga, I'm going to put you up on charges."

"Oh, thanks a lot, Sophia!" Olga said. "Thanks a lot!"

"You'll spend the rest of your time in the squadron in a little cabin with other people who have committed crimes," Sophia said. "Because you raised your right hand and said that you swore to obey orders. You don't want to go onshore. I know that. But the choice is between going and spending years in a cell. And it *will* be years, Olga. I'll make sure of it. You'll be old and white and gray by the time you see a town like this again."

"I thought you were my friend," Olga said, crying.

"I am," Sophia said. "And I'm your commander. And you *are* going to get in the boat. And you *are* going to cut out some of those yachts. And you *are* going to sweep the town. Because if I let *you* slide, *nobody* will get on the boats. Nobody will get those yachts. And one of those yachts will find more than the number of people we'll lose getting them. That's it. Cold, hard, math. And that's what all this Navy shit is all about. When it gets down to something like tomorrow, it's about *forcing* people to do things they don't want to do because the alternative is *worse*."

"And I suppose you'll just stay on the boat, fat and happy?" Olga said.

"No," Sophia said. "Tomorrow, at least, I'll be leading the away team. Frankly, I'd rather do that than sit on the boats and watch my people go out. Lieutenant Chen wanted to lead it but I convinced him not only do I have more ground combat experience, he *needed* to be on the boats. I want to make sure they're here when we get back. And what I really want to do is go find some harbor that's not teeming with sharks and catch a tan and drink some rum and maybe do a little diving. But that's not what we get to do right now.

"What we get to do is go find people who are dying and hopeless. So that in a few weeks, some of them will be back, hopefully, helping do the same thing. And maybe, just maybe, if we get enough of them, one day we can go find that beach that's not black fucking volcanic sand surrounded by friends-eating sharks and drink some rum and talk about Cody.

"But now, it's Navy shit. Cold, hard, math. And tomorrow, you're going to be getting in that dinghy, in a shark-filled marina, and cutting out yachts. And if you really want to honor Cody, instead of shooting sharks, remember to keep your damned *balance* and don't *feed* them. The correct response is 'Aye, aye, Ensign.'"

"Aye, aye, Ensign," Olga said.

"Last thing," Sophia said. "If it had been you in the water and Cody sitting here, what would he have done tomorrow?"

Olga thought about that for a while and shrugged.

"He'd have gotten in the dinghy," Olga said.

"Because Cody was always about the God damned mission," Sophia said, choking.

"Oh, don't you cry, too," Olga said. "We're never going to get anything done if you start crying."

"Like a river," Sophia said. "And all we've got to do right now is play bait."

"I should have screwed him," Olga said. "I was going to. I was just playing hard to get."

"Yeah, probably," Sophia said, shrugging. "But that was yesterday. For tonight... Well, I'm going to have to clear with a hangover in the morning. Let's have a wake..."

"Bloody hell," Sergeant Major Barney said as the military "fast-boat" inflatable finally slowed. It had been going balls to the wall most of the night, more or less bouncing from wave top to wave top. And not regularly by any stretch of the imagination. Barney's kidneys felt as if they were going to bleed for a week. But the "flotilla" was finally in sight, the only electric lights they'd seen since leaving Tenerife. "I thought Ferrets beat you up. I hope to never have to repeat this experience."

"Gotta love the ocean, Mick," Chief Schmidt said. He'd slept like a baby most of the ride or at least seemed to have. "Think of her as a mother. An abusive one."

"Ah, well, that makes so much more sense, Yank, thanks," Barney said. "But how do *you* handle it? I *had* a mum and dad."

"Flotilla, Fast Twenty-Nine."

The kid driving the boat was, well, a kid. He couldn't have been more than twelve. But he seemed to know what he was doing. He'd found the flotilla at least.

"Oh, come on," the kid said. "Somebody's got to hear the radio, right?"

As they neared the flotilla they could hear music playing. Loudly. And there were people on deck dancing to the music. It looked like a party, not a military operation.

Zombies apparently wanted to join in. The flotilla was broken into two groups, one by a marina and one by some beaches to the north. Zombies were roaming both the marina and the beaches, obviously trying to join the party.

"*Yeah, what's up?*" a slurred voice answered. "*And what's a fast twenty-nine? Sounds like a band . . .*"

"Fast boat coming up on your party, over," the kid said. "Bringing some reinforcements from Squadron."

"*Yeah, I dunno nothin' about that. Hang on . . .*"

"*S'up?*"

The new voice was female and just as clearly drunk.

"This is Fast Boat Twenty-Nine?" the kid said. "From the squadron? I've got two replacements for you."

"*A'ight. Hey, hey, Paula! Get the flare gun. Go to the boats by the marina. Go to the one that fires the flare. Just tie up alongside. We're having a rockin' wake for Anarchy.*"

The voice was clearly, even deeply, Southern. Between the drawl and the slur it was hard to make out some of the words. "*Git uh flar gone. Duh wun thet fars the flar.*"

"Roger," the kid said. "Uh . . . Fast Twenty-Nine, out. I guess we go to the flare, sirs."

The chief just hung his head at the "sir." There really wasn't any point.

There were three yachts and two gunboats anchored by the marina, bouncing on the light waves. As they approached, one of them fired off a red signal flare, then another. Then another. Then one at the zombies on the shore. That one landed in the midst of them, hitting one of them. The rest scattered from the flame, then chased down the injured one and piled on to eat. The resulting feeding frenzy was a scene from Dante's *Inferno*, complete with red lighting.

There were shouts and applause from the yachts. They were

barely audible over "Welcome to the Jungle" cranked to nuclear level.

Then there was a burst of fire from one of the gunboats. It initially seemed aimed at the infected. Then it was turned on the water, then up as if trying to hit an invisible plane. Then back to the infected still clustered to feed. Tracers were bouncing of rocks and pinging into the air wildly. Lord only knew where the rest of the rounds were going. This produced still more shouts.

"Oh, bloody hell," Barney said.

"Okay, a little loose around the edges I can handle," Chief Schmidt said. "But are we U.S. Navy or fucking hajis?"

"My thoughts exactly, Chief," the sergeant major said. "Bloody fifty just keeps going."

"Uh, do I tie up alongside?" the kid asked. "Are you gonna climb over?"

"Pull alongside the transom deck," the chief said. "That's for boarding."

"The what deck?"

"The trans... Oh, just let me do it!" Chief Schmidt unbuckled from his seat and took the wheel. "Just get ready to handle the lines."

"Okay," the kid said.

"The correct response is 'aye, aye, Chief Petty Officer,'" Chief Schmidt snapped. "And I am not a 'sir.' I work for a living."

"Yes, s— Ok—"

"Try 'Yes, Chief Petty Officer,'" the sergeant major said.

"Okay."

"I would weep, but the ocean is *made* of the tears of men," the sergeant major said.

Some people at the party caught the tossed lines and tied up the boat.

"Permission to come aboard?" the chief petty officer asked. There didn't appear to be an Officer of the Deck. In fact, there was no way to tell who was who. Everyone was in civvies, mostly shorts and T-shirts or Hawaiian shirts. A couple of the chicks were in bikini tops.

"Sure," the woman greeter said. "We figure if you can talk and you're wearing clothes, you're probably not a zombie. Come on over. What's your tipple?"

"I don't mind a drink," the chief said. "But it sort of looks like people have had enough."

"Not even *close*," the woman shouted. "We're having a wake for Anarchy. Besides, it's how we draw in the zombies. Who are you guys?"

"Chief Petty Officer Kent Schmidt," Chief Schmidt said. "And Sergeant Major Raymond Barney. We're coming aboard as Chief of the Squadron and Sergeant Major of the clearance forces."

"Oh, cool," the woman said, holding out her hand. "Paula Handley, recently promoted to skipper of the *Linea Caliente*. Glad to see you guys. We could use some people who know what they're doing. Especially after..." She paused and shrugged and looked around for her drink. "Hey, come on in the saloon. I'll get you a beer..."

"Is Lieutenant Chen aboard?" Chief Schmidt shouted. "We're supposed to report to him."

"I think he's up on the sundeck with Soph," Paula said. "Go on up there. I think there's a couple of bottles up there anyway."

"Okay," Chief Schmidt shouted.

They made their way past the superstructure to the sun deck. There were four people sitting there in mostly darkness, passing a bottle around.

"Is there a Lieutenant Chen present?"

"Here," one of the men said. "You the new people?"

"Chief Petty Officer Kent Schmidt, sir," Chief Schmidt said. "And Sergeant Major Raymond Barney, late of Her Majesty's Light Horse."

"Light Cavalry, you twit," Barney muttered.

"Cop a squat, Chief, Sergeant Major," Chen said, with careful diction. "You are probably wondering about the party."

"I understand it is a wake for your ground clearance commander, sir," Barney said.

"More or less," Chen said. "And we also do it fairly regularly. Not, usually, with this much abandon."

"With due respect, sir, I hope you're not normally that free with fire," Sergeant Major Barney said.

"Depends," Chen said. "I had them stop when they clearly couldn't hit the broad side of the barn. And they did. I really should keep the briefing for the morning but we have ops in the morning. So here goes. We go to these little seaside towns. We anchor overnight where there is a clear field of fire on shore. We then play music, fire off flares, keep all our lights on and, yes, frequently have a little party. At dawn, we fire up the zombies that have been attracted to the shore. We then go in and either cut out more boats or clear the town, depending. I'm of two minds on clearing this town tomorrow. But we're going to have to clean out the harbor of all its large yachts. This is called, Chief?"

"You mean a cutting out expedition, sir?" the chief said. "I don't think we've done that sort of thing since the War of Eighteen Twelve. If then."

"But that is our current mission," Chen said, taking a drink from the bottle. "Littoral clearance and yacht salvage. We then get the yachts in running order, if possible, and continue on to the next town where we have a party, lather, rinse, repeat. With, hopefully, minimal casualties and, just as hopefully, picking up some survivors."

"You're going to have your work cut out for you tomorrow, Sergeant Major," one of the women said. The one from the radio. The accent was strong. "There's a lot of enthusiasm for killing zombies. And sharks. Not so much for grabbing boats."

"Ensign Sophia Smith," Chen said. "She will be in charge of the away team tomorrow. When it comes to working with the boats, I listen to Lieutenant JG Paris, who grew up in a yachting family."

"Hey," Elizabeth said, waving. "Welcome aboard."

"When it comes to pretty much everything else, I listen to Seawolf," Chen said. "She's been doing this since she and her father and sister captured the... What was it, Sophia?"

"*Tina's Toy,*" Sophia said, thickly. "Put a bit of a burr under Da's saddle."

"That would be Captain Smith," Chen said.

"The boss," Sophia said. "I'm getting too old for this shit."

"How old are you, ma'am?" Chief Schmidt asked.

"Fifteen," Sophia said, taking a drink. "A fifteen-year-old who's seen more dead bodies and chewed up children and shit that nobody should have to see than the sergeant major there. Guaran-fucking-teed. *And* I was in charge of the away team when Cody went in the drink."

"And we have been attempting to convince her that it was not her fault," Chen said.

"I think you're trying to convince yourselves," Sophia said. "I know it wasn't. It was just...shit happens."

"No life preserver, ma'am?" Chief Schmidt asked.

"No," Sophia said. "No point. We've tested it. You can't do the job with a type three; you can't access your gear. And we wear Marine ballistic protection, not those Navy flak jackets. With that and the weight of ammo and gear, an inflatable won't support you. And if you go in the drink, it's the first thing you've got to take off. When there's a specifal... specfical... really bad maneuver like climbing a boarding ladder, we'll rig up with floats and a safety line. Floats if we can. But he was just cutting out a fucking inflatable and slipped. And that was that. Rusty and Olga got to watch him get torn to mincemeat on the fucking bottom."

"Bloody hell," Barney said, shaking his head.

"Then we had to fish him out with a grapnel," Sophia said, taking another drink. "What was left. That was, by the way, *this afternoon*, Chief. Sergeant Major. So you shall forgive us, I hope, if we drown ourselves in really good booze. Now, what do you drink? And if you answer 'I don't,' I swear to God I'll see if you can outswim the fucking sharks."

"I'm trying to figure out if I'm still a recovering alcoholic," Chief Schmidt said. "My wife of forty-three years finally convinced me I had a problem. On the other hand, she is no longer with us. But you go right ahead, Ensign."

"I take it back, Chief," Sophia said. "I'll go find some of the tea I usually hold back for my sister. Or we've got some Coke."

"Coca-Cola would be great, ma'am," the chief said. "I would normally say an officer should not get a chief a Coke, but I'm not sure I'm going to be able to stand up again without help."

CHAPTER 24

Now all you recruities what's drafted to-day,
You shut up your rag-box an' 'ark to my lay,
An' I'll sing you a soldier as far as I may:
A soldier what's fit for a soldier.
Fit, fit, fit for a soldier
Fit, fit, fit for a soldier
Fit, fit, fit for a soldier
Soldier of the Queen

"The Young Recruit"
Rudyard Kipling

"Oh," Sophia croaked, holding her hands over her ears to blot out the sound of the guns. "I have got to either give up drinking or give up early mornings."

The sun was just rising over the marina of Puerto de Gulmar and it was another fine morning in the Canary Islands. Seabirds squawked over the dead bodies of infected as fish jumped to avoid the sharks that were swarming to the flowing blood.

"More water, ma'am," Sergeant Major Barney said. "When is the rest of the team arriving for the operations meeting, ma'am?"

"After they finish firing and secure, Sergeant Major," Sophia said. She took a sip of her coffee and grimaced again. "And hopefully after the Tylenol kicks in."

The chosen target zone was a small beach outside the entrance to the marina. The guns had finished off the infected on the beach and the *Golden Guppy* raised its three anchors and pulled out to sea. There was another group of infected at the end of the seawall protecting the marina. The problem was, if the *Guppy* fired from its current location, it would be firing into the marina and probably hit some of their target vessels. It moved out to sea, into the rolling combers, and prepared to engage again. This time, it was doing so without anchoring.

The fire was much less on target, with rounds going over the zombies as well as below. The problem with "below" was the large rocks of the jetty. They had various angles to them and tracers went everywhere, including towards the anchored boats.

"*Guppy, Division. Check fire, check fire, check fire. Try it again, anchored.*"

"I told 'em that wouldn't work," Sophia muttered, picking up the radio. "Catenary is a bitch. And we don't have all day. Division, *Señorita*, over."

"*Señorita, Division.*"

"Recommend pull into the marina entrance, fire from there. Very little wave action, over."

"*The tide is going in,* Señorita. *They'd have to maintain position to fire against the flow, over.*"

"Permission to approach for close rifle fire. There are only ten or fifteen. And I can maintain position against the tide. Over."

"*Roger, stand by.* Guppy, *clear and lock all weapons and stand off.* Señorita *approaching for close rifle fire. Confirm.*"

"*Division,* Guppy. *We can get this, over.*"

"*Wasn't a request,* Guppy. *Confirm.*"

"*Clear and lock all weapons then stand off, over.*"

"*Roger. Division out.*"

"And so we're moving," Sophia said, raising the anchor. "Sergeant Major, I assume you can still fire a rifle?"

"Yes, ma'am," the sergeant major said. "And I even was given an opportunity to zero."

"I'm going to back in," Sophia said, turning the boat around. "Get Olga, and you and she fire 'em up."

"Yes, ma'am," the sergeant major said.

∽ ⊖ ⌒

There was a nasty little eddy at the entrance caused by a combination of the wave action and a small metal wall that was probably to prevent silting. But Sophia finally found a stable point.

"Okay, this is as good as you're going to get," she shouted.

"We may have to discuss uniform at some point," Sergeant Major Barney said.

Olga had turned out in shorts and a bikini top with her LBE thrown over.

"Yes, Sergeant Major," Olga said.

"How do you normally do this?" he asked.

"The only time I fired from the boat I was up on the flying bridge," Olga said. "And I didn't hit many. We were anchored but the boat was rocking."

"There is a technique for that," the sergeant major said. "Unfortunately, I wasn't a Marine and I've never studied it. We'll use the deck up front. What's it called?"

"The sundeck, Sergeant Major."

The sergeant major followed her up to the sundeck, trying not to pay too much attention to the butt and legs.

"Prone position," he said, getting down creakily. It had been a bit since he'd done this and he mentally made the note that he was going to have to figure out how they were going to engage in physical training. Not to mention general discipline and uniform standards. "Slow, aimed, fire. We have time."

"Yes, Sergeant Major."

"Go ahead and load, then open fire," the sergeant major said. He wanted to observe her technique.

"Open fire, aye, Sergeant Major," Olga said. She charged the weapon, then took careful aim. There was a crack and one of the infected stumbled. It didn't go down, though, so she fired again. That time it went down.

"Bloody five five six," the sergeant major muttered.

"Lieutenant Smith, Faith that is, calls these things Barbie guns," Olga said, taking another shot.

The sergeant major looked through the Aimpoint scope and considered his shots. He knew he shouldn't do it, but he went for a headshot. Fortunately, he hit.

"Very nice," Olga said. "I'm not quite that good."

"Luck," Barney said. "And about twenty-four years experience."

He picked out another that wasn't moving much and dropped it with another head shot. That seemed to be working, the range was no more than forty meters and Ensign Smith was keeping the boat comfortably steady. He fired again.

"Okay, I *know* I hit that one in the bloody head," he said, just as the infected dropped.

"Barbie guns," Olga said. She was just using two or three rounds in the body to drop hers.

"They shouldn't be able to survive being shot in the bloody *head*," Barney said. "Not even for a few seconds."

In less than ten minutes from when the boat had entered the marina entrance, all the infected were down. More than half of them from headshots from the sergeant major.

"Position is clear, ma'am," the sergeant major called.

"Roger, Sergeant Major," Sophia said. "I'm going to move into the turning area for the conference. Might as well be comfortable."

"We still have infected leaking into the area," Lieutenant Chen said. "But the presence is down. Sergeant Major, aware that this is your first such operation, would you prefer to suggest an action plan or have Ensign Smith present hers?"

"I'd rather the ensign present hers, sir," Sergeant Major Barney said. "I do have thoughts but it is my first time on such an operation and I would like to have the ensign's insights."

"Sophia?" Chen said.

"The primary purpose of this mission is the recovery of the ocean-capable yachts," Sophia said. "Most of those are tied up along the breakwater. As such, I would suggest putting in a primary security team at the base of the breakwater, probably with a 240 and some rifle support, then go through and clear and remove any infected from the yachts. If we place a gunboat alongside one of the yachts, oriented to fire parallel to the breakwater, they can support if there is a heavy response by infected. If there are still too many, have inflatables in place to support the retreat of the security team. I would recommend the sergeant major primarily be with that machine-gun and rifle security team. That's the point that is most likely to have major infected response and Anarchy was our only person fully qualified with the 240. He trained Rusty on it, so I'd suggest Rusty as the gunner. I'd suggest the *Guppy* as the support boat with the chief onboard to maintain control of the fire from the gunboat. Leave all the *Guppy*'s gunners aboard, the ground team taken from the *Wet Debt* and the other boats with security. For the defense team I suggest use most of the *Wet Debt* crew. For the clearance team... Olga and I can handle that."

"Sergeant Major?" Lieutenant Chen said. "Comments?"

"I think the overall plan is good, sir," the sergeant major said. "However, the ensign should not be involved in active clearance, with respect, ma'am."

"Light clearance like this isn't hard, Sergeant Major," Sophia said. "But it is adrenaline-pumping. And when you have adrenaline pumping, you get ADs. It takes a steady nerve. Olga, despite her apparent flightiness, is pretty steady. I've done it plenty of times. Rusty has done it some. The rest of them aren't experienced at it."

"Choose someone else, Ensign," Lieutenant Chen said.

"Yu?" Sophia said. Then: "To be clear, Seaman Recruit Leo Yu from your boat, sir."

"Yu is a good steady hand," Chen said, nodding.

"Better him than Steinholtz, that's for sure," Sophia said.

"Two seaman recruits," the sergeant major said, frowning.

"What we tend to have is seaman recruits, Sergeant Major," Lieutenant Chen pointed out. "And they haven't been through recruit *training*. There hasn't been time. For an example, our schedule calls for cutting out the vessels, clearing this town, recovering survivors and making it to the next town by no more than twenty-three hundred hours, local, so as to start the next party and attract the infected. And so on and so forth."

"You have to have some time for training, sir," the sergeant major said.

"Tell that to the commodore, Sergeant Major," Chen said. "Who, in fact, agrees. And also notes that if we'd taken time for training, we might never have found you. Or me. Or any of the security specialists, seamen, et cetera. We're not going to be able to clear the entire Canary Islands before we leave. We know there are more liners moored in marinas throughout the islands. This more or less *is* training."

"Understood, sir," the sergeant major said, frowning. "Well, then, we'll have to hope for the best and plan for the worst I suppose, sir."

"That's the spirit, Sergeant Major," Sophia said, smiling tightly. "What's the worst that could happen? A zombie apocalypse?"

"Where do you want to land?"

The inflatable was crewed by another bloody twelve-year-old. And a nervous one at that. Everyone was nervous, which wasn't enjoyable for Sergeant Major Barney. Nervous troops did tend to AD. He had a vision of one of these bloody ponzers shooting out one of the bloody pontoons and them all going in the drink. Because there were, yes, sharks. They seemed to be following the bloody boat.

"On this end," Barney said.

"Why here?" Steinholtz asked. "It's a long damn walk down that pier."

"Because I bloody well said 'land here,' Seaman Recruit!" Barney boomed. "Is that good enough for you, Seaman Recruit, or would you like a bloody valentine with it?"

"Sure, sure," Steinholtz said.

"Quit looking so nervous, you lot," Barney said, shaking his head. "We've got a bloody damned *gunboat* backing us up, we've got a bloody *Singer* and so far there aren't any bloody zombies to shoot. This isn't taking down a Taliban stronghold. We're picking up some yachts from a bloody marina. I won't say this will be a walk in Hyde Park but take a bloody breath, follow orders and we'll all come back heroes. Right? Right. Just pull the bloody boat up to the damned pier if you will, Coxswain!"

"Yes, sir, Sergeant Major," the driver said.

"And would people quit calling the chief and me 'sir'?" the sergeant major said, shaking his head. "The chief and I work for a living."

"But . . . you call a chief sir, Sergeant Major," Yu said. "Don't you?"

"What?" Barney said. "Since when?"

"Isn't that like a Master Chief?" Yu said. "And the Master Chief in Halo always was called 'sir.'"

"What?" the sergeant major said. "What the bloody *hell* is *Halo*?"

"The video game, Sergeant Major," Olga said, clearly trying not to laugh.

"DOES THIS LOOK LIKE A BLOODY VIDEO GAME TO YOU, SEAMAN RECRUIT?"

"Well, now that you mention it . . ." Olga said, trying to keep a straight face.

The sergeant major just held his hands to the sky and growled.

The yachts that were the target were tied to a narrow pier separated from the breakwater by a stretch of water about ten feet wide. There were bridges from the pier to the breakwater, which had a road on top of it, at regular intervals.

The sergeant major stepped ashore first and caught the tossed line from Olga. He held it in one hand as the group got out of the inflatable, then tossed it back into the boat. This was only part of the "security team." The rest were in the second inflatable with the ensign.

"SR Zelenova on point," Barney said. "Up to the first bridge then Zelenova and Yu break off and the rest up on the breakwater."

They got to the first bridge and Olga continued down the pier followed by Steinholtz.

"Steinholtz," Barney snapped. "Get up on the breakwater," he said, pointing.

"By myself?" Steinholtz said.

"Oh, God Lord," the sergeant major snapped. "We're all bloody following *you*! That's what point means you bloody poofter! Cross the bloody bridge! It's not exactly the Rubicon!"

"What?" Steinholtz said.

"Just cross the bloody bridge! It's not as if there are zombies! The road is bloody clear!"

"Actually, there are, Sergeant Major," Olga said, pointing. A lone infected had finally found its way to the flock of seagulls feasting on the dead and was now loping down the breakwater. It had a ways to go to get to the group and was still better than two hundred meters away. "Well, one."

"Can I shoot 'im?" Steinholtz said, racking a round into his weapon.

"Oh, let's just *wait* here and let Steinholtz try to *shoot* the bloody zombie," Sergeant Major Barney said, crossing his arms over his weapon. "Go ahead, Steinholtz. Try to shoot the bloody zombie. Why not? We've all day."

Steinholtz raised his weapon and started firing. And firing. And firing.

The zombie had slowed. Not because it had been hit, but because it was emaciated and clearly out of energy. If it even noticed the group it wasn't apparent. And it definitely didn't notice the fire.

"Steinholtz," the sergeant major said, pushing through the

group and placing his hand on the weapon. "Before you run out of bullets, we'll just cross the bridge, shall we?"

"But it's..." The infected was still more than a hundred meters away but he was clearly unhappy getting near it.

"Cross the bridge, Steinholtz," Barney said, giving him a light push. "We're going to have a demonstration of why one doesn't attempt to fire from a *rocking* platform if one has a *solid* platform available."

He got the reluctant former security guard to cross the bridge then got him down in the prone position on the dirt road of the breakwater. The zombie had closed to maybe seventy-five yards and was starting to speed up with fresh meat so close.

"Now, take a deep breath and shoot the zombie in the chest, Steinholtz," Sergeant Major Barney said. "One round only."

Steinholtz fired. And missed.

"Oh, good Lord. You missed *that* shot? Try it again. You're jerking your trigger. Slow squeeze, Steinholtz..."

This time the seaman recruit managed to hit the infected. The zombie was nearly dead from dehydration and malnutrition and it dropped with one round.

"I got it!" Steinholtz said.

"At under fifty yards with a gun capable of aimed fire at four hundred," the sergeant major said. "We're clearly going to have to work on marksmanship."

"I'm better with a pistol," Steinholtz said, starting to stand up.

"I did not give you permission to *get up*, Seaman Recruit Steinholtz," Sergeant Major Barney said. "While you're down there, you can give me twenty push-ups for your inability to follow the *simplest* orders. And a one and a two..."

CHAPTER 25

The young recruit is silly—'e thinks o' suicide;
'E's lost 'is gutter-devil; 'e 'asn't got 'is pride;
But day by day they kicks 'im, which 'elps 'im on a bit,
Till 'e finds 'isself one mornin' with a full an' proper kit.

Gettin' clear o' dirtiness, gettin' done with mess,
Gettin' shut o' doin' things rather-more-or-less;
Not so fond of abby-nay, kul, nor hazar-ho,
Learns to keep 'is rifle an' 'isself jus' so!

"The 'Eathen"
Rudyard Kipling

"Having fun, Sergeant Major?" Sophia said. She'd brought her group up to the breakwater and was passing the sergeant major and the sweating Steinholtz.

"Just getting a few things clear, ma'am," Barney said. "Seaman Recruit Bennett has already set up the Singer. If you could keep an eye on things for a moment that would be excellent. Be up there in a trice."

"I think I've got it under control, Sergeant Major," Sophia said, grinning, then keyed her radio. "Olga, what's the status on the first yacht?"

"Door's locked to below," Olga said. "Topside is clear. Engineer is working on the lock now."

"Can we spare some people, Sergeant Major?" Sophia asked.

"One two-man team," the sergeant major said. "Hill and Hadley unless you object, ma'am."

"That will do," she said. "I'll go get them."

"If I may, ma'am," Barney said. "Seaman Recruit, get up off your face and run down to the security team. Get Hill and Hadley. Have them report back to the ensign. Do you understand those orders?"

"Yes, Sergeant Major," Steinholtz said, getting to his feet.

"What were your orders, Seaman Recruit Steinholtz?" Barney asked.

"Go get Hill and Hadley?" Steinholtz said.

"If I may, Sergeant Major?" Sophia said. "The way we do that in the Navy is that the correct response to a direction such as that is 'Go and get Hill and Hadley, aye, Sergeant Major.'"

"Really, ma'am?" Barney said.

"Yes, it's called a repeat back," Sophia said. "Makes sure they got the order that you gave instead of what they heard."

"Well, in this case, that would make sense," Sergeant Major Barney said. "Because what I told you to do was RUN and get Hill and Hadley, Seaman Recruit. So, here is the 'direction.' Run and get Hill and Hadley. Have them return to meet with the ensign. Is that clear?"

"Now what you say," Sophia said, "is 'Run to get Hill and Hadley, aye. Have them return to meet the ensign, aye.'"

"Run to get Hill and Hadley, aye," Steinholtz said. "Have them return and meet you, aye."

"Go," Sergeant Major Barney said, pointing. As Steinholtz started to trot down the breakwater he shook his head. "WHAT IS IT ABOUT *RUN* THAT WAS *UNCLEAR*, SEAMAN RECRUIT? Shall we promenade, ma'am?"

"Oh, let's, Sergeant Major," Sophia said.

"I'd say arm in arm, ma'am, but people might talk," the sergeant major said, strolling down the avenue. "What was it you wished Hill and Hadley for if I may inquire, ma'am?"

"I thought they could check the boats topside while Olga and Yu wait on the mechanic," Sophia said. "Then Olga and Yu can check below. When the doors are locked, there's rarely an infected in the boat. At least, alive. Or survivors in a situation like this. But it's a little less nerve wracking checking topside than below."

"Thank you for the explanation, ma'am," the sergeant major said. "It makes a great deal of sense."

"Thank you, Sergeant Major," Sophia said.

"But if I may so detail them, ma'am?" the sergeant major said. "That is, in fact, what I am for."

"So I should have said 'tell Hill and Hadley to check topside?'" Sophia asked.

"Ma'am, you can run things any way you please," Barney said. "You are the away team commander. However, if you wish some guidance, ma'am, you can tell me 'Get a team to check the topside' and I shall be pleased to manage the rest. That is, in fact, my purpose in this great endeavor. To take your directions and expand upon them with it is to be hoped intelligence and wisdom. Ma'am."

"Well, here come Hill and Hadley," Sophia said as the two walked up.

"You wanted something?" Hill asked.

"Sergeant Major?" Sophia said.

"First, when reporting to an officer you salute, especially under arms," the sergeant major said. "The correct method of reporting is 'Reporting as ordered, ma'am.' With a salute. So, try that once more, with feeling."

"Reporting as ordered ... uh ..." Hill said as he and Hadley saluted then dropped them.

"You do not drop the salute until the officer salutes in reply," Barney said. "Ma'am, if you would hold off on that until I complete this training evolution, please?"

"As you say, Sergeant Major," Sophia said.

"So, salute again," Barney said. "Then repeat after me, 'Reporting as ordered, ma'am.'"

"Reporting as ordered, ma'am," Hill said, saluting.

"Do I salute?" Hadley asked.

"Technically, no," Barney said. "But there is rarely such a thing as too much saluting. Now, ma'am, if you would return the salute, please?"

"Roger," Sophia said, saluting.

Hill dropped his salute.

"And you don't drop your hand, Hill, until the ensign drops hers," Barney said. "So ... back to saluting and now, ma'am, if you would drop yours. Thank you."

"Is there really a point to this?" Hadley asked.

"First, never ever question one of my orders when we are in the midst of an evolution," Barney said. "Do you understand that, Seaman Recruit?"

"Sure," Hadley said.

"Seaman Recruit, are you familiar with the term, 'front leaning rest' position?"

"No," Hadley said.

"That is the push-up position," Barney said. "Assume it. Arms extended."

"Seriously?" Hadley said.

Barney darted forward, at an angle *opposite* the security specialist's weapon barrel and shoved his face into Hadley's.

"GET DOWN ON YOUR FACE *NOW*, RECRUIT!" he screamed. "DOWN, DOWN, DOWN!"

Hadley got down.

"Repeat after me, Recruit," Barney said, kneeling down so his face was by the recruit's ear. "I WILL COMPLY WITH THE ORDERS GIVEN AND NOT ASK STUPID BLOODY QUESTIONS!"

"I will comply with the orders given and not ask stupid questions!" Hadley said.

"I'm a little deaf from years in Her Majesty's Army," Barney said. "SO I CAN'T SODDING HEAR YOU!"

"I WILL COMPLY WITH... I WILL COMPLY WITH MY ORDERS AND NOT ASK STUPID QUESTIONS!"

"Recover," Barney said, straightening up. "That means get up, you stupid poofter. At attention, you too, Hill, side by side, arms cupped..."

When he'd gotten them to understand the position of attention, he started to circle them.

"Yes, there is a point to not dropping your salute until an officer has returned it," Barney said. "In the old days, and we seemed to be back to them, officers could not trust their enlisted men. Fragging, as you Americans call it, is a very old tradition. By forcing the enlisted to keep their salute until returned, especially and *always* under arms, it gave the officer a moment more to reach for his weapon in the event that the enlisted was likely to attempt to kill said officer."

"Seriously?" Sophia said, laughing. "I heard it was a gesture of respect between two warriors."

"Which it is, ma'am," the sergeant major said. "But when two warriors meet, there is *always* tension. The reason that you do not ask questions, unless specifically told to ask questions, is that in many circumstances there is not time for questions or thought on your part. You do not know, now, enough about how to do your jobs to have any really useful input. You think you have useful input. You do *not*. Any idea you may have is more than likely idiotic. An example of that is Steinholtz attempting to hit an infected at four hundred meters on a rocking platform. And because of the narrowness of said platform, he was blocking everyone else from continuing the mission. Which I already explained to *him*. So you do not ask questions unless you are told you can ask questions. I do not want to hear the word 'why' come from your lips, again, *ever*, unless you are specifically told you may ask questions. Do you understand? The correct response is 'Yes, Sergeant Major.'"

"Yes, Sergeant Major," they chorused.

"You *always* salute an officer," the sergeant major continued. "You do so because that officer can tell you to *jump* into that shark-infested marina and if you do *not* do so when she orders it, I *shall* shoot you for failure to follow an order. I will *not* hesitate. And that officer *always* salutes back. Because that salute should remind them that they have the *awful* responsibility of giving orders that may lead to your deaths. This is *not* a bloody video game. There's no . . . what's that word? There is no respawn.

"Yesterday, this officer gave an order that led to an unfortunate loss. It was the right order, there was nothing wrong with it. But she bears that responsibility for her life. *You* were not responsible. *I* was not responsible. If one of you dies, *today*, I am not responsible. I may or may not *feel* responsible, but I am not. *You* are not. That officer *is*. That is her burden. That is what you acknowledge with that salute. That you don't have to think and worry and plan. That you don't have to bear the responsibility for a mate's death. That it's on your officers. Your job is to follow her orders and keep your bloody mouths shut. She doesn't need your input and it's not going to help. All it will do is add to her stress load which she does not *bloody well need*. Is this all perfectly clear? Again, the correct response is 'Yes, Sergeant Major.'"

"Yes, Sergeant Major," they chorused.

"I can't HEAR YOU!"

"YES, SERGEANT MAJOR!"

"Good," Barney said mildly. "Now that we've got that straight. The ensign gave me an order to get the topside of the yachts cleared with a second security team. You are detailed. Moving carefully and covering each other, you shall clear the topside of the yachts. Is that *clear*?"

"YES, SERGEANT MAJOR!"

"Ensign, do you have any additional information for these two?"

"Make noise before you board," Sophia said. "We've got the area clear so don't worry about drawing infecteds. One of you, Hill, have your weapon loaded and ready. Hadley, shout and yell to wake the dead. Then, if there's no response, safe your weapon and board. Check for open doors. Do not go below. Topside only. Understood?"

"Yes, ma'am," Hill said.

"Together, and the ensign can't HEAR YOU EITHER!"

"YES, MA'AM!"

"And I'd like a repeat back," Sophia said. "From Hill. And not shouted."

"Check the topside, aye," Hill said. "Uh...Hadley's going to yell. I'll cover. Don't board until we're sure there aren't infected. Just check the topside. Uh...I want to ask a question..."

"Not yet," Barney said.

"Questions, comments, concerns?" Sophia asked.

"What do we do if we find an open door, ma'am?" Hill asked.

"Call it in," Sophia said. "Otherwise, stay off your radios except to report the yacht clear. But do check the hatches just to see if they're open."

"Yes, ma'am."

"Hill, you are in charge of the team," Barney said. "If you have further questions, and only if you have important and valid questions, ask for me on the radio and I will clarify. Understood?"

"YES, SERGEANT MAJOR!"

"Very good," the sergeant major said. "Off you go, lads."

"Sorry," Sophia said. "We've really never gotten into the whole discipline thing. Which I know is a bad thing."

"The Army and the Navy have very different approaches to, well, most things, ma'am," Sergeant Major Barney said. "But discipline is important in both, ma'am."

"Am I really responsible for Anarchy's death?" Sophia asked quietly.

"Officially and legally, yes, ma'am," the sergeant major said.

"That is the hard part of being an officer. Had he any family, it would be your job, not mine, to write them a letter telling them what happened, how he died. You have the authority to order them to perform actions which I do not have the authority to order. By the same token, you bear the responsibility of the result of those actions. From all I've gleaned, there was little that you could have done to prevent his death. You were under orders, yourself, to gather the boats. He died as the result of an accident while performing that mission. There will be more, ma'am. That is the nature of this profession and the sea, of itself, takes lives. It is one of the reasons that I am less than sure it is entirely wise placing a teenager in the position of an officer. That is a terrible burden to bear. By the same token, you do the job quite well."

"Thank you," Sophia said, clearly thinking about it. She was watching Hill and Hadley tentatively board one of the yachts.

"If I may add, ma'am," the sergeant major said. "The other problem of being in this position is that you have to set aside such thoughts. It is my job to watch the teams and ensure that everyone is doing their jobs and doing so in such a way that they, probably, are not going to kill themselves. Speaking of which, I need to get up to the defense team in a moment. However, your job, ma'am, is to put aside anything but anticipating future issues and plans. Let me handle this. You think about what is next. Because, among other things, I haven't a clue about any of this and don't know what is probably going to go wrong."

"Yacht's clear. Dead batteries. Fuel. Some stores. No infected. Mechanic's working on it. As usual, he's afraid of the dark. What do you want us to do?"

"Stand by," Sophia said. "Division, can we get another repair crew? We've got four yachts. Topsides are clear on at least two so far. Doors are locked. They're all going to need batteries. Over."

"Away Team, Division. Roger, we'll scrounge up another mechanic."

"Have Hill and Hadley stop checking topsides," Sophia said. "One of them can stand by and help the engineer on the first yacht then the other on the second."

"Yes, ma'am," Sergeant Major Barney said. "We need more than one frequency. Hill, Sergeant Major. Status."

"Topside is clear. Door's locked."

"Send Hadley back to the first yacht. You stand by on the second, the one that you are on. Just wait there. Over."

"*Ok— Roger, Sergeant Major.*"

"*Uh...Sergeant Major, Rusty. We've got an infected coming down the way...*"

"Gunboat," Sophia said, looking through her binoculars. "That's on me, I think."

"Very well, ma'am," Sergeant Major Barney said. "but if I may...Singer Team. Stand by. Gunboat should take care of it. Do not fire unless ordered."

"*Uh...Roger, Sergeant Major.*"

"We're Singer Team, right?" Rusty said.

"Hell, *I* dunno..."

"*Guppy*, Away Team, over."

"*Away Team*, Guppy. *Yes, we can.*"

"If you would, please," Sophia radioed. "Nuke 'em from orbit. It's the only way to be sure."

"Aim," Chief Schmidt growled, pointing at the oncoming infected. It was approaching more or less directly at the gunboat's position. "If you cannot hit that target with your first burst, I will find a new gunner and you can just spend the rest of your career humping ammo."

"Yes, Chief," the seaman recruit said, sweating.

"One burst," Schmidt said. "Take your time."

"Yes, Chief," the gunner said.

"Wait," the chief said. "Your sight's off for this range." He clicked the ladder sight. "You'd have fired over."

"Thanks," the gunner said.

"Fire."

The burst, fortunately for the gunner, hit the infected with one of its rounds.

"And you get to keep your job," Schmidt said, taking off his earmuffs. "For now."

"Thanks," the gunner said.

"That would be...what?"

"Thank you, Chief," the gunner said and gulped.

"Better."

∞ ⊖ ⌒

"Okay," Sophia said as the last yacht cleared the marina and joined the growing flotilla. "Now we need wheels if we're going to clear this town."

With the yachts cleared, the team had gathered at the point where the breakwater reached the shore for a little huddle.

"Very well, ma'am," the sergeant major said. "If I may?"

"On you, Sergeant Major," Sophia said, nodding.

"First, all but Zelenova Team and Singer Team, drop your magazines and clear your weapons."

"Sergeant Major?" Rusty said, raising his hand. He had the 240 slung.

"You're not in bloody primary school, Seaman Apprentice," the sergeant major said. "Seaman Recruit Steinholtz, what is the proper way to ask a question?"

"Permission to speak, Sergeant Major," Steinholtz said.

"So, Seaman Apprentice," the sergeant major said. "Try it again."

"Permission to speak, Sergeant Major?" Rusty said.

"Permission granted, Seaman Apprentice," Barney said.

"Uh..." Rusty said. "I forgot what I was gonna ask..."

Sophia turned around and covered her mouth to keep from bursting out laughing. She coughed instead.

"Bloody hell..." Sergeant Major Barney said, just getting warmed up.

"Sergeant Major!" the assistant gunner said, quickly raising his hand. "Permission to speak, Sergeant Major!"

"Permission bloody granted," Barney said. "And it had better be bloody important!"

"Are we Singer Team, Sergeant Major?" the AG asked.

"Oh, yeah," Rusty said. "*That* was it..."

"Yes," Sergeant Major Barney said, nodding. "You and Seaman Apprentice Bennett are Singer Team. That was my mistake. Singer is British Army slang for a machine gun. Now, everyone but the *machine-gun* team and Olga's team, clear your weapons. And don't bloody ask why. You know why. Right. Hadley, carry the jumper cables. Steinholtz, carry the battery. Zelenova team has point. Then the ensign, Singer Team, Hadley and Steinholtz, myself and Hill. Is that clear?"

"Clear, Sergeant Major," Olga said.

"There's gates on this marina," Sophia said. "Get them closed so we have a secure fallback point."

"Yes, ma'am," Barney said. "SR Zelenova, move out."

The reason the infected had only been trickling in to the marina was clear when they got to the gate. There were two. The larger rolling gate was locked. The smaller swing gate was jammed by a small car that had hit the partially open gate and rolled over, blocking the entrance. The passenger side window had been smashed out.

"Yu," Barney said. "Climb up on the car and see what the other side looks like."

"Nothing, Sergeant Major," Yu said, looking around. "Some cars scattered around. I don't see any infected."

"Orders, ma'am?" Barney asked. "Do we clear the gate or try to get the other open?"

"Can we clear it?" Sophia asked.

"Oh, *yes*, ma'am," the sergeant major said.

"Clear the gate, Sergeant Major," Sophia said, stepping back.

"Singer team, drop your Singer," the sergeant major said. "Jumper team, drop your gear. Over *there* to the side you bloody idiots, not in the bloody way. Zelenova team, outside and keep an eye both directions. Hill team, that's Hadley and Hill, over the car to the far side. Singer Team, take the bonnet side. Steinholtz, that side, I've got this. Now, the trick is for everyone to lift on command, with your knees...The command will be a two part, prepare to lift and lift. Team, prepare to lift...Lift! Walk it to the water...careful..."

The Fiat 500 only weighed 2400 pounds. Six reasonably in-shape guys could lift it easily. Once it was out of the gate, they set it down.

"Keys are in it, ma'am," the sergeant major said. "Tip it upright and try to get it started?"

"We're going to need cars that are a bit bigger," Sophia said. "But might as well just to get it out of the way."

"Right, and here's how you do *that*..."

After several months upside down the Fiat wouldn't start but there were plenty of other cars abandoned outside the gates.

"Orders, ma'am," the sergeant major said as the abandoned small SUV finally caught.

"The way the Marines usually do this is two-man teams," Sophia said. "I don't think we should split up, though. Find a car with a sunroof. Put the Singer up there. Put that in the lead. I'll take that one. Then the rest of the teams, two to a car. Wait..." She stopped and thought. "Stand by. Division, Away Team."

"Away team, Division."

"We can secure this marina. There are gates and we can get them closed. Request additional support for hand-off of refugees at the marina gate. We'll handle the town. Over."

"Roger, away team, we're observing that. We'll unload the security element from the Guppy to hold the gate, over. Also going to check on the fuel situation. One of these yachts is nearly dry."

"Thanks, Division. Seawolf out. Okay, that's got us a secure point to fall back on. We'll go as a group forward. If we find refugees, we'll send them back with a two-man security team. Does that sound like a plan?"

"Sounds like a plan, ma'am," Sergeant Major Barney said. "All right, you horrible lot...!"

"*Hola!*" Sophia said as an emaciated man staggered out of the apartment complex. He was being helped along by Olga and Yu. "*Buenos dias!*"

"*Buenos dias, verdaderamente,*" the man said. "*Bendice a la Armada de Estados Unidos!*"

There were four more refugees with him, each skinny as a rail. But most people they found were. The apocalypse had been the best diet plan in history.

"*Bendiciones para los habitantes de las islas Canarias,*" Sophia said. "Sergeant Major?"

"Hill, Hadley, get these people back to the marina, then catch up."

"YES, SERGEANT MAJOR."

CHAPTER 26

"Before we move you over to the other boat, you need to go through a decontamination shower."

Thomas Walker covered his shades-covered eyes with his arms against the sun and just reveled for a moment at the touch of sunshine. There were thin clouds that cut down on it a bit but that was for the good. After so long in that fetid hold it was glorious. The smell of rotting flesh had become so common he barely noticed it. What he mostly noticed was the strong, fresh, wind from the sea. It smelled like wine it was so clean.

Thomas Walker wasn't his real name. It was a common alias he'd used over the years. So common, he'd stopped using it years before the Plague. He knew why he'd instinctively given an alias when the crap hit the rotary impeller. He was out in the cold. Until he was sure what he was dealing with, he was staying under cover. Right now what he seemed to be dealing with was some sort of militia, not the pre-Plague military.

The other reason was, this was a new world. That was what none of the idiots he'd shared the compartment with for six long months could understand. Who you had been, what you had done, accomplishments and failures, no longer existed. The only thing that existed, now, is who you really were.

For now, he would be Thomas Walker, English as a Second Language Instructor, and just go with the flow.

The harbor of Santa Cruz de Tenerife was crowded with boats and ships. There were two megayachts, a dozen smaller yachts, two supply ships, a small passenger liner and a tanker all moored in the channel. Around and between them zipped at least a dozen inflatables.

What he noticed, first, was that one of the megayachts was the *Den'gi Ni Za Chto*. That was Nazar Lavrenty's yacht. So the oligarch was apparently involved. Not something in the group's favor: he couldn't imagine Lavrenty changing his spots. An American flag was flying from it, but flags could be changed. There were some uniforms, all U.S. Navy and he'd seen one Coast Guard driving a boat. Uniforms could have come from a salvaged vessel. Although it would take a ballsy militia to loot a Navy ship. Or complete idiots, like the Somalis. The team that found them identified themselves as United States Marines and they had the sound. Except for the woman who he'd pegged as teenage girl despite the encumbering gear. Teenage girls were not Marine lieutenants. Or, perhaps they *were* in an apocalypse. New world. Which was rather exciting, since he had been getting bored with the old one.

"There are some clothes, not much, over here," the man said. "Grab a pair of shorts, a shirt, a towel and one of the plastic trash bags. Put the shorts, shirt and towel on the table by the shower. Get in the shower. Put your clothes and personal effects in the bag. Then turn on the water. You get one temperature, which generally feels scalding at first. You can take as long as you'd like, we refilter the water, but please clean off quickly. We've got more survivors coming through. Do *not* drink the water. It has decontamination chemicals in it and while it won't kill you, it will make you throw up. If you're really thirsty, right now, there are bottles of water. So grab some clothes and let's get moving."

"May I ask a question, sir?" Walker said, raising his hand.

"It's gone," the young man said. "It's all gone. It's the first question I asked, too. It's what everyone asks. If you don't believe me, try to get one of the Zodiac guys to drop you off on the shore. Ask the zombies. Whatever place you're asking about, we probably don't have contact and we don't know. There's some Yanks who are in a headquarters somewhere in the U.S. Omaha or something like that. They're sort of in charge but they can't get out. Now, we really need to do the showers so I can get you over to the boat and you can get some food, a bunk and people who are there to answer your questions."

The response sounded rote. The guy had answered the question before. A lot.

"Decontamination shower" had some rather unpleasant historical connotations. But he could smell the chemicals and there was enough spray around that if it was mixed with, say, Tabun, the guy running the shower would have been doing the dying cockroach.

Thomas grabbed a pair of Navy PT shorts and a Marine T-shirt. Someone had found a well-stocked U.S. Navy ship. Presumably the Hole had given them permission to loot it.

The shower was, as advertised, hot. And that was good after spending months in a hold with limited, and always cold, water.

He showered quickly. He wanted to just sit under the water for an hour. But he washed grabbed his towel, shorts and shirt, put them on and got out.

"Put the towel in the bucket, please," the young man said, pointing to a blue bucket. "They get laundered and reused. What compartment were you in?"

"L-1438," Thomas said tossing the towel in the barrel.

The kid pulled out a piece of plastic and a Sharpie and carefully wrote L-1438 on it.

"Were all you in the same compartment?" he asked, handing it to Thomas.

"Yes."

"Right," the kid said, pulling out more plastic and starting to write the compartment on them.

"May I ask the purpose of this?" Thomas asked.

"They keep people in the same compartment together at first, mostly," the kid said. "You may bloody hate your compartment mates but they're the only people you know at first."

"Okay," Thomas said. "What now?"

"Wait for the rest of the blokes to get done," the kid said. "Unless they call for a group to head over to the boat."

"How many you got?" an older man said, walking up.

"Just this one, right now. Five when they get done showering."

"You okay going on your own?" the older man said. He was

wearing a U.S. Navy uniform with rank tabs for a petty officer third class but no name tag.

"Yes," Thomas said.

"Zodiac's ready to go with some others," the man said. "Come on."

He led the way around the corner to the promenade deck of the liner and pointed aft.

"See that group by the gangway?" he asked. "That's the stair thing. Join them. Okay? Or you can wait."

"I'll go with them," Thomas said.

The group, with the exception of an older man wearing a U.S. Navy uniform and no rank, was also dressed in T-shirts and shorts, holding plastic bags. From there it was possible to see another decontamination shower, a larger one. There was one of the fire-gear and MOLLE covered "zombie hunters" under the shower, still holding his M4, being doused down. The water was running off him blood red.

Thomas briefly wondered if he'd just taken a shower in zombie-blood contaminated water.

"Right, the Zodiac's here," the man in uniform said. "Make your way down the steps, carefully, and into the boat."

The boat wasn't, technically, a Zodiac. It was a Brig designed to carry four and a driver. Thomas found it interesting that a sailor was calling it a Zodiac and not a RHIB. Language changes were already occurring. He pushed 'RHIB' to the back of his memory since using the term might betray his cover.

There were six in the group. People needed help getting in. Everyone could barely see.

Thomas waited until the other passengers had found seats before boarding. He stepped lightly onto the boat and dropped into a spot on the deck. He was wedged between an older man on the deck and a fortyish woman sitting on the front seat.

"Wrap the blankets around you if you get cold," the kid driving it said. "You're going to have to leave them in the boat."

The blankets were USMC green wool blankets and already damp. Thomas decided to forego.

"Everyone keeps saying everything's gone," the woman next to him said. "It can't simply be gone. *Something* had to survive!"

"I don't know, lady," the kid said, pulling away from the float-ing dock. "There's zombies all over on the land and there's not much in the way of radio stations. Some ham operators, pretty much. There's some that say they're, like, king of some place I've never heard of, but there's not much."

"Submarines?" Thomas asked.

"There are subs," the kid said. "So I've heard. I've never seen 'em but other people have. The boat I'm taking you to used to be owned by some rich Russian dude. He tried to jack the boat that found him. It's one of the real 'Navy' boats. Some of the boats are run by civilians and some of them are Navy. Anyway, the guy tried to jack this Navy boat and a sub surfaced and told him they'd open fire if he didn't surrender. So then I guess we jacked his."

"So there are Navy ships?" the woman asked.

"Sorta," the kid said. "They found a Marine ship, which is where the Marines and a bunch of the loot came from. But it's still floating somewhere out there. The boats are all salvage. Some of them are Navy, some of them are civilian. Something about who can have what guns. Like, I'm a civilian. I didn't want the whole 'three bags full' thing. But my boss is Navy. But he was an Army dude when he was a kid and he's never been in the Navy before. It's all sort of like that. Sort of fucked up but it mostly works."

"I'm confused," the woman said.

"Okay," the kid said. "The boat you're going to, it's called the *Money for Nothing*. It's got a Navy dude in charge of it but the captain, the guy who runs the boat, is a civilian. But the Navy dude, who's the operations guy for the squadron, had never been in the Navy before this. So if you're confused, you're not the only one. Like I said, it has to do with who gets guns."

"Controlling legal authority?" Thomas asked.

"That's it," the kid said. "Like, they're clearing out some of the little towns here in the islands and to do that you've got to have... what he said. Somebody told me it's sort of technically an act of war but we've got permission from somebody or something."

"So did you live here, before?" the woman asked.

"Oh, hell no," the kid said. "I was on a cruise ship, too. We abandoned ship when the zombies took over. I was in a lifeboat that got found by one of the Wolf boats. And let me tell you, that fucking sucked. Being in the boat, I mean. Look, there's a pamphlet they give you when you get to the boat. Just wait till you read it then ask questions, okay?"

The inflatable pulled up to the waterline transom deck of the yacht and people were helped out. Thomas took the offered hand of a man he pegged as an Indonesian and probably a steward. There had been four stewards and two Indonesian waitresses, initially, in the compartment he'd been stuck in along with six other passengers. Two passengers as well as one of the stewards had "turned." During the subsequent six months he had, slowly and painfully, "learned" the dialect that was common to the other ten survivors.

He'd never let on that he spoke two other dialects of Indonesian and had been able to understand what they were saying two hours after they'd closed the compartment.

"Hello, my name is Nadia..."

The young woman was good-looking, even beautiful, with a strong Slavic accent. She also was noticeably pregnant. So were the two Indonesian waitresses. Thomas figured even if humanity was mostly wiped out, there was about to be one hell of a baby boom.

"I'm to be your guide for a short time as you get acquainted to Wolf Squadron. The first step being to get you some food and answer any questions. But the food, first. If you could follow me, please?"

They were led into the main saloon of the yacht. It was showing definite signs of wear but it was still more luxurious than any of the compartments on the cruise ship.

"So this is how the other half lives," the fortyish woman said. Thomas could tell she was bristling a bit at the Russian girl. She wasn't pregnant which meant she was either fixed or no one in the compartment was interested. Given that there were four other men with her, she was probably fixed.

"There is soup," Nadia said, pouring a cup and handing it to the woman. "There will be more in a moment but some people have not had much to eat and this helps their stomach. There are three kinds, tomato, chicken and lamb. The Americans generally prefer the tomato or the chicken. Help yourself."

"Can you...What's going on?" one of the men said.

"This is always the problem," the girl said, smiling. "Do you feed the questions or your stomach first. Here is a pamphlet," she said, picking one up and handing it to the man. "Please to read. Then ask questions."

Thomas read the pamphlet while sipping a cup of tomato soup. There had been tomato soup in the compartment but *hot* soup was delicious. Most of the information he wanted was in the first section. Given what his compartment had been like, he could see why there was a waiver on UCMJ actionable offenses. It was probably on a case by case basis, though, he'd have to read the reg.

It brought up the question, though, if he should make contact. The problem being, the most the Hole would have had was a two star flag duty officer. And if he popped up, they'd expect him to take over this jugfuck, retired or not. He wasn't sure he wanted to. There was a reason he'd retired. If he wanted to do anything, it was kill freaking zombies or cruise around on a boat. Not sit in an office and figure logistics. On the other hand, he was getting a little long in the tooth for that. It looked, however, like this was a legitimate operation, if a bit cock-eyed, not a pre-Westphalian militia.

"What about Britain?" one of the men from the group asked.

"There is currently no contact with the British government or any government organizations other than those listed. We recently freed some people from the Canary Islands including a policeman. He is the closest we have to a member of the government of Spain. There is a group called Sons and Daughters of Britain in Exile which meets regularly on Wednesday nights. Their chairman is a former member of Parliament and who is, more or less, the prime minister in exile. Although he is quick to point out that all he is is the chairman. There are similar groups that meet on other nights from other countries. On the bulletin board there is a list."

"So we're still trapped on these boats," the woman said.

"Yes," Nadia said. "For the time being. There have been some small towns partially cleared here in the Canary Islands. The next objective is to clear the U.S. Navy base at Guantanamo Bay in Cuba. The purpose of that is obtaining supplies, equipment and, hopefully, additional trained personnel. Beyond that, the commodore has said that 'it depends.' The eventual goal is to free both the United States and Europe from infected so that we can...restart, yes?"

"How the hell is he going to free up the entire United States?" one of the men asked.

"Again, that depends," Nadia said. "Right now, in the south harbor, there are what are called 'mechanical clearance devices.' Zombie traps is what most people call them. They are containers that have been turned into essentially, pardon, sausage grinders."

"Oh, my God," the woman said, putting her hand over her mouth.

"Light and sound to draw the zombies in?" Thomas asked.

"Yes," Nadia said. "And one-way gates, yes? Then, well, blades driven by a motor. All very efficient. The commodore has said that there are other plans for interior areas. But we are still few. And he prefers not to detail them as they will change, yes? It all depends upon what we find. Who we find who are willing to help."

"Three days off," Thomas said. "With nothing to do?"

"There are books," Nadia said. "There are TVs in the rooms and there are channels that play movies. Eat, rest. Get back your strength. On the third day there will be an orientation and you can choose to help or not. After that, you see a human resources counselor. I will warn you that in most cases, you must first be part of the forensics cleaning teams. These are teams that clean out the boats and compartments. It is . . . At first it is quite unpleasant. I still do it. But it is important. We have to have somewhere to live that is not filled with the filth that the zombies leave. And after a while you get used to it. We wear a sort of plastic coverall and masks. It is not the worst thing in the world."

"So to get any of the better jobs, we have to muck out compartments?" one of the men said angrily.

"Unless you have specific skills, yes," Nadia said. "There is a shortage of persons with trained skills in engineering, electrical systems, plumbing, welding and boat handling. For those you must either have proof, such as a master's ticket, or pass a test that shows you have the skills. Are you an electrical or mechanical engineer, sir?"

"No," the man said. "I'm a solicitor."

"There is, unfortunately, an overabundance of those, sir," Nadia said drily.

"And if we tell them to fuck off?" the solicitor asked. "What then?"

"There are interior staterooms on the *Boadicea*," Nadia said, smiling. "Six to a stateroom, sometimes eight. Minimal rations and water to drink. Bit like being back in the compartment, yes? Some people choose that. At least for a time. If you choose to help, the most you spend on cleaning is a week. It, again, helps out and it has to be done. Someone has to do it."

"Do we have to take the three days or can we just see the counselor?" Thomas asked.

"You can see the counselor at any time, sir," Nadia said, her brow wrinkling. "But generally people take a few days off before getting to work."

"Where's the HR office?" Thomas said. "I mean, you said any time."

"Well," Nadia said, frowning. "The next thing we were going to do was get you registered. You have to do that before going to the counselor's office, I think."

"Where do I register?" Thomas asked.

"Over here," Nadia said. She led him to a computer terminal and gestured to the seat.

"Were you ever in the United States military?" she asked.

"A long time ago," Thomas said. "But my personnel files got burned up in a fire in St. Louis. You probably don't have them." *They'd* better *not have them.*

"Well, type in your Social Security number," Nadia said. "That has many records associated with it."

Thomas typed in a totally bogus Social Security number. He knew it was bogus because he'd had it "issued" to him at one point. If they had that one, they were *really* connected. And to more than the Hole.

A screen asking for personal information came up.

"Okay, I guess they don't have it," Nadia said. "What did you do? They're looking for security and clearance people."

"I was a truck driver in the Army," Thomas said. Which was only a little white lie. He'd driven trucks plenty of times.

"Fill in the information then go forward in the saloon and fol-low the signs," Nadia said, pointing. "If you change your mind, we'll be here in the saloon for about an hour. We were going to have lunch. It is tuna."

"I'm sure I can find chow," Thomas said. "It's been a pleasure to meet you, Nadia."

"You as well, sir," Nadia said, shaking his hand. This was clearly a first. "If you have any questions, I'll be right here."

"Got it," Thomas said, typing. It wasn't a strong skill, but he could do it.

There were questions after the screen was filled.

"Have you ever been a member of the military of any nation or a member of law enforcement?"

He thought about that for a second and clicked "No." That was looking for zombie fighters. One of the things they were looking for was boat captains. He'd decided that was what he wanted to do. And he had enough experience, he could probably fake his way to it. He'd kill zombies if it came up. Plenty of zombies to kill and plenty of time.

New Screen: *"Mark any skills for which you have formal training and experience."*

There were a bunch of those. He selected civilian offshore boating; knot tying; knowing he couldn't conceal the skill for long, he clicked civilian shooting; mountaineering for the heck of it—what the hell, it was true and he'd trained people in it; Commercial Driver's License; and linguistics. He left off electronics, computer programming, explosives or demolitions, professional diving, operations management, helicopter pilot, strategic analysis, intelligence gathering, intelligence analysis, strategic intelligence analysis, executive level operations and business management. But he found it interesting they were on there.

Thomas followed the signs to the HR office. There was a desk in the corridor manned by a young woman behind a computer, and a short line. The people were dressed pretty much the same as he was but he could tell they weren't fresh off a boat.

He waited until he got to the woman.

"Like to see an HR counselor," he said.

"Are you with compartment R-765?" the woman asked. Another Russian chick.

"No, I just got off the boat," Thomas said. "L-1438. I just signed in."

"Oh," the girl said. "Name?"

"Thomas Walker," he said.

"You are just off the boat," the girl said. "Are you sure you don't want to take some time?"

"Positive," Thomas said. "And I don't even mind cleaning compartments to get a job. I've been sitting on my ass for six months."

"Go to the open cabin and have a seat," the girl said. "There are computer terminals. On the areas that you listed as being qualified there are short quizzes. Answer the quiz, then a counselor will see you."

"Okay," Thomas said.

He went to the cabin and all the computers were busy so he took a seat.

"I don't know you," the guy next to him said. "Not my compartment."

"No," Thomas said. "I'm fresh off the boat. Didn't take the three days."

"You should have," the guy said. "It was nice. Almost like the cruise I bloody paid for. Yank?"

"Yes," Thomas said.

"Well, you're in for a bit of all right, then," the man said. "The Yanks are in charge. I'm sure you'll have a cushy office job in no time."

"I'd rather clean compartments," Thomas said. A person got up from a computer and he waved for the man to take it. "Your turn."

"Already done," the man said. *"Por vous."*

"Merci, mon ami," Thomas said.

CHAPTER 27

The computer did, indeed, have a number of quizzes. There weren't any on mountaineering. The knot section was multiple choice on how to tie certain knots. There was a note that there would be a second, hands-on, test. He finished the test and was mildly annoyed that he'd only gotten a ninety-five. He must have missed one. He made a note to pay closer attention.

"Civilian shootings" was interesting. Most of it was the written portion of the NRA personal defense with firearms test. But there were other questions that were odd and even off the wall. Some of them were phrases well known in the shooting community. "Be polite to everyone and . . ." He picked the correct answer: "Have a plan to kill them." Although he almost clicked "shower the world with random acts of kindness and gentle mercy" just for the hell of it. Some were almost philosophical. "1911 or H&K USP?" "AK or M4?" "Kukri or chainsaw?" There was one question: ".45 or 9mm" that had only one answer: ".45 because there's no .46." He almost chuckled on that one.

He scored a 100 with the note: "This test is based upon the

experiences of personnel currently involved in operations against infected and, therefore, your answer(s): 1911 has been judged INCORRECT. But we gave you a pass on it since it's a cult thing with you guys and the Constitution allows for freedom of religion. Even if you're WRONG. P3L Faith Marie Smith, USMC."

"P3L?" Thomas said, leaning back. It wasn't a rank he'd ever seen and he'd seen pretty much every rank. Then he nodded. "Oh. So a provisional third lieutenant is telling *me* what gun to use, huh?"

He also found it interesting that "AK" and "Kukri" were correct.

The boating one was the most extensive. It started with a short test that covered basic boating safety and nautical terms. He scored a one hundred on that one. Then a second test came up. He'd seen it, somewhere, before but he wasn't sure where. He'd never taken this particular test but he'd *seen* it. Somewhere. He realized about halfway through that it was from the master mariner's course book.

He couldn't answer all the questions, which annoyed him. He'd read the book, once, on a deployment when it was about the only thing around to read. But that had been...during Desert Storm on that barge in the Gulf. He started remembering some of the questions after that, his memory was like that, and went back and checked to find the ones that he'd guessed. He found himself humming The Doors "Riders on the Storm" and remembering more. The SEAL lieutenant commander on the barge was a Doors fan and he played it constantly. The song triggered more memories and he went back and basically started the test all over again.

Others had gone to computers and gotten up as he was working on his tests. A new group had come in and a lady came over as he was working on the master mariner's test.

"Sir, are you nearly done?" she asked.

"I don't know," Thomas said. "I'm still only on the mariner portion. There's truck driving and a couple of other things to go. How long is the linguistics test?"

"There are three questions on the language," the lady said.

"Okay, be a while there," Thomas said. "And some of these marine questions are tough. Could you give me a few minutes?"

"Take as much time as you wish," the lady said. "We weren't sure...Just take your time..."

He finally finished the maritime questions and was pleased to see that he'd scored an eighty-nine. That should give him a shot at one of the boat crews. That sounded like more fun than being a linguist.

Then came the linguistics questions. The first question was a screen with click boxes that asked the user to click what languages were "fluent written and spoken."

Thomas paused at that one. The screen had a few he couldn't speak and a bunch were missing that he could. Finally he clicked German, French, Russian and because they were in the Canary Islands and they were going to Gitmo, Spanish. He thought about Chinese, Tagalog and Indonesian. But that would probably leave him translating the rest of his cruise and that was the last thing he wanted to do. They also had Arabic and Japanese but, well, the list was longer of what they *didn't* have that he spoke and could read and write in cases where they had a written language. They were missing Urdu, Dari, Pashtun and Tajik for example. Not to mention Swahili, Kikongo, Lingala... The list was longer of what they didn't have...

There was a test on each of them. Three phrases with multiple choice answers as to their translation. All three were what he would term advanced if he was teaching the course. He even recognized a couple of them from DLI.

That one he scored a one hundred. He damned well should; he'd written these tests before.

There were no tests for truck driving or mountaineering, so he was done.

He took a seat and waited.

"Thomas Walker?"

"You were an English as a Second Language instructor?"

There was a printed out folded-paper sign on the desk that read "Matthew Scott Baker." The placement officer was skinny, which vaguely surprised Thomas until he realized that probably everyone had come off a lifeboat or from a compartment like his.

"Yes, sir," Thomas said. "In England working mostly with Spanish and French managers transferred to England who needed some brushing up on their linguistic skills. But I'd really prefer do something on the nautical side."

"You certainly appear qualified for that on paper," Baker said, shaking his head. "We've master mariners that couldn't remember this much of the test. Do you have a mariner's ticket?"

"No, sir," Thomas said. "I just enjoyed reading and read the book a few times. Also I had a few friends with boats and I'd cadge rides on yachts. I know my way around. I forgot to include I can also cook. I've never been a professional cook but I can find my way around a galley."

"Cooks we have," Baker said. "Even professional Navy and cruise line cooks. People who know how to pass the mariner's course are rare. Despite that, you won't be placed directly into a boat captain's position. Sorry, it's a matter of trust. You have to spend some time crewing on a vessel."

"And cleaning compartments," Thomas said. "I understand the need for that."

"Oh, no," Baker said, shaking his head. "We've got a very high priority for persons who can show *any* ability with these yachts. You're going to the very head of that list based on your answers. *And* civilian shooting experience with a one hundred? You're going to boat crews unless you somehow fooled the tests. I'll schedule you for the hands-on testing phase for tomorrow's class if you're really ready?"

"Absolutely," Walker said. "I don't like sitting around."

"You're scheduled," Baker said. "There should be a message passed to you at your compartment but if that gets fouled up, be on the aft deck at eight AM tomorrow morning. And if you're not on their list, have them call me and I'll straighten it out. Thank you for volunteering; we really need all the help we can get."

"Just proud to be here," Walker said. "Any idea where my compartment might be?"

Baker looked at his screen and shook his head.

"You didn't even get assigned a *cabin*?" he asked.

"No, sir," Walker said. "I just signed in and came down here."

"I can assign one from here, I know I can..." Baker said. He tapped at the keyboard and fiddled for a bit then nodded. "All right, I'm assigning you cabin as well as a provisional boat crew ration level. The only pay right now is how good your quarters and food is. And there's not, truly, much difference. Boat crews, civilian and Navy, get a share of the salvage. So they generally eat well and can pick up some pretties to wow the ladies. I'm also told that when you run into someone you've rescued, they tend to be fairly grateful. I know I was to Seawolf but I'm not going to try to express it physically, you understand."

Thomas didn't but he just nodded.

"Go back to the main saloon," Baker said, taking a print-out from his computer and signing it. "The port side is the . . . Oh, I don't suppose I have to explain port and starboard?"

"No," Walker said.

"On the port side, forward, there's a desk that says 'Reservations.' Go there and they will issue you your rations card and your room key. You may or may not get a room on this boat. But you still need to be back on the transom deck by eight AM. There are those Zodiacs that move around all over. If you end up on a different ship, catch a ride back. All right?"

"All right," Walker said.

"Welcome to Wolf Squadron and good luck," Baker said, shaking his hand. "I'll leave you the small boats. I bounced around in a lifeboat for long enough, this isn't even big enough for me."

"I'm looking forward to the fresh air," Walker said.

"You just got out of a compartment and you're already signed up for crewman training?" the lady at "Reservations" said. "Have you even had anything to eat?"

"I had some soup," Walker said. "There was food in the compartment. And I've been sitting on my ass for six months. I'm ready to do something."

"We're out of cabins on this boat," she said, looking at her computer. "I'll put you on the *Boadicea*. They have some cabins that just came open. They should be clean but they may be a bit whiff. Well, the boat may be a bit whiff. Are you extremely claustrophobic after being in the compartment?"

"No," Thomas said.

"I'll put you in an interior compartment, then," the lady said. "I can put you in a stateroom that way. You get your own bathroom and shower."

"A flush toilet will be luxury in itself," Thomas said. "I thank you."

"This is your rations card and, functionally, your identification for now," the lady said, handing him what looked like a hotel room key. "The people on the *Boadicea* will have to issue you your room key. This will let you get something to eat on any of the ships." She handed him a yellow card on a lanyard. "This shows that you're in training for one of the regular squadron positions. It allows you access to any of the public areas on any of the ships as well as travel from ship to ship. By the ships I mean the ships in the squadron, not the liners such as you came off of. Those are off-limits to nonclearance personnel. Even if you have something that was in your cabin, until you get cleared they are off-limits. Understand?"

"Yes, ma'am," Walker said. "I can imagine you don't want people roaming around on them getting lost."

"Or getting shot by the Marines by mistake," she said. "You can pick up a Zodiac headed to the *Boadicea* on the transom deck. That's the waterline spot at the back of the boat you entered by. And you're scheduled for your first class at eight AM tomorrow. Be back here on time. Understood?"

"Yes, ma'am," Thomas said, taking the IDs.

"Thank you for signing up. There's a big world to save. We need all the help we can get."

"Anybody headed to the *Boadicea*?" Thomas asked.

There were three RHIBs tied up on the transom deck. The presumable drivers were chatting up one of the Russian chicks. The drivers were all young, teens or twenties.

"I am," one said. He had a strong Scottish accent. "But unless you're in a hurry, I'm waiting on some more passengers."

"No rush," Thomas said. It was a nice day to be out of the compartment.

"Did you not just come aboard?" the Russian chick asked.

"I didn't want to sit around for three days doing nothing," Walker said, shrugging. "So I signed up for the nautical course already and they put me on the *Boadicea*."

"That's a fair do, mate," the Scot said. "Must be a tough old bird."

"Just don't like sitting around," Walker said. "Did you take the course? I mean, am I gonna get stuck on a Zodiac?"

"That's the shit, man," one of the others said. "Driving these things is a blast."

"Be a bit less fun when we get offshore, mate," the Scot said. "But, aye, it's one of the choices. Mostly they put young blokes on it, no offense. It's a bit physical for most of the older blokes."

"You take the course, then based on how you do, you can volunteer for Zods," the third said. He was English. Midlands probably but it was hard to tell with young people from England these days. "There's another day training on them if you get it. Like Bran said, mostly they take the young blokes that volunteer."

"Are you Navy?" Thomas asked.

"Not hardly, mate," Bran said. "There are some but they've got the boats that can carry guns. We're just offshore, inshore right now, taxi drivers."

"Yeah, but one of the things we're supposed to taxi is Marines," the American said.

"I need one of your boats for the *Bo*." The man was wearing a U.S. Navy "blue-cam" uniform and had the tabs for an engineering petty officer.

"I'm for the *Bo*," Bran said. "This bloke was headed over as well."

"That's fine," the PO said. "Let's go."

"Right you are, captain," Bran said. "All aboard for the *Boadicea*? Anyone else for the *Boadicea*? Let's cast off."

"You first," the PO ordered. "It's a nautical thing. Senior boards last."

"Roger," Thomas said, climbing in the Zodiac. It was, for a change, a Zodiac.

"Didn't mean to be a dick," the PO said. "Just one of those things."

"Not a problem," Thomas said. "Tom Walker."

"Petty Officer Third Class Larry Baker," the PO said.

"Were you Navy before the Plague?" Walker asked.

"Yeah," Baker said. "But I was a seaman apprentice. Sort of a private in the Navy. What they call an oiler. But they're so desperate for people who know one end of a boat from the other, I'm a PO3 now."

"Were you on a ship?" Walker asked.

"The *Iwo Jima*," Baker said. "It's a Marine Assault Carrier. Then I was in a fucking lifeboat for four damned months before anybody found me. Fucking sucked."

"Not a sub, then," Walker said.

"No, the subs that weren't infected are still closed up," Baker said. "We're headed to Gitmo mostly so we can, hopefully, find a working lab to produce vaccine. There was a really good hospital there for the detainees. They think they can use it to make vaccine."

"Oh," Thomas said. "That makes sense. Are you working on the boats?"

"I'm one of the guys in charge of the engine room on the *Bo*," Baker said. "Working for a pretty smart civilian engineer. I was over at Ops trying to wangle some parts. Or, rather, get them to send somebody into the *Festival* to get some parts. I *really* don't want to go crawling around the engine room on the *Festival* looking for an oil pump. But unless we can get them to send a salvage team in, it looks like I'm gonna have to."

"Parts for your main liner would seem to me to be important," Walker said.

"They said the same thing," Baker said. "Also that there's a lot of stuff that's important. And the pump isn't out yet, it's just old. So...I think I'm going to have to go into the fucking dark and try to find Barry's pump. Or he's going to make my life hell."

"Sounds like you need to talk to a Chief," Walker said.

"I would if we had any," Baker said, shrugging. "The only chief we've found was a retired guy on one of the liners. And they sent him off to the small boat squadrons down the coast. I'm going to go brace the gunny, I think. I sort of knew him on the *Iwo*. I knew him, don't think he knew me. I'll ask him if he could free up a couple of Marines. It's fucking dark in there and there are zombies. I'm not going to take a fucking Beretta in there hoping for the best. I'm not."

"If I didn't have some sort of class coming up, I'd offer to cover you," Walker said. "I can use a Beretta. Prefer a 1911 but I can use a Beretta."

"If you're available and I can't find Marines, I might just take you up on that," the kid said. "There's a liquor storage compartment that's barely been touched from what I hear. If we're taking in a pallet to get out a pump, we might as well fill it, right?"

"As long as we get the pump," Walker said as the Zodiac reached the floating dock on the liner.

"What was that name again?" the kid asked.

"Walker," Thomas said. "But I'm going to be taking the nautical class so I don't know how much time I'll have."

"Zero," the driver said. "Bloody zero. Runs from early morning to late at night."

"Shit," the kid said. "I guess I'll need to find some Marines, then."

The cabin wasn't bad but it was interior. And while he wasn't claustrophobic, Thomas was about tired of four walls. He used the delicious luxury of a flush toilet, with toilet paper, took another shower, then took a walk.

There was a dining area that served from morning to midnight according to the posted schedule. He decided to check out the food. A middle-aged guy swiped his card and looked at the readout.

"You can eat as much as you'd like," the guy said, handing him two printed tickets. "But eat everything you take. The tickets are for the bar if you want some booze."

The food was bland and clearly canned. Some of it had the look of being from Navy rations. The only thing fresh was baked mackerel. And there was a lot of it.

"Where's the fish come from?" he asked the server.

"Some of the boats just brought it in," the girl said. She was English, southern England. "It appears that submarines can stun fish with their sonar. They stun them and the boats pick them up."

"They're going *active* to go *fishing*?" Thomas said, his normally bland expression flickering.

"They're out of food, too," a woman said tartly. She was American and apparently in charge of the chow line. "The subs are. They mostly do it to feed their crews. We get what's left over."

"Okay," Walker said. "That makes a little more sense."

He took some of the mackerel and looked for a table by the windows. They were mostly occupied but most of the people were probably European and thus wouldn't mind sharing. One person, one table was an American thing.

There was a self-serve soft drinks stand, Pepsi products, and a bar with wine and beer. He decided he could really do with a beer.

"You look like you're fresh off the boat," the bartender said, looking around then waving away the ticket. "Hang onto it. You can use it later."

"Thanks," Walker said. "I am. And I signed up for the nautical course."

"Good luck, mate," the man said, drawing a beer. "I tried that and quit on day two. Bloody ballbuster that is. You're not cleaning first?"

"I studied for the master mariner's test one time," Walker said. "And I remembered enough of it they put me in the class right away."

"I'll just sit here and pour, then," the man said, pouring himself a beer. "Leave it to you."

Walker went to one of tables by the window with an open seat and gestured to it with his tray.

"May I?"

"Please," one of the men said, waving to it. "I suppose you're another enjoying a last evening of freedom?"

"Yes," Walker said. "Taking the nautical course tomorrow."

"We'll be together then," one of the men said. "Robert O'Toole. No relation to the actor."

"Tom Walker," Thomas said.

"I am celebrating my first night of *not* cleaning up zombie crap," O'Toole said, taking a sip of his beer. "The people who do that full-time have my respect. I don't care if we're using rubber gloves, masks and suits. There are things a man should not have to see. I don't remember seeing you, Tom was it? Were you on one of the other boats?"

"I just got off the *Nordic Venture*," Walker said. "As in a few hours ago. Signed in, went to HR and volunteered. When I took the mariner's test they sent me over to take the course right away. I studied for the master mariner's ticket one time and I remembered some of it. That excited them. So, no, no cleaning up zombie crap for me. I offered to, but they wanted me to go straight to the course."

"Lucky bloody you," the first man said. "Rick Ewald. I'm starting on cleaning zombie poo tomorrow morning. Apparently all that a man with a bachelors in business is good for."

"They've got lots of positions that need managers," O'Toole said. "And it's not nearly as bad as being in a compartment."

"I understand the nautical course is a ballbuster," Walker said.

"You've been talking to Timothy," the third man said. "He's a bit of an idiot but he draws a good beer. Steven Schaper, at your service, Mr.... Walker?"

"Yes," Tom said. "At yours, sir."

"Tim is cut out for a life of working as a clerk," O'Toole said. "But he's a hard worker. He cleans in the day and draws at night. You get points for both, you see."

"Points?" Walker said. "Fresh off the boat."

"Chits, points," Ewald said, gesturing to the drink tickets. "You get points you can trade for drinks or better clothes or food. Even accommodations. They've become the de facto currency. There's even a bit of an exchange."

"Bit different with the boat crews," O'Toole said. "One of the reasons to join. Take, oh, clothes as Rick pointed out. You're salvaging boats at sea as well as doing rescue. If there's something your size, you can grab it. And from what I hear, the boats always have the good liquor. If they have time they'll strip a boat bare then bring the stuff back here. What they don't want, goes to the stores. People who handle the stores tend to get next pick. The ladies who wash the clothes that are brought in pick out anything they'd like to keep. Then if your job doesn't involve either of those, well, you can trade chits. There's a bit of a marketplace down in the Atrium. Prices fluctuate depending on what's come in but it's all quite legitimate. The commodore encourages it from what I've gleaned."

"Otherwise it's functionally a communism," Ewald said, shrugging. "From each according to his ability, to each according to his need."

"Or a bit like the military," Schaper said. "You get rations cards for different ration levels, better or worse accommodations depending on your rank as it were."

"I suspect there's a good bit of graft," Walker said.

"Figuring out the difference between graft and efficiency in an economy like this is difficult," a voice said from behind him.

Walker had known there was someone behind him but tried not to actively notice.

"Commodore," O'Toole said, starting to get up.

"Oh, please," the commodore said, waving. "You're not Navy and I'm not the bloody Queen. Captain John Smith, United States Navy, sir. These gentlemen I've met but I don't recognize you."

"Thomas Walker," Walker lied. But he shook the captain's hand.

"You're fresh out of a compartment, Mr. Walker," Smith said, tilting his head. "But you've got a yellow card. Graft?"

"I volunteered for the nautical course, sir," Walker said.

"Right off the boat?" Smith asked.

"Right off the boat, sir," Walker said.

"Good for you," Smith said. "I most sincerely thank you. Lord God do we need every helping hand we can get."

"You're welcome," Walker said. "But could you explain your comment on graft?"

"The term is broad," Smith said, pulling up a chair. "For example, we recently busted one of the quarters people for accepting sexual bribes for better quarters. That is a nonvaluable form of graft. On the other hand, when the market in points and chits started, some of my officers wanted to shut it down. I told them no and made it official. We're even looking at setting up something like an SEC to monitor it."

"I volunteer, sir," Ewald said. "I worked the Exchange in London."

"Name?" Smith asked, pulling out a green notebook.

"Ewald, sir. Richard Ewald."

"I'll put you on the possible list," Smith said, closing the notebook. "It won't be a high points job but it's a desk job. Getting back to graft. There's a very underground market in things like parts. Any military tends to have that but especially ones that don't, as we do not, have a standard and steady logistics stream. My masters was on the Defense of Malta and specifically keeping their planes running. The reason I named my younger daughter Faith. Their real supply line was almost entirely what you would refer to as graft. Trading what they officially got, or stole, for what they needed. The main comparison was the British Army in Crete. They had a similarly poor supply line but much tighter control on their resources due to a very professional commander and an active inspector general. The fact that they could not, in fact, keep anything running was not the only reason they lost, by a long shot, but it was part of it. And when the commander in Malta changed to one who put his foot down on 'black marketeering,' it became nearly impossible for the crews to keep their planes running."

"The engine room on this has an oil pump that's iffy," Thomas said. "Not out, but iffy. There's one that they want off the *Festival*. Are you saying that they should, what, steal one? I'm interested, not arguing."

"That's worth looking into," Smith said, making another note. "We need this thing to make the crossing. And I doubt there's one to steal exactly. But if I were they . . . I'm sure that they have various items they could trade. They can requisition material that is in short supply and thus valuable. All they really need to do is pass around that they need it. There are 'unofficial' salvage people who would get it for them. Most of them have day jobs that give them access to the liners and salvage bits that people want or that they think they can trade.

"Alternatively, we'd have to send in an official salvage crew, backed by Marines, who would otherwise be finding people like yourself, Mr. Walker, or our few capable Navy security people.

Frankly, an 'unofficial' salvage and some back-scratching is the more efficient route. Do you begin to grasp the concept? I'm not saying you're not intelligent..."

"No, I get it," Thomas said. "I don't even disagree. I'm just surprised to hear a Navy captain supporting back-channeling."

"I was a history teacher before this," Smith said. "And an Aussie para. I doubt that most Navy captains *would* support it. But I am unusual. And we cut down on it when someone is clearly causing issues. But...Mr. Ewald, is it?"

"Yes," Rick said.

"You understand markets," Smith said. "There is a person who has various exchangeable goods or services who needs something fulfilled that he cannot fulfill easily. How would you handle it?"

"Find someone who could fulfill it and broker the deal," Ewald said. "But I'm going to be cleaning compartments tomorrow. And I don't know anyone who can fulfill it. I'm not even sure what they're looking for."

"Find the chief engineer," O'Toole said. "Ask him what, exactly, he needs. Then find some of these 'unofficial' salvagers and broker the deal."

"I suspect by now that that particular deal has come and gone," Steve said. "If Mr. Walker, fresh off the boat, knows about it, the word has gone around. That is one thing that is currently traded and has always been a currency: information. But it is, more or less, the future of the free market. Salvage is what we are going to be doing from now until we die. There's little that is worth manufacturing given all the potential salvage. Only disposable commodities are going to be produced in the foreseeable future and many of those are going to be a glut.

"As long as no one strips a critical ship or depot, it's all good. And we're never going to put any of these liners back in service. But that is why I don't want to cut down on 'graft,' Mr. Walker. It's a more efficient method of supply. As long as it does not impact the official supply line. If someone pulls the pump then holds it to ransom...Well, I have Marines," he added with a grin.

"Understood," Walker said. "As I said, I even agree. It makes sense. If I had the time, I'd go get it myself. And charge the chief engineer through the nose."

"For which he'd put in a requisition through the official supply line," Smith said. "For things that we're holding that cannot be easily obtained. For example, I make sure we have a lock on the really soft toilet tissue. Currently three rolls of Charmin are trading for one bottle of ten-year-old scotch. And that's all the time I have, gentlemen. I, alas, have to go meet with some gentlemen who are less enthused by the process. Enjoy your evening."

"Thousands of Europeans are working in this squadron and you are doing nothing for Europe!"

Ariel Arsène Laurent was two things for which Steve did not care: French and a solicitor. He was also the head of the *Le Comité Européen pour la Liberté*. Which he had managed to get given a French name. Despite the fact that there were fewer than twenty people of French extraction in the squadron.

"I was just meeting with some of them in less contentious circumstances," Steve said, calmly, holding up two fingers in a V. "However, two facts, Monsieur Laurent. The first is that there are not *thousands* of Europeans in this squadron. The total manning of the squadron is currently two thousand three hundred and eight-six. Of those, eight hundred and change are from countries that could be defined as European, with the exception of Russian extraction. That is less than one thousand, much less 'thousands.' Hundred, yes."

"Hundreds, then," Laurent said, waving his hands in the air. "The fact remains...!"

"The fact remains that I said two facts," Steve said. "Two. The second fact is that the Canary Islands are part of Spain which is part of Europe. So you were, in fact, wrong in both particulars."

"The Canary Islands are not *Europe!*" Laurent snapped.

"The majority of the inhabitants we recovered are European in extraction and Spanish citizens," Steve said. "I have done something for *Spain* which is a member of the EU, or was when there *was* a Spain or an EU, and therefore I *have* done something for Europe. Besides find and secure their distressed citizens, such as *yourself.* Monsieur. But, pray, do continue."

"The fact remains that not a *single* town or village has been freed in Europe!" Laurent shouted. "*When* will you begin the liberation? Is the United States to be fully freed before you even *begin* to consider the people suffering under the scourge of this disease which started in America?!"

"*Avec ce,* monsieur?" Steve said. "With what?"

"You have Marines," Laurent said. "You have the gunboats. You have cleared towns in the Canary Islands. But you have not touched Europe! Are you afraid?"

"Terrified," Steve said. "But, you can feel free, monsieur."

"What?" Laurent said.

"I will give you a division," Steve said, shrugging. "Two gun boats. One yacht. I started with far less. When you need more ammunition, well, we'll keep in touch. Come and get it. Would you like it this evening? I do have many other things I could be doing."

"I do not know how to run any of those things," Laurent said.

"And this is my fault, how?" Steve asked. "But, seriously, I would be more than willing to give you a boat. Sail up to La Belle France. Free towns. Free villages. Go right ahead."

"There is more than France to free," David Murphy said. The Irishman more or less represented the British Isles bloc in the squadron's civilian population.

Not quite behind Steve's back, a democratic movement had started. It made sense except for the fact that they were still a) at sea and b) not exactly out of the woods, yet. He liked democracy except when it looked to derail any forward momentum the squadron might have achieved.

Times like this he wished he had an Eisenhower around. Just being able to speak more than English and Spanish would help.

"Oh, most agreed, Mr. Murphy," Steve said. "Totally agreed. If you're asking me what *I* would notionally do to free Europe, it would be to take it in stages, *starting* from Ireland."

"That is absurd!" Laurent said. "Clearing Ireland, alone, would take..."

"About a year the way I hope to eventually do it," Steve said. "Possibly less. M. Laurent, you don't care for me and the feeling is mutual. But if I thought you would actually take such a offer, I'm not sure I would give it to you."

"So first you offer, then you take it away?" Laurent said. "This is so American!"

"Monsieur, you failed to note my statement that I would be terrified to attempt any action in Europe at the moment," Steve said. "And although you are quick to argue for some sort of Europe First campaign, you might want to consider why moving to Europe, versus the Caribbean, during this time of the year is the lesser choice."

"Weather," Murphy said.

"The weather," Steve confirmed. "We are barely able to manage the squadron's boats in nearly ideal conditions, monsieur. Would you have us take the whole force into the North Atlantic? In *December*?"

"People are dying," Laurent said. "People are wondering about their loved ones..."

"There is a map of the world, monsieur," Steve said, pointing to the wall. "Please show me the spot where people are not. As to numbers of people from where, were it based entirely on population, we should up stakes and head for Indonesia and the Philippines. Or the United States. The States are closer. So. We go to the States."

"The fact that you are an American officer and American forces control all the guns has nothing to do with it?" Daimon Eberhard asked. The German represented many of the "continentals" in *La Comité*.

"Of course it has something to do with it," Steve said, reaching into a drawer. "So does this," he said, holding up a round. "Pop quiz for who knows what I'm holding?"

"A bullet?" Laurent said.

"A round," Steve said. "Bullet, casing, primer and propellant. Specifically, a fifty-caliber Browning Machine-gun round, monsieur. We're using quite a bit of these and we will continue to do so because they are faster than mechanicals at clearing infected from ports. Monsieur, do you know where I can get some more? We still have quite a few, but at the rate we are using them, we will need ten times the amount we currently have simply to clear the ports I've been looking at in Scandinavia and the Baltic."

"No, I do not," Laurent said. "And you are planning on clearing Scandinavia?"

"I have what are described as 'notional' plans going out some distance, monsieur," Steve said. "Mr. Murphy, would you care to venture a guess as to where there are more of these rounds?"

"At Guantanamo Bay?" Murphy asked.

"Guantanamo Bay," Steve said. "Key West. Mayport. Blount Island. Cherry Point. Fort Eustis. Gitmo and Key West I know I can take. Fort Eustis, possibly. Mayport and Fort Stony, the primary objective would be the RO-ROs. M. Laurent, you noted that quite a few of the members of the squadron are European.

Do you know where I can get some master mariners to run the RO-ROs so that I can, in fact, roll off the ammunition, guns, trucks, supplies and tanks that are onboard?"

"Many of your mariners already are," Laurent said. "Which is why if you do not take action to free Europe, soon, you will face a strike."

"But finding any of them is a matter of happenstance," Steve said. "Do you know where there is a stockpile of such mariners? On submarines. *American*. Submarines. Filled with *American*. Naval personnel. And do you know who *paid* for those submarines? The training of their crews? The RO-RO pre-positioned ships? This 'bullet' as you put it? *American* taxpayers, M. Laurent. So, yes, the primary objective is and remains, America First.

"Once I have the sub crews, M. Laurent, and once the summer is upon us, I fully intend to send flotillas, squadrons in fact, to various points around the globe. Including, but not limited to, Europe. Can I guarantee this? No. But when summer comes, I will gladly avail you of your *own* boats to go clear La Belle France. Feel free. You can even leave as soon as we clear Guantanamo. If you are stupid enough to do so.

"But when and where I send *my* ships, *my* men, *my* boats, is up to *me*, gentlemen. And as to your threat to strike, M. Laurent, this is not the land. This is the sea. And the law of the sea says that even *organizing* such a movement is *mutiny*, which is punishable by death. I would not, of course, kill you or any of these fine gentlemen. Nor the captains and mates who performed various acts to show their solidarity. I would simply strand you somewhere until there is some town you can be dropped off upon. Or, possibly, if I am feeling generous, a stout ship and you can find your own star to sail her by. In the meantime, there are people to rescue and deeds to be done by the brave. Good evening, gentlemen."

CHAPTER 28

They that go down to the sea in ships, that do business in great waters;
These see the works of the LORD, and his wonders in the deep. ...

Psalm 107: 23–24 (KJV)

"I need something more than shorts and a T-shirt," O'Toole said, his arms crossed.

The morning wasn't cold but it was cool and there was a stiff wind. Thomas was enjoying the wind too much to notice the cold. Unfortunately, it was from the direction of the liners, which meant it was a bit whiff. But he'd smelled worse for months.

"It sounds like there is more," Walker said.

He'd met the former businessman for breakfast. Breakfast wasn't awful but it wasn't haute cuisine. Reconstituted scrambled eggs and more fish. There was, however, really good freshly made bread.

"I looked at the market," O'Toole said. "They wanted five bloody chits for a pair of jeans in my size. I'm told that if we pass the course we get a free dive into what's available. I'm waiting for that. Penny saved and all that. Where's that bloody Zodiac?"

"I doubt they keep a tight schedule," Walker said. "But I see one inbound."

"Anyone for the *Social*?" the Zodiac driver asked as he pulled up.

"We're supposed to meet with the nautical class on the *Money*," Walker said. "Any chance of running us over there?"

"Yeah, sure," the kid said. "You don't want to be late. The Coast Guard fellas are bloody bastards about being late. Hop in."

The traffic was lighter this morning and the driver cranked the Zodiac to full, making the crossing in less than a minute.

"Hop out so I can run back," he said as he slowed by the transom dock. "Don't bother to tie off. If you can't make that little hop, just go back to cleaning compartments."

"I can make the jump," O'Toole said. He stepped lightly off the Zodiac, followed by Walker. "Thanks."

"Cheers, mate," the driver said, splashing off.

"I suppose that's our future," O'Toole said. "Being a bloody taxi driver. And now I'm wet."

"I suspect we're going to be wet a lot," Walker said. "We've got twenty minutes. Let's go see if we can con some Russian chick out of a cup of coffee."

As it turned out, the coffee bar was free. And the coffee was even good. So, apparently, was the tea.

"Gods I missed this," O'Toole said, savoring the Earl Grey. "The fact that Twinings is no more is a severe blow to the world. I wasn't going to bring it up with the others, but what do you think of the commodore's little lecture last night?"

"I think I need to get into the salvage business," Walker said. "Officially or unofficially."

"I had the same thought," O'Toole said. "Problem being, the bloody zombies."

"The problem being, no guns," Walker said. "I suppose I could use a machete..."

"I was having a serious conversation, Yank," O'Toole said.

"So was I," Walker said. "You can kill someone with a machete. I'd prefer a gun, though."

"So you have some experience in those matters?" O'Toole asked.

"Yes," Thomas said. "But I wasn't interested in being a master-at-arms."

"A what?" O'Toole asked.

"Navy security force," Thomas said. "I'd rather just spend some time on these yachts. Among other things, it will cover the dos and don'ts of salvage in the current climate. There are going to be don'ts."

There were Marines starting to filter into the area and a Marine corporal walked to the coffee bar.

"Good morning, Corporal," Walker said, more or less automatically. He even said it with a bit of command voice and reminded himself he was under cover.

"Good morning, sir," the corporal said. To Walker's surprise, he fixed a cup of green tea.

"Green tea?" Walker said.

"For the lieutenant, sir," the corporal said as a very young looking blonde walked over. She was wearing pips on her collar.

"For you, ma'am," the corporal said, diffidently.

"You didn't have to do that, Derek," the girl said, dimpling. "But thank you."

"Lieutenant," Walker said. "May I ask if you are Probationary Third Lieutenant Faith Marie Smith?"

"Yes, I am," the girl said, looking at him with suddenly dark eyes. The corporal tensed a bit as well. "Why?"

"What is your issue with the 1911 if I may ask?" Walker said.

"You must have taken the firearms test," the girl said, grinning just as suddenly. More dimples. "Seven rounds. Okay, seven plus one. H&K has twelve plus one. And I've been in too many scrums where twelve was better than seven. And you can shoot it underwater. If you get it out in time," she added, darkening again.

"You can shoot a 1911 under water," Walker said.

"Ever done it?" the girl asked. "My Da shot a hammerhead with an H&K. Okay, the polymer frame is an issue. I had one crack on me the other day and finding a new one's going to be a bitch. But other than that, I'm a big fan. Like the response says, it's a religion thing."

"I take it that AK was the right answer," Walker said. "Although, I prefer a custom. The manufactured versions are robust but clumsy. What is your problem with the M4, if I may?"

"Oh, good God, sir!" the corporal said. "*Please* don't get her started on Barbie guns!"

"Barbie guns?" Walker said. "As in, M4 SOP Mod, Barbie for Guys?"

"As in made of plastic by Mattel," the girl said. "*And* they don't kill zombies. They're a bloody toy. AK puts them down with one to two rounds. Barbie guns it's five to seven. *And* they zip right through the target. The United States started going downhill—"

"When the military changed from a round designed to kill the

enemies of our glorious Republic to one designed to piss them
off...." the corporal finished.

"Your quote?" Walker asked.

"My father's," the lieutenant said. "But I agree."

"Do you get many proposals of marriage, Miss?" Walker asked.

"Haven't had one today," the girl answered, grinning. "But Lieutenant Fontana pointed out that fourteen is legal in Arkansas. I told
him if we cleared Arkansas by the time I was fourteen we'd talk."

"'By the *time* you're fourteen'?" O'Toole said. "How old *are* you,
Miss?"

"Thirteen," the girl said. "Almost fourteen. So time's a wastin'."

"And a Marine lieutenant?" O'Toole said. "Bloody hell. We
must be stretched!"

"She's earned it, sir," Corporal Douglas said loyally. "Shewolf
was *born* a Marine, sir."

"Thanks, Derek," the girl said, punching him on the arm.
"Love you, too."

"Fontana?" Walker asked. "One of the Marine lieutenants?"

"He's a Special Forces staff sergeant," the girl said. "He took
a direct promotion to Army First Lieutenant. He's running one
of the Marine platoons since we don't have many officers. Oops,
gotta go. Time to go suit up and kill us some zombies."

"And time for us to make our way to the transom deck,"
O'Toole said. "Don't want to be late."

There was a thirty-five-foot sport fisher tied up to the transom
deck with a man in Coast Guard uniform sitting on its transom.

"Nautical course?" O'Toole asked.

"Climb aboard," the Coast Guardsman said. "If you fall in, you
get an automatic fail when the sharks eat you. Names?"

"O'Toole. Rob O'Toole."

"Walker, Thomas."

"Okay, just grab a seat inside. Be with you at eight."

Eventually, six more people filed into the saloon, followed by
the petty officer.

"O'Toole," he said. "Take the helm. If you hit anything, you
get an automatic fail. If you can't figure out how to drive this,
it is a demerit. Any questions?"

"Yes, sir," O'Toole said. The helm was forward, just off the
saloon. "Where am I going?"

"Head for the entrance to the harbor," the petty officer said, taking a position by the helm. "And listen up. I'm Petty Officer Ernest Paxton. I'm one of the few actual boat drivers that survived on the USCG cutter *Campbell* so I am, for my sins, in charge of this course.

"We're given three days to teach you how to drive these boats, basic safety and how to survive in one of the toughest professions on earth. That is *not* enough time. So we work all day and into the night. If you don't like it, quit. You rotate positions, while the classes are going on. We stop the boat, sometimes, for the quizzes and that's it. All of you will take the helm and you're going to have to drive and listen to the classes at the same time. Some of you will be in the engine room going over that while classes are going on up here. You'll have to catch up on your own time and you won't have much. Walker?"

"Sir?" Walker said.

"How the hell did you score a eighty-nine on the test?" the PO said. "We've got master mariners with tickets didn't score that high."

"I read the book a while back, sir," Walker said. "And I've got a good memory. I'm not a master mariner."

"Damned straight," Paxton said. "But you've got the book down pretty well. The thing about the sea is, about the time you think you've got it figured out, it rears up and bites you in the ass. And the evolutions that they're planning for with you guys are insane. You're not going to be taking over boats immediately. You'll be crew. But even then, what they are planning is crazy. But it's got to be done. It's the only way to complete the mission.

"So we're going to train you, as well as we can, in three days. You will be on this boat *constantly*. You won't be sleeping here but you'll be eating here and otherwise living on this boat. Part of the class is how to survive in a galley. That's actually what that portion is called: How to Survive in a Galley. And...Killian. What's a galley?"

"The kitchen on a boat?" Killian answered.

"Or...? Bradford, what's the other meaning of a galley?"

"I...don't know," Bradford said.

"I don't know, Petty Officer," the PO said.

"I don't know, Petty Officer?" Bradford parroted.

"It's a type of ancient rowboat," the PO said. "And I need a cup of coffee. Find the galley that is not an ancient rowboat and fix me one."

"Yes, sir," Bradford said.

"Yes, Petty Officer," Paxton said. "And we're beginning with basic nautical terms..."

"Which side of the ship is to lee?" Paxton asked. "Bradford?"

"The lef...port, side, Petty Officer," Bradford replied.

"Bradford, Killian, mount the fenders then stand by with boat hooks," Paxton said. "O'Toole, Rogers, on the grapnels. Martin and Bush, heave ho on the grapnels. Walker, you're the captain. Which side are you going to approach?"

The group had been going constantly for the last two days from 0800 to 2200. Man overboard drills. Recovery from lifeboats. How to board a lifeboat. Fire drills constantly. Maintenance. How to survive going alongside another yacht first in harbor then at sea. How to cook in a galley, first in harbor, then at sea. How to stow things away so they didn't come loose in heavy seas. How to come alongside a supply ship and "unrep" in the harbor. Now how to unrep from a drifting freighter. Live. At sea. The freighter had been "cleared" by Navy security and now they were, as a sort of final exam, having to come alongside, board, and pump out the freighter's fuel into their tanks. It had been determined to be diesel, which was not always the case.

For this one, there were additional Coast Guard personnel standing by in a Zodiac. A previous class had managed to set their boat on fire doing this evolution.

"With your permission, Petty Officer, I'm going to circle the boat, first," Walker said. "Port is sort of to lee. Wind's off the starboard bow. I want to make sure I've got the best spot not only to tie up but to enter."

"Go for it," the PO said.

Walker circled the container ship, then lined up for a run.

"Coming in with our port to its starboard," Walker said. "Right aft."

"Damnit," Bradford said. He'd gone to starboard and had already started tying off one of the big balloon fenders. "You could have said."

"You drop it, you get to go swimming for it," PO Paxton said.

"With due respect, Petty Officer, I'd probably have him use a boat hook," Walker said.

"So would I," Paxton said quietly. "But it's incentive not to drop it."

"O'Toole," Walker said. "I want you forward. Rogers, aft."

"Good choices," Paxton said. O'Toole had shown a deft hand with the grapnels, and getting the forward grapnel affixed was particularly important.

O'Toole made his connection but Rogers missed. As usual.

"Heave around on the forward line," Walker said. "Bring us alongside. Bradford, tie off another fender forward. Killian, stand by with the boat hook."

"What are you going to do?" Paxton asked.

"Go to back on the starboard engine and get it hove around," Walker said. "Then have O'Toole put up the second hook. O'Toole, grab the other grapnel."

"Aye, aye, cap'n," O'Toole said.

"I can get it," Rogers protested.

"I believe the acting captain gave you an order, Rogers," the petty officer said.

O'Toole made the toss and the boat was alongside. It was bouncing and rubbing unpleasantly against the much larger ship, but it was alongside.

"Boarding ladder," Walker said. "O'Toole on grapnel. The rest on heaving."

The boarding ladder was up, then there was the question of who was going to board the recently zombie-infested boat.

"I'll go," Bradford said. "But I'm sure as hell not going by myself."

"It takes three to heave up the pump safely," PO Paxton said. "Killian, Rogers and Martin. O'Toole and Bradford will belay from the boat. Walker's in charge."

"I do *not* want to go up there," Rogers said.

"Do you want to pass the course?" Paxton asked. "This evolution is sometimes necessary. We're not even having you salvage the stores. Just get the fuel off."

"Seriously," Rogers said. "What if there are zombies? I mean, how do we know they got them all?"

"Get back on this boat quickly," PO Paxton said. "They're most likely to turn up when you start the pump. This is part of the job, not just tooling around on boats. Now, do you want to pass the course? 'Cause we haven't got all day."

∽ ⊖ ∾

Getting the pump up onto the deck of the freighter wasn't just a matter of pulling it up. If they just pulled it up it would bang like hell on the hull and probably break. The team on the yacht, therefore, had to pull it out from the freighter's hull while the team on top pulled it up. There were problems. There was a bit of shouting. But they finally got it over the side and got fuel flowing.

"Stop the pump," Paxton yelled. "Okay, this time, Bradford, you're the captain . . . after you get it onto the deck without breaking anything."

"How many pumps do you go through?" Walker asked, looking into the water. The pump had disappeared from sight in an instant.

"That makes five," Paxton said, leaning over to look as well. "The mechanics on the *Grace* are getting pissy about it. But at least *this* time it didn't hit the deck, break through, damage the hull which then *cracks* on the freighter's hull and sinks the boat. Okay, Killian, what did you do wrong?"

O'Toole was sitting at the bar in the main civilian saloon on the *Boadicea*, holding a scotch in mid air with his head slowly drifting down then bobbing back up.

"I feel as if I should celebrate," the former businessman said, then snorted a snore.

"Rob," Walker said. "Go get some rest. We're getting assigned in the morning and for all we know, we'll be gone by afternoon."

"I'm too old for this," O'Toole said, downing his drink. "But at least we didn't get Zodiacs. Good night, Tom."

"Good night, Rob."

CHAPTER 29

Big sisters are the crab grass in the lawn of life.

Charles M. Schulz

"The South Flotilla is already asking for more prize crews," Isham said, looking at his notes. "They're sending the boats they found back up here with all the refugees. The boats coming in are short on fuel. They haven't found much. But that's about it for prize crews and they're short handed."

"Not surprising," Steve said. "They didn't have many to begin with. Lieutenant Kuzma, status on the training program?"

"The first group is trained," Kuzma said. "As best you can train people to be skippers and engineers in three days. We're starting another class. But, again, sir..."

"Ask me for anything but time, Lieutenant," Steve said. "When the boats get here, detail them out to them. As crew not captains till they've had some time to adjust. Then pack what you've got left and send them down to the flotilla as prize crews. As for tanking... Have the new skippers tank from the supermax. If they can't tank from one in harbor, they're not going to be able to unrep. Call it a final exam. Mr. Zumwald. You wanted to talk about the outline of the crossing plan."

"Since everybody is busy as a one-armed paperhanger, I've been chatting up the sub skippers for pointers," Zumwald said. "We've got nine subs hanging around the area. What we're looking at is this. One wing, and that's a term of art, will consist of the small-boat flotillas. It will also be, well, one wing of the sweep. The subs will take the other wing with one back to handle any security issues.

"The boat wing will center two flotillas, each with its own megayacht and supply ship. The boats will tank from the mega-yacht and or the supply ship. They'll rotate inwards as time goes by, hopefully filling up with survivors but whatever. When they get to the supply ship, they'll crossload survivors and spare sup-plies, tank up if necessary then probably do fish ops for a day before going back out on the end of the flotilla.

"The megayacht and supply ship will, if necessary, tank from the tanker. We'll need to fill that puppy slap up before we leave.

"Each of the boats will need one, at least, Navy clearance guy for clearing yachts. We'll have a different group doing the picking them up and getting them running.

"The divisions will each have a specialist clearance boat. That will be a fairly fast yacht or one of the fast supply boats with a Zodiac and some Marines onboard. The flotilla will have the Marine boss with the flotilla boss on the flotilla boss's boat and they'll have another one of those Zodiacs. That will be for clear-ing large vessels such as tankers and freighters. They'll generally run back from the main wing about thirty, forty miles.

"The boat will be accompanied by another yacht, which will have survey and salvage people on it. That's the 'prize crews.' If there's a good find, we'll send them out in Zodiacs to pick it up. The sub wing will have a similar group but there will need to be, probably, four to six yachts in that one and most of the Zodiacs. When a sub spots a prospect—they call it a sierra for some reason—the security guys or Marines in a Zodiac head out to it and check it out. If it's worth picking up, then they pick it up or recover survivors, whatever, usual deal. We'll send Kuzma's Coasties to pick it up if it's a yacht. If it's something big we want to keep, we'll send a pro crew from the command ship.

"The command ship is the *Boadicea*. It will handle overflow from the megayachts if they get too crowded. The command group will hang back, probably about sixty miles, from the main line. We can use the rotating yachts to bring back refugees. That's also where the *Grace* will be and the tanker unless it needs to head forward to resupply the other ships.

"God help us if we find a fricking liner; the plan goes out the window then. That's the outline. The devil's going to be in the details and keeping it all going at sea."

"May I interject, sir?" Lieutenant Kuzma said.

"Go," Steve said.

"Unrep at sea is not . . . the easiest thing in the world, sir," Kuzma said, frowning.

"Unrep at sea is bloody dangerous and without an experienced crew, right on the edge of insane," Steve said. "The only alternative, Lieutenant, is forming up in a group and driving straight to Gitmo. All of the boats we're getting can, I'll admit, make that crossing without tanking. However, I have no idea if there are people between here and there still alive in lifeboats. The likelihood gets lower every passing second. But I'm also going to do my best to find them. And taking the time to find them means using up more stores. Which means, in turn, the boats will *have to* unrep. At least once, possibly more often.

"So, Lieutenant, the choice is between unrep or not doing search and rescue. I'm not going to ask you which you would prefer, undergoing a dangerous evolution at sea with inexperienced crews or ignoring a prime imperative of your service. That would be cruel and the decision is made. I'll add, however, that four people, two of them teenage girls, with no experience prior to boarding a sailboat in Virginia managed to not only unrep from a freighter, at sea, but figure out how to convert some pumps so that they could suck out the water and fuel tanks.

"Lieutenant, if Sophia, Faith, Stacey and myself could do it, so can they. Is it going to be easy? No. Are there going to be mistakes? Often. Are we going to lose a boat? Almost assuredly and probably more than one. I'd suggest that in your spare time from honing your class you put your mind to how to do it as safely as possible. If I might make one suggestion for your class, it be that no one passes if they cannot figure out what 'to lee' means."

"Okay, what's it mean?" Zumwald said.

"It's the downwind side of the boat," Steve said. "In general, if you've got a smaller boat snuggling up to a bigger boat, you want to be to lee. The water's smoother. On the other hand, if it's really windy, the bigger boat can sort of roll the smaller boat under. One thing to put into your equation is that if we do hit a squall, all unrep operations have to stop then and there. I chose this time of the year to do this because the southern Atlantic is fairly calm. There is a method to my madness, Lieutenant Kuzma."

"I'm aware of that, sir," Kuzma said.

"And when something happens and you mentally say 'I told you so,' feel free to keep it to yourself," Steve said. "I already know at least half of the problems that can and will occur. I am accepting them, as the squadron commander, in the interest of performing the mission. This is my decision and my responsibility. Yours is to try to make it the least insane decision possible. I don't suppose we've found a cigarette boat, yet."

"Not so far," Isham said.

"When we do, that's mine," Steve said. "Yes, there is an element of greed to that. But mostly it's that I'm damned if I'm going to spend the entire trip on the liner. I haven't met half the people in the squadron at this point and I am going to get out there at the front. I'll do it in an inflatable if I have to, but something designed for long runs in open ocean would be preferable."

"I'll make a note," Isham said. "Find the commander a drug-runner special."

"I'm serious," Steve said. "I'm not getting stuck in the liner the whole trip. That's what *you're* for, Jack."

"I'll stay on the liner," Isham said. "You can have your drug-runner special. If we can find one..."

Isham drummed his fingers on his desk thinking. He didn't really like Smith. He'd gotten to where he sort of respected him, which he hadn't when they'd met. But he still didn't like him.

On the other hand, he didn't like people who worked for him doing a half-ass job and he refused to do one himself. He'd taken this job and he was doing it, he thought, pretty damned well. He'd thought about subtly fucking the guy but it wasn't worth the effort. Not to mention, this was the only game in town. He'd talked to the guys in the Hole, and Wolf squadron seemed like the only thing getting organized in the whole world. They monitored radio and were peering through satellites and there wasn't what you called much in the way of signs of life. Not intelligent and civilized life. That one satellite dude said that he'd been looking at satellite stuff for twenty years and never realized the world could *be* this dark.

Which was the answer to the question. The flotillas weren't finding any cigarette boats as it was going. So ... get somebody else to look ...

He tapped his keys and connected to the *Boise*.

"*Boise*, I need a direct link to Master Sergeant Doehler in the Hole ..."

"Puerto de las Nieves," Doehler said, looking at a screen to the side. "I'd already spotted it. That's the nearest to your flotilla working the east side of the island. It's across the straight on Santa Lucia de Tirjana."

"Where?" Isham asked.

"Look out your window, sir," Doehler said. "Since you *have* one. Big island across the strait southeast of Santa Cruz de Tenerife. It's about forty miles due east of their current position."

"Okay," Isham said. "Spell that name ..."

"Why don't I just send you an e-mail?" Doehler said.

"We're crossing the strait," Lieutenant Chen said, thumbing out the window. "Some place called Puerto de las Nieves. Three large yachts and, specifically, a cigarette boat."

"Oooh," Sophia said. "Who gets that?"

"Your father," Chen said. "He apparently needs it to move around the squadron during the crossing. So ... Plans ..."

"Well, I'll say this for the job," Sergeant Major Barney said. "We certainly go some pretty places."

Puerto de las Nieves translated as "Port of the Snow." It should have translated as "Port of the Cliffs." Tall volcanic bluffs reared up two and three hundred feet over the crystal-clear water.

"And a sort of tricky harbor," Sophia said. "Not the marina part but you get over by those cliffs and I just know there's some nasty rocks."

"We'll target the ferry dock and the inner harbor," Chen said. "First Division will take the inner harbor. I'm going in on an RHIB to check the water. That looks like it could get nasty. Second Division, set up to engage at the ferry dock from inside the breakwater, guns pointed out to sea. First Division stand by."

"I suppose there will be more bloody music tonight," the sergeant major said.

"I could see if anyone has any swing, Sergeant Major," Sophia said.

"I'm not that bloody old, ma'am," Barney said. "However, if you're going to play rock and roll, ma'am, why couldn't it be *rock and roll* for God's sakes."

"Such as?" Sophia asked.

"Beatles," the sergeant major said. "Rolling Stones. The Birds. Even the bloody Beach Boys or Jimmy Hendrix! This modern stuff has no soul, no heart!"

"Would you like some Cream with that whine, Sergeant Major," Sophia said, laughing. "How can you like Rolling Stones and not like Avenged Sevenfold? Among other things, they play guitar better than Peter Frampton and there is nothing *like* a modern drummer compared to those old fogies! Listen to DragonForce some time and tell me that John Bonham could keep up."

"John Bonham, ma'am, was a bloody genius," the sergeant major said proudly.

"I'll tell you what, Sergeant Major," Sophia said. "I'll set up a playlist for tonight that combines the two. We'll discuss it."

"Okay, ma'am!" the sergeant major shouted over "Through Fire and Flames." "How the hell do they bloody do that?"

"Are you talking about the guitar or the drums?" Sophia shouted.

"Yes! I play the guitar and that's *impossible!*"

"I've heard their fingers bleed at concerts," Sophia said. "Well, did. Probably dead. And *I've* done it on Guitar Hero!"

"What the hell is . . . Never mind. It's a bloody video game again, isn't it . . . ?"

"Commodore," Captain Wilkes said, saluting. He was still covered in gear and weapons and thus "under arms." "The last liner is clear. Ish."

"Ish?" Steve said, returning the salute.

"We're sure we got all the survivors out," Wilkes said. "We're also sure there are some infected in the bilges. I'm a Marine, sir, but I would like to raise objection to sending my men, and women, into the bilges just to hunt down a couple of CHUDs."

"CHUDs?" Steve said. "Oh . . . New acronym?"

"You eventually get tired of saying 'infected' and Corporal Douglas points out at every opportunity that they are not the living dead," Wilkes said. "We tried zeds but he figured it out.

The gunny told him to lay off but now we know whenever we say... Sir, the liner is clear, sir."

"Faith once suggested Zylons," Steve said. "Captain, go get your gear off then get some rest. That goes double for my daughter."

"Yes, sir," Wilkes said. "She's a real asset, sir. Motivation goes a long way and motivation combined with... sort of existential fury goes even further, sir. Now if I could just get her to compose a coherent sentence..."

"Later for that, Captain," Steve said. "Three days off for the men and junior NCOs. Up to you on the officers. We've got to detail the distribution of the Marines for clearance on the trip over. But that will wait until you're less bleary tomorrow."

"Yes, sir," Wilkes said. "I'm at that point where you can't decide between shower, bed or food."

"Go, Captain," Steve said, making a shooing motion. "I'd suggest bed."

When the captain had left he picked up his phone.

"Communications, to all flotillas. Return morning Santa Cruz."

"Yes, sir."

He hit another speed dial.

"Isham."

"Marines are done. Three days. Schedule the first planning meeting for tomorrow morning."

"Got it. I'll get a count on the boats. Oh, your cigarette boat is on the way. You're welcome."

"Oh, God, what now?" Faith said at the knock on the door. She was stretched out on her bed, too exhausted to bother picking up a book. "There's nobody here! We went shopping in Santa Cruz!"

"Open the door, Faith," Sophia said. "I *did* go shopping."

"Well, I'm glad *you* had *time*," Faith muttered, getting up slowly. "Hang on."

"I come bearing gifts," Sophia said, shouldering past her. "What's gotten under your skin?"

"You?" Faith said. "I'm exhausted, okay?"

"Good, all the more reason to go to the spa," Sophia said. "So am I. And I need a hot-tub. There's a new bathing suit in there for you."

"I do not like spas, Sister dear," Faith said. "There are bad things in spas."

"This spa does not have bad things," Sophia said. "It has a hot tub and a massage guy named Eduardo who is smoking hot. Put on the suit. You've got ten minutes."

"And who are you to boss me around?" Faith said. "I can and will sit on you and make you cry."

"I've got two weeks date of rank on you, Faith," Sophia said. "Not to mention way more smarts. That's who. Just put on the suit and I'll be back in a minute."

Faith pulled out the suit and contemplated it grumpily. The biggest problem was it was beautiful and she knew it would look good on her.

"I hate her," she muttered.

"So, we're rolling along through the picturesque town of Puerto de las Nieves..." Sophia said, taking a sip of wine.

Faith had to admit that the hot tub was better than the dinky little tub in her room. And the suit really did look good.

"Really was picturesque. Beautiful place. Hardly any infected. Hadn't found any survivors, yet. We weren't split up, all moving along in a convoy of, you know, Fiats and Toyotas, whatever we could pick up."

"Been there," Januscheitis said, taking a pull on his beer. "Take it it didn't go well?"

"So, we'd cleared the *town*. Freaking gunners had made piles of infected. But there were two little towns off to the side. And you know how the infected come to those flocks of seagulls."

"Like, well, seagulls," Lieutenant Volpe said.

"So we come around a corner and there's, like, this *wall* of zombies," Sophia said. "I'm in the lead in a little Toyota RAV4 with Rusty out the sunroof with the Singer and all I can think is 'roll up the windows!' For some reason, 'open fire' doesn't even cross my mind. So, that's what I say. 'Roll up the windows! Back up!' And I'm on the radio, 'Roll up your windows, back up!' And all of a sudden it *occurs* to me that there's a guy with a *machine gun* stuck out of the sunroof for a *reason*...'"

"And they say you're the smart one," Faith said, shaking her head.

"Didn't he open fire, ma'am?" Januscheitis asked.

"No rank in the spa," Faith said. "Jan owes a quarter. Unless it's one of the ones with a bazillion screaming zeds. Then rank is fine."

"No, he *didn't* open fire, Jan," Sophia said. "Because the sergeant major had been putting the fear of God into everyone. And, besides, it's Rusty. He's not the sharpest Halligan tool in the shed. So I kind of go, 'Uh, Rusty?' 'Yes, ma'am?' 'You can open fire.' 'Oh, thanks!' And it wasn't even a real wall. About twenty. Rusty pretty much took care of it. I'll leave the ground combat stuff to you Marines."

"I was sorry to hear about Specialist Mcgarity, Miss," Januscheitis said. "He was a good man."

"He was," Sophia said, taking a sip of wine. "For God's sake, watch your step boarding."

"Heh," Faith said. "Watch your step in the bilges. I still think Pag pushed him."

"Oh?" Sophia said. She really was tired of discussing her sole casualty. She missed Anarchy, which was as much a reason not to talk about it as any.

"The bilges on these things are massive," Lieutenant Volpe said. "I don't think they used to be filled with sewage but they are now. And oil and occasionally zeds. So Corporal Derek Douglas has decided he is on a one-man crusade to eliminate the word 'zombie' from the vocabulary. This is not a zombie apocalypse. These are not zombies. They are not the living dead and do not, particularly, eat brains."

"The gunny told him if he rolled his eyes one more time behind his back he was going to scoop them out and feed them to him," Januscheitis said. "That was right after the gunny had used the z-word."

"So there was a little 'incident' in the bilges," Faith said, grinning. "They'd just popped a deck hatch to check a portion of them and Derek...slipped. Or, possibly, was pushed."

"He wasn't injured," Januscheitis said. "He was just covered in oil- and crap-filled water. Which since he was in the water got in under his gear. And it still stinks."

"Which has got him to shut up about the zombie thing," Faith said. "Thank God."

"Oh, I can't wait to get back to cruising," Sophia said, leaning back in the water. "Looking for survivors, do a little fishing, clear some small boats, auto-pilot and just *go!*"

"Meanwhile, we're going to be training on boarding from *Zodiacs*," Faith said. "Which we'll apparently be taking all over hell and gone. While you're catching a suntan on your flying bridge."

"You can catch a suntan on your Zodiac," Sophia said. "Of course, you'll be being beat to hell while you do. Have fun."

"I hate you," Faith said. "I really do."

CHAPTER 30

A soldier will fight long and hard for a bit of colored ribbon.

Napoleon Bonaparte

"From what PO Paxton says about you, *you* should be the captain," Sophia said, yawning and looking at the print-out from the new guy's "nautical training course." "Scored a ninety-eight on the written? That's better than most of our pro captains. Better than I did."

It was ten AM but she'd had a late night partying with the Marines. Even Faith had finally gotten into the act. Which sort of pissed Sophia off since Faith was a way better dancer. And she could *drink* better than Sophia, who had been *practicing* for God's sake.

The new crewman was both fairly good-looking for an older guy and oddly... unnoticeable. He should have been sunburned after going from a compartment to the nautical course but instead was just starting to brown. Eyes so blue they were nearly black, grey-shot black hair and she could look him in the eye standing up which meant he was short as hell for a guy. There was something about him she couldn't put a finger on. She'd been raised to be a paranoid and compared to most of her generation she was. But in this case what should have triggered paranoia, "something odd," was instead triggering a feeling of... relief? She had the oddest feeling that the man, unnoticeable though he might be, was going to be a real asset.

347

❦ ⊖ ❧

"I'm a quick study, ma'am," Walker said. He was trying not to laugh at the situation.

"The only question I've got is can you take orders from a fifteen-year-old?" the girl said, looking up finally. "According to this, you've also got some civilian shooting experience and you're a vet. Which is great. But I've been fighting this damned war since the last sign of civilization fell. So can you, will you, do what you're told when a fifteen-year-old girl tells you to do it?"

"There was a saying in the Army, ma'am," Walker said. "Respect the rank, not the person. But you have been doing this job the whole time and you're still alive and sane. So I respect both. And I've taken orders from people younger than myself. Yes, I'll follow your orders, ma'am."

"Sorry," The ensign said, shrugging. "We got a guy came down with the prize crews and he did *not* have that attitude. Which was why I pitched him off my boat as soon as we got back. There can only be one captain on a boat. And they took most of my crew down in Gulmar. They'd been with me for *months*. Paula and Patrick went back to when Dad kicked me off the *Tina's Toy* to take over a boat. I'm not handling the transition very well. But...welcome aboard the *Bella Señorita*."

"Thank you, ma'am," Thomas said. He really was trying not to chuckle that he was now working for one of the youngest officers in the DoD. One of the youngest in history if his recollection was correct.

"If I may ask a question, ma'am?"

"We don't usually stand on that much ceremony, Walker," The ensign said. "But go."

"Aren't you one of the youngest officers in Navy history?"

"There was a fourteen-year-old probationary third in the War of Eighteen Twelve," the skipper said. "But my sister has him beat. There hasn't been one younger than sixteen since. That young was more of a British Navy thing. They had a *twelve*-year-old Lieutenant put in charge of a prize crew during the Napoleonic Wars from what one of the Limeys told me. That kid had to be peeing his short pants. But, yes, my sister and I are sort of throw-backs. Da points out that this is also the smallest and most desperate the Navy's been since the War of Eighteen Twelve."

"A valid point," Walker said. "But historically interesting."

"We are living history," The ensign said, shrugging. "Each and every one of us. The founding fathers and mothers of a new nation. Which Da points out at every opportunity. Usually adding 'conceived in liberty' although we're pretty much all stuck in conditions of tyranny. The next step is meet the rest of the crew. We also have a new quote engineer coming aboard. We'll see how that works out. And Olga is staying aboard, thank God. That much I insisted on."

"Olga?" Walker asked.

"Seaman Apprentice, just promoted, Olga Zelenova," the skipper said. "She's from Chicago, sort of. Ukrainian by birth but grew up in the States. She...can take some getting used to. Guys usually sort of drop their jaws and follow her around with their tongues out. But she's actually pretty good at clearance. I got her the promotion 'cause she was one of the few people I could trust at my back. And she can drive the boat well enough to stand watch and she doesn't mind doing the chores. Now if I could just get us a real cook."

"I'm an okay cook, ma'am," Walker said.

"I'm not bad," The ensign said. "Neither is Olga. But I'd like more or less a full-time cook. We're going to be doing pretty much continuous operations and I'd rather have someone handling the galley who has just that job. It's not what they're saying we need. I don't think they're right. So I'm going to grab a bottle of hooch and go wheedle HR. Olga!"

"*Mon Capitan?*" Olga said, popping her head up from below. "I wasn't eavesdropping. Much."

The girl was wearing bikini top and shorts. Tom successfully managed not to leer. It was tough, but he managed. The knife scars were rather surprising though, especially given that they were too old to have happened because of the apocalypse.

"This is Tom Walker," The ensign said. "Show him around the boat. I'm going to go see if I can scrounge up a cook."

"Will do," Olga said. "Hello, Tom, welcome to the *Bella Señorita.*"

"Between the captain and the clearance specialist, the boat is well named," Tom said. "Before we take the cook's tour: Ma'am, I met your father the other night."

"Was Da his normal charming self?" the skipper asked.

"He was," Walker said. "However, it was an interesting subject. Why sometimes doing things...off the books was better than officially."

"Basis of Da's master's thesis," the ensign said. "Your point?"

"The compartment I was in included two Indonesian waitresses," Walker said. "One of them, Batari, was also a cook. She's currently doing forensic cleaning. But I'm sure I could persuade her to join us. Several issues: She hasn't been through the nautical course. The answer to that is she practically grew up in a galley. Her father had a fishing boat in Indonesia. Issue: She's pregnant."

"By you?" the skipper asked.

"I believe the phrase is, 'what happens in the compartment stays in the compartment,'" Walker said. "There were four other males in the compartment. The best I can say is possibly, I'd lean so far as 'probably,' and there was no rape involved."

"Lucky her," Olga said.

"So what are you saying?" the ensign said. "Go steal her?"

"I understand boat crews get to scrounge more or less at will," Walker said. "I think she'd prefer that to working for chits on one of the ships. Who is going to say I can't bring her over to the boat? I doubt anyone's going to miss one Indonesian cook."

"How pregnant?" Olga asked.

"About six months," Walker said.

"Fast work," The ensign said. "That *sounds* a bit like rape."

"There wasn't much to do in the compartment, ma'am," Walker said. "You can ask her if you'd like. She speaks a bit of English. And I know where to find her this evening. That way you don't have to waste your time wheedling HR."

"I didn't really have time for it anyway," The ensign said. "We're getting flotilla assignments this afternoon and having a meeting on the crossing. Okay, if you think you can scrounge a cook this evening, great. I'm all for it. And if she's anything like Sari, Da's cook, all the better."

"So do I still get to show him around the boat?" Olga asked. "He's cute. And he's small. I bet he can fit in all sorts of spaces in the engine room."

"She's mostly a flirt," The ensign said. "Mostly."

"After you, Miss Seaman," Walker said, gesturing for her to precede him. "That way I can watch your butt while ignoring what you're saying."

"I zeenk I zee the beginning of zee beautiful relationship," Olga said.

"*Vos yeux sont de la couleur de la mer du Nord,*" Walker replied.

"Oooo," Olga said. "It speaks French."

"It also speaks Ukrainian so I can know what you're saying about me in your sleep," Walker said.

"No hanky panky till I see if the new engineer is a prick," The ensign said.

The new engineer was a Filipino female.

"Celementina Rosamaria Starshine Sagman," the girl said, shaking Sophia's hand. "At your service, ma'am."

"You're a mechanic?" Sophia asked. She didn't look like a mechanic. She looked like a China doll and younger than Sophia. Her documents said twenty but the ensign was having a hard time believing them. And she was, unsurprisingly, pregnant. So much for that being an issue.

"My father was a mechanic, *si*," Sagman said. "I grew up in the shop. I was a maid on the *Festival*. But I am a good mechanic."

"Scores are high," Sophia said. She was starting to wonder if Da was pulling strings in that regard. Walker's scores had been through the roof. "Is that going to be an issue?" she asked, gesturing awkwardly at the young woman's round belly.

"I will perform my duties, ma'am," Celementina said. "I have been working with it already. This is not . . ." She shrugged. "I am Filipino, ma'am. We don't have the same attitude about it that some women have."

"American?" Sophia said. "Or Western in general?"

"I was not meaning to be offensive, ma'am," Celementina said.

"I get your point," Sophia said. "In the U.S. we'd say 'suck it up and drive on.' I guess Filipino women just . . . do. Okay. ROWPU is running slow. See if you can get it figured out. I've asked for a replacement but there aren't any with the same capacity. At least that they're willing to give up. It's probably the filters but that's just a guess. And we don't have any spare ROWPU filters. So . . . try to figure it out. Once we start at-sea clearance, if there is any at-sea clearance, we might be able to find a new one or some filters. But for now, we need this one working. Tanking water is a pain."

"Yes, ma'am," the mechanic said. "Are there tools?"

"Pat should have left most of his," Sophia said. "And, again, if not wheedle, beg or borrow. We could maybe go raid one of the liners. That's how we roll."

"Yes, ma'am," Celementina said. "I am used to this."

"And I'm off to a meeting," Sophia said. "Walker!"

"In the engine room, ma'am," Walker yelled back.

"Grab the inflatable," Sophia yelled. "You're running me over to the *Bo*."

"Yes, ma'am," Walker said.

"Ma'am," the mate said on the way over to the liner. The inflatable was a twenty-five-foot Brig Eagle center console. It had the name "Anarchy" written on the side in flowing script. "Since I'm here, mind if I go try to find Batari?"

"The cook?" Sophia said. "No time like the present. We could definitely use a full-time cook."

"I shall endeavor to provide, ma'am," Walker said. "When should I pick you up?"

"They'll radio the boat," Sophia said. "Should be at least two hours. Probably more. You'll know when all the other boats start flocking around."

The floating dock of the *Boadicea* was crowded with boats. It took some time to get the ensign to the dock.

"Be available in two hours, max," Sophia said.

"Roger, ma'am," Walker replied. "I'll wait for some of this to clear down to board."

"See you in a few," Sophia said.

The meeting was in the theater and there was a seating chart. The flotilla and division commanders were down front and the boat captains were to the rear, port, organized by boat names, alphabetically. The Marine contingent was starboard along with engineering and support. She found her seat and chuckled. Each of the seats had a yellow pad, clipboard and a pen on them. Just in case the attendees forgot they'd need to take notes.

She sat down and looked at the skipper next to her. He was an older guy she didn't know. There were getting to be more and more people she didn't know, which was encouraging.

"Ensign Sophia Smith," she said, offering her hand. *"Bella Señorita."*

"James Dave Back," the captain said, shaking her hand. *"Bare Naked."*

"I hope that's the name of your boat and not a Freudian slip," Sophia said, chuckling.

"I was told it had become tradition not to rename your boat," Back said. "So, yes, boat name."

"That's probably my fault," Sophia said. "At least in part. I used that as an excuse to keep the name '*No Tan Lines*' on my second boat."

"Second?" Back said.

"I'm on my third," Sophia said. "The first was a thirty-five and they retired it. Then I had a mechanical out-and-away on the lines and there was this *sweet* ninety-footer just *aching* for a new crew..."

"Wait," Back said. "Smith? Seawolf Smith?"

"Don't let my sister's stories fool you," Sophia said. "She liiies."

"Quiet down," Isham said up front. "Time to get this started..." He paused as the murmur of conversation continued.

"AT EASE!" Gunny Sands boomed.

"Thank you, Gunnery Sergeant," Isham said. "Welcome to the first full captain's meeting of the Wolf Squadron. My name, in case you don't know me, is Lieutenant Commander Jack Isham. I'm the squadron Chief of Staff. A small smattering of applause is welcome since I got promoted this morning."

"Oh, he's going to be insufferable for the next couple of weeks," Sophia said, clapping politely.

"Know him?" Back asked.

"Loathe him," Sophia said, smiling. "Capable. Real ass."

"There are a series of promotions to announce before we begin since they affect the management of the upcoming crossing," Isham said. "Hold your applause on these, we have to get through this meeting as quickly as possible. Chen, Zachary, Lieutenant Commander, USNR. That's a permanent position, Zack, approved by the NCCC. Not frocked as the Navy says. Garman, Charles, Lieutenant Commander, USNR. Kuzma, Robert, Lieutenant Commander, USCG. Volpe, Michael, Captain, USMC. Paris, Elizabeth, Lieutenant, USNR..."

Sophia knew all of them and wanted to applaud every one. She found herself trying not to cry.

"You okay?" Back asked.

"These are all great people," Sophia said, sniffling. "Just...great people. I'm so happy for th—"

"Smith, Sophia, Ensign, USNR..."

"*What?*" Sophia said.

"Oh, HELL yeah!" a voice shouted. This time, there was applause.

"I thought..." Sophia said, sliding down in her chair. "I thought they were going to wait."

"No time, people!" Isham said, holding up his hands. "Besides, there's only one more to go..."

He waited for the buzz to die down then looked at his list. Sophia knew he was trying not to growl. And why.

"Smith, Faith Marie, Second Lieutenant, USMC."

When the cheering had died down, Isham said, "And now the reason for the promotions, besides being well deserved." He brought up a PowerPoint slide. "This is the overall manning of the squadron. As of this morning, we have seven ships and sixty-three auxiliary craft, which is what the smaller motor yachts are now being called. Since that means that Lieutenant Commander Chen, for example, was handling twenty-seven boats in his 'flotilla,' that has now been changed to a wing. There will be three flotillas in Wing *Alpha*..."

Sophia automatically looked for her name in the chart and found it: Commander, Division 7, Flotilla Four.

"Oh...shit."

"Flotilla Four," Isham said. "North Wing. You are entirely response boats. The primary search vessels will be submarines. Each division will be assigned to one sub, spread out so as to act as a secondary search group. Each boat will have at least one Navy clearance specialist and the division command boat will have a Marine clearance team as well. Captain Volpe will be in overall charge of your Marines. You'll change subs during rotation. Stay back from the subs. Two reasons. One, we don't want them getting contaminated. Two, their radar turns out to be about as powerful as their sonar. They said something about 'having kids with two heads' if you got too close. They'll be scanning by periscope and radar but they'll only have about ten to twenty miles on visual, depending. You need to maintain a good watch at all times..."

"There will be not a pass in review but a group photo taken prior to leaving harbor. Uniform is NavCam, MarPat or work blues, for Navy, Marines or Coast Guard, respectively and as to civilians, you can wear the usual riot of colors..."

⚬◯⚬

"Last item," Isham said. "Awards. By orders of the Joint Chiefs, who had to remind our glorious commander that there were such things, award recommendations were circulated among the officers of the squadron. These were reviewed at squadron level. Some were either increased or decreased. I'm given to understand that in the past, virtually any award recommendation was automatically downgraded. That's not what happened. We don't know how the JCS made their decisions but most stood. Some were upgraded. None were downgraded."

There was a bit of a buzz at that, mostly from the professionals explaining the concept to the newbies.

"We've all been here a long time and because of the number of actions that have taken place, there is a stack, literally, of these to go through. So quiet down. Two additional notes. The NCCC, being a civilian, can give purely civilian awards. Several civilians are up for awards as well..."

"Is there a bump in pay?" someone shouted.

"Ah, there is why some people stay civilians," Isham said. "And no. Second item. The Congress of the United States has to approve new awards other than campaign ribbons. The *DoD* can on its own create new skills badges. The difference is a designated skill versus a particular action. One notable skill badge, so I am told, is the Combat Infantryman's Badge. The Marines don't generally have many skill badges. You're a Marine, that's your skill. Take it or leave it. In this case, there have been two new skill badges created by the current JCS with the approval of the NCCC, which are available cross-service.

"The first is the Sea Savior Badge. That is primarily for small boats who do at-sea rescues. The badge is in three levels of award, Basic, Senior and Master Savior. The levels are based upon how many people came across the transom of a small boat crewed or captained by an individual from another boat. Persons picked up from land do not in most cases count. There is a silver civilian award and a gold military award. Prior civilian experience accrues so if you're a member of the military who did at-sea rescue prior to joining the military, your 'points' accrue to your military badge. The badge design is a cross surrounded by a life-saving ring. Senior has a star on top. Master is a star and wreath.

"The second new skills badge—I keep wanting to say 'merit badge'—is the Boarding and Clearance Badge..."

"Oorah!" the Marines shouted, more or less as one.

"And, yes, the Marines *are* going to *tend* to get these," Isham said. "This skills badge is based upon deck area cleared in large vessels with significant belowdecks spaces including but not limited to, freighters, liners and military vessels. I'm reading this from the notes, people. That's what it says. As with the Sea Savior Badge, the Boarding and Clearance Badge counts prior civilian experience. There was apparently some debate on the design but the JCS finalized on a gold crossed Halligan tool and grapnel with a fouled rope representing its connection to the United States Marine Corps."

"Away boarders!" Gunny Sands boomed.

"Oorah!" the Marine contingent replied.

"Again, Senior has a star surmounting it, Master has a star and wreath. And, Gunnery Sergeant, here's one for the books. You *don't* get a Master Boarder badge. Badge *is* to be worn on daily undress uniforms.

"The Hole took all our records and ran them through a computer algorithm to come up with these badges. Before we begin, let me warn the Marines that most of you are *not* going to get even a senior level clearance badge. The 'points' on both are based on how many feet of deck were cleared or people pulled over a transom divided by how many people were involved and their time involved. We're going to take this in the order I've worked out. Each individual is going to come up and get pinned with all their awards and badges at once. Persons getting the least in terms of level of award and number are going to go first.

"Last item before we begin. A general 'I was there' award has been struck for clearance operations in and around the Canary Islands as well as actions in the North Atlantic prior to the Canaries. The North Atlantic Campaign Medal has a civilian counterpart that civilian crews who have operated in the area can wear at their choice. We're having a hard time producing all of them but we'll get it done. Those are going to be handed out through the chain of command later.

"Captain Smith, if you could take the stage to give the awards."

Sophia had recommended Olga for a Silver Star, the only award she knew. She'd been gently informed by the flotilla commander that that was over the top. They'd settled on a Navy Commendation Medal with V device for Valor. She'd been told that it had been approved but the award would be at a later date in the flotilla. She wasn't even sure what a NavCom was.

The first award that caught her attention was:

"Sergeant Joshua Hocieniec," Isham said. "United States Marine Corps. Six awards, one badge. First Award: Silver Star Medal for clearance operations on the liner *Voyage Under Stars*. Within hours after being rescued subsequent to being stranded at sea for two months, then Lance Corporal Hocieniec volunteered to join a small team on clearance of the massive ocean liner, *Voyage Under Stars*, to effect rescue of remaining crew and passengers. For three weeks, with little rest and no breaks, the lance corporal drove on with the mission, clearing two million feet of deck area and terminating, with the rest of the team, an estimated two thousand infected personnel, participating in the expenditure of over twenty thousand rounds of ammunition when he was not engaging in hand-to-hand combat with infected. During the course of the operation, one hundred and forty-two persons were rescued.

"That's the last time I'm going to read the full text," Isham said. "We've just got too many to go through.

"Second award: Bronze Star Medal with Valor. For clearance operations on the USS *Iwo Jima*..."

"New award: Wolf Squadron Formation Medal. For operations as part of Wolf Squadron prior to clearance operations on the USS *Iwo Jima*. Mostly civilians are going to get this award. Hell, I think *I* get one...

"New Award: North Atlantic Campaign Medal..."

Sophia was glad to see that Hooch was getting the recognition he deserved. She remembered how bad the *Voyage* was. The whole team would come back to the boats every night just dead with a look of absolute horror in their eyes.

"Last award:" Isham said. "Skill badge. *Senior* Boarder Badge."

"Oorah!" the Marines boomed. "Away Boarders!"

Listening to the litany was a time-capsule of the last few months and it was starting to wear on Sophia's nerves. She really didn't want to be reminded of the *Voyage*, the *Iwo Jima*, the thousands of empty lifeboats and yachts and freighters that she had found. She found herself shrinking into her chair, wishing it would just end.

"McGarity, Cody, Specialist, United States Army," Isham said. "Bronze Star with V Device. Posthumous. For actions in clearance in the Canary Islands operating area. Accepting the award, Ensign Sophia Smith..."

"Hold onto this, honey," Steve said, when Sophia accepted the award. "It's possible that some family survived. If not... Keep it."

"I will, Da," Sophia said, clutching the award to her chest. "Thank you. I didn't even think about it..."

"That's what senior officers are for," Steve said. "Grab your seat again. But don't get comfortable.

"Fontana, Thomas, J., Lieutenant, United States Army Reserve, six awards, one badge...

"Silver Star, for clearance operations before and on the liner *Voyage Under Stars*...

"Senior Boarder's badge...

"Smith, Faith, Second Lieutenant, United States Marine Corps, six awards, one badge. Three civilian awards, five military..."

"Six?" Sophia muttered. "Six? Seriously? For *Faith*?"

"From what I hear, she deserves them," Back said.

"But *six*?" Sophia said.

"Navy Cross. Leading combat teams in close-quarters clearance of ships in the North Atlantic. This award reflects civilian experience in clearance of vessels prior to the lieutenant being commissioned. Basically, she *really* got it for the *Voyage* and the *Iwo*...

"Bronze Star with V device. Leading clearance teams on littoral clearance missions in the Canary Islands operating area...

"Navy Commendation Medal...

"Bronze Star, Second Award...

"Wolf Formation Medal...

"North Atlantic Campaign Medal...

"Last Award: Skill Badge. *Master* Boarder Award. First one awarded. Over the course of her civilian and Marine career, Lieutenant Smith has cleared or led forces in clearance of over nine million square feet of enclosed space combat at sea."

"OORAH!"

"Smith, Sophia, Ensign, United States Navy," Isham said. "Six awards, one skill badge..."

"Oh," she said.

"Time to go get covered in glory," Back said, grinning.

"Defense Distinguished Service Medal, clearance and rescue operations as master of a Navy auxiliary vessel, from formation of Wolf Squadron. This award reflects prior civilian experience...

"Bronze Star, with V device, for commanding Navy security and clearance teams in the Canary Islands operational area...

"Navy Commendation medal, with V device...

"Last Award: Skill Badge: Master Sea Savior. First one awarded. Over the course of her civilian and military career, as both a crewman and master of small boats, Ensign Smith has contributed to the rescue of over one thousand persons from small craft at sea, including many of the people in this room..."

"Oorah!" the Marines boomed. They generally felt that Sophia showed there *was* a good side to the Navy.

"Whenever you get to thinking about all those empty boats," Steve said to her, pinning the award on his daughter to a round of enthusiastic applause. "Just rub this badge and know how many you *have* saved."

"Yes, Da," Sophia said, her face working to hold back the tears.

"We've got a long road ahead of us," Steve said. "If these little bits of cloth keep the wheels turning, that's worth it. And I think we're finally done. Except for a couple of surprises."

"Surprises?" Sophia said.

"I'll take the mike, now, Jack," Steve said.

"Oh, really?" Isham said.

"Really," Steve said. "As some of you may know, Lieutenant Commander Isham and I did *not* start out well..."

"Got *that* right!" Faith said loudly.

"I outrank you, now," Isham said, pointing a finger at the lieutenant.

"But this whole lash-up wouldn't work without Lieutenant Commander Isham putting in long hours of skull sweat," Steve said. He took an award out from under the podium. "Lieutenant Commander Jack Isham, Front and Center."

"I don't need a medal, Captain," Isham said.

"You're getting one anyway," Steve said. "Just one, though. By direction of the acting Joint Chiefs of Staff with the approval of the National Constitutional Continuity Coordinator, Lieutenant Commander Jack Isham is hereby awarded the Defense Superior Service Medal for operations in the Atlantic Ocean Area. Congratulations, Jack."

"I'm not even sure what a Superior Service Medal *is*," Jack said. "Wait, I read the matrix..."

"Just take it, Jack," Steve said, pinning the medal on the

lieutenant commander's uniform. "If we ever get dress uniforms, you can start building up fruit salad. And I think we're done."

"Oh, no," Isham said. "You have your surprises and I have mine, Captain." He snapped his fingers and Stacey came out of the wings with a stack of award boxes. "Captain John Steven Smith, front and center."

"Crap," Steve muttered.

"By the authority of the National Constitutional Continuity Coordinator and the Chairmen of the Joint Chiefs of Staff," Jack said. "Captain Steven John Smith is hereby awarded the following awards or badges.

"Silver Star, for establishment of Wolf Squadron and clearance of vessels at sea. This award reflects both military service and prior civilian actions.

"Defense Superior Service medal...

"Navy Medal...

"Bronze star...

"Senior Boarder's badge, primarily reflecting prior civilian service...

"Senior Savior's Badge, primarily reflecting prior civilian service...

"And we're done," Isham said, grinning.

"Thanks," Steve said. "Now I feel like a generalissimo."

"It's well deserved, honey," Steve said. "Seriously. You've been doing a wonderful job."

Steve had taken the opportunity to have a family dinner. With the way they were planning on doing the crossing, it might be the last for a while.

"I think most of the people think it's nepotism," Sophia said.

"It was almost the opposite," Steve said. "We'd discussed across the board promotions due to the increase in the size of the squadron. When Jack sent the list up for the NCCC's approval, it came back with both your names penned in and a note asking why we were failing to promote good officers."

"How does the Nick know we're good officers?" Faith asked. "It's not like he's here."

"There's a good bit of back channel going on through the subs," Steve said. "I don't mind it; the pros want to know that I'm not going hog wild. And we're about the only entertainment the subs and the Hole have these days. So, yes, the Nick knows who you are and the officers in the Hole can make some rational judgments as to whether you're doing your jobs and are worthy of promotion. Under Secretary Galloway says that your reports are getting much better, Faith. I'm putting Lieutenant Buford in charge of ensuring that improvement continues. And that you continue your schooling."

"Ugh," Faith said. "And I was looking *forward* to this float."

"Sophia, your new deck crewman was an ESL teacher," Steve said. "From the test scores, he has to be a fairly smart fellow. So I'm going to put him in charge of continuing your education as well. If that doesn't work out, we'll figure out something."

"And running a division and a boat," Sophia said. "Da, this is getting worse than that walk in the rain."

"Don't remind me of that," Faith said.

"There will be universities again someday," Steve said. "Somewhere. And when there are, you're both going. You have to be prepared, however. Now...we all have duties. Stay safe, please."

"We will, Da," Faith said. "As long as the fricking toy you put me on doesn't sink."

"We have a cook?" Sophia asked, stepping into the Zodiac and sitting down quickly. "Get us gone from this mob, Tom."

The new crew member had picked up some threads on his expedition. He now was wearing a bright Hawaiian shirt and cargo shorts that appeared a size too large for him. On the other hand, there was a bag in the dinghy that had a blue jumpsuit in it.

"We are out of here," Tom said, puttering through the crowd of boats. Fortunately, they were all inflatables and while he occasionally bumped other boats, they were, well, inflatables. The sponsons just bounced off each other.

"Batari Dian Eko, Ensign Sophia Smith."

"It is a pleasure to meet you, Miss Eko," Sophia said.

"It is a pleasure to meet you, Acting Ensign," Batari said carefully.

The cook was, if anything, more round than Celementina. This was going to be interesting.

"My mistake, hang on," Tom said. He chattered at the cook for a moment.

"I apologize," Batari said. "I am not good with the rank. Congratulations on your promotion, Ensign."

"Thanks," Sophia said. "It was a complete surprise. So was the promotion to division commander."

"My automatic reaction based on my previous service is to flinch," Tom said. "You're not ready to command thirty-two thousand men. Then I remembered with the Navy that's a three- or four-element unit. Three boats?"

"Yes," Sophia said. "And you're going to be getting some personal orders to assist in my continuing education."

"I'm not surprised your father is interested in that," Tom said. "Being a teacher as he was. I can handle pretty much anything you need taught."

"I was taking Chemistry," Sophia said.

"Analytical or experimental?" Walker said. "And I don't know where we're going to find a lab but I can probably gin up some doozy experiments with explosives."

"Not on my boat," Sophia said, laughing. "Where did you learn explosives?"

"I've been around the block a few times," Tom said. "Let's say that while a zombie apocalypse is my first *apocalypse*, disasters I've seen a few. ESL teacher is a somethingth career. I can and have taught a good number of classes. It will be an honor continuing your education, Ensign."

"And we have a group photo op the day of the float," Sophia said. "And I need to get ahold of my two new division boat captains and actually meet them. They were somewhere in the crowd but there was no way to find them."

"Which boats?" Tom asked.

"*Negocio Arriesgado* and *Finally Friday*," Sophia said. "I don't know either of the skippers. Rainey and McCarthy. Both civilians."

"Should we just call it the *Risky Business*?" Tom asked.

"Probably," Sophia said. "I'll get up with them when we get back to the boat."

CHAPTER 31

Once upon a night we'll wake to the carnival of life
The beauty of this ride ahead such an incredible height
It's hard to light a candle, easy to curse the dark instead
This moment the dawn of humanity
Last ride of the day

"Last Ride of the Day"
Nightwish

"Well, I can guess what people are going to call *this* division," Lillie Rainey of the *Negocio Arriesgado* said, taking a sushi roll from the tray. The skipper was above average height for most women, although shorter than Sophia's towering sister, "well endowed" and with fiery red hair that must be natural. The one real oddity was a tattoo planted squarely in her cleavage. So squarely most of it was invisible. All that was really visible were two wings. Sophia was mildly curious what the whole tattoo looked like but not so much as to ask her to, ahem, "spread."

LeEllen McCartney of the *Finally Friday* was slightly shorter than Rainey, still taller than their "boss" with dark black hair shot with gray, dark hazel eyes and a figure that hinted she'd been at the least athletic before the Fall and possibly a female weight lifter.

Both were pregnant.

"The Pussy Patrol?" Olga said. "The Pregnancy Patrol? The Bun Brigade?"

"Ease, SA," Sophia said. "Olga is my clearance specialist. And nearly entirely incorrigible."

"Then we'll get along," Rainey said, grinning. "Trade?"

"Not on your life," Sophia said. "She's one of the few people I trust around me with guns."

"Seriously, trade?" Rainey said. "I've got a security guy but I'm not sure I'd trust him to fight his way out of a paper bag. Don Knotts seemed more competent."

"Which brings me to a point I need to make," Sophia said. "Few points. The first is security of the boat. The security people are, technically, along for light clearance. Light means up to about a hundred-foot yacht. If it's a ship or a megayacht, that's heavy clearance. Let Marines handle it.

"They're also along for boat security. Most rescuees are grateful to be off whatever you've rescued them from and just want to get their feet back on dry land or even a larger boat. Some food, a bunk, shelter from the elements, they're golden at least for a few days. You've both been there, I take it?"

"I was on the *Voyage*," Rainey said, patting her tummy. "What happens in the compartment stayed in the compartment. Except for my little bun. Just say I was quite thrilled when your father came along."

"Same here," LeEllen said. "I take it that's not always the case."

"Besides certain oligarchs that tried to jack my boat, I've dealt with, well, a lot of people," Sophia said. "Most of them are great. Some of them aren't. What happens in the compartment, stays in the compartment. Or should. Some of them think that they can keep acting like they did on the lifeboat. Sometimes they were 'somebody' before the Plague and try to order you around. Sometimes they can't handle women as authority figures. That's particularly the case with non-Western cultures but you've got idiots in all societies."

"Amen," Rainey said.

"Step on it," Sophia said. "*Hard*. You're the skipper, do not accept *anyone's* shit. Not even an ounce. If you have the vaguest thought that there's a real threat, go armed. Hell, go armed most of the time when you've got passengers. Keep weapons locked down or on your persons, with a lanyard or combat harness, at all times. Do not assume that the meek are not an issue. I've had people who were the 'quiet' one on a lifeboat go off. If the person cannot figure out that they're back in civilization, even if the 'civilization' is a boat, lock them up, chain them down, tie them up, and call for pick-up. You can be as high-handed as you'd like short of shooting them. And you *can* shoot them if they become a real threat to your boat or try to grab a weapon. But do not let *anyone* subvert, undermine or, especially, *overrule* your authority. Is that understood?"

"Yes, ma'am," LeEllen said, a touch oddly.

"Got it," Lillie said. "I'm all for going armed."

"Skipper McCartney?" Sophia said. "Question?"

"No," McCartney said quickly, then shrugged and sighed. "I didn't have a question; I was just...You're...Some people think you're an ensign 'cause you're your father's daughter..."

"Most, I'd guess," Sophia said.

"I'd heard from some people who worked with you, even before I got transferred to your division, not to think of you as some regular teenager," McCartney said, biting her lip. "Sorry. My daughter was not much younger than you..."

"I'm sorry for your loss never covers it," Sophia said, wincing. "We were lucky. Some of it was planning but a lot of it was luck."

"My point was," LeEllen said, "I couldn't help thinking 'Oh, God, teenage girl.' I'm...sorry for that thought. It was not deserved."

"It is, sometimes," Sophia said, shrugging. "I've been doing this a while, though. Most of it is rote. The running a division thing will be a new experience. Which gets us to a few more points. Security..." she looked at her notes. "Ah, we're going to be back of beyond and we're looking at a month's float. Satellite imagery indicates some boats out there but we never know what we're going to find. Watch your consumables. Fuel especially. The *Pit Stop* is going to be an oceangoing, well, *Pit Stop* for emergencies. It will be extremely embarrassing if the emergency is 'Uh, I'm out of gas.' I like you both and you seem like great people. Run out of gas twice without good reason and I'll get you replaced in a heartbeat. Understood?"

"Yes, ma'am," McCartney said.

"Absolutely agree," Rainey said.

"Food, water, fuel and a running engine," Sophia said. "The Holy Quaternary of boating. But first and foremost are fuel and a running engine. All the rest you can fix easily if you can get from Point A to Point B. On the running engine...we're just going to have to take our chances. We don't have geniuses for engineers in general and we don't have a real supply line for parts. If you find a boat that has parts, strip them. In fact, strip every boat that has anything like supplies. Food, clothing, booze, toilet paper..."

"I'm sort of a packrat on things like that," Rainey admitted reluctantly. "I usually grab the sheets and towels."

"Good," Sophia said. "Do that. Even if we're going to use the boat, strip it. If we use a boat, it generally will need to be refueled. That's one point where you can run out. If it runs but is out of fuel and you're below a half a tank, put a beacon on it and leave it. If it's got gas but putting enough in it will drop you past a half a tank, ditto. Hopefully we'll find a freighter with diesel or something.

"When, if, we get rotated back to the main wing support ships for crew rest, we're going to have to offload, and I quote, all our damned stores. Lieutenant Commander Isham was insistent on that."

"All?" Rainey asked. "Including my cabernet collection?"

"That's the point," Sophia said. "You and each crew member can, by my orders, stash about a footlocker's worth. But, yeah, that's it. The ships need the supplies so we're going to have to give up more than we're used to. Which is why, yep, strip any boat, any freighter, anything we find. By the same token, it is possible to overload these boats. If you're to the point of overload on supplies, unlikely, I'll send you back to the *Grace* or the *Shivak* to unload. And, yes, Lillie, you have to give up the supplies."

"Damn," Rainey said.

"Think of it as charity," LeEllen said.

"Or think of it as duty," Sophia said. "Part of our job is being the gatherers for this little flock."

"Wow," Rainey said. "We're back to the most traditional gender roles possible."

"What?" LeEllen said.

"Hunter gatherer society?" Rainey said. "Men hunted, women gathered?"

"Men *killed*, women gathered," Sophia corrected. "Men brought in less than ten percent of goods to the tribe in really traditional hunter-gatherer societies. With the exception of special conditions like subarctic zones and plains where large ungulate hunting was a mainstay, men really didn't contribute much in the way of game. What they were hunting was men and women from other tribes. Men to kill, women to steal. Sorry, did a paper on it in school. My teacher really hated it but I still got an A 'cause it was so well researched."

"Oh," Lillie said.

"Yeah, not just a pretty face," Sophia said. "I've been teaching myself calculus when I've got the time. I find it soothing. Never mind. Last points, usual stuff. Fire in a boat: bad. When you strip boats, even if you're not grabbing much, grab fire extinguishers. I'm going to scream and holler to hold onto as many as is feasible. The big industrial ones are the bomb. We really should give them up for the ships but I want at least two in every boat if we can swing it. Salt water goes outside the boat. Keep an eye on your bilge pumps. If you're pumping a lot, you've got a problem. There are ways to fix it but that's advanced seamanship. Call your division commander if you've got a leak or anything similar. Ditto a fire onboard, even if you get it put out. *Any* emergencies, day or night, call me. Sometimes I know the answer, sometimes I don't, but I still need to know. Even if you're embarrassed by it. Understood?"

"Understood," LeEllen said.

"Roger," Lillie said.

"Tomorrow morning we have this stupid group photo op," Sophia said, shrugging. "We've sort of done them before but not since we've been a real 'squadron.' It is going to be, I assure you, a madhouse. Just don't ding your boats and don't let anybody else ding your boats. Then we're out and away. If you can't start your boat tomorrow morning...I like you and you seem like great people, but... Make sure your boat is good."

"Got it," Lillie said.

"Any questions?" Sophia asked.

"Nope," Lillie said.

LeEllen just shook her head.

"Be up early," Sophia said. "We're going to be jockeying around all morning. Be prepared for a lot of hurry up and wait..."

"Skipper McCartney," Sophia said as the meeting broke up. "Moment of your time?"

"Of course, Ensign," LeEllen said.

Sophia waited until the saloon cleared, with a significant glance at Olga saying "be elsewhere."

"Or should I say 'Colonel McCartney?'" Sophia asked.

"Please don't," LeEllen said with a grimace.

"Most people are automatically reactivated," Sophia said, sitting down. "I sort of need...clarification?"

"I'm one of your skippers, Ensign," McCartney said. "No more, no less."

"But you were a colonel?" Sophia said.

"U.S. Air Force Academy, twenty-four years as an Air Force officer," LeEllen said. "Retired as a colonel. Same rank your father holds now."

"Sooo..." Sophia said. "We need skippers, don't get me wrong. But I'd say Da needs staff officers more."

"There's an issue," McCartney said, shrugging.

"You got court-martialed?" Sophia asked.

"No," LeEllen said, snorting. "Got a couple of people out of them." She looked at Sophia and shrugged. "I guess you really do need some background. I was an SJA colonel. I retired as the OIC of the MDW SJA office. Not the *national* SJA, just the SJA for MDW."

"Just the fact that you know all those acronyms points out that you might be useful to the cause somewhere other than driving a boat," Sophia said. "That's a backhand way of saying I have no clue what you just said."

"I was a military defense lawyer," LeEllen said, smiling. "Like a public defender, but for military personnel facing charges."

"Okay," Sophia said. "And the rest?"

"I was in charge of the Washington DC office," LeEllen said. "That's where I retired from. Took up boating and then..."

"Zombie apocalypse," Sophia said. "Better than being in DC. So why not come back as a colonel?"

"Don't get me wrong when I say this," LeEllen said, frowning. "I support what we're doing here. I even support how we're doing it. That does not make anything that we're doing actually *legal*."

"It's not?" Sophia said, grimacing. "I thought we had...what's that term?"

"Controlling legal authority?" LeEllen said, chortling. "It's not. Not really. Not fully and legally. That's the point. I know what 'controlling legal authority' and the difference between 'Laws of

Land Warfare' and regulations are. And I know what the U.S. military is legally allowed to do and what it is *not* allowed to do."

"Like...what?" Sophia asked.

"It might, possibly, be legal to slaughter civilian persons some of whom are and some of whom are not American citizens without due process," LeEllen said. "If we had a clear Congressional Mandate of such. Possibly. But what we are effectively engaging in every time we kill an infected is genocide."

"So what in the hell are we supposed to do?" Sophia asked, a touch angrily.

"Exactly what we're doing," LeEllen said. "I agree with the plan, I agree with the program. But it's not, technically, legal. No matter if the NCCC says it's 'okay.' That's why I said 'Oh, hell, no, I'm not taking back a commission.' It probably doesn't matter but my legal side has been screaming every time I see *half* the stuff we're doing. Seizing vessels willy-nilly. Clearing foreign towns without clearance from the legal government. No Rules of Engagement at *all*. Again, it's a zombie apocalypse. You do what has to be done. But the hell if I'm going to do it as a *commissioned officer*. Not with my understanding of the issues. For you, probably doesn't matter. Above your paygrade. But if I came back as a colonel, with my background and expertise, I'd be obligated to object and basically be a pain in the ass. *Obligated*. Required. And we really don't need that. So I said 'Bring me back as a civilian and I can ignore it.'"

"That's...weird as hell," Sophia said.

"Law's like that," LeEllen said, grinning and standing up. She threw up a salute. "By your leave, Ensign?"

"Carry on," Sophia said, throwing a salute back. "Skipper."

"*LOBO DE MAR, LOBO DE MAR!*" Sophia boomed over the loudhailer. "STAND OFF! STAND OFF! I DON'T KNOW WHERE YOU THINK YOU'RE GOING, BUT YOU'RE NOT EVEN IN THE RIGHT PART OF THE HARBOR!"

"THE NORTH END, YOU IDIOT!" the skipper boomed back. "THIS IS *OUR* SECTOR!"

"THIS IS THE *SOUTH* END! LOOK AT YOUR GOD DAMNED COMPASS IF YOU DON'T BELIEVE ME! THE NEEDLE POINTS NORTH! NEEDLE! NORTH! WHICH WAY IS THE *SODDING* NEEDLE POINTING...?"

∽ ⊖ ᵔ

"We're going to have to do this as a pass in review," Lieutenant Commander Kuzma said. "We can't get them arranged otherwise."

"Have the photo team set up on the end of the cruise liner pier," Steve said. "Move them out as planned, *Boadicea* first..."

"Flotilla Four, all divisions, over."

"Division Seven, over," Sophia said when it was her turn. She was trying not to laugh at the cluster fuck the harbor had become. Zodiacs with swearing officers were zipping all over the harbor trying to get the boats arranged. So far there had been no major collisions, which was a miracle. Her own division was, she was sure, in the right spot and properly aligned with their forward and stream anchors down. Not so much the rest of the squadron.

"Prepare to weigh anchor for pass in review. Man the rails when passing the breakwater. Repeat back."

"Weigh anchor, aye," Sophia said. "Pass in Review, aye. Man rails passing breakwater, aye."

"Stand by for orders to move out."

"How's this look?" Olga said. She was wearing a U.S. Navy tank top and LBE with a bikini bottom and carrying her M4. She posed holding onto the flying bridge's folded-down Bimini top with the weapon stuck upwards.

"Technically, it's supposed to be Navy Cam," Sophia said. "They can send me a reply by endorsement..."

"Divisions, Flotilla Four, Man the Rails! And don't let anyone fall overboard!"

"Sundeck for pass in review," Sophia said over the intercom and the division frequency. "And I want *everybody* up on deck."

The end of the cruise liner pier had a nearly four hundred meter gap between the last liner and the tip of the wharf. At the very end there were four photographers and two video cameras recording the passing of the squadron. But that wasn't what caught her eye.

Her Da was standing there, at attention, in front of a Marine Flag Party, in Navy dress whites, holding a salute. It had not been an easy "evolution" getting all the boats out of the harbor. Some had, as she had expected, broken down already. There were close calls. It had been an hour since the "pass in review" order.

But her Da had been, she was virtually certain, standing there in the sun at attention, holding that salute, the whole time. And would until the last boat cleared the harbor. And he'd probably personally carry the flag. She was reminded of a certain hike in a thunderstorm. Da was like that sometimes.

"All military personnel, hand or weapons salute..." flotilla ordered over the loudhailer. "SALUTE!"

Sophia rendered a hand salute but kept one hand on the helm and her eyes forward. Which meant she was also looking at her crew. She had the vague feeling that Olga was regretting her choice of uniform. The security specialist was at attention with her rifle held vertical. She was having a hard time maintaining the position of attention, swaying a bit and occasionally having to catch herself. But she was right in there. And she appeared to be crying.

What got Sophia, though, was Walker. He was wearing his Hawaiian shirt with a Lakers ball cap he'd picked up somewhere and a pair of shades. But his back was rigid straight and he was at attention and holding a perfect salute. And he didn't seem to have an issue with the incoming swells. That was muscle memory. The kind of muscle memory you didn't get with a guy who had been an enlisted truck driver twenty years ago. That was "Gunny" or "Chief" muscle memory. Fixed that way, there was something about him. She couldn't put her finger on it but she was suddenly wondering what the hell she was doing in command instead of him.

"Order arms," Sophia said as they passed the tableau at the end of the wharf. There were swells coming in and she didn't want anyone going in the drink. "That means stop saluting, Olga. Fall in and secure all weapons."

"I should have worn my uniform," Olga said, coming up on the flying bridge. Her mascara had run. She had been crying.

"Yeah, probably," Sophia said. "But that right there was an Olga moment. And this was about seeing who we *are*, not who anybody wants us to be."

She watched as Walker went below.

"The question being, who *are* we?"

EPILOGUE

"Captain," General Brice said. "I'm glad to see all your people, if not boats, survived to make it out of Tenerife."

"The fact that this lash-up works at all is the surprising part, General," Steve said, shrugging. "The occasional Keystone Kops moments are to be expected. I take it you got that via the subs in living color?"

"Satellite," Brice said. "Happened to be making a pass. Speaking of which, we're not terribly busy down here and have been using them to do a bit of diplomacy."

"Still having issues with General Kazimov?" Steve asked. "I'll get his subs the vaccine as soon as possible."

"The general is no longer an issue," Brice said, frowning. "It seems that he nearly made good on some of his threats and subsequently suffered from lead poisoning. Committed suicide by shooting himself twenty-three times in the back or something similar. Colonel Ushakov is a rather charming rogue who sends his regards to Seaman Apprentice Zelenova. He apparently was an acquaintance, even friend, of her father and is unsurprised she is 'a little tigress.'

"The diplomacy aspect was mostly targeted on the Chinese. One of the realities of our condition previous to the Plague was that, well, we had much better satellites than anyone else in the world. And with the permission of the NCCC and since we're not going to be able to make them again in somewhere between fifty years and never, we've been sharing rather copiously. If for no other reason than this little video. You might want to dim your compartment lights."

The picture started with a shot of the earth's surface, by night, dated the day the Plague was announced. There were more as the plague progressed and the sparkling strands of light slowly began to turn off, portion by portion, Africa went before South America went before Asia went before North America went before Europe until the entire world was cloaked in pre-industrial darkness. Then the shots zoomed down, pre-Plague satellite and file images of New York, Beijing, Moscow, Tokyo, filled with people and life and laughter, the cities bright by day and night with a billion incandescent and fluorescent and neon and LED lights proclaiming to the heavens that Here Was Man.

Then the same cities, in satellite shots, with streets choked with decaying vehicles, and raven-picked bodies, and infected roaming the deserted streets.

A world cloaked in darkness.

The somber music swelled as a single satellite passed over India, then Africa, picking out shots of dead Mumbai, Cairo, Casablanca, then paused and seemed to shift, zooming in and in and in...On a single point of light that on further zoom was a hundred ships and boats crowded into a harbor.

In all the world, there was a single point of light.

Wolf Squadron.

"Mind if I borrow this, General?" Steve asked, his eyes misty.

"Of course," Brice said. "Pass it around. Your people need to see it. They need to understand."

"It's easy to curse the dark, ma'am," Steve said. "We'll light a candle instead."

Riding the day, every day into sunset
Finding the way back home

TO BE CONTINUED